D0935076

THE
ALICE
FACTOR

THE ALICE FACTOR

J. ROBERT JANES

J. Robert Janes

Stoddart

First published in 1991 by
Stoddart Publishing Co. Limited
34 Lesmill Road
Toronto, Canada
M3B 2T6

Canadian Cataloguing in Publication Data
Janes, J. Robert (Joseph Robert), 1935 –
The Alice factor

ISBN 0-7737-2415-X

I. Title.

PS8569.A64A75 1991   C813'.54   C91-094799-6
PR9199.3.J35A74 1991

Cover Design: Brant Cowie/ArtPlus Limited

This book could not have been written without
the help and patience of Niagara's librarians.
To them I owe my sincere thanks.

The Alice Factor is entirely a work of the imagination, though it deals with a very
real situation. For historical and industrial authenticity, the names of real places
and some companies have been used, but these are seen in totally imaginary
ways that suit the story and no offense is meant. Occasionally, for the same
reason, the name of an actual person will occur, but all are deceased and, again,
their use is totally imaginary.

Printed and bound in the United States of America

To Willi,
who is not the Willi de Menten of this story,
but will know where it came from

Part One

Summer – Fall 1937

I sent a message to the fish:
I told them, "This is what I wish."

One

A LIGHT RAIN FELL, misting the windowpanes and giving the city of Antwerp its midsummer gray. In the street below, puddles had begun to form.

Hagen saw himself reflected in the glass against the rain. Rawboned, that untidy shock of sandy hair down over his brow again — he'd have to get it cut — a halfback in a gray business suit, a prospector, a salesman of industrial diamonds.

Alone, like himself, the Dutchman crossed the street, ignoring the traffic, the rain and the puddles. A portly, determined man of sixty, one so socked into things he'd forgotten his umbrella and rubbers.

Four floors below the office, the front door slammed. The lift began to rise. The tall, old buildings with their fine Flemish gables seemed to frown at Hagen with the cumulative emphasis of five hundred years of trust and tradition.

Condemned, he listened for the lift, knowing he shouldn't see the Dutchman, shouldn't even give him the time of day.

From the foyer came the alarm as Arlette Huysmans cried out, "Please, you cannot go in there, *mijnheer!*"

The Dutchman grunted something sharp and pushed his way past her. The rain got worse. The puddles began to grow. Like lead, the water outlined the cobblestones as it sought the open grille of a sewer.

Hagen spoke in Dutch. "Arlette, it's okay. I'll see him."

Transfixed, she stood in the doorway, fresh-faced and innocent, the color rising in her cheeks. "De Heer Wunsch . . . Mijnheer Hagen, he has said . . ."

Hagen grinned to ease her mind. "It's all right. Honest it is."

Klees tossed his briefcase onto a chair and sat down heavily. Dragging out a handkerchief, he mopped his brow and florid, fleshy cheeks. Tried to catch his breath.

Anger hardened the pale gray eyes. A redness rimmed them. "So, and why is your superior, de Heer Wunsch, not in the office? He and I both agreed to this meeting. It was made for today, at this time."

"Mijnheer Klees, if you'll permit me to ask, why do you come to us with your problem? Why not take it to someone in Amsterdam?"

3

Wheezing, the Dutchman unbuttoned his coat and held his chest. "The traders in Amsterdam are nervous."

"Bernard's in London on business."

The breath was forgotten. "London, *ja*, of course. And *what* is he doing there?" Another wheeze. A deep one.

"I can't say."

Klees stuffed the handkerchief away and leaned well over the corner of the desk that separated them. "Well, I can, my young friend. He is buying hope and maybe, too, a place for himself."

"So?"

The man drew in a breath. "So I need someone to do the same for me."

The faded blond lashes flickered. The eyes swept over Hagen. The breath was held — begged for the oxygen it contained.

Hagen glanced uncertainly across the room toward the door, then lowered his voice. "You mean, you can't pass up what's happening. Come on, *mijnheer*, you know as well as I that refugees have been slipping out of the Reich at an alarming rate."

A wariness crept into the Dutchman's gaze. "The Jews have much to offer. Someone has to buy it."

Caution entered. "Buy what, *mijnheer*?"

"Jewelry. Diamonds. What else?"

"Small things, eh?"

"Yes, small things."

"And you'd like us to look after them for you?"

"Yes."

"Rough and cut stones then, no jewelry."

Startled, Klees grunted half in anger, half in surprise. "What do you want me to do? Destroy the pieces? My God . . ."

"When the time comes, you may wish you had."

Klees heaved a sigh. "Very well. Rough and cut stones, no mountings." Would Hagen really go along with things?

The halfback's hands spread as if to catch a ball. "London might not be as safe as you think. America might be better. Why not take them there?"

It was a possibility — far better than London. Much safer . . . Klees's laugh was humorless. "Can you see me carrying a suitcase full of stuff through their customs without a visa?"

"You've money. Buy yourself some papers."

The Dutchman's gaze narrowed. "You are naive. It is not so easy. Besides —"

"Besides, there's the matter of your record, *mijnheer*. One doesn't steal diamonds from a member of a bourse. One gets ostracized that way."

Damn him! "Please, I am only asking as . . . as an old friend of de Heer Wunsch. You will tell him, *ja*? Here, I will give you a card where I can be reached. He will understand and do as I say. It is not much to ask. Just a vault beneath the streets of London."

Just someone to take the diamonds over. Someone who had the clearance to do so.

"How much are you willing to pay us?"

Must he continually be forced to beg? "Ten percent. Dillingham's need never know. It is business, *ja*? Just like during the Russian Revolution when the bear shed his coat only to let it grow back in again."

"How do you really come by the stones?"

"Friends, associates. I cannot say."

The Dutchman fished for a cigarillo. Hagen said, "The answer's no, *mijnheer*. It can never be anything else, and you're only too well aware of this."

Klees took a moment to study this salesman of industrial diamonds who had the reputation of his father. "Times change. Old friends should not be made to beg, Mijnheer Hagen. Just tell Bernard that I was in and ask him to allow me the courtesy of an answer from his own lips."

The coffee was black and strong; the deep brown eyes were wide and searching. An anxious frown still furrowed her brow.

"Has everyone gone?" he asked.

"Yes, all but de Heer Levin. He . . . he has asked to see you, Mijnheer Hagen."

She was young, not quite twenty-three years old and at times so serious. "Arlette, please call me by my first name, at least after hours."

He had taken off his jacket and had rolled up his sleeves. The straps of the suspenders were broad, and where they met the shoulders the white shirt was creased.

"That man . . . de Heer Wunsch, he has . . . he has asked me to send him away. I . . . I do not think it right of you to have . . ."

She dropped her eyes, felt so foolish now.

Hagen set the cup and saucer down and waited for her to finish.

She blurted, "You are such a good man, Mijnheer Hagen. I did not want to see you get in trouble."

There, she had let him know how she felt about him and must now await the rebuff.

She'd never see the smile or know in it the kindness he felt. "Wait here, will you? Let me go and have a word with Lev, then I'll walk you to the tramcar after we lock the vault."

The shop was in the back of the building, on the same floor. Alone among the rows of benches, Ascher Lev was bent over his wheel, faceting a stone.

Hagen quietly cleared his throat. Lev let him have it but didn't take his eyes off the stone. "Is it right that you should keep an old man working like this? If you wish to spit, please do so outside."

Hagen chuckled. Lev continued to work. The sound of the grinding — diamond on diamond paste — rang in the empty air. With a thumb Lev applied a little more of the paste to the rapidly rotating scaife.

The diamond, cemented to its dop, was given a minute adjustment. "It is best we work, you and me. Richard, you are going to see our friends next week. Düsseldorf, Essen, Hanover, Hamburg — Kiel, no less and the shores of the Baltic — then Berlin, ah, Berlin. I should be so lucky. Did I ever tell you I used to go fishing on the Spree?

"There, I thought not. Yes, me, Ascher Levinski, now Levin — Lev to you and the others. Pretty soon they will shorten my name to nothing if I'm not careful."

The cutter swung the dop back, gave the stone a tiny squirt and squinted at it through his loupe.

Lev was nearly seventy. Kept on through the darkest years of the early thirties, he had watched with dismay as one by one his fellow employees and friends had had to be let go. No one had wanted diamonds then; only now, in the summer of 1937, was the business in gemstones beginning to reestablish itself.

Seven finishers worked in the shop under Lev's direction. Seven out of a possible fifty. Most worked with the industrial stones, shaping them to the varied needs of industry.

He looked tired and worried. "Go home. Leave that, will you? Tell me what you want. Is it about Rachel?"

"You know it is. You, too, have a conscience. Richard, this thing with the Nazis has been building for years. So I tell her — I, me, Ascher Levinski — Rachel, do not marry him.

"Love . . . she says it is for love. She is thirty-eight years old, unmarried, and she talks of *love*? A bookseller, no less. A poet. A pauper. What is a father to do?"

Moisture clouded the sad blue eyes in that thin and angular face that was all chin, nose, high forehead and sunken cheeks.

"She is on the Motzstrasse, Richard, not far from the cathedral. Number 87. Upstairs, yes? On the fifth floor. You can't miss it. An easy walk, if you like to hike. Yes, at night. Here, I'll write it down for you."

Somehow he'd have to be told. "Lev, can't you trust me to remember the address?"

The cutter shut off the wheel and held his eyes a moment to ease the strain. "Yes. Yes, that would be best. You will memorize it and then my Rachel will be safe. If she and Moses won't come with you, then bring them by force."

"I'm going by train."

Lev took it in his stride. "So much the better. Tell them to leave everything. Tell them to tell our friends they are going for a holiday. Yes, that would be best. Perhaps if you were to . . ."

"They'll have trouble at the border."

"Yes, trouble. Perhaps it is best if you just go and see them. Rachel makes a lovely honey cake."

"Lev, I'll do what I can. I promise. Now give me that thing and let me put it in the vault for you."

Unsettled by the cutter's request, coming as it had on the heels of the Dutchman, Hagen quietly returned to his office. Arlette was sitting in one of the leather armchairs over by the windows. Her long legs were crossed, she was staring pensively out into the gathering dusk, hadn't heard him at all.

"Arlette, what did de Heer Wunsch tell you about the Dutchman?"

She leapt, uncrossing her legs and getting to her feet in one swift but graceful motion. "Only that he was not to be trusted." Had Richard seen into her thoughts?

"And am I?"

"Yes. Yes, of course. Please, I . . . I don't know what you mean."

She was still upset. "Does anyone else know that he was in there with me?"

"No, but . . ."

A look of abject dismay swept over her and she turned from him toward the windows. "It is as I feared. You have been tempted."

"Not in the slightest. Now come on. Let's lock up and get out of here."

The vault, a walk-in safe with timers, alarms and a double combination-locking system, was across the foyer from her desk. He paused to check his office. Satisfied, he switched off the lights and locked the door. Then we went into the vault to put Lev's diamond away.

Arlette noted the time and wrote it down in the logbook, but Richard began opening drawers, now this one, now that one. When he found what he was looking for, he held the white paper packet open before her.

Ten emerald-green macles, the flat, cushioned-shaped triangular stones, these of from two to four carats in weight, lay in the palm of his hand. Their clarity was like that of ice. Even when uncut they had such fire.

He prodded the diamonds with a finger. "They're so very beautiful, aren't they? But they're flawed. They're not good enough to be cut into gems."

She knew that it was because of stones like these that de Heer Wunsch had been able to offer her a job nearly a year ago. But she didn't know where this discussion was leading, and it worried her to see Richard so intense.

"Arlette, listen to me. What de Heer Klees had in mind was nothing. Already the Germans are stockpiling chrome, manganese, copper, tin and zinc — you name it. These, too." Impulsively he crumpled the packet in a fist, then apologized and put it carefully back in the drawer.

Selecting a vial of crushing boart, the stones that would be made into grinding and polishing powders, he shook out a mass of the tiny cubes — some light yellow, some green, gray, white, pink, so many colors. "Gem diamonds are nothing, Arlette. Nothing! It's the industrials they'll need. If only we could stop the Nazis from getting them."

A salesman of diamonds? "What will you do?"

His shoulders lifted in a shrug she knew so well. The grin was there again, both to put her at ease and to laugh at himself, at fate. "I don't know. Go on selling to them until we have to stop, I guess. That's why de Heer Wunsch is in England. There's talk of moving the Antwerp diamond stocks to London."

They looked at each other, and a stunned silence crept over her as she realized he had trusted her with the secret. He had asked her to forget about the Dutchman. "It's getting late," she said, a whisper.

Hagen gently took hold of her by the wrist and emptied the vial into her hand. "When the time comes, Arlette, the Nazis will do almost anything to get these. What de Heer Klees is dealing in won't even matter because it can never be enough."

There was a binocular microscope on the grading table in the vault. Bringing some of the boart into focus, he asked her to look at it and tell him what she saw. "Don't be afraid. Just say what you think."

His left hand still cradled the base of the microscope. Her knee touched his and a tremor ran through her.

Hesitantly she began. "They are all of the same size but . . . but there are many shapes."

Again he said, "Don't be afraid. Say what you think."

"There are cubes and modified cubes. Some of the faces have pyramids through them and beveled corners and edges."

The gentleness of his voice came to her. "Those are all poorly formed octahedra. The stones have been screened. That's why the sizes are all about the same."

"Some are rounded but all are . . . "

"Trust yourself. Go on, say it. We'll make a sorter out of you yet."

A sorter . . . "Their surfaces are dimpled. They look greasy."

"Anything else?"

"Inclusions?"

"Good. Now take a look at these. Feast your eyes."

Hagen found the paper of macles and placed three of them in front of her. Looking down into them she was again struck by their clarity and depth of color, only more so. It was like diving into an emerald-green sea or an aspic of mint and she so small . . .

Only then did Arlette notice the flaws, the inclusions of other minerals, the fine sunbursts of tiny cracks that made them unsuitable for cutting into gems.

Hagen slid a few small, clear white octahedra into view. Again she noted the inclusions, much more easily now. "Probably rutile, a titanium oxide," he said. "Concentrated along the cleavage planes in rows of tiny black dots as the crystals formed under very intense pressure and temperature."

If ever anyone was fascinated by diamonds, it was Richard. His whole life had been involved with them. "What are you trying to tell me?" she asked.

The dark auburn hair had spilled softly forward as she'd leaned over the microscope. The deep brown eyes gazed steadily at him.

Confronted by her, Hagen realized he had had to speak out to someone he could trust. A haunting beauty lingered. Something Spanish, something French and Dutch as well. The dusky eyes and long lashes were darker than her hair.

"Only that by looking at a rough diamond you can often tell where it came from. The Germans, Arlette . . ." He glanced down at his hands. "Alternate sources — ones that are outside the normal trading channels. It's only a thought but if they should succeed in finding another source, the shape and look of the diamonds would tell us where they were getting them from."

He was really worried.

"Those cubes are all from the Congo, from Mbuji-Mayi, the largest deposit of crushing boart the world has ever seen. The Congo, Arlette. The Belgian government . . ."

His voice trailed off as if he had said too much, but committed to telling her now, he gave a shrug. "The macles are from South Africa, the source of most tool diamonds. Without the boart, the Germans can't grind and mirror-polish the harder metals or sharpen the tungsten carbide tools they use to cut so much of their steel. Without the tool diamonds, they can't true their gun barrels, cut armor plate, precision optical glass, radio oscillators, high-temperature ceramics or draw wire. So many things, Arlette, so many uses."

The white blouse of fine Flemish lace rose gently. The fine dark brush of her eyebrows arched. "And the diamonds de Heer Klees would have you take to London for him?"

She wasn't the type to have listened. She'd have sat at her desk, worrying herself sick because the reputation of the firm and of himself would have been at stake.

"Klees is nothing. He's just a small-time crook, a thorn in a much greater problem."

"The Nazis."

"Yes."

"And Lev?" she asked.

Hagen knew he couldn't keep his feelings from showing. "I've got to try to convince Lev's daughter and her husband to leave the country while they can."

The rain had stopped, the day was gone. Mirrored in the puddles, the wrought-iron street lamps were amber, the stepped and bell-shaped crowns of the guild houses were darkened silhouettes against the night sky.

Arlette stood at the curbside with hands in the pockets of her mackintosh, waiting for Richard to lock the outer doors. Stray droplets fell and she heard these with a sense of alarm, startled that they should be so loud.

Dillingham's was on a side street, off the Pelikaanstraat, in the heart of the city's diamond district. The tall windows of the bourses faced northward. Viewing gem diamonds required a pure, white light to avoid false colors and bring up the flaws — she knew this, had thought she'd come to know quite a bit. But in those few moments Richard had treated her as an equal.

His steps clattered on the stone staircase. Impulsively he slid an arm under hers. "Are you still upset with me?" he asked.

She shook her head but found she couldn't look at him. "It is nothing. It's just the times — that man...de Heer Wunsch...Will you really walk with me to my stop?"

"Aren't you hungry?"

Startled, she hesitated, then gave a slow, soft smile as the reality of what he'd just said swept over her. "I will have to telephone Madame Hausemer. She's very strict with us girls, but she's nice, Richard. You would like her, I'm sure."

The landlady was a Walloon, from the French-speaking half of Belgium. The boardinghouse would be above a shop or a bakery. He hadn't thought much about where Arlette lived, and realized then how little he knew about her.

In silence they walked along the street. There wasn't much traffic at this time of night, but soon the clubs, cafés and bars would be doing a roaring business. Antwerp had several large department stores, Europe's first skyscraper, scads of good restaurants, the opera and the theaters, but still retained the fine old Flemish architecture of its ancestry. Balustrades of stone, bas-reliefs on every cornice, busts, statues, superb art galleries...

And always there was the presence of the diamonds. The greatest trading and cutting center in the world.

It was enough. It continually made him glad to be a part of it.

They passed one of the bourses, and she saw him look up at it and knew he was thinking of the high ceilings, of a silent cough, the crackling of thin paper, the dry rattle of the stones.

"*Mazel* and *broche*, Arlette. Luck and prosperity. Each weekday the traders sit on either side of long and virtually empty tables with thousands scattered between them in a few rough stones."

Much of their work was done in secret, and they spoke always in whispers that strived to echo but often produced only a collective hum.

"Luck and prosperity," he said again, a little sadly this time, "because so often luck is required when dealing with rough, uncut diamonds."

The Diamond Exchange was a club, a close-knit fraternity where one had every opportunity to prove oneself but a mistake could cost so dearly. Word traveled fast. Brother accepted brother.

Everything was controlled by the cartel whose head offices were in London. Security was tight. The cartel held a virtual monopoly on the trade, owning the mines and controlling the distribution even to the point of once thinking, in their darkest days, of dumping diamonds into the sea just to keep the prices up.

Dealing with Klees — even letting him into the office — carried risks that were far too great. He would leave a signed memo on Bernard's desk. He would have done so anyway, in spite of Arlette's warning.

Lev's daughter was another matter. It could only cause trouble for him and interfere with business — one had to be practical. Bernard and he had many Jewish friends, but Bernard would be forced to preach caution.

Best not to tell him then. He'd leave that to Lev. Best to see Rachel at night. Dieter Karl might lend him the Daimler for an hour or two, no questions asked. But would Dieter be in Berlin? Would it be right to put him at risk? They'd seen so little of each other lately.

Rebelling at the need for security in such a simple matter, Hagen asked himself what would happen here if war came?

Virtually all the trade in diamonds was in Jewish hands. Bernard and he were among the exceptions, and he knew that a part of his success in the Reich was due to this.

"Are you upset with me?" asked Arlette, her voice timid.

He shook his head. "It's this trip that's coming up. I've got to go on thinking things are normal when I know they aren't."

"Will there be war?"

"I don't know, Arlette. I really don't."

"De Heer Wunsch says you are much better at selling than he is. He says that you understand the trade in industrial diamonds far better than anyone else in Antwerp and that you are also much more able to handle the Germans. I think, too, that he knew I could not stop de Heer Klees and that you would deal with him properly."

She still couldn't leave it alone, was haunted by the thought that he might fail them. Ever since he'd been given a seat in one of the bourses people had been watching out for him. Trust... the whole business was based on mutual trust. Yet the Dutchman was proof of what was happening.

To distract her he asked, "Will you go home for the holidays?" Dillingham's would be shut down for the first two weeks of August. Holidays were a religion to the Belgians.

Glad that he had changed the subject, she tossed her head and answered eagerly, "Yes, to Ostend, to the shop of my father. I will help him a little, and my mother, too, with the house. Maybe Willi will take me sailing in his new boat. Yes, I'm sure he will. Then we'll go to the beach for a picnic. And you?" she asked, as they paused in the middle of the street to let the traffic go by.

"I haven't thought about it. London maybe. I really don't know."

Willi... Why had she mentioned Willi de Menten's name to him? A butcher's son...

Hagen took her by the hand, helping her across a puddle next to the curb and catching her when she jumped. Together, they rode a tramcar along the Meir toward the Grote Markt and the cathedral. It seemed the most natural of things to do with Richard, seemed as if they really did belong together. But then he led her away from the cafés and theaters to a little place around a corner.

There was music — American jazz — beer, students, tobacco smoke, much talk and sin. Sin everywhere.

As he headed for the back of the place, he shouted over his shoulder, "I come here sometimes."

"Oh?" It was all she could find to say. And then, she shouting too, "Richard, how am I going to telephone Madame Hausemer from a place like this?"

He gave a sheepish grin and then that shrug. "I'll ask Cecile to let you use the one in her office."

Cecile Verheyden was absolutely gorgeous, shockingly so, and straight out of the films. A tall, slim, bare-shouldered blonde with striking deep blue eyes and a loose and easy smile.

Leaving a lingering touch on Richard's arm, the woman led the way upstairs to her cluttered office, then closed the door and pointed to the telephone.

Arlette had never been in a place like this before and knew it must show. As she put through her call, she tried not to throw worried glances at Cecile and Richard but failed.

This was a side of him she hadn't really expected. They were laughing, the two of them — the woman confiding little things, teasing and flirting until... Her cheeks growing hot in a rush, she was forced to turn away and stammer, "*Madame*, it... it is me, Arlette. Yes. Yes, I'm through work. No... no, I'm all right. I have not missed the tram. *Madame*, I'm sorry I haven't called you sooner. I had to work late. Yes... Yes, there was some trouble but it's all right now. No, I will not come home alone. Yes, Richard" — she flung a desperate look his way to see him pause — "Richard Hagen, Monsieur Wunsch's assistant, will see me home. *Madame*, I know you have not met him. It was an emergency. We thought some of the diamonds were missing. We have had to go through all of the logbooks but everything is fine now. Please do not worry. No, nothing was stolen. *Nothing!*"

Dear God forgive her the lies. They had tumbled from her so easily. Now what would happen? There would have to be more explanations. Once a person lied, they had to do so again and again until everything came crashing down on them. Everything!

Cecile Verheyden was in her early thirties. That she loved or had loved Richard Hagen was all too clear.

"So you are their receptionist and secretary?"

"Yes."

The woman burst into laughter. "Richard, how could you? She's just a child!"

"Cecile, lay off it, will you? Come on, we're hungry. Where's that famous hospitality?"

The blue eyes flicked to him, to Arlette and back again. "My God, you're serious. Forgive me, please."

The meal was good — a fish soup that was more like a stew, fresh bread and butter, the inevitable baskets of *frites* but served with buttered filet of sole and fresh green vegetables whose sauce was perfect.

Arlette ate quickly, out of nervousness, but when Richard reached across the table to still her hand, she swallowed hard and watched as that gentle smile lit his gray-blue eyes and spread to his lips.

"Relax. Cecile's just a friend. Don't be put off by her manner."

"She is very beautiful."

"So are some diamonds. I ought to know. I've spent enough time looking for them."

"Since the age of seven, with your father. In the Congo — Mbuji-Mayi and Tshikapa . . ."

She dropped her eyes, felt awful now, waited tensely for him to rebuke her.

"What else did the firm's file on me tell you?" he asked quietly.

"That . . . that your parents, they were American. That . . . that you still travel on an American passport even though you were brought up here and in England, even though you speak Dutch and German very well, English, too, and . . . and French."

"What else?"

"That . . . that your passport might be useful to the firm. That . . . your father, he was killed in the war."

"He was a sniper, a sharpshooter. Another one got him."

"That your mother, she has married again and lives in England on an estate, a very nice estate, but that you . . . you do not get along with her and . . . and think of yourself as one of us."

"A man for the times. A sucker."

"No! Richard, please. Do not do this to me. I shouldn't have read your file. I know it was wrong of me but . . ."

She couldn't say it and lowered her eyes in shame. "Please take me home."

"Hey, come on, Arlette. I'm not angry with you. I'm not about to tell de Heer Wunsch you've been reading the company's personnel files."

"Only yours," she blurted.

Up, down, up, down. One minute she would think that maybe, just maybe he might care a little for her; the next, she felt despair. And now? Hope again.

She managed a weak, apologetic smile.

Richard was thirty-four years old — eleven years older than she — a mining engineer, a geologist, a prospector, so many things. He was tall, and boyish still, a superb dancer, Lev had once said. The thick, sandy hair was always flopping over his brow. Sometimes it made her secretly laugh to see him irritably push it away; at other times she longed to cut it for him.

He had a good, strong face — pleasant and disarmingly handsome, with high cheekbones and a broad brow that would normally have been burnished by the sun. The scar beneath his lower lip and to the left revealed a cut that had never been stitched, and she knew that it had happened when he was out in the bush.

There were other scars, one on his brow above the right eye, another on the bridge of his nose, which had been broken but did not show too much.

"Do you really know how to handle explosives?" she asked suddenly.

For just a second his expression darkened and she saw him look down at his left hand. There were only three fingers there: the thumb, the first and second ones. No others. Dear God, what had she done?

The fuse had been too short, too fast, the sun ... the sun ... but that was a long, long time ago and the vultures had flown away.

"Come on, let's get out of here. I haven't touched dynamite in years, and I hope I never have to again, because I don't in all honesty know what I'd do."

The boardinghouse was down by the river, near the quays and beyond the Cathedral of Our Lady.

Hagen found his thoughts confused. Though very young, Arlette had upset him in an unexpected way. It had been good to be with her and yet it hadn't been. Too close for comfort. Besides, with the news, it was no time to be mixed up with anyone.

He didn't want to see her hurt. "Arlette..."

"Please, I know what you are going to say. It's not the time, not the place. If you were to take up with me it might affect your work and then, why then de Heer Wunsch would not think so highly of you."

Her smile was very brave — resigned to things now. Hagen walked her up the steps, but when Madame Hausemer went to open the door Arlette held it shut and fiercely said, "*Madame*, please! Just a minute."

Then she did what she had never done before, even with Willi de Menten. She looked steadily into Richard's eyes and bravely said, "Please kiss me. Just once, so that I will know what it's like."

Her lips were warm, hesitant at first and trembling, but when he put his arms around her she moved in closely, couldn't stop herself. Nor could he leave her yet. Damn!

"Arlette..."

"Shh! Now you know how much I love you."

Just before noon the train crossed the border into Holland. All along the Albert Canal there were barges, some brightly painted, others coal dirty; some tied up, for it was Sunday, others constantly on the move.

Lines of washing had been taken in. Geraniums in pots stood about the tidier decks along with patchworks of vegetables and herbs, even a few cages of chickens and rabbits. On one of the barges a grandfather smoked his pipe in quiet contemplation. On another, a thin waif of a blond-haired girl of eight or ten had just rescued her cat from the wheelhouse roof.

Hagen tossed her a wave, but the child didn't respond. Too much had happened already. Like her parents, she'd be worried.

Continuing to stare at the train, the girl braced her bare feet and clutched the cat more possessively as the barge rocked gently.

Just upstream of her, the guns of the Belgian fortress of Eben Emael faced the canal. Built in 1932, largely by German subcontractors, the fortress had been placed strategically at the junction of the canal, the main roads to Brussels and Antwerp, and the River Meuse. Great stock was placed in this fortress by the Belgians, but Hagen wondered about it. Not only was the field of fire sadly limited, but its guns couldn't even cover the bridges adequately. As for the skies, eight machine guns waited patiently for the monoplanes and biplanes of the Great War to return.

He swore, a thing he seldom did. The girl and the fortress soon passed from view. Left alone with his thoughts, he brooded. Not even lunch in the dining car, in the company of the stalwart *Bürgermeister* of Stolberg could distract him.

Just before Aachen they crossed the border into Germany. A different scene, a whole new world.

Unable to sit any longer, Hagen got up and began to pace about the room. Laid out on a table, scattered on the floor nearby, was everything he had brought with him — all his clothes; the latest high-speed cutting tools; grinding wheels and powders; diamonds, diamonds and more of them; the order books and address cards; the contents of his wallet, even those of his pockets.

"Look, for the hundredth time will you please contact the Baron Dieter Karl Hunter in Munich? He'll vouch for me. That letter from the Reich Ministry of the Interior entitles me to travel to Düsseldorf, Essen, Hanover, Hamburg, Kiel, the Heinkel factory on the Baltic and then Berlin."

"What is your business, please?"

Jesus Christ Almighty! "I've already told you that."

"Then tell me again."

Exasperated, he sat down across the desk. Calming himself, he gave the purpose of his visit.

A member of the Geheime Staatspolizei, the Secret State Police, the man didn't appear interested. As he explained things anyway, Hagen tried to penetrate the reasons for the delay. He'd covered himself; he'd been very careful. They'd never bothered with him before, so why should they now?

Otto Krantz was a Berliner, a heavy man, a beer drinker with puffy gray, unfeeling eyes, florid cheeks, pudgy fingers, a gold wedding band, state-issued wristwatch and short iron-gray hair. A squat bull of a man. Muscular in spite of the excess weight that his middle years had brought.

Wearing a crumpled, nondescript gray business suit, he was colorless. In a crowd no one would bother to notice him.

Krantz examined the passport. He favored his jowls in thought, crammed a stumpy finger under the collar of his shirt, tugged at it until the button Frau Krantz had sewn there must surely burst.

Berlin had pulled him out of the obscurity of East Prussia to find a man called Richard Hagen and get to know him. Nothing else. No explanation of why he'd been chosen for such a task or of why Hagen should require such attention.

"How is it that you travel on an American passport?"

"Because I'm a citizen of the United States."

"Yet you work in Belgium?"

Round and round it would go, the same questions, the same pedantic, plodding, excruciatingly thorough mind.

Krantz lit a cigarette, then passed a battered, bullet-dented silver-plated case across the table, only to see Hagen shake his head. "It's not something I do."

"Oh? Why is that, please?"

Hagen grinned but made the mistake of saying it would take too long to tell him.

"We have all night."

"But my train, damn it! I've got to be in Düsseldorf this evening. I'm due at the *Gusstahlfabrik* in Essen before noon tomorrow."

"Why?"

Krantz examined his fingernails, then took out a trooper's wooden-handled penknife and began to clean each nail.

"The Reich Ministry of Industry needs the products I sell. Without them, it's doubtful even the *Gusstahlfabrik* of the Krupps could manage."

"So?"

"So I'm on a business trip. Look, I've done this sort of thing lots of times before."

"How many times, please?"

What the hell was behind the questioning? What did the Gestapo really want?

"I think it must be my thirteenth trip in the past two years. I don't know. Look, I never bothered to count them. I've worked for the firm too long for it to matter."

Eighteen trips, my friend. Eighteen, thought Krantz but didn't say so.

The telephone rang. Krantz laid a meaty hand on the receiver and gave him a cold, cod-eyed stare as if to say, You'd better be telling the truth the next time.

Fishing the passport toward him, he listened disinterestedly to the caller. From time to time he glanced from the photograph to Hagen and back again.

When the Berliner hung up, he did so with a finality that troubled. "How is it that you are a friend of the Baron Dieter Karl Hunter?"

"I met him on safari a little over three years ago. We went shooting together." We did a lot of other things, too, thought Hagen, but didn't enlighten him further.

The Gestapo arched his eyebrows and sucked on a tooth. "Well, it seems you have friends in high places, Herr Hagen. You are free to go."

Krantz gave a shrug, a plastic grin that grew into a generous smile and a laugh that began low down and rumbled upward as if the whole thing had been a great joke.

Only when he came to the card de Herr Klees had given him, did the Berliner revert to his former self.

Hagen cursed himself for having forgotten it.

"I should ask who he is, Herr Hagen. It's just a matter of routine. We policemen . . ." His voice trailed off. Their eyes met. Hagen's gaze didn't waver.

"Herr Klees is a former acquaintance of my director's. As the director was out of the office, I met with him and promised to pass his card along. I simply forgot to leave it with our receptionist."

"May I keep it?"

Shit! "I'm sure Herr Wunsch is aware of the address, but just in case he isn't, maybe you'd better copy it down and let me keep the card."

"Yes. Yes, that would be best. Then we will both have it."

The telegraph kiosk at the main post office in Essen seemed set out in broad daylight. The clerk behind the wicket greeted the request with undisguised suspicion and reticence.

"I've clearance," said Hagen, sliding the letter from the Reich Ministry of the Interior and his passport under the grille.

The man took his time. These days one had to. "To send such cables is not so easy anymore," he grumbled, pinching the fleshy nose in thought.

"Look, I know you have to be careful, but it's only to my mother. She had a bad cold and I forgot to telephone her before I left Antwerp. You know what summer colds are like. Her chest isn't all that good. She's not so young anymore and I'm her only son."

The clerk knew all about mothers. Who didn't? He also knew a wind when he felt one.

"Why not telephone her from here?"

The man's fleshy lips parted, the pale blue eyes returned to their puffy folds. Like a basking turtle waiting for the tide, he stood motionless behind the grille.

Hagen gave him the look he reserved for all such turtles. "Because, though the Reich is far ahead of everybody else, international calls still take far too long to place."

"You could try a blitz call." Why don't you? implied the clerk.

Was it suspicion and just plain stubbornness or orders from above? "The cost," said Hagen evenly. "The cable. Why not simply send it?"

"You're a foreigner. All foreigners are suspect."

"Even messages to their mothers?" scoffed Hagen.

The turtle returned the shrug and said nothing. So much for Germanic efficiency!

"Send it or I'll be onto the Führer and he'll fry your butt in grease."

"The Führer does what he has to. I do what I'm told."

"Then you won't send the cable even though I've got the clearance?"

Again the man pinched the fleshy nose. "I didn't say I *wouldn't* send it. I am merely questioning you on the necessity."

Turning from him, he took the cable over to the desk, hitched up the elastics on the arms of his shirt, pulled down the translucent green eyeshade he wore and sent the thing.

TO WINDFIELD MRS LOIS ANNE INVERLIN COTTAGE BLACK DOWN HEATH PORTESHAM ROAD DORCHESTER ENGLAND FROM HAGEN RICHARD KAISER WILHELM HOTEL ESSEN

MEANT TO CALL STOP FORGOT STOP SORRY STOP DID YOU MANAGE TO SHAKE YOUR COLD STOP HOPE MY GERMAN CUS-TOMERS ALLOW ME TO SELL THEM SOMETHING STOP CHEERS HAGEN

From the Father William poem in *Alice's Adventures in Wonderland* he had chosen two lines: "Pray, how did you manage to do it?" and "Allow me to sell you a couple?"

When decoded, the message would read: STOPPED AT BORDER / QUESTIONED

Nothing else, not for now. But at least they were still letting him send things out, and this he had absolutely had to know.

Hagen turned away from the microscope to rest his aching eyes. Since sending the cable five days ago, he had worked from dawn until well after dusk matching industrial diamonds with the jobs they were sup-posed to do.

The vastness of the *Gusstahlfabrik* at Essen was spread all around him, over eight square kilometers of smokestacks and furnaces, hot-metal working, cold-metal working, drop forges, shearing and rolling mills, deep drawing and spinning . . . sheds and sheds of assembly lines.

Only in the lab was there comparative quiet. But, then, he only came up here once in a while, descending always to view at close hand the high-speed lathes, drill presses, wire-drawing dies and grinding wheels that had each needed diamonds either as the cutting edge itself, or in the trueing.

"Jake, what are your boys doing with these octahedra? Every one of the points has been ripped off. I can see the chatter marks."

The works' foreman, a fourth-generation employee of the Krupps, a real dyed-in-the-wool Kruppianer, twisted his grimy cap uncomfortably. Signs and posters exhorted everyone to be careful of what they said, especially to foreigners.

Yet Herr Hagen had always been most careful — one to whom a man could talk. He would have had the necessary clearance from above.

"It is the new gun barrels. The steel is so much harder, so much more costly."

"How fast are the lathes turning?"

"Eighty-six RPM. It is fast, ja? I have said we should slow them down, but Herr Vogel, my supervisor, insists it is your diamonds. He says they are — forgive me, Herr Hagen. He says they are being cut by Jews."

"Would that make a difference?"

"You know what I mean."

Hagen grinned, putting the foreman at ease. "Let's go and have a look."

Relieved, the burly foreman led the way. Once on the working floor, he felt at home. He knew every centimeter of the works, loved the bustle of earnest labor, the smell of grease, hot cutting oil and freshly turned metal. They passed through a maze of rolling stock. Bars and billets were stacked everywhere. Overhead cranes continually came and went. Always present, the sound of a drop forge grew steadily until Jake yanked on a door. Instantly an earth-shattering sound came at them, shaking the walls and the floor. Repeatedly the forge gave out its shrieking lament.

"Makes you want to piss, eh, Jake?" shouted Hagen.

"To shit, ja?" laughed the foreman, making shuddering motions as he squatted and wiggled his backside to the delight of the men operating the forge.

Then he lifted his fist as the forge relaxed, and wiped his brow. The thing was colossal. Down and down it came, again and again, hammering out armor plate, pounding it into shape with utter ruthlessness.

Hagen shook his head to clear his ears. Leaving the forge behind, they came out into the comparative calm of regimented rows of tanks, some all but complete, others only partial skeletons. PzKw Is and IIs, 7.5- and 10-ton tanks, the Mark IIs armed with 20 mm cannon. But now the 20-ton Mark IIIs, and bigger still, the 23-ton Mark IVs, which were armed with 75 mm cannon that fired high-explosive shells. There weren't many of these larger tanks, not yet. But haste, there was so much haste. Like ants, men swarmed over them. Like demons, stricken by some sort of orderly madness, they worked, knowing that at least they had jobs in these difficult times and that maybe, just maybe things would get better.

Sloped armor gave the plates greater thickness against enemy shells, deflection, too. But who was the enemy? Who was it all meant for?

At 500 meters the 75 mm cannon could penetrate 40 mm of armor plate.

From out of the constant din came the foreman's shout. "It is the 50 mm cannon barrels the general wants to mount on the Mark IIIs, Herr Hagen. This way, please."

They went through yet another shed. Side by side with the tanks, Kruppianer were turning out cannon barrels and shell casings. Every three minutes one of the casings would be jammed into the chuck, spun into the cutting tool to have its top threaded to take the detonator that would explode the shell on impact.

In one area, once an island of vacant space, a dozen or so workmen were operating a battery of stamp presses punching out helmets as if they were minting coins.

It would be a marching army, too, yet where were the trucks they'd so desperately need? The assembly lines were still there, lost in the works, but they hadn't been enlarged. Instead, the *Gusstahlfabrik* and other similar works were concentrating on heavy guns and tanks, half-tracks and other motorized armor at the expense of plain, simple transport.

At ease among the men and the machinery, and liking it, Hagen rolled up his sleeves and pitched in. Trueing the gun barrels involved running a reaming tool inside them while each barrel was turning on the lathe. The reamer would work for hours, then suddenly one of the diamonds in the head would catch and break.

Lowering the speed had helped a little. Backing off on the advance of the reamer had eased things, too.

"It is the metal, *ja*?" shouted the foreman. "It is too hard."

"It's the same as for the 75 mm cannon barrels, isn't it?"

A nod.

"How's your power supply?"

Every once in a while the lines became overloaded. The drawdown caused a drag that was followed by a surge of power. For just a split second the added torque caused one of the diamonds to catch and break along a cleavage plane.

"Back off on the speed. Slow it right down. Try 30 RPM and let's see what happens."

Three hours later, at 56 RPM, with good, sharp octahedral points and a much reduced rate of advance, things had improved. Though the process was not perfect, General Guderian, the expert in tank warfare, might just get his 50 mm cannon barrels for the Mark IIIs after all.

Smoke billowed about the first of the furnaces, filling the air with the stench of sulfur. As the taphole was ruptured, a shower of sparks preceded the flood of molten metal that raced to find the molds. Then the taphole was plugged, the furnace tilted back for recharging, and another melt produced.

One pour was much like another. The line of furnaces at the *Gusstahlfabrik* was so long, the screen of smoke and dust obscured the far end of the building.

From the head of the stairs, Otto Krantz looked into the distance as sweating, bare-armed, asbestos-aproned men labored in the heat below him.

Hagen was what he'd said he was. Then why the interest, why the special attention? Why that cable to his mother if not to ask after her health?

An element of uneasiness crept in. The flames, the smoke, the stench of sulfur didn't help.

Krantz fished out the Dutchman's address. Berlin had said help could be called in, that he'd have a free hand. Why not pay the Dutchman a little visit and have a glass of beer?

It couldn't hurt. Talk but don't ask. Just have a look. Yes...yes, that's what he'd do. Then he'd take a little side trip to Antwerp just for fun.

The Villa Hügel — the house on the hill — was huge. Lit up by floodlights and viewed through avenues of tall trees, its depressingly narrow and heavily lintelled windows looked out on the world with the stolid detachment of a prison.

In 1869 there had been no trees on the hill. Being sixty years of age, Alfred Krupp, the cannon king, hadn't had time for seedlings. Whole groves of mature trees, their roots bagged in burlap in the dead of winter, had been moved to the hill.

In April of the following year Krupp had laid the cornerstone only to find the Chantilly limestone from the quarries outside of Paris jeopardized by the Franco-Prussian War. Undeterred, he had supplied the cannons to kill the French and yet had continued to get the stone by detouring it through Belgium. He had even kept the French stonemasons who had been working for him.

It was an honor to have been called to the house. It was also a disquieting puzzle.

The man who would one day be called the Krupp was at the back of the garden, sitting in the darkness of the little summerhouse he had had built for himself. The sounds of a wireless broadcast crackled faintly. The speech was being given at another rally in Nuremberg. Hitler had just spoken of *Lebensraum*, the need for living space. East into Russia, but to get there one had to cross Poland or Czechoslovakia, and if either should prove too difficult, would he not turn westward to the Low Countries and to France?

Had the war to end all wars really been such a dismal failure?

Krupp reached out to switch off the wireless. Hagen waited for him to speak.

Alfried was thirty years old. Since 1931 he had been a member of the elite SS Fordernde Mitgliedschaft, the sponsoring members. He was a skilled pilot, a member of the Nazi Flying Corps, not of the Luftwaffe, though a colonel all the same, a *Standartenführer*.

As yet, however, he hadn't formally joined the Nazi Party. Of this Hagen was fairly sure, though many of the other industrialists had taken this final step.

He liked fast cars and was reported to be madly in love with a woman who had not only been divorced — a family taboo — but whose sister had run off to Latin America with a Jew.

Out of the darkness came his voice at last. "The Führer is impressive, is he not? The man's oratory never fails to stir the masses."

Hagen was cautious. "I was here in March of last year when ten thousand of your men gathered in the Hindenburg Bay to cheer him and to sing 'Heil Hitler Dir.' "

"The locomotive works. Yes, that was a sight. Tell me, Herr Hagen, what do you think of our works?"

"They're impressive, a city within a city, but then they're only a part of the Krupp interests."

"And the Reich? Do you think it will exist for a thousand years?"

Instinctively caution entered his voice. "I don't know, Herr von Bohlen und Halbach. I'm just a salesman, not a politician."

One might have scoffed at such an answer. The man in the corner said nothing.

Shy with strangers, awkward even, Alfried Krupp was not the easiest person to talk to. Of the same generation as Martin Bormann, Heinrich Himmler and Reinhard Heydrich, he had graduated with honours from Aachen. He was a certified engineer who had not only studied chemistry, physics and metallurgy, but had done so extensively, even if his chasing around the resorts of Europe had interfered a little with the progress of these studies.

No slouch. Not this quiet man. What did he really want?

"Tell me something about diamonds."

Hagen let a pause register surprise, shock even at such a general request. Krupp was far too busy for generalities and must, of necessity, know quite a lot about diamonds.

The cigarette glowed. To fill the pause, Krupp made an attempt at casual banter. "It is nice here in the garden at night. So quiet I can hear the works humming in the distance."

"What, exactly, would you like to know about diamonds?"

"Start by telling me about the Belgian Congo. Can we get tool diamonds from there?"

Hagen hesitated. Krupp said, "Please, there are no hidden microphones. You may speak freely."

"Very well, I will, Baron. If you mean outside of the established trading channels, then no. It's impossible. As for the Congo and its tool diamonds, no again. It's true that about forty percent of the diamonds from Tshikapa are of gem quality and that this signals a high percentage of tool diamonds, but the whole production is quite small."

"And there are no other deposits? It seems to me..."

"Mbuji-Mayi."

"Yes, that is the one. Rumored to be soon the largest producer in the world."

"Virtually all of the stones are not just industrial, Herr von Bohlen, but what we call crushing boart. Much of it ends up in the grinding wheels your people use to sharpen the tungsten carbide cutting tools."

"Then it's essential to us, but have we a problem getting tool diamonds from there?"

One could see nothing but the cigarette, the silhouette of the man. "I've just answered you, Baron. Most of what we sell — that is, of the high-quality tool diamonds — comes from South Africa."

"From De Beers, from the Diamond Corporation, the cartel."

"Yes, but you know as well as I do, that they'll soon control the deposits in the Congo as they do elsewhere."

"And the Diamant Boart, this new Belgian company of which your firm is an affiliate?"

"Merely a company to explore and promote the use of crushing boart from Mbuji-Mayi."

"Is it true this company stocks in excess of thirty million carats of this boart in Antwerp?"

In round figures about two-thirds of a ton, or at fifty percent space between the crystals, a volume of just over twelve cubic feet. Roughly the size of an average cedar chest.

Enough to cart away, if one wanted to, without too much difficulty.

Enough to last the Reich for several years. Was that what the Germans had in mind? The Antwerp stocks themselves — not just the boart but the tool diamonds and the gems? It was an unsettling thought.

Krupp repeated his question. Hagen answered levelly, "I can't say, Baron. They wouldn't tell me that sort of thing. After all, I'm somewhat of a competitor since I work for Dillingham's."

The future cannon king allowed himself a laugh. He drew on the cigarette, stubbed it out, then decided to light another.

Momentarily that thin, aristocratic face appeared out of the darkness.

"Richard, listen to me. Whatever the Ministry of Industry needs from you this time for the national stockpile, I will personally see that the order is doubled. In fact, I have a special request. *Der Firma* is prepared to order a year's supply of diamonds to fit all our own requirements."

They weren't just worried, they were scared. "Some types of tool diamonds are in short supply."

Was this caution from a salesman? "Then get them for us. The Dresdener Bank in Berlin will issue you a line of credit. So, too, will the Deutsche Bank."

Krupp's impatience was all too clear. "It's not just a question of having the diamonds, Herr von Bohlen. For specialties like drawing wire or making the cutting and shaping tools and the grinding wheels we have to employ highly skilled workmen. Dillingham's has only a staff of eight in the cutting shop, another ten in the fabricating shop. I'd have to go outside the firm to fill the order."

"Do so, but use discretion lest we force the prices up too high."

He'd have to stall them somehow. A year's supply must mean war. "I'll have to talk to my supervisor, Baron. Can you give us a little time to get back to you with an answer?"

"Time? Why should you need time? The request is handsome. I would have thought —"

"The holidays are coming up. You know how the Belgians are. You and I would work right through but they won't. There's another thing. I'll need payment in advance, in gold. I'm sorry, Herr von Bohlen, but the firm will insist on this."

More caution! "To insist is to say you do not trust us."

"Not at all. It's merely a precaution against a run on prices should one develop. Our bankers don't always advance against sales no matter how confirmed."

In the face of such an order the salesman was being difficult. Krupp paused to draw on his cigarette. He thought to say, But I've already offered you lines of credit, then thought better of it since Hagen had patently ignored the offer. "Tell me, there is talk the traders in Antwerp and Amsterdam are nervous. Have you heard anything of a move to London?"

"They're always nervous. Show me a dealer with a paper of Jagers in his pocket and I'll show you a nervous man. Even his shadow frightens him."

"Then you've heard nothing of this move?"

"Nothing, Baron. If I had, I'd be looking for another job."

"And are you?"

"Perhaps, but I should tell you that I've a seat on the Diamond Exchange and am very well fixed where I am. Your order, if we do succeed in obtaining it, can only help to keep me there."

"Good. Then it's settled. Tomorrow you will come to the office where we will provide you with a list of our requirements."

Hagen was out on the lawn, heading for the lights of the villa, when Krupp called after him. "Brazil. You did not mention Brazil as a source for us, nor did you say that at Mbuji-Mayi there are some tool diamonds."

It was late when Hagen got back to the hotel. Taking one of the postcards from the desk, he sat down to draft out a message. With tons of mail to be checked, the odds were the thing would arrive in England. Another cable so soon after the last one would only arouse suspicion, but just to be on the safe side, he'd mail the card from Hanover.

The meeting with the Krupp had unsettled him. During the Great War of 1914-18 the British naval blockade had successfully cut off the Germans from the industrial diamonds they had so desperately needed. Vowing never to be caught again, they had developed tungsten carbide, a remarkably hard material that could do many of the jobs formerly done by diamond.

The problem was, of course, that the only thing that would cut and shape a tungsten carbide tool or true one of its grinding wheels was diamond.

The Germans could still be hamstrung and they knew it. But did the Krupp's concern really mean war, or was it merely the astuteness of the industrialist in providing for all eventualities?

No matter how hard he tried to convince himself otherwise, Hagen knew the maelstrom was beginning.

To Mr. Frank Albert Winfield, 10B The Mews, Magpie Lane, Oxford, England.

Dear Frank,

Thought you might like to admire the view from my window. So much of history is being made here, it seems a shame people like yourself don't write it down. Still, I guess there isn't anything tougher than the fourteenth century. I only hope that with events so much in the news, your students can listen all day to such stuff!

Cheers, Hagen

That would tick Frank off. Hagen knew his stepfather needed that now and then.

Except that Frank lived in Dorchester and he hadn't had digs in Oxford

for some time, though the porter still remembered him and Duncan...
why, Duncan would collect Frank's mail and take it down to him.

From "The Walrus and the Carpenter" poem in *Through the Looking Glass* he had taken "admire the view" and "it seems a shame"; from the Humpty Dumpty poem, "write it down."

"Anything tougher than," and "can listen all day to such stuff!" had come from the Father William poem in *Alice's Adventures in Wonderland*.

When decoded the message would read:

KRUPP PLACES DER FIRMA ORDER YEAR'S SUPPLY DIAMONDS / QUERIES CONGO AS SOURCE / MOVE TO TRANSFER ANTWERP STOCKS TO LONDON

Two

ARLETTE LIFTED HER EYES from the cabinet. The file had been in the right drawer, but out of place and tilted up at one end. The name tag had been broken off. Ah! What had happened?

She had come to steal a last look at Richard's photograph, to read again the lines that said so much about him. *"Mbuji-Mayi, Tshikapa in the Congo...the River Gbobara in Sierra Leone...Tanganyika...South-West Africa and the Coast of Namaqualand...Minas Gerais, the Mato Grosso in Brazil..."* Where hadn't he been?

"An expert in trace indicator minerals."

De Heer Wunsch might have had the file out, but he wouldn't have been so careless. No, this had been done in haste. Someone else had wanted to look at Richard's file.

"Cause of accident: unknown but believed the result of illegal prospecting.

"Health: excellent except for infrequently recurring bouts of malaria."

There was only she, de Heer Wunsch, Lev and the other men in the cutting shop. All the rest of the work — the sintering of the diamonds into grinding wheels, or mounting of them into cutting tools — was done at the fabricating shop down by the docks.

"Has ambitions of forming his own mining and prospecting company. Has made excellent connections to this end but still must overcome the stigma of his father..."

This morning the door to de Heer Wunsch's office hadn't been properly closed.

Had someone broken in?

"Enjoys the company of beautiful and intelligent women." Nightclub owners like Cecile Verheyden! Women of experience.

What was she to do? Tell de Heer Wunsch that she had disobeyed all the rules and had gone into his desk for the key to the filing cabinet? Had done so time and again?

To see the photograph of the man she must leave.

Lev was sitting in the shade at the top of the fire escape. Timidly Arlette asked to speak with him.

"Me?" he said. "I should be so lucky. Here, please, sit down. Do you like herring? On toast? It is good, yes, but better if you — hey, listen and I'll tell you what to do. You take a slice of rye bread —"

"Lev, I'm not getting married. I must talk to you, please?"

"So, I can see you're not hungry. Is it Richard? Has a cable come through from him already?" Had Richard run into trouble?

She shook her head but still couldn't bring herself to tell him.

"Is it because you have decided to leave us? For... what was it now?"

"Another job. In...in the Browning Works at Liège, assembling..."

"Guns."

"Yes, pistols and...and revolvers."

She wrung her hands. Everyone was so upset with her and now... why now she must tell them all she was not as good as they had thought.

Lev unfolded the newspaper and held it before her. On the front page was a stark photograph, a grim reminder of the Spanish town of Guernica.

The buildings were in ruins, the streets filled with rubble.

"That child. Do you see that child?" he asked. "Dazed and frightened out of her wits. Terrified."

She knew what he was implying. "Please, I cannot stay here. It would not be good for Richard. I must leave, Lev. You know I must."

"Bombed by German fighter planes, Arlette. Seven thousand people lived in that town. There were also three thousand refugees. And when did the German Condor Legion choose to attack? At four-thirty in the afternoon on market day, no less. For sure it was on April 27, and only now has the Reich Ministry of Propaganda chosen to release this photograph so that our humble press can make us better aware of the atrocity. Annihilated, they say. Wantonly destroyed. All those people..."

"Lev, someone has been into the personnel files. I think they may have photographed Richard's file."

Bernard Wunsch was gray, with thinning, slicked-down hair, a heavy mustache and dark brown eyes. He had a rather rotund face, a comfortable paunch, bags under his sad, grave eyes and the pallor of too much dedication to his work.

Lighting yet another cigarette, he irritably puffed on it, letting the acrid smoke billow around him as he waved the match to extinguish it.

"How many times have you looked at that file?"

Arlette bowed her head in shame. "Ten...twelve — twenty! I'm not sure. Please, I...I meant no harm. I knew I shouldn't do a thing like that. I knew the personnel files were not...not for my eyes."

"And your decision to leave us is because you are infatuated with de Heer Hagen?"

Infatuated! "Yes. He . . . he does not feel this way toward me. I am sure of this. At least I . . . I do not think he does."

"But in any case you've decided it's best for you to leave us?"

"Yes."

Wunsch glanced at Lev. It had taken courage for the girl to have come forward. Worry, too, over Richard.

Blast it! Had Hagen been messing around with the girl? "You're not pregnant, are you?"

"No! I . . ." Hurt more than if he had simply struck her, she bowed her head and wept.

"Bernard, go easy, eh? Arlette's been an excellent receptionist. It's just this . . . this sort of thing. It's made her nervous."

Lev laid the newspaper on the desk. Wunsch nodded grimly but went right back to the matter at hand. "He must have had keys to the front door and the offices."

The diamond cutter nodded and reached to take the newspaper back, only to leave it. Sometimes Bernard needed to be reminded of things.

Wunsch telephoned Richard's landlady, and when he got through, asked if she'd mind checking the apartment. "We need another set of keys, Madame Rogier. Richard usually leaves his in the bureau when he's away on business. Yes, they should be in the top drawer."

He covered the mouthpiece. "She will go and see if he has taken them with him to Germany. If so, then the Gestapo have stolen them and the rest is a foregone conclusion, unless he himself was into the file for some reason."

Arlette flung up her tear-filled eyes. If ever there was a girl in love it was she.

"Richard has not done this. Please, the file, I . . . I looked at it yesterday. It . . . it was all right then."

The girl was attractive. Richard might find her quite suitable. An anchor. Not the avant-garde, the demimonde, the artists and nightclub owners.

"Hello? Yes . . . Yes, Madame Rogier. I see. The keys are there. Good. I will be around later to pick them up. No, there has been no trouble."

An uncomfortable silence settled over the office. Arlette hurriedly wiped her eyes but didn't look up. It had been like the Inquisition. *Pregnant* . . . was she *pregnant* with Richard's child? She, a girl who had never . . . "I wish I was, but I'm not! Now may I go, please?" She got up quickly.

Startled by her statement, by the obvious anger of it, both of them watched her leave the office. Not until the door had closed, did Wunsch speak. "Lev, you will notify the others in the building. See that all the double locks are changed and the alarm systems are checked — at our expense. I want no trouble with this. I will go to Madame Rogier's and find out if perhaps someone hasn't been in and borrowed Richard's keys only to return them to allay suspicion. Have only three sets of keys cut for us. One for yourself, one for me and the other for Richard. From now on we must keep a better watch on things. The time for innocence has passed."

"And the girl?"

"Try to persuade her to stay on with us. It's understandable she is upset, but if it doesn't affect her work, we could perhaps find the heart to make allowances."

"Then you'd better tell her that yourself. I'm only a diamond cutter." Muttering, "Guernica... just some pisspot little town," Lev went to see about the locks.

Wunsch looked sadly at the front page of the newspaper. What manner of men could have done such a thing?

The scratches kept showing up during the fifth stage of grinding. The surfaces would be perfect until this stage, then suddenly one stray particle of coarser grit would tear across the metal and ruin the whole thing.

Hagen held the flat, plate-sized ring under the tap and watched as the water beaded on the metal. The surface, some two inches across and very hard, had an almost mirror polish except for the scratch. Taking a clean chamois, he began to carefully dry the surface.

Outside the window the land was flat, but in the distance, along the shore of the Baltic Sea, there were moundlike dunes of light brown sand.

The laboratory was on the second floor, off in a separate wing from the rest of the giant Heinkel factory. For several days now they'd kept him busy among the production lines where rows and rows of Heinkel He-111 bombers were being assembled.

As yet they hadn't told him what the part was for, only that the tolerance of the surface had to be better than one in ten thousand.

It had to be a bearing surface of some kind — for a new kind of bombsight perhaps. The main part of the instrument would rest on bearings that would, in turn, move over the ring in its housing.

"Walter, this isn't happening all the time. Only once in a while. How's the air-cleaning system?"

The assistant foreman, a taciturn Rhinelander of forty-five, was terse as always. "Excellent. Three times a shift we change the filters. All my men wear the special suits, just as we are doing now. It has to be in the grit."

"But you didn't buy it from us, did you?"

Rows of grinding and polishing machines endlessly worked on similar rings under the watchful eyes of several technicians. "It's Herr

Klausener, my supervisor, Herr Hagen. He has insisted we try making our own grades of powders."

Hagen couldn't quite hide his surprise. "By crushing and grinding boart?"

The foreman shook his head. "No. By buying the cheaper ungraded powder in bulk and making our own oil separations."

The next step would be for them to import the boart and crush and grind it themselves.

Indicating the trouble they were having, he said, "You're not saving any money, are you?"

Walter Fritsch gave a shrug. "Me, I only do what I'm told. I haven't the wisdom of a director of engineering and guidance systems."

Rockets perhaps? "Let me see the times of settling, Walter. For some reason every now and then a tiny bit of that number-four is getting over into the number-five."

Precision grinding was done in stages, beginning with the coarsest grit, then progressing stage by stage through to the finer and finer grits, and finally to the polishing stages. The diamond powders were sized to very fine tolerances by settling in olive oil. After a thorough mixing, the ground diamond dust was then allowed to stand for ten minutes, after which the mixture above what had settled was decanted. All the finer sizes thus passed over into the next settling container and the remaining powder, after washing and drying, was classed as number-one.

Number-two took thirty minutes; number-three, one hour; number-four, two hours; number-five, ten hours; and number-six, until the oil above was absolutely clear.

By the use of the simple law of gravity the particles could be accurately sized.

Fritsch led him downstairs to a windowless, airless bunker where special rubber mats had been installed to prevent damaging vibrations. A lone technician, startled and blinking at the intrusion, cautioned silence as he decanted number one, then two, then four, timing these to a production schedule that had been chalked on a board.

"Martin, this is Herr Hagen, the diamond expert. He has suspicions that tiny bits of number-four are getting into the number-five."

Hagen shook his head to put the technician at ease. "Not suspicions, Martin, just a thought. Why don't you run through things for me? Walter, suppose I meet you back in the lab in about twenty minutes?"

Fritsch got the message and grumpily left the room. Everything appeared to be in order. Left alone with the technician, Hagen became his easygoing self. "They ever let you near that beach out there, Martin?"

"Sometimes. After work on Wednesdays and on Sundays. My wife and I take our little boy. He likes to play in the sand. It's nice. No people. Not like the Workers' Clubs."

The "Strength through Joy" holidays. "I sure could use a bit of sun myself. What time do you get off on Wednesdays? The usual?"

"At six, yes, but I keep my bicycle right outside the building. In twenty minutes I'm home and we're on our way."

"Boy, I envy you. It seems like I haven't had a holiday in years. Must be rough, though, waiting for these powders to hurry up and settle."

The technician smiled hard. Hagen felt sorry for him. "Look, don't worry. Why not get here fifteen minutes earlier on Wednesdays? Then the timing would be okay and you wouldn't be decanting stray number-fours into the number-fives."

"You won't tell Herr Fritsch, will you? My wife . . . she didn't think it would matter so much if I hurried one batch a week."

"Relax. I'll tell Walter the problem lay in the mixing. Just see that it doesn't happen again."

Hagen went to leave, only to hesitate. "Say, maybe you can tell me, Martin. What are you guys using the amber for? There must have been a fortune's worth in those bins I saw them off-loading this morning. I wouldn't mind getting a piece for my girlfriend."

The technician smiled with relief. "It's from East Prussia, from ancient mines that are now under the Baltic. There are flies in some of the pieces. Flies, can you imagine that? I'm going to make my wife a necklace for her birthday."

"It's a perk then — scrap for the boys and their wives?"

"Ah, no. It's for the insulation on the electrical wires. Apparently it's the only thing that works at altitudes above eight thousand meters. Amber dust, can you imagine that? They grind it up and melt it to make the insulation. It seems such a waste."

"You couldn't let me have a piece, could you? Mum's the word. Just so that I can show my girl what it looks like."

They found one with an embedded fly among the cluster of pieces in Martin's lunch pail. Hagen got rid of it in the first dustbin he passed.

The Baltic was ice-blue in the early-morning light. As the Stuka climbed to its service ceiling of eight thousand meters, it appeared as an angular black dot in an all but infinite sky.

The sound of the engine faded — came now and then, broken by the extreme altitude and the rushing of the onshore breeze.

Then it died away altogether.

Hagen waited at the edge of the landing field. As he looked straight up,

Dieter Karl Hunter gripped him by the elbow. The airplane hung motionless for the longest time, then the pilot tipped it over and started down.

Falling like a stone, gathering momentum with the increasing whine of its engine, the Stuka plummeted straight at them. Dieter released his grip. "Now notice what happens, Richard. Listen."

"Dieter, what're we standing here for? That guy may not be as good as you think!"

"He's one of the best. You'll see."

Hagen's mind flashed back to Africa, to the two of them standing alone on the veld as a white bull rhino had charged. Dieter hadn't budged then; now Hagen knew he couldn't do so either. On and on the plane came, plummeting at them until to the scream of its engine was added the piercing wail of a siren.

Unable to stop himself, he flung his hands over his ears. The sound of the siren was excruciating. Tears ran from his eyes. He began to yell inwardly, Got to keep on looking at it. Got to try . . .

With a bang, the Stuka bottomed out at four hundred meters in a rush of air that made him shut his eyes. Through the webs of pain he heard Dieter's laughter.

"I told him you wouldn't run. There, you see, the same old Richard."

Hagen knew he was visibly shaken. "That was the Krupp, wasn't it?"

Again there was laughter, the laughing wink of gunmetal eyes. "So, he asked, and I said, 'My friend will not run.' "

"How much did you bet him?"

"Mmm, a little. Ten thousand marks. Come now, Richard, don't be tiresome. I know how you feel about taking unnecessary risks, but it was all just a joke."

The Stuka landed at the far end of the field and began to taxi toward them. When it drew near, Alfried Krupp cut the engine, and with a final swing of its propeller the plane came to a stop.

Dieter spoke quietly as the canopy was slid open. "We are having breakfast at the Flying Club, and then you are to come to Munich with us for a little holiday. Your work is finished here, Richard. Be sure to compliment him on his dive."

The Daimler sped through the night. Since breakfast they'd been on the road. All talk had long since ceased. The Krupp von Bohlen was again at the wheel and, though he drove very fast, he did so exceedingly well, but all his concentration was required.

Hagen, having the whole of the back seat to himself since they'd last changed drivers, now had time to reflect. Alfried had listened politely to Dieter and him. It was as if the shy and future cannon king had wanted to share some of the freedom they'd once had.

Twice during the trip the Krupp had asked about Africa. Hagen had let Dieter tell his version, wishing not to contradict him but also to show, by additions here and there, that he was supportive.

Not once had work been mentioned, nothing of the sweeping changes that were all around them or of the hierarchy that had come so firmly into power. Only too obviously Dieter and the Krupp had agreed on this beforehand.

Instead, the talk had been of hunting, fishing, racing cars, women and good times. A whole day of it and some. Right across the country from the Baltic Coast near Warnemünde to Munich. A country of great beauty and much misery still. A country in turmoil, searching for its soul and fast forgetting that it had one.

Only the lights from the dashboard glowed. There were no other cars on the road at this time of night, just an occasional glimmer from a tiny village nestled in the wooded hills or by some forgotten stream.

At twenty-nine years of age Dieter Karl was the youngest son of a wealthy Munich industrialist. Having three older brothers and two sisters, one of whom was just a year older than he, Dieter had enjoyed being the baby in the family but had let none of it affect him in the slightest.

He was tall, though not as tall as the Krupp von Bohlen, with whom he had attended classes in engineering at Aachen and taken in the ski resorts of southern France and the gambling tables of Monte Carlo. The jet-black hair was short and parted in the middle, the forehead strong, the dark blue eyes fascinating to women, the nose ramrod straight. No dueling scars. No visible scars of any kind. Just the bluish shadow of a beard that never seemed to go away even with the closest shaving.

There were touches of arrogance, but these were infrequent and directed only at those who deserved the cutting edge of his tongue.

Hagen liked him immensely. Though completely different, he was almost the equal of Duncan McPherson, with whom boyhood days in Scotland had been shared. But Dieter would soon be on the other side unless things changed for the better.

"You are quiet, Richard. Thinking of some woman?"

"Yes, as a matter of fact, I was. The receptionist in our office."

"Pretty?"

He gave a snort of laughter but was surprised to find that he wanted Arlette kept as a private matter. "I suppose so. I hadn't really thought of her that way. No, I was just thinking I'd better send a cable to let the office know there's been a change in the itinerary. They'll expect me to be in Berlin on Monday, not sunbathing on the shores of the Tegelsee with Irmgard and Dee Dee. They'll be at the house, won't they?"

It was Dieter Karl's turn to laugh. "Why else have we come all this way to rescue you?"

The Villa Hunter overlooked the gardens of the Castle Nymphenburg, the legendary summer residence of the princes of Bavaria.

As Hagen started down the staircase, laughter filtered through the house and he knew the girls must be having breakfast on the sun porch.

It would be good to forget things, good to see them again. Yet the presence of the Krupp continued to trouble him. It seemed an inordinate amount of time for the head of Hitler's latest four-year plan to examine the character of a diamond salesman.

There were two entrances to the sun porch, which was built in the shape of an L. Only Dee Dee was in sight, her left side to him. The wavy, jet-black hair was pulled tightly back off the smooth, high brow to fall in curls about her slender neck.

As always, Irmgard's best friend and Dieter's current lover made him take a second look. The milk-white skin, high color on the cheeks, the finely chiseled face with slightly jutting chin were matched by lovely red lips, a broad smile and an animated manner of talking that was, in itself, a study in motion.

Flashing dark, dusky eyes betrayed a nervous intensity.

An actress, and a good one, a Bohemian not just of the avant-garde but whose ancestors had come from that region, Dee Dee Schroeder at thirty years of age was a stunning woman both on and off the stage. Her skirt was navy blue, pleated below the knees, the thinly red-white-and-blue striped jerkin falling around her hips to emphasize the leggy look of what was beneath.

The white silk blouse was ruffled on the sleeves and at the cuffs, the collar broad, floppy and open to expose the base of her throat. A nest of silver chains Dieter had brought from Cairo led to a single pendant. From time to time as she spoke or gestured, Dee Dee would suddenly retreat to the pendant, grasping it tightly as if to steady herself.

After he had watched her do this several times, Hagen realized something was troubling her.

Irmgard would be seated opposite her, the two girls having been friends since childhood and always carrying on like this when they got together, but was there someone else?

And where were Dieter and Alfried?

Hagen searched the grounds but couldn't see them anywhere. A timid hand reached for the cream and he heard Dee Dee say, "Oh, sorry, Liza," and saw her turn the pitcher so that the fingers could close about its handle.

He gave a chuckle, as much by way of letting them know he was there, as of laughing at himself. Of course, Liza Berle was the woman the Krupp was rumored to be madly in love with. Dieter had arranged the whole thing and had typically said nothing. A quiet weekend unknown to the Krupp family, who didn't approve of the liaison. Dee Dee would probably be nervous for Irmgard's sake.

"Richard!" The broad, square shoulders, the rangy, easygoing look of him, that grin ... Dee Dee pushed herself away from the table and flung herself into his arms, hugging him too tightly. "Oh, Richard, Richard, how good it is to see you."

She kissed him on the cheek, kissed him again and again, and all the time he held her, he felt the trembling.

Gently he chucked her under the chin and trailed a hand reassuringly down her arm. "What is it? What's wrong?" he said quietly.

She gave her head just the tiniest of shakes and touched his lips. Moving in on him again, she said, "We need you, that is all. Now come, don't be so serious. Come. We've someone for you to meet."

Irmgard Hunter was the same age as Dee Dee. Her lank, light brown hair was worn back off her ears in rebellion at fashion and family. Her face was strongly boned and Nordic but reminiscent, too, of the Hun. The lovely hazel eyes were sometimes gay and mischievous as now, sometimes sad, far-seeking and shadowed by despair.

She had the blush of youth and the outdoors in her cheeks, the ghost of a summer's tan, no lipstick. "Richard, so it is you at last. And how long have you been studying a certain woman?" Namely Dee Dee.

Liza Berle was blond, shy, somewhat matronly and feeling decidedly out of place. Giving her a sympathetic look, he took her hand and lightly kissed the back of it. "*Fräulein*, you mustn't pay any attention to these buffle-heads. It's a pleasure to meet you."

Ignoring the rush of "Dee Dee, isn't he gallant?" "A fop, Irmgard. An absolute fop," he said:

"They're always like schoolgirls when they get together. They need a good, long hike in the mountains to straighten them out."

Her voice was mellow and quiet. "You are the Richard my Alfried has spoken of. The American."

"In good terms, I hope?"

"Yes, of course. Alfried and the Baron Dieter Karl von Hunter are having a stroll on the grounds. They will join us shortly."

Irmgard nudged Dee Dee under the table and gave Hagen a dark look. "What about me, Richard? You have not bothered to even kiss my hand."

He took her by the shoulders, intending to give her a brotherly kiss on the forehead, but she pulled him down, locked her eyes fiercely on him and hungrily kissed him on the lips.

The breath eased out of her. Still she clung to him, swallowing with difficulty. "There, now maybe you will understand how much I've missed you."

The moment passed. They all laughed, lightly at first and then with gathering gaiety, for it had all been done in fun.

Or had it?

Hagen drew a chair toward himself and sat down at the head of the table. Irmgard called one of the maids over, and in her best authoritarian style ordered, "Sausages, Gerda. Two eggs, scrambled, please — and juice, pancake flakes, brown rolls, jam — make it black currant this time — oh, and coffee. A big cup, too. A full pot for he is almost a Belgian, this one, though he eats like an Englishman."

"You know me well."

Her eyes grew sad and distant. "I should. You are like a messenger from the outside world, Richard, and I..."

"Irmgard, please."

"Dee Dee, shut up! I need to know of the outside world, Herr Hagen. What is happening there, please?"

He would have to try to pass it off. Glancing at Dee Dee and Liza, he winked. "Nothing much. If you ask me, this is where things are happening. New roads — everywhere people building them, whole crews of teenage boys."

"The *Arbeitsdienst* — after their stay in the Hitler Youth they are drafted into work gangs for the glory of the fatherland. There are shortages, Richard. Breadlines... Not everyone is so healthy-looking as those teenagers."

Dee Dee gave her a rueful look and turned to talk to Liza. Hagen knew he had to say something. "There are shortages everywhere, Irmgard. Ranks of the unemployed. When I was in England last, I heard Welsh coal miners singing in the streets of London. They had walked, if you can believe it, all the way from their villages and towns. Never have I heard men's souls lift themselves like that. It was as if they had to use the beauty of their voices to object to their poverty."

"It will all end soon. Soon there will be work for everyone."

What was the matter with her? "Including Dieter?" he asked, leaning back to let the maid set the start of his breakfast before him.

"Including Dieter. Father is adamant that my younger brother should not go into the armed forces. All the rest of the family have important jobs in our factories. They make uniforms for the Reich, Richard, silver braids for the arms, flashes for the tunics and badges for the caps. But something equally important must be found to keep Dieter out of things. This, of course, he does not believe."

"Maybe he'd enjoy the army." Richard was being cautious.

"He'd only get killed."

Again he found himself wondering what had happened to set her off like this, particularly in front of company she didn't know.

Dieter and she were so very close.

His tone was apologetic. "Yes, of course, he might get killed. I hadn't thought of that. But there won't be a war in any case, will there?"

Liza Berle watched them with bated breath. Dee Dee seemed to sense the danger for she said quite brightly, "No, of course there won't. Why should there be? Germany's only doing what is right. Everyone knows this."

"So, we must find something for our boy to do just to keep him out of mischief and away from the pretty girls," he said, waving his fork at them.

The meal was good, the sausages excellent. He worked at eating, hoping that the impasse was now over. Irmgard studied Dee Dee; Liza picked at the tablecloth as if pecking at indecision, then shyly offered hope.

"I think this may be why my Alfried has wished to meet privately with your brother, Irmgard. Alfried is very worried about the shortages of materials, yes? He needs someone who is free of other responsibilities to be a sort of troubleshooter..." Her voice trailed off in embarrassment. She felt foolish for having spoken out.

So Dieter would be working for the Krupp...

Dee Dee entertained them with the tale of a complicated love affair that involved a Polish cleaning woman, a cluttered closet that could not be locked and a fat Jewish stage manager whose wife was suspicious.

Alfried and Dieter finally joined them, the Krupp announcing that it was a distinct pleasure to share the weekend with them.

Now, however, everything became very formal, the laughter subdued. Cigarettes were produced, and Dee Dee took to clutching the pendant all the more.

When Hagen finally caught her eye, her fingers fled from it immediately. Over and around them the talk politely flowed, he adding bits and pieces as required until, on impulse, he reached out and took the pendant in hand.

The silver work was exquisite, a two-headed Celtic symbol like the Roman Janus, with the heads back to back, one looking outward, the other inward. Both with the bleakest of expressions.

"That's from the La Tène period. The sculptor's seen it in a museum and copied it."

Irmgard didn't smile, but watched the two of them. The Krupp and Dieter talked quietly. Liza was forgotten for the moment.

Was it an age of symbols? he wondered. The crooked cross of the swastika, the double zigzag and death's-head of the SS? The banners and flags that were everywhere?

Irmgard had commissioned a friend to make the pendant, of this he was certain. But why give it to Dee Dee when it was far more her sort of thing?

The runic symbol for self, a sort of capital letter *M*, was incised in the space between the heads, but on turning the pendant over, he found the symbol for joy.

"Only through knowing the self is there joy and true peace of mind."

"You're too deep for me, Irmgard. I'm just a salesman."

"Oh? For your sake, Richard, I hope you are."

"What's that supposed to mean?"

"That questions are being asked of everyone, you in particular."

The alpine meadow was far above the lake but not nearly as high as the stunted fir-clad slopes and *felsenmeer* that rose steeply behind them.

After breakfast they'd taken the car and had driven south to the very edge of the Bavarian Alps. The scenery, as always, was magnificent. Sheep bells tinkled in the distance, and from somewhere far below them came the lonely sound of an ax.

Hagen was glad the two of them were alone. "What sort of questions?" he asked cautiously.

Irmgard looked away. Sitting cross-legged in the middle of a slab of gray, lichen-encrusted rock, she reminded him of a Norse goddess, a Valkyrie.

A questioner.

He followed her gaze. Far in the distance, down across the tree-clad slopes and avalanche trails, the heavily timbered tower of an old gristmill rose through the forest.

"Why can't you answer me?" he asked gently. "I've nothing to hide."

"I love my brother, Richard."

"So do I. We're the best of friends. You know that."

"Dieter has asked me not to tell you."

"That I've been followed this time? That the Gestapo stopped me at the border? That Franz Epp, the Krupp's head of internal security, has probably done a job on me? So what? I'm clean. I only sell diamonds, Irmgard. Nothing else."

"There was a cable for you this morning. Dieter has asked me not to give it to you until you are about to leave us. I'm to have forgotten, to have said I purposely forgot because I wanted you to stay. Which I do. Dear God, I hope you know I do."

To give himself time to think, he began to pack up the lunch. They had left the Krupp and Liza to themselves in the cabin at the hunting lodge Dieter had rented. He ought to appear angry, not wary . . .

Suddenly sick of the continual need for caution, he said rather harshly, "Can't I even trust my friends enough to let me relax and enjoy their company as I always have in the past?"

That had hurt, and he could see this in the way Irmgard clutched her knees.

Richard waited, hoping she'd tell him. She wished he'd fall in love with her, wished he'd take her to bed.

From the breast pocket of her shirt Irmgard pulled the cable. "Dieter just wanted you to do that, Richard. To relax and be with us. To remember all of this —" she swept an arm around "— and know in your heart of hearts that we are still your friends."

TO HAGEN RICHARD C/O VILLA HUNTER MUNICH
FROM WUNSCH BERNARD DILLINGHAM AND COMPANY ANTWERP
REQUEST YOU BYPASS BERLIN THIS TRIP RETURN OFFICE IMMEDIATE CONSULTATIONS STOP DO YOU SUPPOSE THEY COULD GET IT CLEAR?

She watched him closely as he read the cable, then turned away more quickly this time, to search the distance for the truth and hold his soul cupped in her outstretched hand.

She couldn't possibly know.

"You're hiding something from us, Richard. I have seen it in your eyes. I was afraid of this."

She seemed so sad this trip. He'd have to put her at ease, would have to laugh it off. "Afraid of what, for heaven's sake? Irmgard, this is a police state. You know that as well as I. What you haven't realized is that it's made you suspicious of even your closest friends. This is a straight business cable in response to one that I sent Herr Wunsch at the request, I might add, of the Krupp von Bohlen und Halbach."

"The new cannon king. The profiteer of arms, the maker, Richard, of wars. Without us, the industrialists, the Nazis would be nothing."

"Yes. Now what gives? What sort of questions are being asked about me?"

She tossed her head and breathed in deeply. "The last line. Neither Dieter nor the Krupp can make sense of it. They fear perhaps it is some kind of code."

He shook his head. Folding the cable, he tucked it away and gave her an honest shrug. "It means just what it says. Can the Krupp get clearance for the deal."

"Oh!" she exclaimed. "Even I have puzzled. I'm sorry I doubted you,

Richard. It wouldn't have surprised me in the least to have discovered that you were some sort of spy."

Her grin faded. Steadily they looked at each other, and he saw the fear come back into her eyes and wondered at it.

"Dieter would be so upset if that were true, Richard. So, too, would the Krupp, of this I am very sure."

"You're very serious this visit. That two-headed Janus was really meant for you, wasn't it?"

"You know the shit the Nazis say! They're bastards, Richard. Pigs! They've got us working for them and we're scared."

"Is Dee Dee upset about something?"

"Didn't you see the way she laughed when she told us that story? Can you imagine how it must have hurt her to lie like that? She's one-quarter *Jewish* and terrified everyone will find out, poor thing. Already there are whispers about her. No longer do the good parts come her way. It's stupid, Richard. Criminal!"

He held her close, and she buried her face in his shirt. Dee Dee and Dieter waved and then began to call and run toward them. Caught on that slope he felt so very alone.

"Richard, Dieter is going to Brazil for the Krupp. Get her out of Germany. Make my brother take her with him."

The light was fading rapidly, the rain coming soon. All over the city people would be running to take shelter from the storm.

As the first and distant rumbles of thunder came, Bernard Wunsch turned away from the window. "Lev, I really wish you'd sit down, just this once."

"Then please tell an old man what has happened?"

"Must you always use age to get the better of me? You're hardly much older than myself."

"Bernard, we've known each other a long time. Long enough for me to know you must talk to someone you trust."

Irritated, Wunsch ran a hand over his thinning hair, then used a knuckle to straighten the ends of his mustache — clear signs that he was worried.

"I'm almost certain Richard's flat was searched — no, do not look so alarmed. I have —" he touched his forehead "— a certain feeling for this sort of thing. Nothing was forced. Neither the door nor the windows, but the skylight that lets out onto the roof was slightly ajar. Madame Rogier has told me Richard sometimes leaves it open for the cat, but me, I'm not so sure."

Lev hardly breathed. "So you took a look around his place?"

"Yes, but I've not had the courage to tell you this. Instead, I've worried over it for days and days, watching always his progress in my mind. When the cable came in from Essen to say that he was sending me something in the mails, and then one from Munich to say there'd been a change in his itinerary, I decided I'd have to answer him.

"Lev, listen to me. Richard doesn't have many things. A couple of photographs of him and his father out prospecting. A group shot of the two of them in the bush with his mother. One of his friend, the Baron Dieter Karl Hunter, another of that boyhood friend of his, that tutor in archeology at Oxford, Duncan McPherson. Then his books — you know how much he likes to read. Well, let me tell you, Lev, he has hardly any books."

The man before him seemed to shrink, to whisper now. "Please . . . what are you getting at, Bernard?"

Wunsch reached for a pair of slim little volumes, something a child might read. They were bound in red leather and embossed with gold letters on the spines and the signet of a chesspiece on the front covers. "Isn't it a bit unusual for a man like Richard to have copies of *Alice's Adventures in Wonderland* and *Through the Looking Glass* on his desk at home?"

Lev held his nose, pinching it as always when struck by a thought. "So?" The sad blue eyes looked across the desk. "Don't keep an old man in suspense, Bernard. I might have a heart attack and then what would you do? Call the police or an ambulance?"

Smoke curled from the forgotten cigarette. The thunder came.

"Codes are funny things, Ascher. Sometimes a word, sometimes a seemingly innocuous sentence slipped into an otherwise straightforward message. During the war I had experience with such things. But, to be frank, I do not want to believe such a thing of Richard, but then, God help us, I do, though I would, of course, have to dismiss him immediately."

Lev swallowed with difficulty. Richard a spy . . . "What've you done, Bernard?"

"Sent him a cable. Included a couple of lines from a poem he had marked in this." Wunsch lifted one of the little books. "From *Through the Looking Glass*. It is an appropriate title, is it not? The looking glass . . ."

"What lines?" croaked Lev.

"From 'The Walrus and the Carpenter,' a delightful poem. I must confess it made me smile, but I had great difficulty in choosing an appropriate passage. To fit such words into a cable is not so easy as one might assume."

Bernard had been a cipher clerk during the war, not an intelligence officer! "Bernard, you read too many novels. This is nonsense."

Wunsch held up a hand for silence and opened the book to read him the lines in English. "They are on the beach. Just the two of them, the

Walrus and the Carpenter in great discussion, and they are looking at the sand and wondering how on earth one could ever clean the place up.

" 'If seven maids with seven mops
Swept it for half a year,
'Do you suppose,' the Walrus said,
That they could get it clear?' "

"You'd best explain things, Bernard. At the end of the day I don't think too clearly. It's my eyes. They seem to be going on me."

Wunsch set the book aside. "It was just a gamble, you understand. But because of the break-ins, I've had to try to warn him. If he is gathering information and using this poem as some sort of code, he'll realize he's in great danger."

A gamble. Two lines chosen with difficulty from a poem that had been marked. "What is it you want from me, Bernard? Praise for doing the right thing when you ought, really, to have warned him right away? Or sympathy, knowing you may well have blown his cover? If he is a spy. *If*. I'm not so sure of this. In fact, I'd go so far as to say I very much doubt it. Richard's not the type. He's far too kind and generous, far too conscious of others. Besides, he holds no loyalty to the British, not after what they did to his father."

"He holds none to the Germans, either, not after what *they* did to his father."

A weary sadness crept in on them. Wunsch stubbed out the cigarette and cleared his throat. "Lev, I've asked you in here to tell you that because of what has happened I've had to tell Richard not — I repeat not — to go to Berlin this time."

"Ascher, I'm sorry. Believe me, I know how much Rachel means to you and Anna, but Richard's life may well be in danger. He may be far too important for us to let our personal lives interfere."

So there was something else, and Richard would be only too aware of it.

Lev couldn't keep the bitterness from his voice. Self-protection knew no bounds. "Will they let you traders take the Antwerp diamond stocks to England?"

Wunsch was aghast. "How is it that you know of this?"

"Do you think I'm blind? Me? Ascher Levinski who spends three-quarters of his time shaping tool diamonds so that Richard can sell them to the Nazis?"

"Please, you mustn't say anything of this. Besides, it hasn't been decided."

"So it's true. You will try to ship the stocks to London but not the cutters and polishers."

Wunsch heaved a sigh. "It's the other members of the Exchange, Lev.

This has been a collective decision. For myself, I've tried to make them include all the skilled workmen that are so desperately needed, but — " he spread his hands in defeat "— the British are being stubborn. In all probability they won't take any of us, and they may not even agree to take the diamonds. Only time will tell, and there may not be much of that."

Lev indicated the little books. "Have you told Arlette of this business?"

"No, of course not. The girl suspects nothing more than that someone has been into the files. When Richard returns she'll be gone from us in any case. This has been her decision, Lev. I couldn't stop her. She still feels it would be best for him if she left our employ."

Tongues of misty rain swept down from the mountainside, making the forest slopes dark and brooding. Out over the lake the early-morning light was gray and cold.

Hagen gave his rod a flick, sending the fly some thirty feet toward the shore. There were just the two of them, all alone on the lake. Dieter sat in the stern; he stood in the bow to stretch his legs. The rowboat drifted with the wind.

Somehow he had to get another message off to England. Something must have happened at the office. Bernard knew nothing of the code.

The rain came stronger now. A gust rocked the boat. He braced himself and pulled up his collar. Then he flicked the rod again.

"Richard, the Krupp is nervous, yes, about having gone over everyone's heads and offered you the deal of a lifetime. It's only natural he should have wished to read your cable. You must admit that last sentence doesn't quite flow with the rest of the message."

"Bernard simply tacked it on as an afterthought. Dieter, how many times must I tell you that Herr Wunsch simply expressed his consternation at the size of the order? Personally, I can't blame him. Initially the Krupp requested I supply *Der Firma* with a year's supply of diamond products, but when I got to the office he had something else in mind. To supply the *whole* of the Reich with a year's supply won't be easy. Not only are some of the stones exceedingly difficult to get and shape, but the very size of such an order, if known, would create panic buying or worse still, hoarding by the dealers."

Dieter gathered in his line. "So you *have* a code. You communicated the order to Herr Wunsch in secret. Therefore he had to reply in code as well."

"You're being worse than Otto Krantz, a singularly unpleasant fellow I met at the border, at Aachen."

"My response to Herr Krantz's call was what released you."

"And I'm grateful, but that's what friends are for."

"Richard, listen to me. I've told the Krupp nothing could be farther from your mind than to engage in some sort of petty information gathering, yet I have to warn you that a certain hesitation still remains."

"In spite of our standing under his Stuka?"

"Perhaps because of it. Now, please, tell me how, if not in code, you communicated an order of that size to your director knowing that secrecy was of the utmost importance?"

So that was it! Given the logic of the thing, the German mentality demanded he use a code. They would assume the last sentence of Bernard's cable was in code and they'd now be satisfied with that explanation even if he didn't tell them what it meant!

Hagen was tempted to go along with things, to create a fabrication just to ease their minds.

"Dieter, what is it with you people? Do you honestly think the members of the Diamond Exchange would stoop to tapping each other's cables and telephones? That business works on absolute trust. I simply cabled Herr Wunsch from Essen and told him I was sending something in the mails for him to consider. I then sent him the estimates the Krupp had given me, and I asked Bernard to begin putting out feelers so that when I returned to the office I could take over in his absence. Not even an order of that magnitude would stop him from taking his vacation. That's another reason he's anxious for me to return."

"Then there is no code?"

He seemed so disappointed. Hagen shook his head. "But I'm going to have to send him a reply. It wasn't right of you to ask Irmgard to withhold that cable."

Richard had access to so much. Every factory, every works. "I'll take the answer into town for you. Irmgard must do some shopping. We can send it off while the Krupp and Liza are still sleeping."

"Am I not allowed to send it myself?"

Dieter moved to take up the oars. "Look, I know you have clearance, Richard, but it would be better for me if you didn't this time."

"Then can I ask a favor?"

"Of course. You know that."

"I must send a cable to my mother. She's expecting me to visit them early in August, but with the Krupp's request to attend to, I'm going to have to put her off."

"What about Berlin? Will you be joining us there, or will you be returning to Antwerp as requested?"

"Berlin's essential. Not only do I have customers who are waiting on me, but you know as well as I, the Krupp will want me to meet with his bankers just to reassure them everything will be all right if the deal should go through. The guarantees will have to be staged. They're really a formality, but Herr Wunsch will understand my hesitation to proceed without them. So, too, will he understand why I must go to Berlin."

"Irmgard will be pleased. She and Dee Dee both seem to have acquired an urgent need for you, Richard. I feel quite left out."

The time had come. "Dee Dee's in trouble, Dieter. No — don't stop rowing. Just take us out a little more and I'll try another cast."

The oars dipped, the rain made its gentle patter on the lake. Richard took up his rod, and they began to fish again.

Finally Dieter asked, "Well, what is it? What's the trouble?"

Hagen told him, and Dieter noticed that when he did so, he faced the opposite shore. A man consumed with his fishing, a salesman who knew enough to know that someone could well be watching them.

"She's afraid, Dieter. Why not get her out of the country?"

Dee Dee one-quarter Jewish ... who would have thought it possible? "I don't know. It isn't necessary."

"You know as well as I that it could be. Dee Dee's one of us, Dieter. We need to do this for her. You're still in love with her, aren't you?"

"I'm not sure. I ... I don't know anymore. I thought so. I still do. Let me think on it, Richard. These things are not so easy. There's also the matter of her parents. Knowing Dee Dee, I doubt if she would leave without them."

"Aren't you going to Brazil?"

"Irmgard's not very adept at keeping things to herself. She's the one who ought to go to Brazil. Yes, it is correct that I'm going there for the Krupp. We must have rubber. The synthetic stuff is still not good enough."

Rubber and diamonds ... "Will you see what you can do? She hasn't asked for this, Dieter. She doesn't know anything of it."

TO WUNSCH BERNARD DILLINGHAM AND COMPANY ANTWERP FROM HAGEN RICHARD OBERAMMERGAU STATION BAVARIA BERLIN IMPERATIVE STOP RETURNING NIGHT TRAIN FRIDAY STOP HOLD INQUIRIES UNTIL THEN STOP SCENERY BEAUTIFUL STOP FISHING NOT TOO BAD STOP FOOD EXCELLENT AS ALWAYS

"The company — he has not mentioned the company, Dieter?"

"He's enjoying it too much. Now come on, Irmgard, don't sulk. Richard has an interest in you, of this I'm certain."

Laying the other cable on the counter, she read it once again, then handed her brother the copy she'd made.

TO WINFIELD MRS LOIS ANNE INVERLIN COTTAGE BLACK DOWN HEATH PORTESHAM ROAD DORCHESTER ENGLAND
HAVING A PLEASANT RUN THIS TIME BUT VERY BUSY STOP

GREATLY FEAR I'M UNABLE TO COME AS ARRANGED STOP WILL
DO EVERYTHING I CAN TO PUSH FOR A COUPLE OF DAYS MID TO
LATE AUGUST STOP WISH I COULD BE MORE DEFINITE BUT
THAT'S THE WAY OF THINGS STOP TELL FRANK TO KEEP THE
CORKSCREW HANDY STOP AFFECTIONS TO YOU BOTH.

"I didn't know he felt so warmly toward his mother, Dieter?"

"He doesn't, but why tell Frank to keep a corkscrew handy? Surely his
stepfather would do so?"

"You're being too German, too cautious. Richard is only teasing his
mother. You know very well he keeps his stepfather at arm's length."

"And his mother."

Unknown to them, the message read:

TROUBLE ANTWERP OFFICE / QUESTIONS BEING ASKED /
REICH NOW ORDERS YEAR'S SUPPLY

"*Bitte*, Dieter. Please. It's so good to be alone with you."

The rain fell steadily now, and from the bedroom window in the loft, a
gray light filtered in to them.

Hunter held Dee Dee from himself, locking his thumbs into her
armpits so that her weight rested on him and her arms were wrapped
around his own. "Kiss me again. Please," she said with that desperate
urgency only she could give .

"In a minute. I want to look at you, Dee Dee. Sit back. I want to
remember this moment."

"You sound as if it will be our last! I wish you wouldn't. It's bad
enough you're going away."

His eyes lingered on her body. Dee Dee nervously wet her lips. As she
watched him, she clamped her knees more tightly against him. "Is there
something wrong with me?" she asked. Irmgard must have told him, or
Richard . . . Yes, Richard had been the one to let him know about her
grandmother. It was so unfair. Jewish . . . part Jewish!

The duvet slipped from her shoulders. Goose pimples began to rise on
the milk-white skin, exciting him.

She straightened up and arched her back. Eyes on her breasts, he
smiled, thought wicked thoughts perhaps, or thought he must leave her.

In a whisper she said, "Touch them. Wet your fingers."

Did he really love her? Sometimes Dieter simply took her for the
taking. Sometimes they made love with a passion that could only be
lasting.

When he touched a nipple, she caught his hand and held it to her
breast. Leaning back, she stirred his erection.

He brushed his hands over her flanks. Cupping each breast, he caught the nipples and made them hard — strained to sit up, and hungrily found her lips.

She drank him in. His hands slid down over the firm soft contours of her seat, gripping her now. She found her voice. "I want to come, Dieter. I need it."

"Then come. Let me watch."

"Please . . ."

Hunter lay back and grinned up at her. Flattening a hand against the smoothness of her stomach, Dee Dee spread her fingers and pushed them down into the jet-black curls of her mons — wouldn't take her eyes from his.

Parting the lips, she found herself and began slowly to bring herself to orgasm. Several times it failed, several times she touched her nipples or held the base of her throat.

His cock was big and hard between her legs. She could feel it riding up against her.

Dieter gave a chuckle. She heard it as laughter. Harsh and bitter — mocking her and so distant.

Dee Dee bit her lower lip and shut her eyes. It was horrible of him to watch her masturbating, horrible of her to do it in front of him.

Reaching back, she found his cock and squeezed it. He said, "That's not allowed."

She said, "Damn you!"

Smoke crept into her dark eyes, misting them. She held her seat — flattened a hand over a buttock, kept on until the blood pounded in her head and she gave the first of several earthy cries, didn't care anymore, had to do it. Had to!

She flung herself off him and onto her hands and knees. Waited tensely, said, "Damn you, Dieter. Do it to me!"

Hunter pushed her down over the edge of the bed. Kneeling between her legs, he flattened his hands on the cheeks of her rump, spread them, molded them, then slid the hands right up the length of her and drove himself into her.

The blood rushing into her head, Dee Dee pushed herself up against him — strained to do so and gave a stifled scream, a broken cry of ecstasy.

Again and again he slid himself into her. Moaning, tossing her head from side to side, she tightened her muscles and wept as he came inside her. Wept for all the good times they'd had, for all the promises.

Afterward, lying cradled in his arm, he smoking a cigarette, she heard him ask, "How do you find our Richard this time?"

She traced an uncertain finger through the curls on his chest. "Distracted. Worried. Why do you ask?"

"No reason. Only curious. Did Richard say anything about that mining company he's always dreaming of? We could help him, Dee Dee. I'd like to do that for him."

She laid her head on his chest, listened to the beating of his heart. "He's quiet this time. Me, I don't think he's interested anymore. Resigned to working for his firm perhaps. Yes, resigned to that and preoccupied."

"Tired?"

"Yes, tired and run-down. Irmgard is worried about his malaria. Perhaps that is what's bothering him."

"Isn't he taking mepacrine? It'll help. It always does when he goes into the tropics. He takes it for several weeks beforehand. Quinine and sulfa are only good when he has an attack."

Had someone stolen the mepacrine from Richard's suitcase? she wondered. Nothing was sacred anymore. Nothing. It would be just like the Gestapo or the Sicherheitsdienst, the Secret Service of the SS, to have done such a thing if Richard was gathering information. But then, of course, that could not be.

Hunter drew on his cigarette and held in the smoke a long time before brushing a hand over her hair. "Doesn't Irmgard suit him? What's she said?"

Dee Dee turned suddenly to look at him. "That they will probably play chess while we fuck like dogs and that she will let him win or he will let her."

"She didn't say dogs. She said make love. Irmgard's a romantic."

"And so is Richard."

"Then we must see that the two of them come together."

The rally was in the Tiergarten, in Berlin's sprawling central park. There were masses of troops, crowds of cheering people. Lines of torches lit the sky while on a platform, under a golden eagle, the hierarchy of the Third Reich sat in silence as their leader ranted on and on about peace.

The crowd remained spellbound. Not a soul moved, not a horse among the mounted guard.

Imperceptibly, Hagen moved closer to Irmgard. Dieter was running his eyes over the stage. Dee Dee was leaning back against him.

Flanked by Goering, Himmler, Heydrich and Rosenberg, the Führer paused, his clenched fist uplifted. Hess stood some distance away, with Bormann and Goebbels.

And not a sound, other than the flapping of the banners and now, from somewhere distant, the lonely, wounded howling of a dog.

Then, as if to shut out the canine insult, the Führer nodded and the place erupted with "Peace! Peace! *Sieg Heil! Sieg Heil!* One Führer, one Germany!"

Hitler beamed. Goebbels began to applaud. The band struck up the ancestral "Deutschland, Deutschland über Alles." All up and down the broad avenues the people linked arms and swayed from side to side. Mad with joy, most of them would go home believing their Führer had honestly meant peace.

Hagen scanned the faces around him. Since he'd come to Berlin there hadn't been a chance to get away for even an hour or two. If only the girls weren't with them. If only there weren't blank faces in the crowd...

Goons. Thugs. He picked them out, surprised to find so many clustered near.

Weighing the options, he put his arms about Irmgard and kissed her ear. "I promised to call on the daughter of one of our employees. Let me lose myself in the crowd. I'll meet you all back at the Kakadu. We'll have a drink and then go on to the Kranzler for a bite to eat."

"Richard, don't! Please..." She couldn't take her eyes from the stage. "Something's wrong. I feel it. We're being watched."

"She's Jewish, Irmgard. Her father's afraid for her."

"Then go. Do what you can. The crowd's breaking up."

The Tiergarten was huge, wild in parts, tame in others. Riding trails crisscrossed and circled the lowlands or went up into the woods. Down in the hollows, near the ponds, the sounds of the crowd and traffic fell away, and he could hear the gentle trickle of water as it flowed over one of the little dams.

The ponds were in series. Those toward the Unter den Linden were a shade higher than those toward the zoological gardens. Hagen followed the sound of the water. When a shadow moved, he froze. When another appeared among the trees off to his left, he knew they'd stuck close to him.

Steadily he walked out of the woods, found a cindered path and began to make his way along it toward the Potzdamer Platz.

They fell in behind him, the two of them.

Under one of the lights he was asked for the time. Then the two of them walked on ahead and left him standing there.

About thirty or thirty-five. Tough. Hands in the pockets of their coats. Collars up. No cigarettes...

Hagen turned, and when they looked again, he was gone.

Number 87 Motzstrasse was just off the Nottendorfplatz, not far from the cathedral. As Lev had said, the place was on the fifth floor. What he hadn't said was that the tenement was run-down, that the street was dark, and that the stairs, seen from the porch, rose precipitously to the first of several landings.

Satisfied that the lone car parked down the street was empty and had been so for hours, he struck a match, found the bell and rang the flat.

Nothing happened. Again he tried the bell, this time pressing it a little longer.

Still there was no answer. He thought of trying one of the other flats, thought of leaving.

Time . . . he'd have to take the time.

Cursing the place, he tried the outer door and found it open. The lock had been broken ages ago, so, too, the buzzers.

When he reached the fifth floor, there was only a small landing. Three doors led off this. The name was scratched in the dark brown paint. He knocked.

They didn't answer. It was now nearly midnight and he'd been away too long.

Looking back down the staircase, he caught a breath. It was a hell of a drop.

He knocked again, this time a little louder, a little more sharply. Still there was no answer. Only on the third attempt did a woman's voice timidly ask who it was.

"Rachel, I've come from your father."

The door opened in a hurry, the woman tearing at the locks. With tears in her eyes, Frau Tannenbaum blurted, "We thought it was the police. Come in. Please. I'm sorry, so sorry. Papa . . . Papa, how is he?"

Once started, she couldn't stop talking, though he tried to impress upon her the need for haste. She was tall like her father, with the same sensitive blue eyes, but with the long, dark auburn hair of her mother, braided into a rope that was clutched in embarrassment. "My night-gown. I'm sorry. We were asleep. Moses —" she turned to her husband "— Moses, ask Herr Hagen into the sitting room."

Behind her, lost in the hallway, Moses Tannenbaum clutched his skullcap as if still not sure of what to do with it. He wore the beard and look of a rabbinical scholar, had the wounded brown eyes of a haunted man.

Hagen dispensed with formality. "Apply for visas. Emigrate. Get in wherever you can. That's the message your father asked me to give you."

"And did he tell you the doors were closed?"

This had come from the husband. Hagen paused to reassess the situation. The bookseller slipped his yarmulke on. "The Nazis want to kick us out, Herr Hagen, but the countries of the world are reluctant to take us in."

"Will you leave if I can manage to sponsor you?"

"Of course."

"Even if it means leaving the shop?" This had come from the wife.

"You know that, Rachel."

"Look, I can't promise anything, but I'm going to England soon. I'll try to see what I can do."

Tannenbaum shook his head. "Save your breath. The British don't want us."

"What about Belgium?" Again the head was shaken. "Brazil — there might be a possibility there."

"We'd need money." Moses shrugged to indicate the flat. "As you can see, we have none."

"There'll be money waiting for you. Consider it a loan." It would complicate things, but given the circumstances, what else could he do?

Irmgard and Dee Dee had got to him.

"Say nothing of this, please. Even to your very best friends. Just keep it to yourselves."

They thanked him warmly. Rachel asked him to wait a moment more. After she disappeared into the kitchen, he heard her cutting something and then wrapping it.

"There...for my father. Please. You take it with you. It's only a bit of honey cake, but it'll tell him more than words or my letters that we're well and now so full of hope."

The street was empty. The car had left. From the direction of the Nottendorfplatz came the sounds of traffic. Otherwise the night was still, the wind gone.

A cat, a stray, wandered from an alleyway only to dart across the street and disappear into the darkness. Not liking the look of things, Hagen walked briskly away from the tenement. When he passed a boarded-up building, he knew he had his man. Short, squat and wearing a fedora. Standing by a door, cupping a lighted cigarette in one hand. As still as the night yet letting himself be seen.

Otto Krantz — he was certain of it. The Berliner would be chuckling at his discomfort.

The steps began when he was some distance away, and until he reached the bright lights, Hagen knew he was being followed.

Dieter and the girls weren't at the Kakadu. He ran his eyes over the huge semicircular bar and the crowded tables. Pretty blond and brunette waitresses were everywhere — they never hired anything else in this place. There were men on the make, women too. Business was booming as usual.

"Do you wish a table?"

"Yes. Please. For four. No, make it for five."

A number. Any number...

He let the waitress lead him to a table. He tipped her well, then took off his coat. Leaving the honey cake on the table and the coat over the back of a chair, he headed for the washrooms, pausing only to order a round of drinks for the friends who hadn't shown up.

In the back, he shoved open the door of the men's room, then made for the kitchens at a run. Once out on the street again, he managed to find another taxi. Krantz wasn't far behind him. As the taxi turned a corner, Hagen had a last sight of him standing at the curbside enjoying life, a man on holiday, a Berliner...

At the Kranzler Restaurant there was no sign of Dieter and the girls. Something had gone wrong. He should never have left them, never have asked Irmgard to distract her brother.

Dee Dee lived in Charlottenburg overlooking the Lietzensee. When in Berlin, Irmgard often stayed with her. As he paid off the taxi, Hagen could see that the lights were out in the second-floor apartment.

The hall light was out, the door to the flat slightly ajar. He warned himself not to go in, to leave while he could. The doors should have been locked.

Dee Dee was lying facedown across the bed. Her arms were outstretched, her head turned away from him, the hair spilling forward in a tangle over the edge of the bed.

Blood had trickled from a cut behind her ear.

"Dee Dee..."

He couldn't bring himself to move.

"Richard...oh, Richard. Dieter..."

The front of her dress had been ripped open to the waist. "Dieter went after you. Irmgard tried to stop him, but they...they came at me. One had a knife. They said they were going to teach me a lesson. They took me into the trees and they..."

A policeman had finally heard her screams and had blown his whistle. She had run from them and had somehow managed to get home.

She hadn't been raped. "Lie back and try to rest. Let me get you a drink. It's over, Dee Dee. Nothing more's going to happen to you."

Grimly he went through to the living room and switched on the lights. Still in his tuxedo, Dieter Karl was sitting in a chair. For a moment neither of them spoke, then Dieter said, "Where were you?"

"I went to see the daughter of one of our employees. She's Jewish, Dieter. I didn't want to cause you any embarrassment."

"Then don't. From now on be honest with me, Richard. If you need such help, you've only to ask."

"Where's Irmgard?"

"Gone home to Munich for her own good."

Daylight came at last, and with it a burst of sunlight that lit the living room and all the lovely things Dee Dee had gathered around her.

Hagen sat alone in a chair. Above the mantelpiece there was a still life by Cézanne, a magnificent thing, so simple though. A blue pot, some apples, a kitchen table. The warmth ... a mother's voice. Children somewhere ... Why couldn't life be like that?

The mantelpiece was of white, draped alabaster, with fluted panels at the sides and Greco-Roman carvings along the top. A tall, beautifully shaped porcelain vase from China complemented the painting.

There were small, gorgeous pieces of sculpture, other paintings, one by Degas, another by El Greco, a Dürer ...

If she had to, Dee Dee must be made to leave it all behind.

Dieter brought them coffee and said that she was still sleeping. At a knock, Hagen went to answer the door.

It was another cable.

TO HAGEN RICHARD C/O REICH MINISTRY OF INDUSTRY BERLIN

FROM WUNSCH BERNARD DILLINGHAM AND COMPANY ANTWERP

DUTCH PROBLEM HAS RETURNED STOP INSIST YOU VISIT AMSTERDAM STOP REPORT CIRCUMSTANCES TO COMMITTEE ON RETURN STOP URGENT REPEAT URGENT STOP THIS MUST BE SETTLED

"What does it mean?"

He gave a noncommittal shrug. "Just an unhappy client. We get them now and then. This one's fussier than most."

"And the Committee?"

He didn't avoid Dieter's gaze. "Someone's complained about me to the governing body of the Exchange. It's nothing, Dieter. It's just another problem. I get them all the time."

Three

THE MORNING EXPRESS from Berlin was right on time. At Cologne, Hagen changed trains, catching the popular Rheingold Express as it went north, back down the valley of the Rhine to Emmerich and the Dutch border.

As usual at this time of year, the train was crowded. People from all walks of life used the express, which passed daily through Germany from Amsterdam to Basel and return.

Moving through the corridors was difficult; finding a compartment with any space at all, nigh on impossible.

There was so much laughter, so much excitement, but then Hagen noticed a corner space by a window. Using German, he asked if it was free. A woman and her son, a young Wehrmacht corporal on his way north to a border posting, a corpulent, cigar-smoking Bavarian — all eyes momentarily lifted to him, no laughter now.

Squeezing into the seat by the window, Hagen found himself looking into the haunted, unsettling eyes of the boy.

The train began to move. The boy turned away. Elsewhere the sounds of holiday-makers filled the corridor. Here there was only a strained and uncomfortable silence.

Hagen shut his eyes. Dear God, he felt tired. Malaria? he wondered, cursing the person or persons who had lifted his pills. Would the Gestapo be waiting for him at the border? Would they let him go? Increasingly the strain was beginning to tell. He'd have to find out what had happened with the Dutchman. He'd have to deal with it.

With a jolt, the train stopped and he flung his eyes open only to find himself staring into those of the boy.

The train began to move again. A switch perhaps. Nothing more . . .

Realizing what must be troubling the boy, he raised his left hand and said in German, "I lost my fingers in an explosion. Some sticks of dynamite."

With an effort of will that was supreme, the boy held his gaze and remained silent.

Puzzled by his response, Hagen glanced at the mother. The woman was exceedingly well dressed.

He looked to the time-ravaged hausfrau who sat next her by the compartment door, endlessly knitting a bulky turtleneck sweater. The Bavarian turned a page of his newspaper. The corporal cleared his throat. The boy took to looking out the window, the mother to twisting and untwisting the diamond ring on her finger, a Jager of at least four carats, a beautiful thing that didn't match the plain gold wedding band at all.

Sensing his scrutiny, she became even more nervous. The twisting increased. The fingers interlaced, unlaced, and then the twisting began again.

She didn't have a chance. They'd catch her for sure.

He turned away to stare emptily out the window. Against the movement of the wheels he could hear the hausfrau's knitting needles. He thought of the U-boats he'd seen under construction in the shipyards at Kiel. Type IIs, still some of those, the small, coastal submarines of 250 tons. But alongside these there had been the Type VIIs, a concentration of effort now in making the latest in the line of 750-ton submarines that were ideally suited to the open ocean and the shipping lanes of the North Atlantic.

The Germans had to be planning a war on such a scale as to make the 1914–18 conflict appear tame. But what had prompted them to do this? What made the hausfrau knit as if she were damned?

The train passed the shade of a water tower. Reflections momentarily revealed the compartment. The boy's mother was staring at him. Hands in her lap. Still at last.

He thought of the East African Rift Valley, of other train trips, of his father shouting bits of history, the volcanic origins of the terrain, the shooting, the blacks . . . all of it as if to a friend, an equal, while his mother had sat like a thorn between them.

The woman dropped her eyes, realizing he was looking at her. Hagen turned to the boy. "We'll soon see the windmills on the flats across the river. Did you come this way before, or is it your first trip along the Rhine?"

The mother chose her words carefully. "He can't hear you, sir. The boy is deaf."

Hagen said he was sorry to hear this, and asked if they'd been to a clinic in Switzerland.

"Yes. The doctors say there is nothing that can be done. My son was deaf at birth."

Dee Dee's eyes had held that look. "I was deafened once myself — at about your son's age, but only for a week or so. I can't remember much."

"An accident?" she asked.

Glad to bring her out of herself a little, he smiled warmly. "My greatest fear was that I'd never be able to hear again. Then one morning I awoke to the sound of vultures."

He had said it so good-naturedly, yet still she couldn't help blanching. "You must have been very happy."

"I was. I thought they were feeding on me, and when I found they weren't, I realized I could hear. But tell me, which clinic were you at?"

He could laugh at himself; he must be all right. "The Friedrich Liebermann Clinic in Zurich. They are specialists in matters of the inner ear."

She had said it well enough, and that was to her credit. But still he wondered what she was hiding.

He knows my son isn't deaf, she told herself. He knows we are lying.

When she carried on the conversation, he listened again to her accent and tried to place it. The east, along the Polish border. East Prussia, yes. A long way from home. "And yourself?" she asked. "Where did your parents take you for treatment?"

The smile he gave put her momentarily at ease, but his words were troubling. "It happened in the Belgian Congo, so there was no treatment. Once my mother discovered that I could hear again, she took me to America."

And the father? she wanted to ask, but was too polite. "Would she not have done so otherwise?"

Again he smiled, a little sadly this time. "My father went off to war. It was the fall of 1917. The Americans were supplying the Congo mines by then, so it wasn't that hard to book a passage."

She gave an understanding nod, then went right back to staring at her hands. Again the diamond solitaire was twisted. Again he was left to himself.

The corporal drifted off to sleep. The Bavarian folded his newspaper. The hausfrau with the knitting never stopped.

At the border, under the guise of searching for a murderer, everyone was ordered off the train. For an instant their eyes met, then one by one they each got up.

He wondered if he'd ever see the woman and her son again.

The lines moved slowly. They stretched the length of the platform, and in the heat of the sun many of the passengers shed their jackets.

Beside each person, couple or group was their luggage. Along both sides of the tracks and at both ends of the train, flanking soldiers in gray-green uniforms stood at the ready with their rifles. Between them and the passengers were the strolling dark black uniforms of the Orpo, the Uniformed Municipal Police.

A murderer . . . All up and down the lines the whispers continued. Those who had joked and played the fool were silent. Those like the

Bavarian in a nearby lane were openly perturbed. Most, however, were confused or cowed. Some were desperate.

A murderer...

Hagen moved a pace ahead, dragging his cases along the paving stones. A black Mercedes touring car was parked beside the station house. The driver, a corporal in the SS, polished the chrome.

A murderer...

There wasn't a sign of the woman and her son. Now he regretted having put as much distance between himself and them as he could. Now he wished with all his heart the two of them could escape.

They were searching everything — all the baggage, everyone's papers, their pockets even. This became all too clear when he reached the station house.

He caught sight of the woman and her son down at the far end of the building. Her suitcases were open on the counter. A fat, grumbling customs inspector was pawing through her things. Taking his time, the man frequently paused to wipe the sweat from his brow or tip the hat he wore a little farther back on his head as he looked around.

"Herr Hagen..."

"Oh, sorry. I guess, like everyone else, I'm tired. Haven't you caught him yet?"

"Would you come this way, please?"

People glanced at him, then averted their eyes. He was shown into a room. Behind the plain oak desk there was a chair; on the wall behind it, a portrait of the Führer. A cheap, green-shaded lamp stood on a corner of the desk. There was an empty chair before it and then, some distance from this, a third chair. Empty also. No other doors to the room. No windows, either. No one else but himself.

The door closed behind him. He set his cases down and stood there waiting once again.

Half an hour later he was still waiting. A murderer...

A distracted Otto Krantz opened the cigarette case and held it across the desk. Shreds of tobacco lay in one corner. Behind the clip, the cigarettes were separated by the bullet dent.

Hagen shook his head and waited for the questions to begin.

Lost in thought, Krantz closed the case but left it on the desk between them, couldn't seem to take his eyes from it.

In October 1918 the front at Ypres had seesawed with each day. One sniper out in a no-man's-land that still defied description had caused them so much trouble. They'd hunted each other, the two of them out there all alone in the mud and shit. The man had nearly killed him. Thanks to the cigarette case, it had been the other way around.

But until today, until Heydrich's little visit to this far corner of the Reich, he'd hardly given the matter another thought.

Now he wasn't sure of things. Had he been the one to kill Hagen's father? Was that why Heydrich had hauled him out of the obscurity of East Prussia? There'd have been the divisional records, the citation for bravery, but not names attached to names. Surely not?

Match Hagen with a man who would be certain to handle him? Was that it?

The idea smelled of Heydrich. The Dillingham file on Hagen had given enough on the father to make him wish he'd never had the office broken into and the file photographed.

"Herr Krantz, what is it you want with me?"

Anger leaped only to fade. Damn Heydrich anyway! "It's not every day I find myself at a table with five drinks and no one else to enjoy them. Did you have to choose Gilka Berliner Kümmel for all five?"

"My friends like it. It's a good way to start off the evening."

"Eighty-six percent proof and the taste of caraway and cumin seeds? *Gott in Himmel*, Herr Hagen, did you honestly think I'd drink them all?"

Amusement briefly lit up Hagen's eyes. "You were following me."

In spite of the worry, Krantz feigned surprise. "But ... but of course. Didn't you know I would be doing so? I thought — "

"No one told me I couldn't go where I pleased."

"But we received a report that certain undesirables would attempt to rob you in the park. My superiors thought it best to have someone close. Surely they have told you this?"

"There was no attempt to rob me."

The Berliner sighed hugely and eased himself forward to rest his forearms on the desk. Adopting a serious attitude, he said, "Oh, but there was. Two men in the Tiergarten. They passed you on one of the bridle paths. One asked for the time, or was it for a light? You do remember, don't you?"

Decoys! So that was how Krantz had managed to follow him to Rachel's.

"I didn't know they intended to rob me. No one told me."

Krantz drew on his cigarette, then plucked a shred of tobacco from his lower lip. Inspecting the shred, he asked quietly, "Now please, tell me why you don't smoke."

"I don't , that's all. They say it shortens the breath."

The cold, cod eyes sought him out. The stumpy fingers spread themselves over the desk. "The truth, Herr Hagen. Your father smoked cigarettes."

"Yes." What did the man want?

"Once too often," said Krantz.

"Yes, perhaps. I really don't know."

"And someone shot him."

"Yes."

How did Krantz know?

The Berliner gathered in the cigarette case. Fingering it, he lost himself again. To think that the long arm of the SD could stretch so far. To think that Heydrich had called him in for such a minor thing.

And now here he was sitting across the desk from the son.

No matter how hard he tried, Krantz couldn't help but feel uneasy. The war was still that close. Why the hell had Heydrich had to choose him for this?

"Ypres, October 13, 1918. Are you bitter that someone from Germany saw your father taking a quick drag and pulled the trigger?"

"He was a sharpshooter. He should have known better."

"So there is no bitterness?"

The Gestapo seemed relieved. "Should there be?"

"Please, I am asking because I have to."

"None, then. Several of your countrymen are my friends."

"So I've been told."

"Look, Herr Krantz, while it upset me as a boy, the death of my father means little to me now."

"He must have taught you a great deal."

"Yes, and of all the things, one stands out more than the others. That nations, creeds and races shouldn't separate the goodwill men must feel toward each other."

Krantz smiled so faintly Hagen realized he'd let himself be provoked into saying the wrong thing. "I bear no ill will toward the German people, Herr Krantz. I wouldn't do what I'm doing for them if I did."

"Of course. Now tell me, please, why is it you went to the flat of Rachel Tannenbaum and her husband?"

The other chair had remained empty all this time. Hagen had the uncomfortable feeling that it had been deliberately placed there to unsettle him.

"Her father works for us. As a matter of courtesy I went to see her."

"So late at night?"

He must refuse to become irritated. Giving a nonchalant shrug, he said, "You know how these things are. Quite frankly, I'd forgotten I'd promised to see her."

"Why?"

"Why *what*? Why go to see her? Oh, merely to say hello and ask how they were. Her father's getting on."

Krantz waved a reproving finger but let the matter pass. "Please list for me all the places you visited in the Reich this time."

"Why?"

"Because I ask it."

Again the Berliner was trying to provoke him into reacting. "Then I suggest you contact the Krupp von Bohlen und Halbach, the Reich ministries of the Interior and of Industry and my friend, the Baron Dieter Karl Hunter. While you're at it, you might tell your superiors that one of the women who were with the Baron Hunter and me in the park was savagely attacked by hoodlums who attempted to rape her."

The Berliner passed a smoothing hand over the desk. He eased the black band of his wristwatch, then clenched a fist in anger, perhaps, or in dismay at such tactics. "This man, Herr Klees. Tell me about him."

"There's nothing to tell."

Again the Gestapo sought him out. "Then why is it that the Gruppenführer Reinhard Heydrich has taken such an interest in you?"

"Me?" he managed to scoff.

"You," said Krantz, leaning back in his chair.

"But I thought they were searching for a murderer?"

"Perhaps they are. Who knows? I'm just a policeman, Herr Hagen. They don't always tell me everything."

"And I'm just a salesman."

"Of diamonds. So, let us finish up this little chat with Herr Klees."

"He's a nobody. He tried to talk us into a deal we didn't want."

"Then why are you heading for Amsterdam?"

The Gestapo would have read the cables from Bernard just as they monitored everything else. "I've clients to call on."

A knock at the door interrupted them. Krantz got up to open it, and Hagen took the opportunity to study the cigarette case that had at times been clenched in that fist.

The silver plate was tarnished. The kaiser's head was badly dented.

The Berliner's voice filled the room. "Ah, Heini, of course. How good of you not to have forgotten.

"Your coat, Herr Hagen, and the tea towel. The cake . . . Please tell Frau Tannenbaum's father that I'm sorry. Another time. Another visit. The boys at the office. You know how they are."

Krantz gave a good-natured shrug and held the door open. The corporal was the one who'd been polishing the chrome.

"You will go with Heini now, Herr Hagen. Please. Just for a moment. The *Gruppenführer* wishes to extend his condolences."

"For what?"

Their eyes met. "For the delay."

Reinhard Heydrich was the head of the SD, the Sicherheitsdienst, the Secret Service of the SS, Amt I, counterintelligence abroad, and Amt II, intelligence at home. A notorious womanizer, an anti-Semite, a plotter, a schemer.

As he followed the corporal from the station house, Hagen experienced a feeling of utter desolation.

The place was now deserted. Heydrich was waiting for him on the platform in full view of the passengers on the train.

Heydrich was thirty-three, tall, arrogant, fairly thin, very blond and immaculately fitted out in a brand-new uniform. His hair was cut short. Parted on the left, it was brushed back off the high, sloping brow, emphasizing the close-set eyes, the long nose, wide, cruel lips and angular, jutting chin, which was clefted.

"Herr Hagen." The heels clicked smartly together. "Heil Hitler."

"Heil. It's good of you to think of me, Herr Gruppenführer."

The smile was there, but the look was that of a wounded cobra.

"Please accept our apologies for the delay. Our Otto will, no doubt, have told you of our little problem."

"If you'll pardon my saying so, Herr Gruppenführer, murders aren't your normal concern, are they?"

"This one was. But . . . he evaded us. No doubt the woman's family will insist we try again. They say she was beautiful. Certainly in death she was."

Hagen wanted to scream at him, What the hell are you on about? but managed to hold himself erect. A somewhat shabby businessman, tall, rawboned and loose, his suit jacket open, looking lost. A whole trainload of people delayed and inconvenienced for this. A classic Gestapo ploy.

"I trust you had a pleasant trip this time?" asked Heydrich. One could tell nothing from the look in those eyes.

"It went very well."

"Yes. A substantial order, I believe, from the Krupp von Bohlen und Halbach. He places great faith in you, Herr Hagen. We must get to know one another, I think. Yes . . . yes, that would be best. To our . . . how should I say it? Our mutual benefit. Yes, our common interest."

Hagen found himself replying evenly, "I'd like that very much, Herr Gruppenführer."

"Good! Then until your next visit, Heil Hitler."

Someone brought his cases and put them on the train. Hagen watched Heydrich until the staff car had disappeared from view.

Krantz said, "Herr Hagen, your train is waiting."

His stomach tightened. A wave of panic swept through him. Nodding, he heard himself say "Thanks."

The Bavarian was reading another newspaper. The hausfrau was knitting like the damned. The corporal pulled his boots in, then got to his feet and put Hagen's cases into the luggage racks. The woman and her son sat there looking up at him. She was ashen. Exhaustion ringed her eyes.

The train began to move and still she found the will to look at him.

Her ring was gone. The Jager had been given to the customs inspector who had gone through her bags. Even with the worry over Heydrich still very much with him, he found he could notice things like this. A customs inspector who could be bribed. The fifth counter over, against the far wall. A diamond . . . Rachel . . . Herr Klees . . .

Had Heydrich and Krantz been totally unaware of it?

Hagen sat down, but still the woman continued to gaze at him. Finally he reached across the compartment and took her gently by the hand. "It's over. You needn't go back. Just try to sleep."

"You knew him. I saw you talking to him. You didn't tell him about us."

Sadly he shook his head. "How could I have done such a thing?"

She closed her other hand over his and for a time, as the train gathered speed and crossed the border into Holland, they held on to each other like that, two perfect strangers, and yet not strangers at all.

The shop was on the Prinsengracht, one of the original canals that had been dug in the seventeenth century to bring freight to all parts of old Amsterdam. Canal houses lined the waterway. Built shoulder to shoulder of red or brown brick and five stories high, their gabled crowns rose precipitously in ornate steps, bells and cornices to jutting hoist beams, red-tiled, steeply pitched roofs and an open, slotted sky.

Directly in front of the shop, across a narrow stretch of pavement and under the leafy branches of a linden, a houseboat lay moored. Barges plied the waterway. Here and there along the canal others were tied up. A scattering of tourists strolled noisily in the midmorning sun. From time to time a clerk or a typist hurried by on a bicycle. Otherwise, the canal was at peace. The trees cast their shade.

Hagen found a table at a small café on the opposite side of the canal. From there he had a good view of the shop. Ordering coffee and rolls, he forced himself to wait.

Heydrich was still foremost in his mind. He still couldn't figure out what the bastard had wanted. To meet was one thing, to do so in front of a trainload of people, another. And Krantz . . . what had been the matter with him?

On leaving his hotel that morning he'd been followed. He had Krantz to thank for having smartened him up. He'd picked out the two of them — older men, good ones, too — then had searched for the third man and found him loitering behind. Dutch fascists. Heydrich already had them in place.

They'd played leapfrog with him, the one moving on ahead, the other two dropping behind, he letting them follow him only so far.

From now on he'd have to be extremely careful.

"Your coffee, *mijnheer*, it is not good?"

Startled from his thoughts, he smiled up at the waitress. "I must have dozed off. Bring me another, will you? It's the sun."

Concern showed in her sky-blue eyes. "You do look tired. Stay as long as you wish."

Would that he could.

Just before noon a woman went into the Dutchman's shop. Otherwise business was dead.

Hagen paid his bill, found the nearest bridge and went back along the canal and into the shop.

The Dutchman was just about to lock up for lunch. "Mijnheer Hagen —" he blurted. "This is an unexpected pleasure. You should have telephoned. You might not have found me in."

The florid, fleshy cheeks tightened. The pallid eyes flicked to the window, to the street beyond the clutter of pawnable refuse, the violins and horns, the guitars, banjos and cameras that hung in weary anticipation of a buyer.

Hagen closed the door and put the lock on, pausing only to hang the Out for Lunch sign. The Dutchman retreated behind the counter by the cash drawer. Hagen took one look about the shop, took in the incredible maze of cast-off tables and cabinets where silverware, china, soup tureens, old books and trays of jewelry lay asleep.

A cluster of seashells caught his eye. The stench of mold, age, sour sweat and stale cigar smoke stung his nostrils. Picking up a butcher knife, he felt the edge. He chose another and then another, as if dissatisfied with them all.

Klees broke at last. "Please, what is it, *mijnheer*?"

"You've been to the Antwerp Exchange and laid a complaint against its youngest dealer."

The Dutchman gave a lusty snort. "I know nothing of this, my friend. What complaint? From me to those stuffy old bastards? Hah, you've got to be kidding. Why would I complain about you? Why would they listen to someone like me?"

He had a point. Hagen set the knife aside and made his way over to the counter. "What, exactly, did you do?"

The pale gray eyes narrowed. The Dutchman eased open a drawer, then flicked a glance to the street beyond and nervously wet his lips. "I went to see de Heer Wunsch to ask again that he help me."

"But he threw you out. He turned you down."

"Yes, that is correct."

"Then what?"

The fingers moved to the drawer again. "I came back here. Nothing else."

Hagen moved a little closer to the counter. Spreading out Bernard's cable, he let the Dutchman read it.

Still the hand lingered by the drawer.

"I telephoned de Heer Wunsch last night when I got in, *mijnheer*. He told me that I was up against it, that you had laid a charge against me and that my seat on the Exchange was threatened. Now talk."

The fingers moved. Hagen shot out a hand and jammed the drawer shut, catching the fingers in a vise!

The Dutchman cried out in pain. Thrown back against the shelves, he knocked some crystal loose. The glass shattered at his feet.

Easing the drawer open, Hagen released the fingers. Then he took the pistol, slipped open the breech, popped the shell and the clip and tossed everything back into the drawer. "I'm still waiting, *mijnheer*. I'm not leaving until you tell me what happened."

Klees winced. Cradling the fingers of his right hand, he stared at Hagen. The pistol...the speed with which the salesman had unloaded it... "You must believe me. I know nothing of this, *mijnheer*. Others must have used my name. Perhaps they made a simple telephone call."

"Who?"

The Dutchman shrugged.

"Has anyone been to see you?"

Klees shook his head. "Am I under surveillance? Please, for the...the sake of others you must tell me."

Hagen gave him a swift look. "You tell me how you get the stones."

The wariness crept back. Again Klees glanced to the street. Satisfied, he said, "The pieces come out of Germany and I buy them when I can. Lately I've been taking the stones from their mountings as you yourself have advised. The deals are honest. I swear they are. I've invested heavily and want only to protect myself. Believe me, you and de Heer Wunsch are my only hope. I've already exhausted all other possibilities. It's really not much to ask. A vault in London, what could be simpler for you to arrange?"

"Who do you get the pieces from?"

"Doctors, lawyers — who knows, it's all the same. They need ready cash, and this I can supply."

"Not from this rattrap."

Klees showed no emotion. "I have other means. Savings. A —"

"A house down on the Oudezijds Voorburgwal?"

"The Achterburgwal. You know the inner city well, *mijnheer*. Perhaps you have visited with one of my girls."

Hagen picked up the cable and began to refold it. "What do you keep the houseboat for? A floating bordello?"

The Dutchman didn't smile. "You know very well the police would not allow this. The houseboat is where I live in summer."

"Show me what you've acquired in the past few days."

"There hasn't been anything in for nearly a week."

"Damn you, let me see it anyway."

"Very well. If you will excuse me a moment, I will just go into the back, to the safe."

"I'll follow, if you don't mind."

Behind the shop there was an incredible warren of junk, piled here, piled there, swords, old muskets, several bass violins, trombones whose slides were dented, trumpets no one would want, packing cases, suitcases and trunks that had been pawned on arrival at the station or left unclaimed and bought at auction . . .

One of the workbenches held the guts of several cameras. Out of these, Klees had been attempting to assemble a salable item.

On a brick wall, across a sea of junk and seen through cluttered, open shelves, he had hung a collection of dolls, perhaps a hundred or more, of all sizes, all shapes. Some had bits of clothing. Most lacked an arm or a leg, even a head. A clown faced outward while his body was cruelly twisted the other way and hung by a thread of stuffing. Another nail held only a Rhineland maiden's braided rope of flaxen hair.

Gobs of mortar protruded from between the bricks, tongues of gray against the red. One naked doll was running, another was pinned to the wall with her knees spread widely and her pants pulled down about her ankles. Yet another hung upside down with perpetually open eyes. One leg had been torn away.

Sunlight fled across the collection, casting shadows from the battered bars of a grimy window. Dust filtered in the light and still the dolls stared at him.

"You've quite a place."

"Yes. Now, please, allow me a little privacy while I open the safe."

Hagen looked at him. "How do I know you don't keep another gun in there?"

"I do, but would I risk a charge of murder when it is yourself who is in trouble? Believe me, *mijnheer*, I've been along the road you travel. I know exactly what it's like."

The office was tiny, cut out of the warren with see-through shelves that revealed again in fragmented glimpses the rack of broken dolls, the dim gray clutter of broken hearts and shattered hopes.

The Dutchman knelt to turn the dials of an ancient safe. Across the desk, under the light, was spread a collection of what had once been antique jewelry. A cigar box held the scrapped mountings of several earlier forays, ready to be melted down and cast into wedges of silver and gold. Another box held a handful or two of second-rate stones. Some glass, some cheap bits of paste. Hagen let them trickle through his fingers.

Klees nudged him aside. "These came in last week. Please, I don't know what this is all about, Mijnheer Hagen. No one has been to see me. I've said nothing to anyone, and I don't know anything about a complaint against you."

Among the pieces was the woman's ring. Hardly a day had passed since he'd last seen her on the train.

Antwerp was beautiful in the early evening. It was a relief to be home at last, even if there was still trouble ahead. Because of the hour and the annual holidays, there was less traffic than usual on a Friday night.

Hagen stood outside the Central Railway Station. The office wasn't far, the meeting with Bernard and the Committee scheduled for nine o'clock. He had a good hour to wait, time enough for a stroll. He couldn't sit still, couldn't eat. He had to get this meeting over with. So much depended on it.

Yet the heart of the city beckoned, and he wanted to feel a part of it again.

When he came to stand outside the boardinghouse where Arlette lived, he had to smile at himself, for his feet and a tramcar ride had led him where his mind had told him not to go.

She'd be off on holiday — at Ostend with her parents. When she returned to work she might, quite probably, find his office empty. In any case he couldn't become involved.

Yet he had to see her.

The guild houses of the Grote Markt reminded him of those along the Prinsengracht. As he passed the corner of a street, two girls of seven or eight were skipping next a faded red brick wall. Unbidden, the images came to mind, the wall space filled with broken dolls, all shapes, all sizes, all races. Arlette . . .

The Nazis would wreck this place. They'd banish light and innocence.

Turning abruptly away, he headed for the office.

The Committee was waiting for him. They had purposely put off the meeting for an hour so as to have time to rehash the situation and come to a consensus before he arrived. It was all too clear they were far from happy.

Jacob Lietermann was the acknowledged leader of the Antwerp Diamond Exchange, a man of great integrity and immense experience. Well into his seventies, he still worked every day, still smoked his cigars when the doctor or his wife were not near and he thought he could get away with such things.

"Richard, you are punctual. That is good in a young man. Yes, very good."

The dark eyes had lost none of their earnestness. A searcher all his life, Lietermann looked only for what was best in men and diamonds.

That look was questioning but then the moment passed.

"You know the others. Isaac Hond, Abraham Merensky and, of course, our Bernard, who has so graciously taken us into his confidence both as to the break-in at this office and to the fantastic deal the Krupp von Bohlen und Halbach has offered you."

A twinkle momentarily appeared in those ancient eyes, flecks of curiosity.

Lietermann noticed the whisper of shock that news of the break-in had brought; he noticed the control, too, and counted these both positive signs. "To sell the Reich a year's supply of industrial stones is no mean feat, young man."

Hagen didn't waver under his scrutiny. "I must apologize, Mijnheer Lietermann — gentlemen — you have me at a disadvantage. I've only just got in. Mijnheer Wunsch has not had a chance to brief me."

That, too, was a good sign, the choice of words, the putting before all else responsibility to one's employer. Lietermann took him kindly by the arm and led him to a chair.

"Richard, this is not a court of inquiry, but a gathering of friends. As you know, we have always settled things among ourselves. Have a seat, listen to Bernard while he tells you of the break-in, then of the charges against you, and lastly of his reasons for confiding in us so that all might have a say in supplying or not supplying the Reich with such a commitment."

The Antwerp Exchange ruled itself by this informal committee of its elders. Isaac Hond was bearded, dressed in a dark black suit as always and with the worried look of the perpetually nervous, for which he had, in truth, every reason, though now there was a scowl he did nothing to hide. It was through him, through this thin, pale little man, that all the important decisions of the trade passed. He had a mind for prices, for the trends and styles that set the trade in Paris, London and New York.

Abraham Merensky handled the delicate relationships that existed not only between the Exchange and the cartel in London, but between the dealers in the Antwerp bourses and between them and their workers. It was to him that fell the settling of squabbles, the righting of wrongs and the meting out of appropriate disciplinary action. The overseeing of the apprenticeships in each of the shops also fell to him, a task that was not always easy. Like the others, he had an exhaustive knowledge of the trade. He, too, was getting on, and Hagen, as he listened carefully to Bernard, wondered what these men would really do if the crunch were to come.

They'd best all go to London first so as to keep their businesses intact. And then, what then? New York or Israel.

From behind his desk Bernard Wunsch summed things up. "So, Richard, you see we're not without our reasons for concern. Not only have the office and your apartment been broken into and your file almost certainly photographed, but some anonymous person has telephoned Mijnheer Merensky and laid charges against you not only of illegally trading in diamonds but of assisting de Heer Klees in the transport of stolen gemstones."

"The stones aren't stolen — at least, not technically. Klees buys them from destitute refugees who are on the run."

"But are you dealing with him, Mijnheer Hagen?" asked Merensky.

"Of course not. On my way home, I went to see him to clarify things. Klees emphatically denies he telephoned you."

Isaac Hond was adamant. "The caller has said there will be proof."

"Did he appear in person? Since when would you convict a man on such flimsiness? I told Klees we'd have nothing to do with him. Bernard was left a memo to this effect."

Wunsch gave a nod and reached for his cigarettes. Richard was handling himself well, but there was still more to come.

Merensky cleared his throat and gripped the arms of his chair. "Then perhaps, young man, you'd be kind enough to tell us why someone should wish to discredit you in our eyes?"

"Richard, have you done anything in the Reich you shouldn't have?" asked Wunsch.

What was the matter with them? "Of course not. I'm far too busy. Bernard, you of all people ought to know that. Look, I honestly don't know why anyone should want to do this."

"Perhaps," breathed Isaac Hond, letting the word fall softly as he glanced from one to the other of them.

It was Lietermann who interceded. "Richard, is there something we should know? Have the Nazis..."

Hagen hoped his look of concern would suffice. "They know we're thinking of moving the Antwerp stocks to London. Don't ask me how they found out. I certainly didn't tell them, but the Krupp asked me of it and he questioned me on alternate sources."

"Should the Reich find itself cut off again without a ready supply of industrial diamonds," interjected Merensky, studying the cigar he'd taken out. He let his words hang in the air, knowing they would drive the others to remember the Great War and the blockade.

Then he said bitterly, "Damn the Nazis, Jacob. What the devil are they up to?"

A big man, with pallid jowls, Merensky clenched his fist and broke the cigar.

"Abraham, please. Your blood pressure," cautioned Lietermann. "Some coffee, Bernard?"

"Something a little stronger for me," snorted Merensky. "A cognac, young man." He snapped his fingers. "I know full well Bernard keeps a bottle in that cupboard."

It was Hond who, not looking at any of them, said, "So, I have told you this already, Jacob. Me, I have said the Nazis would find out about our wish to move the diamond stocks to London. They have their spies everywhere — the break-in here, the theft — yes, we must call it that — of Mijnheer Hagen's file is evidence enough. Now they will try to scuttle our plans. Our businesses will be ruined."

"Isaac, please. It's not a disaster yet," cautioned Lietermann. "Richard, I take it the Gestapo paid some attention to you this time?"

Unsettled by the question, Hagen said warily, "Yes... yes, that's true. Normally I've been given a fairly free rein. We send the Reich Ministry of the Interior my itinerary. The Germans then check it out and — "

"The German security services," interjected Isaac Hond.

"Yes, the Gestapo, the Sicherheitsdienst — the Abwehr, for all I know," countered Hagen. "Someone checks the itinerary and the ministry provides me with the necessary letter of approval."

"Someone checks *you* out, Mijnheer Hagen," said Merensky. "Please, we're not fools."

Hond replenished his coffee, pausing as he did so. "But this time the Gestapo kept an eye on you?"

Again Hagen found himself having to say, "Yes... yes, that's correct."

Hond jabbed at him with the sugar spoon. "So why, please, should someone want to discredit you in our eyes?"

"In all honesty I don't know, sir."

"Oh come now, young man. Come now," interjected Merensky.

"Richard, you won't have seen the newspapers yet," said Bernard anxiously. "That Brussels rag the Nazis own has slapped a photograph of you and Heydrich on its front page. The handshake of goodwill."

Betrayal was in Bernard's dark brown eyes.

"They're trying to suggest to us that not only are you not to be trusted, Richard, but that you are one of them."

This had come from Lietermann but all of them were the accusers.

Hagen ran a weary hand over his brow, pushing aside the boyish hank of hair. "I'm just a salesman, gentlemen. I'm not one of them. How could I be? I'm one of you and I always will be."

It was Isaac Hond the worrier who quietly said, "You've done amazingly well with them, Mijnheer Hagen. This latest request of the Krupp's only serves to emphasize their continued faith. So, what are we to think when we see you saying 'Heil Hitler' to the head of the Sicherheitsdienst, the Secret Service of the SS!"

"That he's a very difficult adversary for us to have to face, and that for some reason — one we may never know — he's decided to make a point of meeting me and of letting everyone — not just yourselves, gentlemen — know of it. Incidentally, I didn't say 'Heil Hitler.' I said 'Heil,' as I always do when forced into that particular corner. I also didn't know my picture was being taken."

At a curt nod from Merensky, Wunsch reluctantly opened a drawer and took out the two little books he had found in Richard's flat. For a moment he ran his fingers uncertainly over them. *Alice's Adventures in Wonderland* and *Through the Looking Glass*. Things were at such an impasse he regretted ever having questioned Richard's possession of the little books.

Yet he had to say it. "Richard, there is a very obvious reason why Heydrich should take such a personal interest in you. Could it be that he feels the German Military Intelligence Service are not doing their job? We are all aware of the fact that men such as yourself must have Abwehr clearance, though it's never admitted by them. The matter of moving our diamonds to London would, I assume, also be a matter for the Abwehr, not the Sicherheitsdienst?"

"I don't know, Bernard. Your guess is as good as mine."

"No, it isn't, Richard. Yours is infinitely better."

He couldn't waver. "I'm sorry, Bernard, but I simply don't know what you mean."

Wunsch felt the little books again. "Several of the poems are marked. Though it's not common knowledge, I myself have some experience in these matters. Such things are used for secret communications. Are you gathering military-industrial intelligence for the British, the Americans or both?"

Hagen looked sadly at each of them. He wanted to confide in them but couldn't.

"I wondered why that broken passage from 'The Walrus and the Carpenter' had been included in your cable, Bernard. Gentlemen, I can appreciate your concern, but those books were read to me as a boy by my mother. We had to travel light while prospecting. Even in base camp, where my mother and I usually stayed, things were pretty primitive. As a very young boy I came to love those little books, that's all. That's why I have copies of them."

"These are not typical of something that has been knocked about in the jungle, Richard. There are no mildew stains. The termites haven't been at them," said Wunsch.

"Of course they're not mildewed. My mother found those for me in a secondhand shop and sent them on as a birthday gift."

"But there is no inscription!" exclaimed Bernard, being fussy. Damnably fussy.

"She wouldn't have written one. Ever since she left my father we've not got on. Gentlemen, please try to understand that my actions have always been honorable and will continue to be. When this happened — " he held up his left hand "— it was the last straw in a marriage that had been steadily deteriorating. When I was well enough to travel, my mother refused to let me stay with my father and took me from him to the United States. I loved my father very dearly. To understand this, you have only to appreciate that he gave me adventures no other boy could ever have had and that he treated me always as an equal. If she had stayed with him, he'd be alive today."

"Still hunting for diamonds," said Merensky dryly.

"Yes. He knew parts of the Congo like the back of his hand. He was in on the discovery of Tshikapa, in on that of Mbuji-Mayi, though others got the credit."

"And the profits." This came from Lietermann of all people.

"Yes. I admit he felt badly about some things, also that the Diamond Corporation has been trying to make it up to me ever since."

"Then you hold no ill will toward Sir Ernest?" asked Hond. Suspicion still.

Hagen met his gaze. "Why should I? Sir Ernest has always been more than kind to me."

Hond was persistent. "And you've no thoughts of forming your own mining and prospecting company — of striking out on your own and being a rebel like your father?"

So that was it. They were afraid Heydrich had tried to bribe him into working for the Nazis. "None at the moment, *mijnheer*. I'm still learning. As for the dream, don't all of us have one? A realist would say it's crazy, my father, that it was essential — that the farther off, the better, so long as there was the dream to keep us going. I love prospecting. It's always been a part of me, and always will be, but for now I'm entirely content to be working for Bernard and yourselves."

It was Lietermann who, seizing the moment, said, "Richard, please give us your thoughts on what is happening in the Reich. Let us have the benefit of your travels."

Hagen talked for nearly an hour, at times earnestly, at times with a sadness whose depth of sincerity could not be misunderstood. Somehow they had to realize time was of the essence, that no matter what the opposition, everything had to be done to clear the way for transferring the diamond stocks to London.

"All their industries are working at capacity. It's awesome. It's the greatest war machine the world has ever seen."

For several minutes there was silence. Merensky stared at the crumbs of his broken cigar; Bernard fiddled with the knot in his tie.

Isaac Hond sought solace in the carpet.

Jacob Lietermann was again their spokesman. "Richard, you must be exhausted. Indeed, if you will forgive my saying so, you don't look well. But if you could spare us another hour? Sir Ernest has cabled a request that you pay him a visit in London. We must decide on this and other matters. Please, you do understand? Perhaps you could visit briefly with de Heer Levinski and his wife. They'll want the news of their daughter I'm sure you bear. Then, on your return, we will not keep you waiting any longer."

Lev and his wife took the news of Rachel and her husband for what it was, an honest appraisal. Hagen said that he was sorry he couldn't have been more helpful. "But I may have a lead on one or two things. I've asked them to apply to Brazil, and I've told them I'll lend them sufficient money."

Lev was grateful but still he had to say, "If they can get out in time."

Hagen knew he had to give them further hope. "There's another avenue. Let me explore it a little more on my next trip. If it looks like we can get them out that way, I'll let you know the moment they're here. The problem then will be in keeping them in this country."

"And the Committee?" asked Lev.

He shrugged. "I'm on trial. The whole thing's a mess."

"Don't worry. Those guys know what's what, Richard. That Lietermann —" Lev touched his temple "— he's smart. They might suspect you of espionage, but this will only make them think you have the ear of important people in London. Even I, a poor diamond cutter, have figured this out, haven't I, Anna?"

His wife gave him an uncertain smile. Lev patted her hand and beamed. "Because of this, you're all the more valuable to them."

Hagen couldn't bring himself to tell them that Krantz had followed him to Rachel's house. "How's Arlette?"

Lev told him that she had left their employ and why she had done so.

"It's not often a girl feels that way toward a man. If I were you..." He looked away. "Bernard, he feels the same as I do. We both think...well, of course, it's none of our business."

When Hagen returned to the office, Lietermann told him that the Committee had unanimously decided to publicly dismiss the charges against him as false and to give him all the support he needed.

"Now you must go to London for us as soon as you can, Richard. Try to convince Sir Ernest, of the urgency of our request. Tell him about the guns and airplanes. Tell him about the Gestapo and the apparent interest of Reinhard Heydrich."

Tell him.

"And what will I tell the Krupp about his request for a year's supply?"

"That you cannot possibly get so many together at one time without disrupting the market, but that you will see what you can do."

Sunlight sparkled on the waves off Ostend. As the sailboat came about, Arlette drew in the cool salt air and said, "It's so good, Willi. Just to feel free like this. Why didn't you tell me the *Vega* was such a boat?"

De Menten laughed. "You're surprised? You really like her?"

"Oh, I do. She's perfect. Such a job. But are you really sure the varnish is dry?"

"Of course it is. I'm sorry you had to wait so long."

Stretching his lanky legs across the well of the boat, de Menten hunkered down out of the wind and folded his hands behind his head. He was glad now that he had kept her waiting.

Arlette felt the 5.5-meter yacht beneath her hand. She lifted her eyes momentarily to the masthead. The bow went up. Spray glistened in the sun.

She knew Willi was studying her. He was the son of a butcher and she had known him nearly all her life. He was thin, wore wire-rimmed eyeglasses, had red hair, freckles, was overly serious at times, overly rambunctious and fun-loving at other times. An awkward boy in the guise of a young man of twenty-six. Sometimes she thought he would never grow up. At other times he seemed ancient. He had a temper, too.

The sun had burned the pale skin over the bridge of his nose and under his sea-green eyes. It had bleached the long lashes, and she wondered how many times he had had the boat out and not said a thing of it to her?

Willi had bought the *Vega* from an estate auction and had worked on her all winter in his spare time. The brass fittings shone. The sails were new; he had sewn them himself.

Yes, he was very capable with his hands. She'd have to give him that. He wasn't handsome. He was gangling, and what started off badly with the short red thatch, the protruding ears, narrow face and long neck only continued down to the big feet that were death on the dance floor.

She was pleased he had fixed the boat so beautifully and had kept it as such a surprise. She was flattered, secretly warmed inside, and men — most men — were not handsome anyway.

But she didn't love him, not in the way she...

"That's a new bathing suit, isn't it?"

She drew in her tummy, hauling on the mainsheet a bit. "Yes. Do you like it?" She wished he'd leave well enough alone, was nervous now.

Goose pimples had risen on the tan she had acquired since coming home for the holidays.

"You know I like it. Especially the front and the back!"

Arlette let go of the tiller and dropped her eyes to her front, threw her hands up to the straps, then watched in dismay as the boom swung toward them.

Petrified, she couldn't seem to move. Her breasts must have shown. She hadn't tied the straps tight enough! She knew she hadn't!

De Menten leaped for the tiller and the mainsheet. The boom swung back. The sail flapped mercilessly, then snapped taut as it refilled.

Coloring quickly, Arlette found him very close to her. Their knees were touching. One bare leg rubbed against her own. "I'm sorry. I should have done better but it...it wasn't nice of you to tease me like that. You're always teasing, Willi."

She was so embarrassed, so afraid of his scrutiny. He kissed her then. The kiss was awkward and not very satisfactory. They might get better, but she had the uncomfortable feeling they never would.

"Don't you like me, Arlette?"

She dropped her eyes, was crying now. "Of course I do."

"It's *him*, isn't it? That guy at the place where you used to work?"

"It is not! I just want to have some fun. I want to sail."

He let her take the tiller again. He said he was sorry, but she could tell that he didn't mean it.

"What'll you do now that you've left Dillingham's?"

"Look for another job. In Liège, I think," she said with punishing severity. "My cousin says there might be something for me at the Browning factory."

"From diamonds to guns, that's quite a change." Liège...it was so far away. "Arlette..."

She tightened up on the sail, gave the jib a passing glance, then examined all the rigging. "Yes, what is it?"

She was afraid.

"What would you say to staying here? My father...he might be willing to let me take over more of the business. We're doing well with the hotels this season. We've got two men working for us now. One of them could take over the deliveries."

"I thought you didn't like working for him? I thought you were sick of driving that van?"

"I am. But there's something else, something really big. Arthur Lund, down at the garage, says he could use me. I'm good with cars, good at fixing engines. In a year or so I'll have my mechanic's papers. Maybe then we could..."

There were crowds of people on the beach in front of the hotels and guest houses that lined the promenade. Some huddled in the lee of their bathing tents, others sat in deck chairs behind striped bits of awning.

As they came abreast of the pier, one of the tour boats sounded its whistle while the other one came in to dock. Soon it would be time for the afternoon ferry from England.

"Willi, I need some time. Please. Just a little. I must find myself another job, yes? I can't expect my parents to keep me."

"Your father says you're needed in the shop."

"He always says that. He's said it since I was a little girl."

"Your mother wants us to get married. She's been talking with my mother."

"Yes, I know. But there's lots of time. Let's just enjoy ourselves. Let's not spoil things."

"I didn't think I was."

"Oh, now you're hurt! All I want is a little time. I need to find myself, Willi. I need to be on my own for a while."

When hunger got the better of them, they made peace with each other and headed up the coast to where the beach was not so crowded and the ragged dunes were piled.

Marram grass seesawed in the wind.

Hagen watched their approach. Beyond the sailboat, almost due west of him, he could just make out the chalk-white cliffs of Dover.

The distance was nothing. The Germans could be across it in no time.

Arlette clambered lithely forward to lower the jib. Willi de Menten furled in the mainsail. When they reached the shallows, Arlette lowered the anchor into the water.

The bow swung into the wind. She slid over the side and hung on, looking up at de Menten and laughing now.

Hagen could see that they'd done this sort of thing lots of times. He had no right to interfere. He ought not to have come.

She stood in the shallows with hands on her hips. "Richard... Richard, is that you?"

He turned and left them quickly, hoping that she hadn't seen him clearly.

The Church of St. Martin raised its spire above the town of Ypres in the distance, while all around them the almost featureless plain of Flanders spread.

Willi hugged the wheel of the battered Citroën van his father didn't know he had borrowed. "Well, what now? What the hell do we do, Arlette? This is crazy. He could be visiting any of the cemeteries. There are thirteen of them. Thirteen! We'll be half the night and all day tomorrow searching for him. And why? What the hell's he to you? A cemetery on a day like this! An idiot! He must be an idiot!"

The argument had gone on like this all the way back to the harbor, to town, the street outside the butcher shop, and on... "Hush. Turn here. My father said he'd be going to the one at Vlamertinge."

They swung into the military cemetery, which was just outside the tiny village, not far to the west of Ypres. De Menten took the van in a mad loop and then another and another, raising dust.

The only other vehicle in the parking lot was an ancient taxi they both recognized. Its driver was a displaced dockworker from Rotterdam, a renegade in shabby coveralls, no shirt and scruffy boots.

Henk Vanderheide believed in bathing inside. He scratched under his fleshy chin, sucked on the fag that clung to his protruding lower lip and looked up wistfully as they pulled in beside him and lurched dangerously to a stop.

Arlette leaned out of the cab, a breath of fresh air on the heat of their exhaust and an engine that had probably rebelled. "Henki, have you seen de Heer Hagen? Where is he, please?"

With a start, he realized she was wearing a bathing suit! Grinning hugely, he jerked a thumb over one shoulder to indicate the nearest path. "He's in among the stones, communing with the departed. You in a hurry or something?"

"Yes."

He drew on his fag, coughed, wheezed desperately and finally said, "Well, you shouldn't be. Not in a place like this. It's far too quiet. Willi, my boy, have you got any beer?"

As she got out of the cab, Vanderheide saw that her feet were bare, her legs...

"Willi, wait for me, please."

Henki let his eyes rove up her backside. The calves of her long legs were shapely, the backs of her knees soft, tender pads, her thighs, Lord Jesus her thighs, were slender, her ass...Oh God, oh Jesus, what an ass...tight like a young green pear.

Willi yelled at her, "I never want to see you again, Arlette! Go to him then. See if I care!" He hit the wheel, bruising a hand.

She yanked open the door and crawled back up onto the seat. "Willi, listen to me. De Heer Hagen is in trouble. I must go and see what he wants."

Dragging her beach coat after her, she remembered her sandals, which were on the floor. Giving a muttered "Mother, please," she slipped these on, tossed Vanderheide a reproving glance and headed for the path.

The two men watched her, Willi with tears in his sensitive eyes, Vanderheide with outright lust, for she walked in that way women who are good in bed walk, slackly, with ease and confidence, as though they know they're going to get it and want only to hurry.

She reached a grove of lindens, went under these and out across the lawn. Regimented headstones flanked her now, row on row, some with holly, others with roses. Here and there Lombardy poplars threw their shade so that some of the stones were darker than the others.

"Richard, what is it? Why did you leave us like that?"

He was standing alone in the shade before one of the headstones. His back was to her, and for a moment he didn't turn.

"You shouldn't have come. I told your father I'd drop in to say goodbye."

He looked so worried.

"Arlette, go back. Please."

"Not until you tell me what's wrong."

"I don't know. Everything, I guess. Maybe nothing." He gave a shrug and smiled then, smiled so gently she found herself loving him all the more.

"Did you come hoping I'd return to work at Dillingham's?" she asked eagerly. "Lev said you would."

He grinned sheepishly and pushed the hair back off his brow. "As a matter of fact, I did, but then, on the beach there I thought...well, I thought I had no right to interfere in your life. Besides..."

Her eyebrows arched in puzzled alarm. Was there someone else, someone like Cecile Verheyden?

A sadness swept over him. He thought of Klees, of the wall of broken dolls. He thought of the German war machine, of the Stuka and its siren. He couldn't drag her into things. It wouldn't be right, wouldn't be fair to her. "Arlette, I don't want to see you hurt."

She tried to understand, tried to comprehend. When he turned from her, she read the inscription: *Corporal William R. Hagen, died 13 October 1918.* "So many of them died here, Richard. Over 250,000 in one battle alone."

"It was a bloodbath," he said grimly.

Taking out his wallet, he removed a mud-stained, single slip of folded paper. "Just before he was killed, my dad wrote me this. He was out in no-man's-land and he was worried. The man he was trying to kill had no name but was good — the best my father had come up against. They'd been after each other for days."

Hagen refolded the thing, found a match and set it alight. "Please don't be horrified. I can't keep it any longer. It would only be dangerous for me if I did."

He was so sad. He didn't take his eyes from her. "Why?" she asked as the last of the letter fell.

Hagen wanted so much to send her away and yet couldn't bring himself to do so. "Because, although I still can't believe it possible, I think I must have met the man who shot him."

Four

THE STONE was a cushioned oval brilliant that had been exquisitely cut, but it was the color that took his breath away. A dark, North Sea blue. A good eight carats. Hagen wanted to shout, Have you any idea how rare that is?

The setting was Edwardian. In addition to the pendant stone, the rope twist of platinum held six clear white, old-mine diamonds, each of at least a carat.

He couldn't believe his luck. As a matter of course he scanned the antique shops whenever he could — it was a part of the business, a part of keeping oneself aware of things.

The soft chuckle and easy manner betrayed the scoffer of too-high prices. Tavisham of Tate, Tate and Tavisham, Old Bond Street, London, smiled benignly. "Just in from the Continent, are you?"

"In and on the run. London seems the usual."

The swift eyes met Hagen's. "Does it ever change?"

"Seems calm enough considering the threat of war. God knows what'll happen if the Germans start dropping bombs again."

Point taken. The shop was cluttered with fine old porcelain and crystal. "Diamonds are always the best of security in such times."

"War does bring out the worried. A pity there are so many of these old pieces on the market."

Damn the man! Tavisham lightly brushed three troubled fingers across his brow, then fastidiously tightened the knot of his tie. "Were it not for the times, we'd simply have put that stone away."

Hagen set the diamond down on the felt cloth, then draped the rope of lesser stones on top of it and glanced at his watch. The meeting with Sir Ernest was in forty-seven minutes. Time enough.

The gray business suit was brand-new. A man of means? Tavisham wondered. "Would you be looking for something suitable for a young lady, sir?"

Again there was that gentle chuckle, the laughter in those gray-blue eyes. "With a war in the offing? No, I'm just interested in where it came from. An estate, I suppose?"

"Fontainebleau, Sir. The piece is French."

The Tavernier then. Lev would swear to it.

Tavisham said, "Seven thousand pounds, sir, and exceedingly inexpensive at that."

There'd be tears in Sir Ernest's eyes. "Two thousand, five hundred. You can keep the old-mine Jagers."

Ah now, he had let him know for certain what was up. Would they dicker like Titans?

Tavisham shook his head.

Hagen let him have it. "Thanks for your time, then. I must rush."

He was at the door when the words struck him. "Three thousand, five hundred."

"Charterhouse Street. You can let me out at Holborn Circus. I'll walk from there."

"Righto, guv. As you please."

The Haymarket, Pall Mall, Trafalgar Square and Nelson's Column passed in succession. Crowds of tourists mingled with clerks, porters, typists and men in bowler hats, all hurrying home from work. News vendors hawked the *Times*, the *Daily Mail*, the *Evening Herald* and others.

The taxi turned onto Victoria Embankment and headed east toward Waterloo Bridge and King's College. Hagen lost himself in thought.

The Hope Diamond was a part of the Great Blue Diamond, the stone Tavernier had brought to France from India in 1668 and had sold to Louis XIV. Already faceted, it had weighted 112 carats. Dissatisfied with its brilliance, the Sun King had had the stone recut to 67.5 carats. The excess, the waste, had been lost — gone forever. No one knew where.

Then in 1792, in the closing days of the French Revolution, the Blue had been stolen along with others. Carried to London, it had disappeared, only to show up again in 1830 as a remarkable dark blue diamond of 44.5 carats and unknown origin.

Rumor had it that they had cut two stones from the residue, one larger than the other. Had the diamond in his pocket been one of them? Had it gone full circle back to France, to Fontainebleau, only to show up in London again? Were the times not those of trouble once again?

It was an absolutely gorgeous stone.

The offices of the Central Selling Organization were along from the Vegetable Market and across the street from the butcher stalls of the Smithfield Market. Though uneasy that the chairman had asked to see him, Hagen found he had to smile. Diamonds and vegetables or sides of beef — it said so much about the man.

Unlike so many of Britain's corporate leaders, Sir Ernest Oppenheimer had worked his way up from the bottom. First as an apprenticed sorter in

London for the firm of Dunkelsbuhler, then as their buyer in Kimberley, South Africa. He had an encyclopedic knowledge of the types of diamonds that came from each of the mines, but more than this, far more, he was an extremely astute businessman.

From Anglo-American to Consolidated Diamond Mines of South-West Africa, to De Beers as chairman of its board of directors.

It was an impressive career that spanned more than forty years. The control that De Beers now exercised under Oppenheimer was all but absolute. What mines they couldn't buy, they convinced their owners to sell them all their product. What promising prospects they couldn't acquire a controlling interest in, they kept at until they did.

Their whole philosophy was to make diamonds scarce and thus of great value. In this Sir Ernest was simply following the dicta of the original syndicate of ten, or those of Solly Joel, its leader in 1917, who bought sight unseen the whole of the czar's diamonds from the Bolsheviks for a quarter of a million pounds and then had simply locked them away for years.

Now nearly ninety percent of the world's diamond production was funneled through the Central Selling Organization's offices.

Having had the third degree from the Antwerp Committee, Hagen wondered if he would now get it from the chairman.

Bernard and the others were one thing; Sir Ernest quite another. He'd want to know what had happened with Heydrich — yes, of course — but he'd also want an analysis of it. He'd want the state of things in Germany to add to all the other reports that filtered through to him. He'd probably — and here Hagen was all but certain — have heard of Krantz's interest in him.

It wouldn't be easy, but with Sir Ernest, as with any good businessman, there was always the unexpected.

This quiet, well-mannered, gentle and unassuming man was waiting at the far end of the sorting room. Hagen sensed the choice of meeting place had been deliberate. The room was long, the man diminutive beyond the seemingly endless row of white, cloth-covered tables on which was gathered in round, flat, conelike piles here, there, everywhere, the week's assortment of rough gem diamonds.

Windows to the north gave the sorters' bench light. Apart from Sir Ernest and himself, everyone except the security guards had long since left for the day.

The walls and the ceiling were white, gray-tinged now by shadows. His footsteps echoed, driving home a message he was well aware of long before he ever reached the chairman.

In 1932 the total world sales of gem diamonds had been a mere £20,000. One by one Sir Ernest had closed the De Beers mines in South and South-

West Africa. Production had fallen to fourteen thousand carats, less than 1/160 of what it had been in 1930.

Even so, prices had continued to plummet, the market to dry up. In spite of this, Oppenheimer had had to continue buying up the production from the mines he didn't control, particularly those in Portuguese Angola and the Belgian Congo.

By 1937 the stockpile had grown to over forty million carats of gem rough — twenty years' supply at the best of times. And now there was La Forminière in the Congo to haunt him. Apart from De Beers, they themselves had a stockpile of nearly thirty million carats of crushing boart alone.

Then, too, there was pressure to move the Antwerp stocks to London and to stop dealing with the Reich.

No matter how one looked at it, the chairman was facing the most difficult time of his life.

"Well, Richard, it's good to see you again."

"Sir Ernest, I hope I'm not late."

They shook hands. The chairman gave a deprecatory wave. "You're never late, and in any case it would only have given me more time to think. So often now one has to rush. I like the quiet of the sorting room best. Then one can see at a glance what it's all about."

Responsibility had aged him even in the past six months. The well-groomed hair was thinner, grayer, the mustache now completely iron gray. The brow was permanently furrowed, the eyes faded with a still and distant dream.

Looking down the length of the sorting tables, indicating the diamonds before them, he said somewhat sadly, "There are always two questions before us, Richard. How do we sell them, and if we do, how do we maintain their price?"

They exchanged a few pleasantries. Oppenheimer asked after his mother, after Bernard Wunsch and Ascher Levinski.

Hagen said they were well, though both Bernard and Lev were worried about the international situation.

Oppenheimer nodded sympathetically. "You people are so much closer to things in Belgium."

"Sir Ernest, the Nazis must be planning war on a scale never seen before. If so, the market for gems that's only just beginning to reestablish itself will evaporate."

"My thoughts exactly. A lot of old stones are suddenly coming on the market. Will it become a tide, I wonder?"

Taking the pendant from his pocket, Hagen handed it to the chairman. At once Oppenheimer was intrigued. He sought the north light only to find it all but gone. Using one of the lamps, he examined the facets, the style of the cutting. Then he drew out a loupe and went to work.

Fifteen minutes later he was using microscope, diamond light, fluoroscope and set of calipers. By then they had removed the stone from its setting and had weighed it at 8.7139 carats. Oppenheimer's enthusiasm refreshed him. It had been good to work on something together, good to talk about the situation in Europe while busy with a totally different problem. It pleased him to know that Richard had remembered his passion for collecting colored diamonds.

"Richard, the depth of the blue is right for the Kollur Mine, but the weight is too high."

"It's possible, Sir Ernest. Two stones were cut from the residue. Ascher Lev has always maintained they'd surface someday."

"Ascher Lev. Has he lost the end of his name or something?"

Hagen grinned. Oppenheimer went back to studying the diamond, then asked what he'd paid for it.

Richard could be blunt when he wanted.

They spoke again of the overhang, of the old gem diamonds that were coming onto the market and interfering with the normal course of business. "We're being forced to buy them as well, Richard. It's not the best of situations."

In silence, they looked over the tables where perhaps a quarter of a million carats of gem rough lay waiting to be absorbed. Oppenheimer let the silence grow as he held the blue before him. It had such color he hated to leave it, but things had to be said.

Setting the stone down on the table between them, he turned decisively from it to give Hagen a piercing look. "Richard, what's this business I hear of with Reinhard Heydrich?"

"He knows the Krupp has asked me to supply the Reich with a year's supply of industrial stones."

"And what, exactly, did he say to you?"

"That the two of us should get to know each other, that it . . ."

"Go on, Richard. Everything."

Hagen nodded. "That it could be to our mutual advantage."

"Yet if I understand de Heer Lietermann correctly, Heydrich's Sicherheitsdienst may well have been responsible for trying to use de Heer Klees to discredit you in the eyes of the Committee?"

"Perhaps Heydrich wanted to apply the stick as well as the carrot? Perhaps his people had nothing to do with it."

"Perhaps he wanted to shake us up? Was that it? Perhaps he merely wanted to show friendship with an American? There are so many perhapses with a man like Heydrich, Richard, you'd do well to be wary."

Oppenheimer gave him a moment before saying, "Is he about to offer you a job?"

"I don't know, sir. I only wish I did."

"Would he have heard of this talk to move the Antwerp stocks to London? It's only talk by the way. King Leopold and his government are adamantly opposed to such a move lest it be perceived by the Germans as a breach of Belgium's policy of neutrality."

"Heydrich must know of it, Sir Ernest."

Again there was that moment's pause, the careful searching of him. "We're trapped, Richard. You, the Committee, all of us, by governments over which we have no control. Britain hedges, Belgium hedges, Germany makes its secret moves, and we, poor mortals, do what we must."

Sell diamonds. "Sir Ernest, the Germans are thinking of alternate supplies. I believe that soon they'll be sending someone to Brazil. If I know him, it won't be long before he realizes he has to head for the Congo."

"La Forminière, yes. The deposits at Mbuji-Mayi. Well, he might have some trouble there. Did you know we've just concluded a long-term agreement with the Belgian government?"

Hagen hid his surprise. "No, I didn't, but like others I assumed some arrangement might be in the offing."

"De Beers will buy all the stones from Mbuji-Mayi and Tshikapa, both the gem rough and the industrials, including the thirty million carats of crushing boart the Diamant Boart have in stock in Antwerp. In return, we've agreed to supply the Antwerp dealers with the best of each year's production of high-quality gem diamonds from our mines."

Impressed by the extent of things, and the secrecy under which the agreement had been made, Hagen spoke his thoughts aloud. "That ensures Antwerp will remain the cutting center of the world unless..."

Oppenheimer nodded grimly. "Unless there is a war. Try not to upset the Committee unduly, Richard. They're nervous enough. Keep an eye on the Nazis and send us a signal if you think we ought not to wait any longer."

Among the diamonds on the tables were those that when cut and polished would be Jagers, the clear white stones. Oppenheimer picked up a small handful and let them trickle through his fingers. "I had a cable from America yesterday, Richard. We've done all the market studies and things look good. Do you know what we're about to accomplish?"

"No, sir, I don't."

The chairman's look was distant, his thoughts lost to the dream. "We're about to embark on an advertising campaign that's designed to persuade the average American woman to want a diamond engagement ring. Up to now such a thing has been a matter of choice or chance, most couples preferring not to bother with a ring and certainly not with a diamond. Pearls, yes. Rubies — perhaps something a grandmother might give the girl. Imagine then the transformation in the eyes of each of those millions of girls when they know, Richard, that the box they have just received will contain the rarest and most precious gemstone of all. A pure white, absolutely clear and beautifully faceted diamond."

Oppenheimer tossed a hand. "I'm convinced this will succeed, and if it does, we'll have an almost unlimited market for stones of a size that has previously been hard to sell at the best of times."

The smaller ones, the kind the average Joe could just afford.

"We're going to convince them, Richard, to hold on to their diamonds not just as an investment in their marriages, but in their financial futures. We're going to eliminate once and for all the threat of that blessed overhang that haunts us!"

They were miles ahead of everyone else in their thinking. That's what it took.

In silence they strolled the length of the sorting room — passed by a fortune or a pauper's sum. There were diamonds with yellowish tinges, others that were a light coffee shade. Those that were clear white had been sorted from those that were colored. Among the fancies, those very rare and beautifully tinted stones, there were those of a deep emerald green, others of a soft and delicate rose, others still of a citrine yellow, a lemon yellow, a canary shade.

There were even some clear black stones with a hidden fire that only the cutters and polishers could release. There were blue stones, too, but none as fine as the one he'd purchased.

Oppenheimer said it for the two of them. "Fontainebleau . . . isn't it odd that your diamond should have come from there?"

On the way to Hagen's club in St. James's, Sir Ernest asked him about his gathering intelligence for the very few that would listen. "I'm not unaware of the way things are here in England, Richard. The people don't want to believe Hitler means anything more than what he claims — namely, peace. The government, far from being totally ignorant, is very well aware of the situation. But there are those who would preach more than this, those who would urge rearmament at a far faster pace. If you are gathering information for them, then Herr Heydrich will have a great deal of interest in you. For the sake of us all, I sincerely hope you aren't."

"I'm just a salesman, and up to now I've been allowed to travel freely within the Reich. I can't help seeing their war machine in action. After all, I'm an essential part of it. Heydrich is not an easy man to comprehend."

"And Mr. Churchill?"

"He knows nothing of me, nor have I any thoughts of trying to meet with him."

"Then perhaps my information is incorrect. We want you with us, Richard. You know there's a place for you here. Why not consider it? A move to London would do you good."

"I will, Sir Ernest. I'm grateful for the opportunity."

"Then stick to selling. That's what you're paid for."

"Would you like to acquire the stone?"

Oppenheimer sadly shook his head. "I have too many. When things ease up a little, why, yes, I'd take it kindly if you'd sell it to me. At a handsome profit, of course."

Hagen was surprised that the chairman hadn't asked him Dieter Karl's name. Instead, he had told him about the arrangement with the Belgian government and La Forminière.

Rain . . . constant rain. The river swollen beyond its banks, the red mud clinging to the boots, the knees, the hands. So heavy . . .

Rain. The din of it. The way it got into everything, the bread, the tea, the porridge, the meat, the punky wood, the hammock at night.

Rain. The racket it made. The way it ripped apart the leaves so high above them. The way a sudden deluge hit the shoulders and stung the skin.

Rain on the backs of the blacks. Rain puddling on the ground behind them as they squatted and shit themselves. Rain in their haunted eyes, the terror of the unknown. Rain on their naked flanks. Rain in the singing of them as they fought to keep their loads and the long, long line of them followed the river.

Rain. The smell of it. The sweet, sickening stench of everything. The warmth, the heat, the cold.

From the streambed of the Tshiminina to that of the Tshikapa, then down the Kasai to the Lulua and up the Lulua to its juncture with the Luebo and the trading post.

Rain on the jungle thatch. Rain dripping through on him. Rain. The cold. The shakes. The heat.

Rain . . .

"Richard. Richard, listen to me. It's malaria, son."

The chills, the shakes coming on him so suddenly. Defenseless now, frightened, weak. Cold, hot, cold, hot. The bitter taste of whisky and quinine . . .

Rain. The sound of it.

Hagen shut his eyes and ran a shaky hand across his brow. As the late-morning train left the outskirts of London, the sweat clung to his fingers.

The diamonds of Mbuji-Mayi had been a disappointment. The year had been 1917 — just forty years after Stanley, the country still largely unexplored, the bush often hostile. For 155 days they had been on the trail, only to find at the end of it handfuls of diamonds that had had no value at all back then.

After the malaria had passed, they had left the trading post and had cut overland. The rain forest had finally given way to open woodland, brush and savanna. The sun had burned down.

Mbuji-Mayi had lain on a low plateau. There had been diamonds in the gravel of most of the streams, diamonds virtually everywhere they had dug their grid of test pits through the ocher-red lateritic soils to the beds of old rivers now long since moved on. Ten, fifteen, twenty and thirty meters down, the diamondiferous gravels had all been thin, the stones seemingly spread over an immense area.

Never one to leave a region until he had worked it to death, his father had dammed off a bend in the Katsha River and had made it swing west of them. With the riverbed baked under the glaring sun, they had set the blacks to work screening the gravels and panning the coarser sands.

All the indicator minerals had been there, the tiny brown crystals of zircon, the deep red grains of pyrope garnet, uvarovite, too, and ilmenite. Diamonds . . . lots and lots of diamonds.

Each pan, each nest of screens had held them. By the end of a month they had had handfuls of crushing boart — cubes with dimpled surfaces and weak, greasy colors of yellow, brown, green, black, gray and white. But not one gem, not one good, clear crystal that might have helped to pay for things. Just boart. A bust. Damn!

Had they been employed by La Forminière it would have helped. Had they had permission, that, too, would have helped.

As it was, not only had they been in the territory illegally, they had done so over the governor's expressed refusal to let them prospect.

The concession, the right to search for diamonds, had gone to others.

The cofferdam had kept the river away long enough. Hagen recalled how he had placed the charges at intervals along the length of it. By the age of fourteen he'd done this sort of thing often enough. But now he was to do it entirely on his own.

"What delays did you use, Richie?"

The black powder fuses had burned at a rate of one foot per minute. "Sixteen feet on number-one, twelve on number-two, and eight on number-three. I can run between them, Dad. By the time I get to number-four I'll still have six minutes to get clear."

His father had cast an eye over the naked bed of the river to the cofferdam beyond. No one had been around. The blacks had all been moved well away. Since leaving the trading post they hadn't seen another soul. Even so, they both looked upstream as far as the bend would allow.

"All right, son, go and light them."

On the silence of the day had come the excited murmurings of the blacks.

Number-one's fuse had sputtered as it caught. Number-two's had ignited. With number-three there had been trouble. Finally in desperation he had cut a foot of it away and had got it going.

Running then, he had made it to number-four. Again the fuse had sputtered.

He'd got it going, had started to run, to get clear . . .

"A boat! A bloody boat!"

For one brief second the bend, the chocolate-brown river, the green haze of the scrub and the sky beyond had appeared before him.

Then he had heard the beat of the drums. A canoe . . . white pith helmets . . . rifles . . . the governor . . .

"Richie, don't! Richie!"

Hagen shut his eyes and wiped the sweat away. The fever raged. His shirt was soaked with sweat.

He remembered the day, the river, the flotilla of canoes and how it had drawn nearer and nearer to the cofferdam. He remembered how he had thought they would all be killed.

The burning fuse had been at his feet, the cutters in his hand. He had run from charge to charge and had cut the fuses, but number-one had been too short. Number-one had had to be dug out of the boulders and earth with bare hands clawing, clawing now, the fuse burning faster and faster, he shouting at himself to throw the dynamite into the river, to throw it as far away from the canoes as he could . . .

They had found him downstream on a sandbar lying face into the sun with the vultures circling above him.

Others had moved in on the prospect, and his father had gone off to war.

"Porter, could you get that bag down for me?"

"Right you are, sir. Now watch your step. Will there be anyone waiting for you?"

"My mother, I should think."

"That's what mothers are for."

"Not this one."

She was standing at the far end of the platform, her ash-blond hair cut short and pinned back by barrettes, the suit of dove-gray tweed, her figure still that of a willow wand.

As he walked toward her, all the bitterness of his father's death and her remarriage within one week of it made her swim before his eyes.

Hagen wished she hadn't done it. He wished he could bring back the past. If only he hadn't shaved. If only he stank of gin and beer and sweat. If only he'd just come out of the bush...

"Hello, Mother."

Lois Anne Winfield — Mrs. Frank Albert Winfield — threw her stern blue eyes swiftly up at him and saw the grin, wanted to smack it from his face. How could he do this to her? How could he? "Richard. Oh, Richard, for God's sake, you've got malaria again. Couldn't you have waited? Couldn't you have come to see me just once without reminding me of your father?"

Reaching up, she felt his brow. Reaching down, she took the suitcase from him.

Then she stood there looking at him. "Darling, why? Why must it always be like this? I was so looking forward to seeing you."

"Where's Duncan? Didn't you tell him I was coming?"

He was still the same, still intractable, still blaming her for everything. "Get in the car, damn you! I'll have to call Dr. Simpson as soon as we're home. I only hope for your sake *and* for your stepfather's and mine that he's not off birding again."

"Mother, I asked about Duncan. I have to know if you told him."

"You're in no condition to... Oh, for heaven's sake, he's not at the gate house — hasn't been there in ages. He's at Maiden Castle, at the hill fort again. At least I think he is, and at times like this I wish to hell he'd stay there and leave us alone. You've got to go to bed. The fever has to break. Please try to behave for once."

"I can't. I've got to see Duncan. You should have told him."

"I did! I drove down there as soon as I got your wire, only he was someplace in France. The girl didn't know where."

"Then I'll drop you off at the house."

"Richard, you can't do that."

"Mother, I have to see him."

"Later. When you're better, and not before then."

By nightfall he was delirious and running a temperature of 105°F.

"Richard... Richard, please try to calm down."

"Brazil... Duncan, I shouldn't have asked Dieter to take Dee Dee to Brazil. I should have got her out myself."

"Richard, I warned your father not to take you back into the bush."

"Munich... I've got to get back to Munich, got to ask Irmgard about Dieter. Can't take that chance. Can't let them know what I'm doing."

"The dynamite. Richard, listen to me. Darling, I knew something was going to happen to you. I begged your father not to take you with him."

The panic left him to be replaced by an icy calm. "Krantz, Otto. Berliner, about fifty-five or sixty years of age. Ex-soldier. Tough. Thorough — painstakingly so. Gestapo. Get me everything you can on him, Duncan."

His voice fell away. He gave a gentle smile, then laughed cruelly at himself. " 'The time has come,' the Walrus said, 'to talk . . . of shoes — and ships,' and guns and tanks!"

She caught her breath, but he said nothing further, and after a while she thought he had finally drifted off to sleep.

As if the day, the moment, were long ago and he but a boy, Lois Anne Winfield saw him lying there in a thatched hut in the jungle. Dirt was everywhere. Dung was everywhere, but neither he nor his father gave them any notice. They never did.

Flies . . . dear God, why did there have to be so many flies? Or rats, for that matter? Or snakes? Or the natives, their precious blacks, the Bantu who wondered at the color of her skin and liked to touch it when she least expected?

Richard and she had been reading the Alice books over and over again, because they shut out the world she had come to hate and brought her closer to the son she had feared she'd lose.

"Folke-Wolfe Condor 200. Maximum speed, 224 miles per hour. Rate of climb, 656 feet per minute. Ceiling, 19,030 feet. Range . . . Duncan, the range is 2200 miles. They can hit us from anywhere. The bomb load is 4,626 pounds."

"Richard . . . darling, what in the *hell* have you been up to?"

He was so like his father, so impossible. She wrung the cloth and clamped it to his brow. She sponged him off and tried to turn him over.

Just as she had done so many times before, she whispered, "Sleep . . . sleep, damn you, Richard. The fever will soon pass."

"Arlette . . . can't become involved with her. Must break it off before it's too late."

She shook him hard. "Richard, you're in England! You're safe! No one's going to bother you here."

Fog rolled in from Lyme Bay to blanket the Dorset hills. On Black Down Heath it drifted eerily, smothering the gardens at Inverlin Cottage and all but hiding the many chimney pots that crowned the brooding Tudor manor house.

Hagen stood beside the Bentley that was parked on the circular drive.

The days had passed on into the first week of September, bringing with them the cold, hard shock of reality. The attack of malaria had gradually lessened, the last of the fevers breaking two days ago. But the whole business had left him extremely weak and anxious.

He was lucky it hadn't happened in Germany, lucky only his mother had been there. He knew he had said things he shouldn't have.

Putting on his fedora, he looked up to the leaded windows of the library.

His mother didn't move. In her nightgown, she stood there staring down at him from beyond the glass, and he knew then that he had awakened her, and he felt sorry for this.

She looked like someone out of the Brontë sisters, locked up in this great tomb of a place with only her garden and her husband to keep her warm.

"Richard," she whispered. "Richard, what is it with you? Are you so like your father you care nothing for those who love you?"

He had mentioned a man named Klees and a wall of broken dolls.

Like someone who knows it is useless to speak out in his own defense, he got in the car and drove off without a wave. All too soon he was gone from her, and the gulf between them had widened a little more.

The visibility on Dorchester Road was down to less than thirty feet. When he finally found the weathered signpost with its tilted arrow, Hagen eased the car off the main road onto a narrow lane.

Thistles, a few late asters and daisies grew with goldenrod among the waist-high hay, but beyond the farm gate, the pasture was close-cropped.

Switching off the engine, he got out of the car and stood there listening to the hush of the land.

Duncan was out there someplace, alone in this.

The all but silent patter of the drizzle came to him, the sound of laughter from long ago, and then the first few hesitant words that had passed between two wary boys of sixteen.

Duncan hadn't asked why he had been sent to them, why he had given his stepfather such a hard time, or why he had felt the loss of his fingers so much.

Instead, he had sized him up and swiftly come to a decision. "Can you climb?"

"Of course I can."

"Och, I mean *really* climb. High, like. You'll no be afraid?"

The aerie had been on the cliffs near Lochinver on the northwest coast of Scotland. Once that first ascent was over, they had climbed and climbed, for Duncan's father had kept the place of his wife's birth at Lochinver and every summer had sent his son there to be with her family.

In the fall they had gone to school together, but who would have thought Duncan would become a tutor in archaeology and prehistory with a consuming passion for studying the Celts?

The dark, forest-green MG sports coupé, with its threadbare canvas top, was parked to one side at the end of the lane. Beyond it, a thin, stony trail ran into the fogbound fields and hills.

Maiden Castle was the most impressive of the hill forts that dotted the countryside and occasionally drew the curious. The western entrance had been the most heavily defended. Ramparts rose steeply on either side. Down in the hollows, walking through the fog and the drizzle, he heard no sound save that of the flint underfoot and the lonely, haunting lament of hidden sheep.

With the advance of the slingshot, and death at more than sixty yards, the Durotriges had enlarged the ramparts, both heightening them and deepening the intervening moats.

And yet the efforts hadn't been enough. In A.D. 43 Vespasian and the Second Augustan Legion had overrun the fort.

Across the flat interior, across the thirty-five or so acres where a settlement of five thousand souls had once been, there was nothing but fog, and through this, as Hagen walked on, the distant cawing of ravens.

McPherson was down in the moat by the eastern gate, between the first and second ramparts. He was lying on his stomach next a freshly opened grave, leaning over what looked to be the remains of a skeleton.

The mud-smeared brown corduroys were drenched, the toes of the collier's boots turned in. The sleeves of the faded work shirt were rolled up exposing the brawny arms. A streak of mud on the back of his closely shaved neck indicated where he'd swatted at a fly. The thatch of dark brown hair had been trimmed by himself. That he didn't care about personal comfort was all too apparent; that he cared passionately for those ever-decreasing hours he was able to devote to his work, only too evident.

Hagen had to grin. Duncan traveled widely to scientific symposia all over Europe, he spoke fluent Italian and French with the harshness of an accent that couldn't be disguised, but at heart he was still a boy who merely liked to find things.

So caught up was he in excavating the grave, he didn't even sense he was being watched.

In 1934 travelers to the Reich had begun bringing back stories of what was happening there. Though few had wanted to believe there was a threat, Duncan and some others had been convinced of the growing menace. Then in 1935 Duncan had contacted him. It had been that simple. Innocent enough. Just keep his eyes and ears open, nothing more. But now ...

"Duncan, a fellow ought to leave the dead lie sleeping in a place like this."

McPherson turned and gave him a wily look. "Up and about, are you?

Well, don't just stand there. Come you down and meet your brother. He's given us the answer, Richard. Now we know why the hill fort fell to the Romans."

The face was strongly boned and squarish, the nose prominent and pugnacious. The dark brown eyes were mischievous and swift. The ears stuck out, the brow was that of a blunt instrument, the build that of a thrower of the caber.

They shook hands warmly, both grinning from ear to ear with relief perhaps, or just because they were back together again. Then the excitement leaped back into McPherson's voice. "Richard, Sir Mortimer's beside himself with delight. We've found twenty-eight of these blessed graves! Men, women and children all hacked to death and him —" he indicated the skeleton "— with a ballista point stuck in one of the lower vertebrae. The proof, Richard. The bloody proof! Wheeler's ecstatic."

Duncan dropped to a crouch, then knelt to scrape away a few last smears of clay, exposing the point more fully and tapping it with the trowel.

"Hot iron, Richard. The ballista was a new invention of war to the Celts, a cart-mounted catapult that fired an iron bolt tipped like this. Every legion had sixty of the blessed things. Think what it must have been like for them."

Hagen thought of Fort Eben Emael, of the Maginot Line and of what he'd seen of the German war machine.

"Duncan, we're totally unprepared. Within the past six months there's been a phenomenal increase in production. Somehow we've got to convince Whitehall the situation is urgent."

Two drovers lingered at the bar. A solitary lorry driver, who must have quit his job or been fired before lunch, had sunk pint after pint over that brief period of time and now waited for the clock to nudge the five-thirty so that he could start all over again.

McPherson indicated the notes he'd taken down in shorthand — Richard had a phenomenal memory for details. The guns, tanks, bomb loads and speeds of aircraft were all there, the privacy of the booth seeming to have enveloped the two of them in its own cocoon.

"Richard, there's someone who wants to meet you — indeed, he insists."

The identity of that someone was all too clear. For a moment Hagen didn't say anything, then that weary sadness he'd felt so often of late crept back in on him. "I've been told to stick to selling. That's what I'm paid for."

"But for how long? Richard, Winston says he must talk to you about the Antwerp diamond stocks."

"I can't see him. For the sake of myself, yes, and for that of my friends in the Reich. It's just too risky."

"But you're our eyes, Richard. Och, we've lost virtually all of our people in the Reich. Those who would help us are now so few and on the run, we can but hope they'll be able to get away."

"There are Irmgard and Dee Dee, Duncan. Dieter too, though for all I know he could be working for the Abwehr. The Krupp thing is excellent cover."

"There's someone else. I can see it, Richard. A girl? Damn it, man, you can't be mixed up with anyone. Women..."

"I know. Of course I can't, but until that's settled, let's leave Mr. Churchill."

"And the Antwerp diamond stocks? Is it that we're to let Heydrich get his hands on them?"

"I'll lose my job. Sir Ernest —"

McPherson clenched his fists. "Sir Ernest will preach caution while secretly wishing something else. Didn't he ask you to warn him? He's party to it then, and won't say a blessed thing *if* he hears of it, which he won't. You have my word on this."

"And that of Mr. Churchill?"

"At least let the two of you talk, then decide how you want to handle things. Don't say no to a man as great as that. Not when he begs you to pay him a visit. Churchill knows full well the risks you're taking."

Duncan had always been able to convince him. "You make it sound like Ben More or Ben Kilbreck."

McPherson grinned with relief. "Perhaps we'll have another go at those wee hills before Hitler takes us on."

"I'd like that, Duncan. Dear God but I would."

Flames leaped from between the newly added chunks of anthracite. In the timbered vault of the ceiling a ghost of shadows flickered.

There were no lights on in the study at Chartwell in Kent, the country house of Winston Churchill. There were no others in the room but Duncan, himself and the man, the legend, the radical.

By the age of sixty-three Winston Churchill had risen to the heights and fallen to the depths of British politics more times than most. As a young man he had been to India, to Egypt with Kitchener, had been in the Boer War as a journalist, only to find himself a hero overnight. With but a brief absence from 1922 to 1924, he had been a member of Parliament since 1900, and for many of those years a prominent cabinet minister.

Hagen ran through some of the positions he had held. Home Secretary,

First Lord of the Admiralty, Secretary of War...his experience and abilities were vast.

But for some years now he had been a virtual outcast among his peers, unpopular because he preached rearmament, a warmonger, some said, because he had dared to speak out against what was happening in Germany.

"Will there be war, do you think?" came the voice, the cigar moving again.

Hagen glanced at Duncan, who gave him a nod. "Mr. Churchill, I'm almost certain of it. The very fact that they're tightening up security indicates something's in the wind. Couple this with the new four-year plan of industry and it seems a foregone conclusion."

"How soon will it happen, do you think?"

"Two years — because they have in hand almost a year's supply of industrial diamonds and are now attempting to buy another. They're also looking for alternate sources and trying to manufacture their own grinding and polishing powders from bulk purchases of boart."

"Is their mood one of war?"

"I can't say — for the generals, that is. For the people, the common workingman, I think not. No, I'd say they're as hopeful and willing to believe in peace as we are."

"Tell me about this new dive bomber they've been trying out in Spain. The Stuka. The Junkers 87."

Duncan would have already briefed him...

"I want to hear it from you, Richard. Everything."

They'd be here until dawn. "Wingspan 45 feet, 3 1/4 inches. Length 50 feet, 1/2 inch. Engine, liquid-cooled, Jumo 211 Da inverted V, 12 cylinder, 1100 HP. Speed, 242 miles per hour. Ceiling, 26,250 feet. Range, 373 miles. Bomb load, one 1102-pound bomb on centerline, four 110-pound bombs on wing tracks. Armament, two wing-mounted MG-17 machine guns, caliber 7.92 mm..."

Churchill appeared not to be listening. That brooding look became darker, more scowling. Then Hagen heard himself saying, "One manually aimed MG-15 in the rear cockpit, same caliber. Spot-on bombing. G-factor crashes have all but been eliminated by some sort of automatic pilot that makes the plane pull out of its dive even if the pilot has momentarily blacked out."

"How will they use it to best advantage, do you think?"

The interest had been there all along. "Ahead of advancing Panzer divisions to take out enemy artillery and machine gun emplacements. In my estimation it's as effective if not better than artillery, and it's much more mobile."

The salesman was impressive. "Describe the look of the plane for me."

Hagen told him of the spatted undercarriage, the gull-wing profile, the closeness of the cockpit, even the smell of the leather.

"Anything else?" asked Churchill. The cigar was poised, the brow still furrowed.

"A siren."

The breath escaped from Churchill. "Why, for God's sake?"

Hagen's gaze returned to the fire. "To terrify people. It's excruciating to hear it."

Quickly he told him of the Krupp and Dieter Karl, and of how he had forced himself to stand there on the landing field.

Churchill was adamant. "The Nazi mind knows no depth to its cruelty. A siren . . . radar?" he asked.

"For heavy guns on their battleships, yes. They are also working on something they call the Freya, an early-warning system, but I believe as yet it can't give them the altitude of the incoming aircraft."

He had traveled the length and breadth of Germany. He had seen and heard so much. "You don't seem too enthused about their radar?"

"It's a low priority with them. I believe they intend to hit first, Mr. Churchill, and to hit harder than any army ever has. Everything I've seen suggests a very rapid deployment of armored troops, a lightning thrust with tanks. The only thing is . . ."

The cigar was clamped tightly, the eyes intent. "Go on, speak your mind, for pity's sake! I need to pick your brains. They deserve to be picked!"

"They're not building the trucks they should. Tanks, yes, and half-tracks, but a fully motorized army would need great numbers of trucks just to carry supplies and reinforcements, and I haven't seen them. Not yet."

The man was a treasure. "Rockets?"

He told him about the amber, about its use as a high-altitude insulating material for electrical wires. "They were working on some sort of guidance system at the Heinkel factory on the Baltic."

"Could you get us one?"

The eagerness, the wish to be a part of things, were apparent, the naiveté, too. He knew of Churchill's stubborn obstinacy, of his wild ideas sometimes and of his bravery, too — no one could dispute those. Still, he would have to be told.

"How could I? The Gestapo have taken a decided interest in me. For all I know, the Abwehr are also interested. To be caught with such a thing . . ."

"That experimental research facility of theirs?"

"In Berlin? Could I get in there, is that what you mean?"

THE ALICE FACTOR • 99

"Young man, you know it is." He would push Hagen now. He would see what he was made of.

"Then you know the answer. It's out of bounds, Mr. Churchill, and I haven't anything to report to you or to Duncan because they don't tell me and I don't ask. If I were to ask, that would indicate an interest in something I ought, really, to know nothing about."

"What about photographs and drawings? Could you get them? I've got to have proof. Those bullocks in the War Office won't believe me otherwise. This government of ours has decided only to be undecided."

"With all due respect, sir, they must know enough already. The chief test pilot of Vickers has seen the ME-109 fly. He was scared to death by the number of fighter planes coming off their assembly lines. Didn't Whitehall believe him?"

"They don't *want* to believe him!"

"Then why should they believe what I say?"

Churchill drew on his cigar and motioned for Duncan to refill their glasses. The time had come to get down to business. "Tell me about the diamonds."

"The Germans need about two-and-a-half million carats a year to sustain present production. That's about half a ton, if you want it in simple terms."

"Half a ton..."

"About nine cubic feet if we assume fifty percent pore space, but diamonds of all sizes, all grades from grinding and polishing powders on up to tool diamonds."

"Their value, approximately?"

"Two-and-a-half million American dollars, five hundred-and-ten thousand pounds sterling. Mr. Churchill, in addition to all our stocks of gem and tool diamonds, there are thirty million carats of crushing boart ready and waiting in the Antwerp vaults. Diamond grinding wheels are the only thing that will sharpen tungsten carbide. Without the boart, they'd be sunk. Those stocks absolutely must be moved to London. If war breaks out, the Germans will make a dash for them. Somehow you must convince the British government to agree to let us move them here."

"The British government..." Churchill took a sip of whisky, nodding his thanks to Duncan. "Some of the people in Whitehall have it in mind to establish a cutting center in Brighton. They want to take over Antwerp's enviable position as the premier cutting center of the world. They want to deal, Richard. To apply pressure of their own while the squeeze is on. Your friends in Antwerp have every reason to be edgy. They'll want to be certain to have their guarantees in writing."

A cutting center in Brighton... No mention of it from the Committee, none either from Sir Ernest. "But De Beers has just concluded an agreement with the Belgian government and La Forminière that offers the best of all gem rough to the Antwerp dealers?"

Churchill was pleased with the reaction to his little coup. "Precisely! Ernest *had* to give the Belgians that to ease their minds about Brighton! You are stepping between the Titans, Richard. Dance with care."

Never mind the threat of war. Never mind that the stocks might be seized. It was still to be business first!

"What's the king of the Belgians got to say about shifting the diamonds to London?" demanded Churchill sharply.

Taken aback by the obvious antagonism, Hagen answered, "He's against the move, as you must surely know. It places us in a —"

"I should say it *does*, young man. Leopold's policy of neutrality places the diamonds in a most vulnerable position. If I were you, I should keep a close eye on him. A half a ton . . . it seems so little, Richard. Pray tell us where they'll get them if war breaks out?"

Churchill had swung from being the lion to being the wily cat of a Smithfield butcher shop. "They're already looking for alternate sources. A lot will depend on how effective a blockade can be mounted and how many of the mines remain open. My guess is that they'll have to turn to the Belgian Congo for the boart, to Mbuji-Mayi, though they'll still have to get the diamonds past the mine security."

"Couldn't they use gem diamonds?"

"There aren't enough of them easily available. Even with the depressed market, they're still far too expensive. Besides, I doubt if greed would allow them to do so."

"What about these tool diamonds? If Brazil's not good enough, is the New York market not up to it?"

"With luck there'll be an embargo in the States, but the Nazis will try to get what they can from there. Fortunately New York's just not that big a trading center. Not yet."

"And the Congo?"

"A small amount of tool diamonds might be obtained from there, assuming again that they could get them past the mine security and the blockade."

Churchill withdrew into a cloud of cigar smoke. When he spoke again, Hagen was unprepared for the question. "How long do you think Heydrich and the Gestapo will continue to let you operate?"

"I don't know, sir. I may never know until it's too late."

"And the Abwehr — have you the whole pack of hounds after you?"

Again he said he didn't know.

Churchill leaned forward to fix him with a piercing gaze. "Well, I do, young man. Tell him, Duncan."

McPherson looked most uncomfortable. He would have liked to tell Richard in his own good time. "Abwehr agents have been asking about you both here and on the Continent. The feelers are out, Richard. They want your leanings, your willingness to co-operate."

"Then Arlette was right. My file was photographed."

"Aye, but by which side? Networks cooperate, but does the Sicherheitsdienst tell the Abwehr everything it knows? The Abwehr's sudden interest suggests that it was Heydrich who authorized the break-in at Dillingham's."

"Are you now about to be caught between them, Richard?" asked Churchill. "Heydrich has made his openers, but will Admiral Wilhelm Canaris of the Abwehr not also have something to say to you?"

Churchill drew on his cigar, savoring the thought. "Normally such a matter as the Antwerp diamond stocks would come under the mandate of the Abwehr — German military intelligence abroad. Heydrich, if I understand my sources correctly, is jealous of the Abwehr and determined to set up within the Secret Service of the SS a counterpart to it. In this he has, I believe, the sanction of Heinrich Himmler, the overall boss of the SS and the closest confidant of Der Führer!

"The Titans, Richard. God give you shoes of silk!"

"Mr. Churchill —"

"Duncan, please don't chide me. If one cannot appreciate the humor of one's desperate straits, one cannot best assess their remedies.

"The Titans, Richard. The Abwehr and the Sicherheitsdienst, the Krupp, the king of the Belgians, the heads of the Antwerp Diamond Exchange, the British government and the greatest diamond broker of them all.

"Pray tell me, young man, would Heydrich try to discredit you with this Klees business simply to stir up trouble and thwart the move to London of the diamond stocks, or would he also, perhaps, not have used this Dutchman to slice you off from your friends and throw you into bed with the Nazis?"

There was no answer that was easy. The problems posed, the sense of entrapment and loss, the sudden futility of trying to win out against it all were too great.

"You've been ill, Richard," said Churchill, his eyes moistening with sudden sympathy and regret for what he'd just said. "Pray do forgive me. Yet the matter, if I may say so, must be faced.

"Gentlemen —" he indicated the two of them with the cigar "— I was never good at mathematics, but I wonder, Richard, are you not the factor that will balance out that equation of Heydrich versus Canaris and cancel each side, so that zero equals zero and neither of them poses a threat to our moving the diamond stocks to London?"

"Pretend to work with Heydrich, pretend to work with Canaris —" began Hagen, aghast at the suggestion.

"Pretend to go along with them," said Churchill, the muse. "Every measure will be taken to protect your identity here. You'll be one of my secret inner circle of advisers. Duncan will be your only contact other than myself. Richard, I want you as my Alice in *Through the Looking Glass*. Duncan will be the Carpenter; myself, the White Rabbit."

Sadly Hagen looked at each of them, knowing it could only end in disaster. "With all due respect, sir, my use of the Alice poems has already been questioned."

"By your director, Bernard Wunsch, and your friend Dieter Karl Hunter. But do they know for certain you're sending code? Did Dieter Karl even recognize the source of that quotation Wunsch sent you?"

"Not yet. I wouldn't be here if the Nazis did."

"Then let the Alice factor decide. Bluff it out. If the worst comes to the worst, tell them that your mother read you those poems as a child and that you and she trade quotes back and forth as a means of reminding each other of the past. If you like, I will personally see that she understands she is not to question your use of her as a letter drop. The same goes, of course, for your stepfather's old address in Oxford."

"We'll need a new code. It'll take time to work it out."

"For now you must continue with what we have. It's good, Richard. They'll puzzle over it, but remember they need you. For us you are in a unique position — for them also."

It was only as they got up to leave that Churchill returned to the matter of Klees. "Is this Dutchman really the end of an escape route we might use?"

Hagen told him it would have to be checked out several times. "Heydrich and Krantz were just too close to it for comfort."

"And this Klees wants you to obtain a safety deposit box for him in London?" asked Churchill.

"Yes."

"Duncan will arrange it."

"But why? It'll ruin my career."

"Richard, it will allow the Nazis to think you corruptible. Play along with Klees. Let the Nazis work to find out you're helping this Dutchman, then they'll think you can be bought. I want to see just how far they'll go to get that half ton of diamonds they need."

Five

LESS THAN A MILE separated the tourists from the fishing port of Ostend. Here there was peace and quiet, no crowds to interfere.

Hagen ran his eyes over the yacht. The *Vega* gleamed among the clutter of fishing boats whose masts were draped with brick-red sails.

Arlette had met him at the pier, shy and extending a hand, saying, "You were ill. I've gone back to work at Dillingham's. De Heer Wunsch has given me the weekend off."

Two days, the Hotel Imperial for him. He'd checked in and they'd come here straightaway, had walked the length of the Digue, the town's impressive promenade, then around the harbor. She'd known intuitively he wanted to be alone with her. No parents yet. Just the two of them.

"I used to come here often, Richard. To buy fish for my mother, and the shrimp the fishermen cook on their way home in the early morning. It's a lovely sight to see the lights of their boats at dawn. These men are poor but they're very good and very proud."

"That's a super yacht, Arlette. Willi's done a beautiful job."

She tightened her grip on his arm, was glad to hear him say this. "Hasn't he? I thought you would like to see it. Have you ever been sailing? Perhaps..."

Why were things so awkward for them? By rights they should feel at ease with each other.

The yacht was over on the far side of the channel beyond the lines of drying wicker baskets and rows of herring in the sun. Richard closed a hand over hers and said again, "It's so good to see you."

As if he couldn't believe it! As if it hurt! "What happened? What's the matter?"

"Arlette..." He couldn't say it. All the way across the channel — for more than three-and-a-half wretched hours of the smoothest crossing, he'd told himself he'd have to say goodbye, that it wasn't right of him to involve her.

Then there she was, waiting for him, and he'd known he couldn't do it. Had hated himself.

"Willi won't mind if we go aboard the *Vega*."

Hagen shook his head. "I would, if I was him."

This time it was she who led him to a small café. The tobacco smoke was thick, the place full of fishermen who eyed him with suspicion until she spoke to several of them in Flemish. Her laughing eyes and easy manner surprised him; she made them feel so good, those poor old men.

Huddled over a small table to one side, the two of them faced each other. At once she was serious again. "So, now you will tell me what's wrong."

"Let's just get to know each other. You're a Fleming."

Arlette tossed her head and smiled. "Me, I'm half and half. My mother is a Walloon, my father a Fleming. That's why I can speak French and German, or Dutch if you like, or Flemish."

"Or English."

"Yes, and I would remind you Ostend is a Flemish town, just as is Antwerp."

He spread his hands on the table. "Do you love me as much as I think I must love you?"

"Is it to be a business deal between us, or do you ask because you cannot believe what I have already confessed?"

Hagen reached for his coffee but set it aside. Never once — not even with Cecile — had he felt this way. "I'm not very good at this, am I?"

"Should you be?"

"Look, I want us to get to know each other. I want..." Oh hell, what did he want?

Arlette saw him drag something out of a pocket. The chain rattled on the table. A superb blue diamond caught the smoke-filled light, a cluster of lesser stones...

She held her breath and tried to stifle the gasp, but couldn't quite do so.

"Richard, are you crazy? In a place like this, you should show such a thing?"

The color had raced into her cheeks. There was moisture in her eyes. "Look, I want you to have it. No strings attached. Nothing. Please. Just have it."

"But...but..."

"We'll put it in the vault. Lev can take the stone out of its setting if you like. You can have something else made."

There were no words to say what she felt. Her fingers trembled when she touched the stone. It had such a deep and gorgeous shade of blue.

"Think about it, will you?"

She shook her head and closed a fist over the thing. Three of the lesser diamonds lay coiled with the braided chain. "Does this mean that you would like us to become engaged?"

How could it? So soon...

He closed a hand over hers. "It means that I think I love you very much, but that I'm afraid for your sake."

Now she couldn't look at him. Now she could hardly find her voice, was conscious of everyone watching them. Everyone! "Then we must do so in secret. Is that what you're saying?"

Hagen rubbed a thumb gently over the back of her hand. "Only that you know I'm worried and that I must have good reasons or I wouldn't be saying this to you."

"Please take me somewhere. Please tell me this isn't a nightmare."

They left the café and went along to the *Vega*. Willi would still be at work. Richard sat in the center well with his back to the side of the boat. She knelt between his upraised knees.

Slowly, hesitantly, with infinite tenderness the girl timidly kissed the salesman. The first touch of her lips on his made her quiver. The next only reinforced things.

She drew away a little and caught a breath, looked fondly at Hagen, then threw caution away and kissed him as Damas had never seen a woman kiss a man before — long and hard and urgently, then tenderly, lingering only to withdraw as if naked between the salesman's knees.

The two of them kissed again, lightly, hesitantly. The girl had that extreme look of smoldering passion young virgins get when in heat. There'd be trouble with unclean thoughts. She'd be haunted by them and yet would let her mind dwell on them until there could be no other solution but to spread her legs.

Karl Christian Damas was one of the SD's key operatives in Antwerp. A Belgian, a Fleming of some forty-two years of age, he was a schoolmaster by trade but a priest in disguise.

Bespectacled, tall and thin, with pale blue eyes and the studious expression of a scholar, he had about him the bemused air of an aesthete bent on teaching the mothers of his young students the facts of art and history while their daughters found out something else.

Berlin had asked him to meet the Dover ferry and take a look at the man called Richard Hagen.

He hadn't bargained for what he'd seen.

Again the couple kissed, the girl resting back on her haunches with hands placed behind her against the deck to brace herself; the salesman touching the skin at the base of her throat as he sought her lips.

Naked, the girl would be beautiful — vulnerable, so many things. She'd have to stare up at him, would have to beg...

She'd say, Please don't hurt me. Please don't. I...

Damas turned away and lost himself among the fishing boats.

Only then did he head for the railway station.

The flat at number 239 the Waalsekaai in Antwerp was nothing special. The river was far too close, the building two hundred years past its prime. Damas had long since removed the priest's collar, but clothes being expensive, had simply put on a tie and had kept the dark suit and shoes.

Hagen the salesman of diamonds, the American — the expatriate? he wondered. Quite handsome, if one fancied men, which he didn't. Quite lost, it seemed, but not just by the young girl who had knelt between his knees. No, lost and deep in thought — worried, yes — but by something else.

Damas went through to the sitting room to glance at the telephone. Berlin would want to know about the girl right away. He had that feeling about it.

Yet rules were rules and Krantz was a stickler for them. The break-in at the offices of Dillingham and Company had been example enough. "Get the keys. Check Hagen's flat before you go busting down the doors. Find the men who will know something about those alarms."

How right Krantz had been.

Though the break-in had been discovered — the girl had been the one to blame for that. A receptionist, a secretary. Pretty, very pretty. She had noticed Hagen's file had been tampered with. She had quit her job too, only to return to it so as to be with the salesman.

Damas loosened his tie. It wasn't easy to get such information. One had to stake out a place. One had to follow people and have contacts, lots of contacts. But there was always talk. Even in the diamond business there was talk. Especially about a break-in.

He found a cigarette and lit it. Naked, the girl would lie across her bed or on the floor in that room of hers. Hit hard enough, she wouldn't cry out...

Stepping over to the telephone, he hesitated — Krantz again — then decided not to risk it.

Locking the door behind him, he hurried from the flat to find a call box. One word, that's all it would take. One word to the clerk at the German embassy in Brussels and Krantz would send someone to see him.

The sound of the telegraph key hammered in the stillness of the night. From somewhere in the warren of trenches a man coughed blood and died.

Everything had been foul and wet. Everyone had felt so very alone.

Then the shelling had begun again, and over the Somme the night sky had been filled with starbursts and the staccato chatter of machine-gun fire.

Bernard Wunsch turned away from the window of their comfortable flat. "The storm will last all night, my dear. You can't even see the lights of the shipping in the harbor."

"What were you thinking of?"

"Me? Ah, the war. The sound of thunder reminded me of the guns, the lightning of the flashes."

That ample woman who had been his wife and companion for more than thirty years set her knitting aside on the coach. "Come and sit by the fire. Stop pacing about like a homeless cat. You're upset and that's not good for you. Would you like me to make you some cocoa?"

"You know I hate the stuff. Make some coffee. Make it good and strong. I must go out."

"It's those cables, isn't it?"

"No, it isn't."

"*Bernard* , you've been looking at them off and on all weekend. Ever since you came back from the bookstalls in the flea market you've been doodling. Did you think I wouldn't notice you'd bought English copies of *Alice in Wonderland* and *Through the Looking Glass*?"

He gave her an ineffectual shrug. "It's the news. Hitler..."

"Herr Hitler — pfft! There is something going on at the office, Bernard, and you're determined to get to the bottom of it."

She could be so stubborn. He glanced at the clock and turned back to the windows. Rain beat against the glass in gusts. If he told her he had to talk to Richard she would only ask further questions. It would be best to be firm. "Martine, this is not for you to know."

"Then for heaven's sake burn your scraps of paper! That wastebasket is full."

The cables had come into the office on Friday, the first separated from the second by about five hours. Had this Irmgard Hunter tried to reach Richard in England as well? Had they, in turn, realized the urgency of things and tried to reach him at the office?

He had struggled with his conscience ever since and had done the unpardonable by stalling.

TO HAGEN RICHARD DILLINGHAM AND COMPANY ANTWERP FROM HUNTER IRMGARD HOTEL BAUR DU LAC ZURICH

JANUS PASSAGE DELAYED INDEFINITELY STOP WILL WAIT TWO DAYS STOP PLEASE CONTACT

Had the woman been afraid for her life? Had the Nazis followed her to Zurich?

Guilt forced him to read the other cable.

TO HAGEN RICHARD DILLINGHAM AND COMPANY ANTWERP
FROM WINFIELD MRS LOIS ANNE INVERLIN COTTAGE BLACK
DOWN HEATH PORTESHAM ROAD DORCHESTER ENGLAND
    DARLING SORRY YOU WERE ILL STOP FRANK DID HIS BEST
TO MAKE YOUR VISIT PLEASANT STOP WISH WE COULD BE
EXACTLY AS WE WERE STOP HOW DELIGHTFUL IT WILL BE TO
SEE YOU OVER CHRISTMAS STOP LOVE MOTHER

Telegram One

Janus? A two-headed Roman god. One who watches both the front and
back entrance simultaneously. One who is the protector of both the
beginning and the end.

Why was Janus being delayed? Why had Irmgard Hunter sent the
cable from Zurich? Why not from Munich? Why not from somewhere
inside the Reich?

Telegram Two

(1) "did his very best to make" — from "The Walrus and the Carpenter" in *Through the Looking Glass*.

(2) "exactly as we were" — from one of the verses the White Rabbit
reads out at the trial of the Knave of Hearts in *Alice's Adventures in
Wonderland*.

(3) "How delightful it will be" — from the Mock Turtle's song in *Alice's
Adventures in Wonderland*.

Passage (1) in plain vertical cipher using four rows and groupings of four
letters (*n* substituted for second *s*):

d	i	n	m	possible meaning:	don't
i	s	t	a		take
d	b	t	k		it
h	e	o	e		to
					him

Passage (1) in plain horizontal cipher using four rows and groupings of
four letters:

d	i	d	h	possible meaning:	take
i	s	b	e		it
n	t	t	o		to
m	a	k	e		him

There were several other futile attempts at decoding, even to arranging
all of the letters in a row and then taking them from both ends and
working toward the center so as to build four-letter columns.

didhisbesttomakeexactlyaswewerehowdelightfulitwillbe

```
d    e    i    b
h    l    i    l
s    i    b    w
```

It was now the evening of September 8, and Irmgard Hunter, the sister of the Baron Dieter Karl, would have waited all weekend in hopes of Richard's call.

"Martine, I have to meet the train from Ostend. I must speak with Richard."

"Then let me burn those for you. I promise I won't look."

He shook his head and went to the fireplace. Taking a handful of his crumpled notes, he began to feed them into the flames. He could make no sense of the passages that had come from England, and this troubled him. The letters must be keyed to a numbered code that in turn meant entirely different letters. It was a level of sophistication that was upsetting. Only Richard and his opposite, whoever he was, would know the answer.

Decoded, the message would read: CONTACT IRMGARD HUNTER / RECRUIT IF POSSIBLE / WHITE RABBIT SENDS REGARDS.

Shadows fell over the Zurichsee. One by one the lights in the city came on, and from the hills that ringed the lake and kept back the snowcapped mountains, an air of quiet contentment settled over the valley below.

As Hagen watched her, Irmgard gripped the terrace railing.

The guest house was on the outskirts of the village of Uetli Berg, about a half-hour's train ride up into the hills from the city. She'd left a note for him at the hotel, asking him to call a friend, who had directed him here.

The house appeared to be empty but for the two of them.

The last of the sunlight etched the strongly featured Nordic brow. It made the thick, wide brush of her eyebrows more hooded, more severe.

But then she flashed him an uncertain smile and extended a hand. "Thanks for coming. My God, I still can't believe you're here. I thought . . . Oh, what the hell does it matter what I thought? I knew you'd come."

"How's Dee Dee?"

The hazel eyes searched his for signs of interest in herself, signs of caution. "Badly frightened. They won't let her leave the Reich, Richard. When we went to get her travel papers, they took her passport away."

"Can't Dieter do anything?"

"Dieter, Dieter — is it always to be up to him? Can't *you* do anything? Look, I'm sorry. It's just that . . . well, I've leased this place for her. Me, the daughter of a Nazi industrialist has had to find a bolt hole for her childhood friend."

"And Dieter?"

She gripped the railing again. "My brother says there is no need to worry. If you ask me, I think Dee Dee's become an embarrassment to him."

Why couldn't Richard put his arms about her? Why couldn't they kiss like lovers? "We'd best go in. It's getting cold."

"When does he leave for Brazil?"

"Soon, I think. Look, can you help me with the finances? They've blocked her money. I — " she swung round now, stood so close to him "— I can't go to my father. Dieter . . . Dieter would only ask why I needed the money."

Hagen took hold of her by the elbows. The blue diamond had drained his account. He'd be overdrawn. He'd have to ask Bernard to cover for him. "Of course. Would a hundred suit? Pounds, that is. I can let you have a bank draft on my trading account. No problem."

His hands were still holding her — reassuringly, damn it! "They'll have to let Dee Dee leave, won't they? She doesn't have to be connected with Dieter. She can just quietly slip away. Then I can come to visit her here, and you can, too. Isn't that right?"

Hagen kissed her brow. She flattened her hands against his chest, moved in closer, wanted him. Dear God, how she wanted him.

"I know I mustn't cry, but I'm afraid for her, Richard. Dieter . . . Dieter isn't himself anymore."

At dawn they followed a well-worn path and climbed in silence to the summit that was above Uetli Berg. Now the whole breathtaking panorama was spread before them. The high peaks of the Bernese Oberland, the Appenzell, the Jura, the Black Forest, too.

They'd spent the night in separate rooms. She'd lain there hoping he would come to her; he'd stayed by the fire for so long, lost to his thoughts.

"When will you be back in the Reich?"

"A month, two months. I don't really know. I was in England, Irmgard. I've not even been in to the office."

Was there someone else? There had been . . . a nightclub owner. A very beautiful woman, Cecile Verheyden, Dieter had said with that look in his eyes, but that had been finished two years ago.

Irmgard reached for his hand and held it tightly. Together they watched the sun rise. "Be careful when you come back, Richard. Remember that things can no longer be the same."

In Zurich he glanced through the message he'd written and then encoded:

TO THE CARPENTER
  SEARCH TITLE CHALET VILLEREUSE UETLI BERG CONFIRM

LEASED HUNTER IRMGARD AND NOT ABWEHR SAFE HOUSE /
ALICE

On October 8 the Austrian chancellor, Schuschnigg, publicly condemned
Hitler's policy of *Anschluss*, the union of the two Germanic-speaking
countries. On the thirteenth of the month the Germans stated they would
respect Belgium's neutrality and would come to its defense if it was
attacked by any foreign power. In return, they demanded only that the
Belgians agree not to go to war against the Reich.

In the Sudetenland the German-speaking population of Czechoslovakia demanded its right to autonomy, and in Danzig, Poland, there were
Nazi-inspired riots against the Jews.

The Japanese war in China had entered yet another critical phase. No
country seemed safe from the madness.

Hagen ran his eyes over the message that had come in to the office from
the Magpie Lane address in Oxford:

SEARCH MADE CHALET VILLEREUSE UETLI BERG / SUBLEASED
TABOR INGE / APPEARS HUNTER IRMGARD HAS TAKEN
STEPS TO PROTECT SELF / EITHER AN ELABORATE ABWEHR
DECEPTION OR CLEAR / PROCEED TO RECRUIT WITH UTMOST
CAUTION

It was raining in Berlin, making gray the austere stone buildings and
wide avenues.

Directly across from a corner of the Tiergarten the broad windows of
the Fuerstenhof Cafe faced onto the Potsdamer Platz, where the early-
morning life of the city would soon pass before him.

Hagen bought a copy of the *Völkischer Beobachter*, the People's
Observer. Over black coffee, rusks and marmalade he watched the *Platz*.

Sometimes it was the best way to get a feel for what was going on. The
traffic tower in the middle of the *Platz* would soon be inundated as nearly
a dozen avenues converged on it.

The request from the Krupp had been brief. Another meeting. Could
he come?

There'd been none of the hassles at the border, not a sign of Otto
Krantz. Indeed, it had been an uneventful trip. Yet he couldn't help but
feel uneasy.

Arlette and he had said goodbye at the Central Station. It had been late
and he'd been worried about her. But she'd stayed on the platform
watching the train disappear, hadn't wanted him to go.

Intuitively she'd known how worried he was.

Across the *Platz*, the flower sellers were arranging their wares. Under the broad awning of a chocolate shop an ancient shoeshine boy had begrudgingly been allowed to set up shop in payment for a few marks and a percentage of the day's take.

The doorman at the Haus Vaterland was making certain the sidewalk and steps were being properly cleaned. Hagen pitied the boy under him.

Life went on. The traffic soon began to swell. A second pot of coffee came, another plate of rusks. One staff car after another passed before him until he suddenly realized there were far too many of them.

In the newspaper there was nothing about a meeting, another rally. Yet the cars had come from all over the Reich, he was certain of this now.

Just what the honorary SS-Gruppenführer Keppler, the secretary of state, was doing at the meeting Hagen didn't know, but the man was proving to be a problem.

"One carat equals one-fifth of a gram, Herr Gruppenführer. To meet the needs of the Reich for one year I must somehow find two-and-a-half million of them."

Alfried Krupp hastened to interject, "That is of all diamonds, Herr Keppler. Approximately thirty percent of those would be what we call tool diamonds. Then there are those we need for bearings and those we need for —"

"Please, Baron, let Herr Hagen finish. You were saying?"

The sounds of impatiently drumming fingernails came to him, a heavy sigh. About the table, in the basement of the Reich Chancellery, seven men were seated besides himself.

Hagen reached for his briefcase and took out a small, much worn wooden box. From it he poured a handful of dark brown, almost black beans, then took a small, hand-held brass balance that was nothing more than a piece of string tied to the center of a short wooden rod from the ends of which the two small brass pans were suspended.

As if to a schoolchild he said, "Those are the seeds of the carob tree, Herr Gruppenführer. Long ago pearl merchants in the Middle East found that when dried, the seeds so seldom varied in weight they could use them as a standard for weighing their pearls. Later the carat, or carob seed, was used for weighing diamonds in the field until the weight became standardized at one-fifth of a gram."

From his pocket he took a vial containing several emerald-green macles. Placing one of them in the left-hand pan, he added five carob seeds to the right-hand pan.

They almost balanced. It was so close...

Keppler nodded. He adjusted the rimless glasses that perched tightly on the bridge of his nose. "May I?" he asked, reaching across the table.

"But of course. Just hold the balance by the string."

The Führer-like mustache, blunt head and stern, unfriendly gaze were clear. No humor there. Keppler knew he was being ridiculed by the others.

Kurt Schmitt, the Nazi minister of Economy, cleared his throat. "Gentlemen, if we could get on with this. Herr Hagen, you've said you can supply us with only one-quarter of the order every six months. That is not enough."

"I'm trying my best to rectify that, Herr Schmitt, but believe me, it's not going to be easy."

"Why? There are some thirty million carats in the vaults of the Diamant Boart in Antwerp right now."

This had come from Franz Epp, the Krupp's head of internal security and counterintelligence. "Yes, I know, but it's simply crushing boart suitable only for saw blades, grinding wheels and powders."

Epp arched his eyebrows impatiently. "Then why, please, can't we at least have a year's supply of those?"

"Because there are others who demand their orders, too, Herr Epp. Because, although the crushing boart is there, it's in the form of cubes, octahedra and granules that must be — "

"Please, what is meant by octahedra?"

It was Keppler again, still holding on to the balance by the string.

Hagen reached into a pocket for another vial and his hand lens. Pouring a stream of boart onto a sheet of paper, he offered the secretary of state the lens, then quickly sorted through the stones with the end of a pencil. "Those clear, glassy, pyramidal-looking crystals are octahedra from South Africa. The yellowish-green and whitish to brownish cubes are from the Belgian Congo. Some of the black to steel-gray granules are from Brazil, others from the Congo as well."

"And the name *boart*?" asked Keppler.

Ritter von Halt, the director of the Deutsche Bank, looked at Keppler as if he were an idiot. Roche, of the Dresdener Bank, was more kindly. "Bastard. It's from the old French word for *bastard*, Herr Gruppenführer."

Hagen was glad Roche had been the one to say it. "Please continue," said Epp.

"By all means. The boart must be crushed and ground and then sized. This takes time — hours, several days. Then the grinding wheels and saw blades must be made to order."

"Why can't we make them ourselves? Couldn't we?"

The making of the tools was a part of the business no one would want to lose. "You'd need the technicians. We're only just getting into sintering. Bonding agents have varying strengths. Day by day our technology is changing, gentlemen. My advice would be to be patient if possible."

"It's not possible."

This had come from Schmitt, the minister of Economy.

Even as his mind raced back to the number of staff cars on the roads that morning, Hagen continued as if nothing of importance had been said. "Then I'd suggest, Herr Schmitt, that we send a team of technicians to Antwerp. If you'll give me a little time, I might be able to sort out the matter with my firm and with the Diamant Boart of which we are an affiliate. They'll not greet the idea with enthusiasm, but let me work on them."

It was an offer he hadn't wanted to make, but it had the desired effect. Franz Epp was blocked, the Krupp immensely satisfied. Rohnert, from the Ministry of Industry, thought the idea good. "If we can do that, Herr Hagen, would it not also be possible for you to train our cutters and polishers?"

So they had got as far as that . . .

"They'd have to work under Jews," said Schmitt. "They're all Jews."

"Not all," offered Hagen. "But if you could look the other way . . ."

Epp didn't buy it. Hagen was a Jew-lover. "Men don't change their skins overnight. Since when would you advise us to take advantage of the Jews?"

Tough, a brawler from the steel mills and cannon works, Epp was the one he feared the most. It would be best to pass it off. "I want to sell diamonds, gentleman. If it takes a bit of training, then fair enough. I'll see what I can do."

"And the gold?" asked Ritter von Halt of the Deutsche Bank.

"Payment is still to be in bullion, in advance. Those are my instructions, gentlemen. Like everyone else, I have my orders."

This they could understand.

"And the delays, the shipping of one-quarter of our order every six months instead of one-half?"

"Gentlemen, please. I'm doing the best I can. Already I've had to meet with clients in Zurich and Prague to try to put them off. On my way home I've got to call into Amsterdam for the very same reason, and when I get back to Antwerp I know I'll be off again to Paris and then to Finland and Norway."

"You don't stay long in one place," said Epp dryly. "You're like a builder of houses, Herr Hagen. You've an answer for everything."

"I can't stay long in any one place. If I did, I'd lose the sales."

As they filed out of the room, Alfried Krupp laid a friendly hand on his shoulder. "It was good of you to come on such short notice, Richard. I appreciate that. We'll talk again."

Wanting a quiet time to sift through things, Hagen let the Krupp go ahead of him, only to find Keppler dragging his feet. As he packed away the balance, he noticed that the emerald-green macle had been pilfered. It happened all the time. Keppler had lifted the stone.

At the most it had cost him 120 marks, about 10 pounds.

Out in the corridor, sounds of "Heil Hitler!" came to them from the direction of the stairwell. Hagen heard them all giving the salute, then saw them part and found himself face-to-face with the Führer.

Keppler introduced them. Hitler held out his hand and he took it in his. The palm was dry, the handshake firm and businesslike. "Führer and Reich Chancellor, it's a privilege."

"You're the diamond man I've been hearing things about."

"Good things, I hope?"

Keppler had been asked to report on the meeting. That was why he'd been there, why he'd pilfered the diamond. To show his Führer . . .

Hitler must have liked the smile for he responded in kind, though he was preoccupied and obviously in a hurry. "You must come to see me some time. My adjutant, Herr Hossbach, will see to it if you'll speak to him. I'm very busy today. Important matters, you understand."

Apart from the protruding, sometimes intense eyes, Adolf Hitler was a singularly ordinary man. The hank of hair over the brow, the pallor were common enough, so, too, the small mustache. Yet he had the power to mesmerize a whole nation. There had been none of the shouting, none of the oratory, simply a quietly normal tone of voice.

Hagen stood aside with the others as Hitler went on down the steps, presumably to find the lavatory or to call on one of his aides.

"Did he really mean I was to see Hossbach about a meeting?"

"He'll have forgotten about it already," said Keppler. "The Führer has too much else on his mind at the moment."

Keppler gave Schmitt a knowing glance, and Hagen knew then that something momentous must have happened.

Horcher's was a sumptuous restaurant but the invitation to lunch, coming on the heels of the meeting, was a puzzle. As he checked his coat and hat, the muted sounds of cutlery and talk were mingled with the strains of a Viennese waltz played by an excellent string quartet.

Once the favorite haunt of foreign diplomats and visiting royalty, Horcher's still retained the plush red velvet brocade and dark oak paneling of its Victorian decor. The waiters still wore their black knee breeches, with red waistcoats, white aprons and white stockings.

Everything was very formal. Under the immense chandeliers, against the glitter of cutlery and crystal, the string quartet went about its business in spite of the changing times and the absence of appreciative listeners.

Some of the conversations held overtones of excitement and false laughter, but for the most part, the tenor of the place was subdued and earnest.

Clearly they'd been given something to think about, and those with sense were a little in awe of it.

Sitting at a table for five against the far wall, Irmgard looked like a beautiful butterfly with a broken wing, Dee Dee like a pillar of salt.

Hagen started out. Guderian...Rosenberg, Goebbels and Himmler were there. Von Blomberg, Raeder, Goering and von Fritsch...Von Blomberg was worried, Goering happy. Raeder was explaining things to Canaris, who turned away to look across the floor at him.

Momentarily he met the admiral's gaze. There was nothing in it. Nothing.

Yet he felt that gaze as he continued on to where the girls were seated. "Irmgard...Dee Dee...this is a surprise."

He kissed them both, felt how cold they were. "Who's joining us?"

"Don't you know?" Apprehensively Irmgard glanced at Dee Dee, who blanched and dropped her gaze to the table.

He shook his head. "Dieter, I guess. The note only said that I was to come to lunch here."

"But we thought..."

Hagen sat down. Nervously Irmgard said to the head waiter, "Herr Reitmann, I demand to know who has invited us to lunch."

Reitmann had the experience of forty years and the wisdom to do as he'd been told. He snapped his fingers. The wine steward brought an ice cold bottle of Steinberger. A waiter brought their soup.

"It is to be a little surprise, *ja*? Just the three of you and then —" he indicated the empty chairs "— perhaps the other guests will join you. Please enjoy your meal."

"Dee Dee, everything's okay. Irmgard and I'll make sure of that."

"And Dieter?" she asked. He could see the hurt in her lovely dark eyes. "We thought...ah, what the hell does it matter? *I* thought he wanted to see me. This —" she indicated the black velvet dress "— was to be for him."

"And this," said Irmgard, "for you."

"You're making me feel as if I'd stood the two of you up. Hey, come on, relax. Dieter must simply have been detained. You know how he is. He's set this whole thing up as a surprise."

"Then who is the other chair for?" asked Irmgard anxiously.

Hagen ignored the question. "Dee Dee, you look absolutely stunning in that dress."

Irmgard had done her hair with a wave down over the right side of her brow. The pale blue satin dress and silver neck chains suited. There was lipstick, too, and a touch of rouge.

The waiter came. She shook her head, and he took her untouched soup away.

Immaculate in a brand-new black uniform, Reinhard Heydrich joined them. As she stood suddenly, Dee Dee's napkin fell into her soup and trailed across the edge of the tablecloth before falling to the floor. Irmgard found herself unable to speak.

"Ladies, please... please be seated. It's lovely to see you all together. Fräulein Schroeder..." He clicked his heels, bowed and kissed the back of her hand. "Fräulein Hunter..." The same. "And Herr Hagen. Richard, it's so good to see you again. Please... please... you are my guests."

He gathered them in, was full of smiles and excuses. "Late as usual. You must forgive me. Richard, I hear you shook the Führer's hand this morning. He was very impressed with you."

A waiter brought his soup, but Heydrich curtly waved it away. "I can't stay. Please, I had intended to but..." He gestured expansively. "A sip of wine. At least I can share that with you."

Heydrich stripped Dee Dee naked with his eyes. He had about him a boldness that was offensive. "Dieter Karl has been called away, I gather. A pity, Fräulein Schroeder. He has much to miss."

He gave her a little smile and then, turning to Irmgard, said, "Your brother's bound to go places, Fräulein Hunter. You should be very proud of him."

"Herr Heydrich..."

She couldn't say it. Hagen did. "Dee Dee wishes to leave the Reich, Herr Gruppenführer. A theater engagement in New York. One of Ibsen's plays."

"But that is good news. Is there some problem, something I should know about?"

Dee Dee found the will to look at him. "They have taken my passport and locked up my money."

"A mistake. I assure you. Come, come now. Please leave the matter in my good hands. There is nothing to worry about. Nothing. Those dolts... Sometimes one wonders, isn't that so?"

The moment passed. They spoke of Berlin, of the Reich. There was to be a reception that evening. He hoped they'd all be there.

Heydrich glanced at his watch, then let his gaze settle on Irmgard. Hagen... could the girl be used? That was always the question one had to answer with the people one met. The girl was healthy, quite passable, and if the reports were true — and he was certain they were — in love with the salesman, though that little favor had yet to be returned.

A girl in Antwerp interfered. A receptionist...

"Your brother, Fräulein Hunter. Really, he should know better."

About what? About leaving Dee Dee in the lurch, about refusing to join

Heydrich for lunch with Canaris looking on? About working for the Krupp, or about something else? Hagen wondered apprehensively.

With a bow, a click of his heels and "Richard, I hope we'll see you again soon," he was gone from them.

Irmgard could hardly find her voice. "I think I'm going to be sick. I feel as if his hands are on my body and I can do nothing about it. Nothing!"

It was Dee Dee who said, "His shadow has passed over all of us."

Water poured off the rider's hat, cape and cavalry boots. A little man, squat, straight-backed and watchful, Admiral Wilhelm Canaris gave the Arab mare a nudge and walked her down through the trees.

Standing by the fountain, at the juncture of four paths in the Tiergarten, Hagen waited for him.

It was 6:30 a.m. Steam issued from the horse's nostrils.

The man who had asked to meet with him at the reception last night was already a legend. At the age of fifty Canaris had seen more of the world, more of life than most men ever dreamed of. Fluent in French and English, he had learned Spanish in 1907 as a young midshipman aboard the *Bremen* in South American waters.

Since then, what hadn't he done? Where hadn't he been? Torpedo boats, the cruiser *Dresden* as its first lieutenant and chief negotiator with the *Glasgow*, under whose guns the *Dresden* had been pounded and then scuttled.

Interned by Chile on the island of Juan Fernándo Quiriquina, he had made a daring and difficult escape across the Andes on foot, on horseback and then by boat down the Paraná River, taking nearly eight months to reach Buenos Aires by Christmas 1915.

Not satisfied to stay more than a few days, he had embarked on a Dutch steamer using a forged passport and posing as a Chilean widower. So good had his cover been, both the British passengers on board and then the military authorities in Plymouth had been completely fooled. Allowed to proceed to Rotterdam, he had easily entered Germany using his Chilean passport.

Since then? Military intelligence in the Mediterranean, working under cover out of Spain, setting up bases and supply lines for submarines, then thirsting for command, a U-boat of his own. Other things. Lots of them.

And now the Abwehr, the German military's secret service.

"Admiral, you wished to see me."

"You're not riding. I was looking for a man on horseback."

Hagen's laughing gray-blue eyes passed over him as he took hold of the mare's bridle and began to rub her muzzle.

"I'm afraid that's what your associates in the SD and the Gestapo are thinking, Admiral. This way, we'll have a few quiet moments to ourselves."

The sausages were excellent, the coffee superb. Canaris had chosen well. Set in the middle of the woods, beside a tiny man-made lake, the Jagdschloss Tiergarten's timbered ceiling rose high above the stone fireplace, in which there was a welcome fire.

"We staff it and own it, Herr Hagen. For us the hunting lodge is a bit of pleasure away from the cares and noise of the city. You need have no fears about Herr Heydrich. For him and his men, the Jagdschloss is *verboten*. In return, we leave such places as are his alone. It is, if you like, a sort of mutual understanding. We may speak freely. No one will hear us."

The admiral loved intrigue. No paperwork man, the two of them had much in common.

"Then perhaps you'd tell me why you wanted to see me."

Canaris gave a fleeting smile. "I couldn't help but notice you with the *Gruppenführer-SS* at Horcher's. Herr Heydrich is a man who can seldom control his impulses with the opposite sex. My informants tell me that after the reception last night he paid the Fräulein Schroeder a little visit and stayed longer than usual. The Baron Dieter Karl Hunter was, I gather, not present."

"And his sister? She usually stays with Dee Dee."

Pleased by the salesman's reaction, Canaris said apologetically, "My men can't watch everyone. The Reich is really not my field of inquiry."

Heydrich with Dee Dee? Canaris could be bluffing. "She needs a passport and permission to leave. I'd be grateful if you'd see what you could do."

"Would Zurich suit?"

"Zurich? Y-yes, of course, although I told Herr Heydrich New York."

The surprise Zurich had created was also pleasing. "Then consider it done."

Needing time to think, the salesman reached for a last piece of toast. Had Heydrich already made a deal with him? Was such a thing even possible?

"Dieter tells me you'd like to have your own mining company. To go back into the Congo would be a mistake. I, too, have malaria. It's God's curse on the wanderer."

Hagen set his knife aside. "Given the right incentives, I'd still be interested."

Canaris gave a slight nod. "How much would you need to set up such a company — assuming you'd be free to do so?"

A waiter came to clear away. Hagen asked for more coffee. "Two hundred and fifty thousand pounds sterling."

"All at once?" *Mein Gott* ...

"Staged, Admiral. Fifty thousand, then one hundred and then the rest. It'd be enough to get the ball rolling, assuming you were thinking of doing so. It's not cheap, and there's no sense in thinking it is. The Congo's a very big place."

"Could you find another Mbuji-Mayi?"

"Not without the sanction of La Forminière and the Belgian government."

"King Leopold, yes. I gather he's opposed to your moving the Antwerp diamond stocks to London?"

"Your informants are ... what should I say, Admiral? Better than Herr Heydrich's? Yes, I guess they are."

Canaris sat back to study him. "Would you leave what must be a very good position so easily, I wonder? You've high-placed friends in London, Herr Hagen. Let's not discount them."

"They want me as a salesman, Admiral, not as someone at the top."

"But surely Sir Ernest Oppenheimer could find something more suitable for a man of your talents?"

"Good salesmen are hard to find, Admiral. When they're as successful as I've been, management likes to keep them selling."

Everything in the Baron Dieter Karl Hunter's reports, and there had been several over the past three years, had told Canaris to proceed with caution.

There had to be some other weakness. A woman? he wondered. Friends ... Hagen's feelings of loyalty to them.

"I'm surprised you haven't asked for a small retainer just to tide you over. Surely a man of the world such as yourself could use a little cash?"

Hagen let his eyes drift away. Then he said what he knew he'd regret. "I happened on a blue diamond while in London, Admiral. It cost me far too much."

Canaris stifled the sudden surge of elation he felt. It was always a challenge to probe a man like Hagen.

Giving the salesman a curt nod, he said, "I think we understand each other perfectly. I'm glad we've had this chance to meet. Yes, it's been most fortuitous. We'll talk again."

TO WINFIELD MRS LOIS ANNE INVERLIN COTTAGE BLACK DOWN HEATH PORTESHAM ROAD DORCHESTER ENGLAND
    FROM HAGEN RICHARD HOTEL ADLON BERLIN
    IT SEEMS A SHAME SCHEDULE SO UNCERTAIN STOP WILL OR WON'T COME STOP TRIP TO FINLAND NORWAY WILL NOT TAKE

MORE THAN FIVE DAYS STOP CUTS IT FINE BUT HOPE YOU'LL
UNDERSTAND STOP I'LL TRY TO TELL YOU AS SOON AS POSSIBLE
STOP PARIS WILL BE DELIGHTFUL STOP WITH THAT BEHIND US
LET'S HOPE FOR CHRISTMAS STOP WILL JOIN YOU SOON STOP
LOVE HAGEN

Decoded, the message would read:

TO THE CARPENTER FROM ALICE

BELIEVE INVASION AUSTRIA DISCUSSED 5 NOVEMBER HIT-
LER AND GENERALS BERLIN / DIAMONDS A PRIORITY / HEY-
DRICH AND CANARIS HAVE MADE APPROACHES / SUSPECT
HUNTER DIETER KARL ABWEHR AGENT / ALICE

Outside the Central Station the broad thoroughfare of the De Keyserlei
and the Meir cut a wide swath toward the port of Antwerp. Arlette
waited to cross over. As always at closing time thousands of bicycles
joined the streams of traffic.

She'd been meaning to bring her bike from home but had put it off for
so long, she wondered if she ever would.

Oh, for sure it would save on the tram fare. But her father . . . Even now
he would look at the bicycle and hope she'd come home to live.

Richard had liked her parents. He'd been so good with them. Yet he
was a stranger to them, an outsider, older than she and an American.
Perhaps most of all they had feared he might take her to America to live.

Richard was not just a superb dancer as Lev had said. He was fabulous!
They'd gone to the Kursaal, then to the big ballroom at the Imperial
where she'd worn the blue diamond pendant. He'd treated her parents to
dinner. They'd watched the two of them dance. Light as a feather and so
close, so dreamy . . .

Then the roulette wheels and baccarat, her mother's eyes wide with
alarm, her father's appreciative.

The traffic stopped. The streams of pedestrians converged, she out in
front a little. Off to her right something moved, but it was only a street
photographer clutching his camera and hovering on the fringes of life.
For five francs they would take your photograph, then contact you later
with the picture. It was a hard way to make a living and not the best kind
of people did it.

The girl reached the curb and began to window-shop. She hesitated
over shoes, thought about a pair of gloves, or was it a new handbag?

For the longest time she looked at men's sweaters. Twice she almost
turned to glance over a shoulder. Once she turned suddenly away.

She began to walk more quickly. Berlin had said to be careful. The girl
was not to suspect a thing.

Jake Van Eyk went on ahead of her and took two other shots. One he sold. The girl passed by. A creature of habit. The same route every night. Some women never learn.

At a nod from Karl Christian Damas, he caught the bitch as she was gazing up toward the cathedral's tower. Light not too bad. God in her eyes, or was it forgiveness?

"Hey, you buy it, my pretty one? For you, three francs, *ja*?"

His voice, the angular look of him as he grew out of nowhere to confront her made her shy away. Grinning, leering, a cigarette dangling, he came at her. An older man...a lecher... "No! I cannot. Now please, let me past!"

"Your name?"

She colored quickly. "I *don't* want it!"

"Address? Hey, I can blow this one up for your boyfriend."

He took another. He embarrassed the hell out of her, and when she ran for a passing tramcar, she didn't look back. Even so, Damas followed her.

It would be good to talk to her, good to get to know her, but he'd wait for that.

By the time she had reached the Grote Markt next the cathedral, she'd settled down.

Berlin would be pleased.

Part Two

Winter 1938 – Summer 1939

The little fishes of the sea
They sent an answer back to me

Six

ONLY THE SOUND of slowly unfolding paper, crisp and dry on the warm, still air, came to Arlette in the grayness of the vault at Dillingham's.

Alone, well after hours, she opened the paper more fully, then caught and held her breath.

The diamonds were a soft rose color — glassies, fancies, Top Cape and Cape — tinted stones of gem quality with excellent clarity even in the rough; fancies because, in the trade, that was what the dealers usually called them.

Against the stark white of the paper, the stones were absolutely exquisite.

Some were modified octahedra — they were not perfect crystals, not exactly the double, four-sided pyramids that had grown base to base. Others were of the more complex dodecahedral form whose twelve sides tended to have curved edges so that the crystals were rounded.

With the industrial stones such shapes as the dodecahedron would be used for bearings, the tiniest ones in watches, but with gems like these, ah no, they were far too valuable, and wouldn't it be a crime to wear such things to dust?

Matched as to color, the stones varied in weight from 0.48 of a carat to 3.74 carats, and there were eighteen of them, more than enough for a necklace, the product of years of patient acquisition.

Taking up the tweezers, she placed the smallest of the diamonds in the left-hand pan of the precision balance. As always, the weights given by the bourse were exact. Each time de Heer Wunsch went to the sights at the Beurs voor Diamanthandel or any of the other Antwerp bourses, it was the same. Though the stones had been weighed, they must be weighed again before logging the packet into the contents of the vault. The only change in routine was that now, after some practice, he trusted her to do the job.

He would pick her up later and sign the logbook to witness what she'd entered; she hoped he'd not be late. The continued crisis over Austria had agitated everyone. It was only understandable that he should have wished to meet with the rest of the Committee.

Things had not gone well in Brussels with King Leopold and his government, nor had they in London apparently. Though still supposedly a secret, the fate of the Antwerp diamond stocks had so permeated the office and shops, one couldn't help but worry.

And Richard . . . Increasingly they seemed to be relying on him to keep them informed of Germany's intentions.

When she was finished the weighing, Arlette numbered the packet before entering the weights into the logbook. Then she put the paper carefully away.

Richard's trading drawer was right below de Heer Wunsch's. She drew it open — a large flat expanse of carefully regimented rows of folded white paper squares, each no more than six to ten centimeters across.

The blue diamond pendant lay among them, nestled on a piece of pure white felt. It was such a beautiful stone. "An investment," Lev had said and had clucked his tongue impatiently. "Not the sort of thing a girl could wear on her finger."

She had worn the diamond only once. It wasn't that Richard hadn't wanted to take her out. The Krupp had seen to that. Richard hadn't left the Reich until the ninth of December. From Amsterdam he'd gone straight to Helsinki, then on to Oslo. They'd had to forward his things.

By the nineteenth of December he'd been in Paris — had he also gone to Zurich? she wondered. By the twenty-third he'd been back in Berlin.

So many places, so much to do.

Arlette fastened the pendant behind her neck and tossed her hair back off her shoulders. Going through to the washroom, she switched on the light to have a look at herself in the mirror.

She touched the stone. It was so cold. Hesitantly she ran her fingers up over the neck chain, pausing at each of the lesser diamonds.

The sound of the lift came to her. Panicking, she couldn't seem to move. The lift continued as she hurried through to the vault, but then it stopped on the floor below, and she wondered about it.

Glancing at her watch, she saw that it was nearly ten o'clock. It was possible someone might wish to drop into one of the other offices, but at this hour . . .

She tried the door to the office. Yes, it was locked. De Heer Wunsch would soon come back.

Still, the uneasiness wouldn't leave her. Hesitantly she took off the pendant and laid it in the drawer. She ran her eyes over the papers and only then noticed that one of them was missing. A paper of three cut Jagers. There was nothing in the logbook to record that Richard had removed it. Only their two signatures and the date of entry.

Searching now — looking in every drawer — she pulled a bottom drawer out too far and found beneath it in the dust a packet of about 150 grams, bound with elastic bands. Couldn't seem to touch the thing.

There were gem diamonds of every size up to about twenty carats, and all of them had been cut and polished.

Her stomach tightened. Tears rushed into her eyes. No matter how hard she tried she couldn't avoid the truth — Richard had been dealing with de Heer Klees. In December he could not have gone directly from Amsterdam to Helsinki as he'd said, but had come back to Antwerp after visiting de Heer Klees and then had gone on from here. It would have been late. The Central Railway Station wasn't far. No one would have been in the office. He'd not have gone to his flat to sleep. He'd have stayed the few hours someplace else and would then have gone on again.

Cecile Verheyden? she wondered, wincing at the thought. Had he gone to stay with her?

He was now at the Man diesel-engine factory in Augsburg. The Nazis made their U-boat engines there, and Richard, just before he'd left the office, had received a cable from his mother in England and had changed his itinerary so as to fit the factory in.

Still sickened by what she'd discovered, Arlette put the packet away and then fitted the heavy drawer in and softly closed it.

The sound of the lift came. It ground slowly down to the first floor. The cage door opened. Through the stillness, she could hear it shut.

Damas held his breath. Standing in the hall outside the office, his fingers were still on the new set of keys he'd had made. The door to the street opened — it had been a close thing. Someone other than de Heer Wunsch coming into the building late like that, but now the girl, who would have heard the lift, would begin to relax.

As he eased the key around in the lock, he felt the bolt slide open and his gloved hand paused. So far so good then. She'd be in there someplace. At her desk, he wondered, or in the vault?

Krantz had said he was to obtain a new set of keys and to check them out. "Nothing else. You leave that girl alone."

Pressing gently, he felt the door give, looked up now at the frosted, dimpled glass across which were the bold black letters of Dillingham and Company, Diamond Brokers.

And then the names of Bernard Wunsch and Richard Hagen.

The girl was in the vault, sitting at a worktable with her back to him, head bowed, hands in her hair. Had she been crying?

Stiff now — tense. Quiet, so quiet.

Damas took in the long chestnut hair, the slender waist, the hips . . .

Turning suddenly, the girl blurted tearfully, "I didn't hear you coming into the office, *mijnheer*. Please, I am sorry. It is nothing. I . . . I will just get my hat and coat. The logbook is open and ready for you to sign. Everything is in order."

Arlette stepped out into the foyer. "Mijnheer Wunsch..." she began. "*Mijnheer*, is that you?"

She tried the door to the office and found it still locked. She heard a step and then another, hurriedly wiped her eyes and got ready to run.

The steps came along the hall to stop on the other side of the door. A dim shape moved. A key went into the lock. A throat was cleared. There was a cough — too many cigarettes, too many late nights. "Mijnheer... Mijnheer Wunsch. Oh, thank God it's you! I have thought..."

The girl threw herself into his arms and hugged him so tightly, his hat fell on the floor.

"It is nothing. *Nothing*, *mijnheer*. It was silly of me. Yes, now I realize that it must have been you I heard."

She started to cry all over again but stopped herself. She couldn't tell him about the diamonds she'd found in the vault, couldn't say Richard must be helping de Heer Klees.

Damas waited until they were gone. Then he left the office to switch off the alarm system before opening the outer door and turning the alarms back on.

Just like a diamond broker.

The car was a decrepit Opel, a two-door sedan. It sat alone in front of the long row of garages that ran at a right angle behind the massive gray block building of the SD's Berlin headquarters on the Wilhelmstrasse. It looked as if it didn't belong, and as Otto Krantz brought the Daimler to a stop ten meters from it, Hagen had a good view of the car.

The paint was a faded Prussian blue, dabbed here and there by attempts at refurbishment. The fenders were badly dented. As the wipers had beat the snow off the windshield, the young engineer at the Man diesel-engine factory had nervously said, "My father was a prominent Social Democrat in Nuremberg. They sent him to Dachau in 1934. I have no choice but to get out."

Never mind that he knew of the silencers the Germans used to muffle the engines of their U-boats, never mind that Duncan had wanted him out. Julius Streicher, the notorious Gauleiter of Nuremberg, had been the deciding factor.

Three Jagers and a ticket through to Klees, but that had been five days ago.

Krantz cleared his throat. Indicating the Opel, he snorted, "Some schmuck we brought in late last night, Richard. At the moment he's trying to figure out why he killed a station guard and thought he could get away with it. If you'll excuse me a moment, I'll just check on the car. Our boys in the lab will have finished going over it by now."

Hagen fought to remain calm. The weak sunlight of mid-February did nothing to brighten the grimness of what had happened. When one of the SS guards walked by with two German shepherds on the leash, he watched as the dogs were led to the car.

Krantz rapped on the window and indicated that he should get out. "Sorry to have kept you waiting, Richard. If you'll follow me, I'll take you in to see the *Gruppenführer*."

The guard said something sharp. The dogs began to bark. Repeatedly they lunged into the front seat. They fought with each other to tear at the upholstery until the guard had screamed and hauled them out.

Apologizing to Krantz, the guard said, "They must have caught another scent."

The gray, cod eyes sought out Hagen. Vapor hung in the air between them. Krantz gave a shrug. "A policeman's duty is never done, Richard. Could you spare me another minute? Come. Come, let's have a look."

Krantz leaned into the car to examine the front seat as if for the first time. "Heinz, here, lost his buddy, Richard. You can't blame him for being interested. Well, will you look at that? Blood all over the place. Must have panicked. These people never learn. Mess up some poor bugger's throat with a pocket knife, then lather blood all over the upholstery and think they can get away with it. Must have been in a hell of a hurry, wouldn't you say?"

"I wouldn't know, Herr Krantz. You're the policeman. I'm just a salesman."

The Berliner crawled out of the car. The dogs moved in and Hagen felt their warm, wet muzzles. They began to whine, then to snarl. One lunged at him and again the guard had to drag the dogs away and shout at them.

Krantz said nothing.

The office was spacious, the man behind the antique limewood desk preoccupied. Immaculate in his black uniform, Heydrich sat rigidly going over some papers.

A Roman torso stood on a black marble column in one corner. Two medieval shields hung on either side of crossed fencing swords high above a blackened hearth. There were some oils, a tapestry, maps and filing cabinets, a battery of telephones to one side of the desk, a teleprinter.

"Richard, how good it is to see you."

Heydrich laid his pen aside and stood to take the outstretched hand.

"So you're back with us. And how is Antwerp?" No mention of the car, none at all of the engineer.

They made small talk, difficult though it was. Heydrich asked about Dieter Karl and Irmgard, and whether they had got away to Brazil.

Hagen said, "I saw them off in December."

"And Fräulein Schroeder? Have you had a chance to call her yet?"

No, he hadn't. "Then we must do a little run around the town together to see a few of the sights."

Heydrich indicated the room. "Wire mesh on the windows, microphones to record everything, even the slightest sound. Alarms, Richard, and hidden buzzers, hidden guns, guards, guards and more of them! Sometimes a fellow just has to get out to relax. But . . . please, what am I saying? A chair? Some coffee?"

As the secretary set the silver service before them, Heydrich made a steeple of his fingers, reminding Hagen that as a young cadet in Kiel, he had played violin duets with Frau Erika Canaris. Both of them were excellent musicians, but it was to those early years that Heydrich owed his ultimate success in the SS.

He'd been under Canaris's orders for two years, from 1922 to 1924. He'd risen to the rank of lieutenant, had been a wireless operator, and finally, in 1930, a communications officer in the Naval Intelligence Service at Kiel. All well and good until the daughter of one of the directors at the I.G. Farben yards had become pregnant and had pointed the finger.

Heydrich had denied the child was his. He was then engaged to a beautiful blonde of nineteen.

The navy had taken a dim view of things and had tried him.

On the street and unemployed at the worst of times, he'd joined the SS and had been sent by a friend to meet Heinrich Himmler at a small farm outside of Munich.

Himmler had asked him to outline how he would set up the Secret Service of the SS, and had given him twenty minutes. Heydrich had done it so well that in another ten minutes he had been given the job.

Their coffee was poured, the woman even stirring the sugar and cream into Heydrich's cup.

The ritual could begin. "Dee Dee's quite a girl, Richard. Dieter Karl should have taken her with him to Brazil."

The cruel lips were wide and full. "If I remember it, Herr Gruppenführer, you were going to see that would be possible."

"Ah yes, but you said she wanted to go to New York, and that wasn't really quite true."

"I didn't know. I wasn't sure."

Heydrich reached for his cup. "Tell me, Richard, is it possible for the Reich to get sufficient diamonds from Brazil?"

"I thought Dieter was after rubber?"

Heydrich waited. The salesman had many uses.

Haunted by the presence of the Opel in the yard, Hagen cautiously said, "The deposits are placers, Herr Gruppenführer. That is to say, not of primary origin. No one has ever found the kimberlite pipes the diamonds must have come from. The mining's not organized. The *garimpeiros* work on their own, washing and panning the gravels and sands. Weeks can go by without them finding a thing."

"You're not optimistic."

"Should I be?"

"Has the Fräulein Hunter written to you?"

"If she has, I haven't received any of her letters. It's a bit early."

The steeple touched the lips in thought. Heydrich came to a quick decision. "I'll be frank. Has she ever given you any indication she doesn't approve of the National Socialist Party?"

The high voice and nervous manner were unsettling.

"Her family works for the Reich. Her brother, as you know, works for the Krupp."

"Yes, but she's outspoken, Richard. There are rumors."

"What sort of rumors, Herr Gruppenführer?"

"Nothing positive. Her brother's in a very difficult position. One can't work for two masters and have a sister like that. Loneliness does strange things to young women. I understand she suffers from acute depression. She'd been seeing a psychiatrist in Zurich, I gather."

Dee Dee must have had to tell him about Zurich, but Dieter working for two masters? The Abwehr and the Krupp? Why had Heydrich chosen to let him know of it?

The fingertips came together again. The coffee was forgotten. "Dieter Karl and she are very close, Richard. Sometimes loneliness can lead a young woman to think things she oughtn't to."

Things like incest? "Irmgard's got a level head on her shoulders and so has Dieter."

Heydrich laughed at this but brushed the thought aside. "Brazil?" he asked. "Will Dieter Karl be able to buy enough diamonds from there?"

"It depends entirely on what he wants."

"Oh, come now, Richard, don't be evasive. We can talk surely? Tool diamonds?"

"He'll get some."

Hagen was clearly afraid. "Is it true the Antwerp traders are thinking of moving their diamond stocks to London?"

"I really wouldn't know, Herr Gruppenführer. I'm just a salesman."

Heydrich fished for a single sheet of paper and ran his eyes over it. The decoders of Amt I, counterespionage abroad, and Amt II, intelligence at home, had been hard at work on the salesman's cables.

Nothing firm yet but some progress. There was also a girl, a photograph of her, a receptionist at Dillingham's.

"Richard, tell me something. In November you went to a *Treff* with Admiral Canaris at the Jagdschloss Tiergarten. How much did the admiral offer you?"

"Nothing, Herr Gruppenführer. Dillingham's pay me once a month."

To scream at him would not work. Instead, he would rock back in his chair. "Let me give you a little piece of advice. Things are going to move very rapidly from now on. Those who choose wisely will go far. The admiral is of the old school, the SS of the new."

"What, exactly, have you in mind, Herr Gruppenführer?" Would nothing be said about the engineer? Were they prepared to go that far?

Heydrich sat forward. "You've traveled widely within the Reich. You've made a substantial deal with the Krupp. A little information. What could be easier?"

"What sort of information?"

"Can Dillingham's really supply the Krupp? It's such a small firm. I would have thought...a consortium perhaps?"

"We'll manage, Herr Gruppenführer. The other traders have been called in. The Central Selling Organization will help."

"Sir Ernest Oppenheimer, yes. He's another Jew."

Heydrich went over to one of the windows. Tall and narrow, it emphasized the height of him, the slender athletic build being marred by the almost feminine hips.

He would give Hagen time to think it over, but could he use the Schroeder woman a little more? She'd said the salesman wasn't interested in Irmgard Hunter. A pity. It might have been so much easier then.

"Drinks in the Eden Bar, Richard. Then perhaps the Kakadu or the Kranzler, or a drive out to Schloss Marquardt, after which a few little places, I think. Yes, something from the old Berlin of the twenties. A few of our more interesting clubs and bars."

He'd let the Schroeder woman talk to Hagen. He'd let the salesman see her in the company of the *Gruppenführer-SS*.

"Dee Dee, why are you doing it?"

She wouldn't look at him. "Because I must. Because for me the choice has been made implicitly clear. Ravensbrück, Richard, that whorehouse on the Damm, or him until he tires of me."

They'd been drunk. Heydrich hadn't been in uniform, but in what he'd called mufti. They'd gone from one disreputable bar to another, the nightclub acts becoming dirtier until at last they'd wound up at his "Kitty House," the small hotel the SS used to entertain foreign diplomats and set them up for blackmail.

Hagen's escort had been a pleasant, intelligent woman of thirty, good-looking, of course, but a thinker, a serious talker, a biologist.

She'd been mildly bemused by the whorehouse and had laughed self-consciously. They'd left Heydrich and Dee Dee there, and he'd taken the woman back to her flat near the university. Nothing more.

Five-thirty a.m. and a head like a split melon.

"Are you ashamed of me?" Dee Dee asked, breaking his thoughts.

She looked ill. "I don't know what to think. You let him take you upstairs in that place. I . . . "

"You wanted to come after me, but you knew you couldn't. You're as afraid of him as everyone else is and he let you know it, Richard. He laughed at you."

She ran from the sitting room and he could hear her throwing up in the bathroom. When he reached her, she was on her knees.

Heydrich's gaze had only become more intense, more impersonal as the night had worn on. Would he work for them? Would he cooperate as so many were?

"The diamonds, Richard. He wants the Antwerp diamonds."

She threw up again and hugged the rim of the toilet, then wiped her lips on her nightgown, didn't seem to care anymore about her appearance.

For a while they stood looking at each other. "I had no other choice. It was my parents or else."

Only the ironmonger seemed oblivious to the snow. Bits and pieces lay about him on the pavement, a range of pulley blocks, a wheel, an auger, several chains and hatchets.

All were laid out like the well-ordered bones of a skeleton, silent in its burial of gently falling snow.

Arlette waited. Turning, she searched the crowded flea market. Yes, the man was there — lost among some others — a Fleming, she was certain of it. The cigar, the fleshy nose, the puffy eyelids and lips, the stalwart build were the same.

He had been waiting for her to leave the office. He had known the telephone would ring and the breathless, frightened voice of a young man would gasp, "My name is Guenther Klass. I'm a mechanical engineer from the Man diesel-engine factory in Augsburg. Please, you must help me. I've a message for Herr Hagen."

"You looking for something? A part for the washing machine? A length of wire for a clothesline?" asked the burly ironmonger.

"No," she leaped. "Just waiting for a friend."

He jerked his head and she moved off. At the bookstall it was the same. Wherever she went, the man would follow. But would he go inside the café? Would he harm this Guenther Klass? Surely not in Antwerp, not in Belgium?

Screwing up her courage, she returned to the ironmonger's and headed for the Café Lindenbos. Because it was nearly noon and a Saturday, the place was crowded.

The young man was sitting near the back. No more than twenty-two, he was tall, thin, dark-haired, dark-eyed and frantic. If she could pick him out so easily, so could the one who had followed her. He looked as if he'd been sleeping in his clothes for more than a month.

"Please, you must listen carefully. Tell Herr Hagen I did *not*, I repeat *not*, come by the route he suggested. I walked over the border. Me, I walked."

In the dead of winter. "Why?"

Suspicion entered his eyes. "How is it that you know about the route? Please, you must tell me."

Pulling off her scarf and beret, Arlette ordered two bowls of soup and a plate of bread and cheese. "I don't know about it. I only ask because I want to know."

Freckles dotted the bridge of his nose. The beard was new and scruffy. At some point he had cut the back of his hand, a cruel gash that was still raw. Barbed wire? she wondered.

He asked if she knew Richard well and she answered, Yes. His German was excellent, that of a Bavarian.

Not until he had finished both bowls of soup did he tell her why he'd left Germany. "The British were supposed to meet me in Amsterdam but I had to come another way."

In the stark silence that followed his mention of Amsterdam, the noise of the crowded café came back to her and the aisle between the tables grew a little clearer.

The man who had followed her was waiting for a table.

"Tell me about this route. Does it pass through a Dutchman named Klees?"

The girl wasn't just sad, she was depressed. Again he looked suspiciously at her. "I can't. I shouldn't have said anything. Look, can you lend me some money — just enough for the train? I'm going to try to get to Paris. I've an uncle living there. He'll see that I get over to England. He'll vouch for me. They can't send me back. They can't!"

He hadn't known Richard at all — had only met him once.

"I wish I'd never done it. I wish I'd never listened to them!"

"To whom?" A swiftness had come into her eyes. Now she held her breath.

"Never mind. It doesn't concern you. Just get me some money. My life..."

People were beginning to take notice of them. "Wait here. I will go to the bank."

"No! I'm coming with you."

As he got up, he stuffed what remained of the bread into a pocket. Out on the street, men suddenly moved from the crowd — one here, another there, Flemings, Walloons, some big and tough, others short and emaciated. Belgians all. Like jackals they bolted after the young man called Guenther Klass.

He made it as far as the square in front of the cathedral and then they threw him — just threw him — in front of a passing truck!

There was a screech of brakes, a bump — some broken glass and another bump. At long last, the sound of an ambulance came to her.

Numb with shock, Arlette pushed her way through the crowd that had gathered. "Does anyone know him? Do you?" asked a policeman.

There was blood all over the road, staining the snow. The wind plucked at a crumpled square of white paper. As Arlette closed her hand over it, she felt the Jagers.

Again she was asked if she'd known him. The tears ran down her cheeks. Angrily she shook her head. "No... no, of course not. How could I have?"

Damas watched the girl as she stepped away from the scene of the accident. Even at a point of extreme crisis, she had used her head. The engineer had thrown something away and the girl had had the presence of mind to have picked it up.

She began to walk sadly along the street. Hands in the pockets of her overcoat, she clutched the paper. Damas moved closer. Berlin would want it. Krantz wouldn't be satisfied otherwise.

The girl stopped suddenly. He stepped aside, turned to stare into the window of a shop. Chocolates, milk-and-butter, vanilla truffles, nut clusters — the Belgium of old, the Belgium of the stupid rich, the blind, the soft and uncaring who couldn't see what was happening, who couldn't catch the magic of the Reich...

Marzipans and rum barrels, toffees Grenoble...

When he picked up the girl's trail again, her hands were no longer in her pockets.

Smoke trailed upward from the forgotten cigarette that lay in the ashtray on the desk.

The questions had gone on and on. Remember...remember... "You must remember."

Like a stone, a great big stone, a fist! The words came back to haunt her and she shouted in anger now, "I can't! Can't you see I can't! He..." She couldn't tell them about Richard. She couldn't!

Lev gently took the cup and saucer from her. "Arlette, what Bernard is trying to say is that my Rachel was going to use this route the young man spoke of. Richard couldn't tell me when he would try to get them out. But if this Guenther Klass didn't use it, then maybe he had a reason for not doing so. Maybe it was no longer safe."

"He was terrified! He walked. Don't you see that because of the Nazis, he walked?"

"Yes...yes, I know. But could the Gestapo have come to his house perhaps? Could he have seen them and run? If so, then the railways would have been denied him and he would have known this well ahead of time. The route might then still be safe."

"I don't know. He was afraid. He said..." She bowed her head and buried her face in her hand. "He said, 'They can't send me back. They *can't!*'"

Wunsch was insistent. "Please, you must try to remember."

Bitter now, she said, "This route, does it involve the Dutchman, de Heer Klees?"

Taken aback, the two men glanced at each other. "What does *he* have to do with it?" demanded Wunsch.

"Nothing. I...I only wondered if the route..." Dear God forgive her the lies, but she couldn't tell them about the diamonds she'd found in the vault. "I only wondered if the route was connected with him. Amsterdam is..."

Wunsch watched her closely. "Is on the route? Juffrouw Huysmans, was Richard planning to use the lines through Emmerich?"

"I don't know. I only ask because Richard, he...he has passed through Amsterdam on the way home sometimes."

"Sometimes." Wunsch said it flatly. Reaching for another cigarette, he flung the empty package into the wastebasket. The girl was hiding something. From a state of trust to one of distrust, the Nazis had got them all agitated. Hitler wanted war — war! "Richard hasn't had anything to do with de Heer Klees, has he? Arlette, you must answer me. The fate of the Antwerp diamond stocks may be at risk."

Lev found his voice with difficulty. "Richard wouldn't do that. You know this as well as I, Bernard. Stop listening to what Isaac Hond has to say or not say at the Committee meetings."

"Isaac has an eye for trouble, my friend, and de Heer Klees is the proof of it."

Sighing hugely, Lev sat back in his chair. Hond had caught Klees thieving from a fellow member of the bourse, but that had been years ago and Richard had had nothing to do with him.

Neither of them said anything. Arlette knew they were waiting for her. She knew they both meant well, that news of the young man's death had shocked them, too. "Can't we send a message to Richard? Can't we warn him that maybe the route is safe but that this Guenther Klass has died because of them?"

Wunsch realized that he had let things get to him and had been too hard on her. "Yes. Yes, of course. Forgive me, my dear. It's this business of Austria. No one seems to know what is going to happen. Richard has requested that we undertake to train German technicians in our work, and this has upset the members of the Committee and made them question his loyalties again. To be frank, everyone is exceedingly nervous."

TO HAGEN RICHARD HOTEL ADLON BERLIN

FROM WUNSCH BERNARD DILLINGHAM AND COMPANY ANT-WERP

URGENT YOU REPLY IMMEDIATELY STOP FIRST PART KRUPP ORDER READY STOP SHOULD SHIPMENT BE DELAYED PENDING CLARIFICATION OF INTERNATIONAL SITUATION STOP AM SENDING CABLE IN MIDDLE OF THE NIGHT SO AS TO REACH YOU BY MORNING STOP HOPE THERE ARE NO CLOUDS IN THE SKY STOP REGARDS BERNARD

Hagen read the cable again. "Middle of the night" and "no cloud(s) in the sky" had come from "The Walrus and the Carpenter."

Silently he cursed himself for ever having left the little books out on his desk at home.

Bernard he couldn't blame, but the Gestapo would read the cable and keep a record of it just as they did everything else.

From the lobby he put through a blitz call to the office. Five minutes later Arlette was on the line and he was hearing her voice again.

Her voice was cold. "De Heer Wunsch is not in the office, *mijnheer*. He waited around all morning for your reply. It is now after five."

"Look, I didn't get his cable until a few minutes ago. Would you tell him that he'd best hold the shipment until I return? I'd like to check it over first and then accompany it back into the Reich to avoid any customs delays."

That might just get him out of the country. Once he'd found the trouble, he could then decide what to do.

Arlette was good at shorthand. He could hear her taking the message down. When she came back on the line, she hesitated, then said, "Van

Haeren's sent that new lamp you ordered, *mijnheer*. Unfortunately the man who brought it accidentally dropped it and smashed the glass. De Heer Levin has told me that if you should call, I am to say you are not to worry, that he has told the store to bring another."

Lev...Oh damn. "Arlette, tell Bernard I'll be back in five days. From here I must go to Dresden and then to the naval yards at Kiel."

Guenther Klass must have gone to Antwerp instead of Amsterdam, but something had happened to him there. Heydrich and Krantz had known this all along, and yet they had led him to believe they were holding the young engineer.

The bar at the Adlon was packed. It was normally the favored oasis of the foreign news correspondents in Berlin, but its regulars were all but lost in the crowd the crisis over Austria had brought. Hardly a day had passed but there had been something new. Schuschnigg, the Austrian chancellor, to Berchtesgaden to meet with Hitler on February 12, their agreement ratified by the Austrian cabinet on the fifteenth. On the sixteenth the pro-Nazi Seyss-Inquart had become Austria's minister of the Interior, salve to Nazi wounds that wouldn't heal.

On the seventeenth, Anthony Eden, the British foreign secretary, had announced Britain would seek Italy's help in the matter. Il Duce had replied on the eighteenth that Italy would stay out of it.

And now Schuschnigg had told Hitler Austria would resist all such pressures.

The reporters were waiting for the Propaganda Ministry's liaison officer to arrive and give them the latest. Normally Hagen avoided the bar simply because, being anxious for crumbs and having to work under the strictest censorship in the world, the reporters would flock to him.

Yet he needed time to think, needed a drink.

"Hard news, Richard. That's what they all want. Care to wet the old whistle, chum? A taste of home?"

It was Bob Darcy of the *Chicago Tribune*, friend of Capone, confidant of Dillinger, a former crime reporter come to witness crime on a much vaster scale.

Hagen took the proffered glass of Kentucky bourbon and had himself a generous swallow. "So, what do you make of it, Bob?"

Darcy's deep-set brown eyes twinkled. "You tell me, friend. From what I hear you're in pretty close. Ed Jakeman of the *New York Times* saw you out with Heydrich and two dolls, one of whom is sitting all alone right over there."

It was Dee Dee, looking pale and anxious in black velvet.

"Care to confide a little?" asked Darcy. "Us Yanks...you know the gen. Pencil through everything, Richard. Come on, be a pal and give a little and I'll lend you this."

A rush copy of Eric Ambler's *Epitaph for a Spy*. "Interesting stuff, Richard. Prescribed reading for a guy in your shoes, I should think. Well traveled. Visits all their heavy industries. Knows the brass, the ropes, et cetera."

"Heydrich's not exactly what you'd call a friend."

"More of an acquaintance, eh? But that babe with the gorgeous body over there is, and if I'm not mistaken, she's been hanging around waiting for a sight of you. You're not on the make or something with Heydrich's latest girl, are you?"

Hagen grinned. "She's just a friend. Thanks for the offer of the book, Bob, but I'll pass. Spying's a little out of my line."

"Hey, did you hear that Carnegie Hall thing of Benny Goodman's? I've got the records, Richard. Krupa on drums, James and Elman on trumpet..."

It was no use. Hagen had found his way over to the girl. The salesman would take her someplace quiet. He had that look about him.

Intuitively Darcy knew it wasn't a time to pursue things. Of all of them in the room, Richard Hagen would know the most, yet he had to let him go.

Darcy glanced at the book. In a world that had gone crazy it would make the most fantastic copy: American Spy Bar-Crawls with Germany's Head of SS Secret Service...

American Spy Caught. White House in an Uproar. Roosevelt Denies Any Knowledge...

Heydrich's girl and Richard Hagen. Trumped-up spy charges were a dime a dozen, but the *Gruppenführer-SS* could certainly make a bit of hay out of it if he wanted to.

The Romanische Cafe on the Damm had once been the rendezvous of Berlin's artists, writers and actors. Left alone, and he hoped, clear of Gestapo listening devices, they had the place almost to themselves.

"Dee Dee, what is it?"

The milk-white cheeks were touched with rouge, the dark eyes empty.

"I just had to see you to know that things were all right between us."

Had Heydrich sent her to find him? He couldn't tell her he'd spoken to Canaris on her behalf.

"Dieter doesn't care about me. Heydrich..."

"Shh! Keep your voice down. Look out at the street."

At the lights, the snow and the people who were hurrying homeward or pausing to search the shop windows for things that were no longer there.

"Richard, I want to help you." There, she'd said it, a first step.

"In what way?" he asked cautiously. Her gaze was searching.

"I'm writing to Irmgard. Would you like me to send her your love?"

Hagen detected the note of bitterness. "Yes, of course. You know I would."

"Really?" she asked sharply. "You've a girl in Antwerp, a lover, Richard. Have you slept with her? Irmgard's got such a crush on you. At least try to be decent."

"Look, I know how she feels about me but..."

"But you're in love with someone else."

"Yes. Did Heydrich..."

"Tell me?" she snapped bitterly. "When that bastard's drunk his lips are not so tight, only more cruel. They know about this girl, Richard. They know her name, know everything they want to know about her."

Grimly Hagen nodded his thanks. Coming on the heels of his telephone call to Arlette, things were beginning to make sense.

Their drinks came, an intrusion neither of them wanted.

"There's something else," she said, a whisper. "He says the Reich will march into Austria if Vienna doesn't capitulate."

"When?"

It was such a tiny question but given with such intensity, the proof of interest if ever Heydrich should ask it of her. "Soon. Very soon, but please, for your sake and mine, keep it to yourself. They..."

He found himself saying, "I'll be in Kiel in a couple of days."

"Then you must wait at least until then before you try to tell anyone else. Later, I think. Yes, later. Now please call me a cab. I must go home."

"Dee Dee..."

"Richard, *please*!"

TO WINFIELD MRS LOIS ANNE INVERLIN COTTAGE BLACK DOWN HEATH PORTESHAM ROAD DORCHESTER ENGLAND

FROM HAGEN RICHARD HOTEL ESPLANADE HAMBURG GERMANY

WEATHER VERY COLD STOP ALL AROUND THE CITY THE FIELDS ARE WHITE STOP SORRY FRANK WOULD NOT LISTEN TO MY ADVICE BUT UNDERSTAND STOP HOPE HE AGREED TO HAVE THE BOOK PUBLISHED IN SPITE OF CUTS STOP TELL HIM EDITORS WILL FORGET THEIR QUARREL STOP PERFECTLY SURE IT WILL BE A SUCCESS AND HE WILL DO IT AGAIN AND AGAIN STOP LOVE RICHARD

TO OPPENHEIMER SIR ERNEST C/O CENTRAL SELLING ORGANIZATION CHARTERHOUSE STREET LONDON ENGLAND

FROM HAGEN RICHARD HOTEL ESPLANADE HAMBURG GERMANY

SUPERB RED 4.37 OLD-MINER OFFERED ANTWERP OVERHANG

SALES EARLY MARCH STOP WILL HOLD FOR YOU ON RETURN IF WISH STOP REPLY DILLINGHAM AND COMPANY ANTWERP STOP REGARDS HAGEN

The customs shed at Hamburg's airport was freezing. Bundled in his hat, knitted scarf, heavy overcoat and galoshes, a fuming Otto Krantz thumbed the cables Hagen had sent four days ago.

The salesman was full of surprises. Expected to leave with the rush, and to go out by rail through Emmerich and on to Amsterdam perhaps, he had pulled a switch and doubled back to Kiel.

To have another look at empty U-boat pens? Krantz wondered. To pay the Klochner aircraft engine factory a sudden visit, or simply to stall what he thought would be the inevitable?

" 'Superb Red,' Richard. What does this mean?"

Lufthansa's Flight 101 to Antwerp, Brussels and Paris was now boarding. Hagen could see the corrugated iron fuselage of the Junkers 52 through one of the windows in the shed. "It simply means a red diamond, Herr Krantz. They're extremely rare."

"So why not cable him when you get back to Antwerp?"

"I forgot to send it earlier."

"Don't piss around with me. I've had just about enough of you. Buying a ticket for the six-thirty from Hamburg to Emmerich and then not carrying through wasn't very smart. You spoiled my supper."

"I had to go back to Kiel. I had no choice. They insisted. Another breakdown. Another order for the shop."

He could let Hagen go this time. He should, perhaps, and he would accept that Heydrich had made it all too clear the responsibility for the salesman rested squarely with him.

Krantz thumbed the cables again. It was irritating to know so little of diamonds. "Red" must mean Most Urgent; "old-miner," some sort of private code Hagen and his Jewish boss in London had devised for Austria.

"Cable your office. You're coming with me."

"Nothing doing, buster. I'm an American citizen. I've business commitments that must be attended to."

The Berliner arched his eyebrows. "Am I to call the Krupp, or should I attempt to reach your friend in the jungles of Brazil?"

Damn him! "I demand to speak to the American ambassador in Berlin."

"Berlin? Ah, that can be arranged. I've a car waiting and can give you a lift."

Hagen knew there wasn't any use in arguing. At least the warnings had got out. Krantz was holding copies of the cables.

Decoded, the message to Duncan would read:

KLASS INTERCEPTED ANTWERP / BELIEVE INVASION AUSTRIA
IMMINENT / U-37, 52 AND 78 LEFT KIEL 27 FEBRUARY 0600 HOURS
/ PENS NOW CLEAR OPERABLE U-BOATS / SECURITY TIGHT /
REQUEST SEARCH LETTERS BRAZIL HUNTER IRMGARD REPLY
ANTWERP EARLIEST SUSPECT MAILS BEING OPENED / ALICE

March 2, 1938

Dear Richard:

Each time I write to you there's something new.

Germany has a very good network of people here. For some, their
families came out years ago — the rubber barons, as I'm sure you
know. For others, the hunters and trappers, the prospectors, it is of
course the lure of instant wealth.

The house where we are now staying is nestled among tall coconut
palms and shuttered against the fruit bats and the never-ending rain.
It's so humid one drips constantly, and both Dieter and I have developed lingering coughs. The estate is very old and situated well outside
of Diamantina, so no one asks too many questions and the traders can
come and go as they please.

Dieter buys what he can. Mostly it is the gray to black carbonado that
comes, they say, from the area to the east of the Río São Francisco. It is
very porous and looks a lot like coke, but when crushed, ground and
separated will yield the abrasive powders he so desperately wants.

The problem is, of course, there isn't nearly enough of it and no such
thing as a steady supply. This makes my brother angry and at times
despondent. He's so eager to do this thing for the Krupp. It's his big
chance and he lets me know this time and again.

Tonight he is meeting with a trader who comes from the deposits
along the Jequitinhonha River, which is to the northeast of us. This
man has come a long way, perhaps as much as 250 kilometers. I really
don't know. But Dieter...you know how determined he can be. If
things look promising, we will go there once the rainy season is over.

Please take care, and if you can, look after Dee Dee for me. I've had
no answers to my letters to her, but of course the regular mails are not
so good, though even here the diplomatic mail gets through so fast it
has to make one wonder.

Will write again as soon as I can. My hopes and prayers for Austria
remain the same.

All my love,
Irmgard

Would Richard understand that "diplomatic" stood for Abwehr? Of course he would. She'd post the letter in Diamantina. For now, though, she must hide it someplace lest Dieter find it.

As before, she had used the address of Richard's mother in England.

The cedar chest was some distance from her room and long before she had reached it, Irmgard had switched off the flashlight.

Crouching, she felt along the bottom of the chest and carefully slid the letter underneath it.

Dieter could no longer be trusted.

There were four men sitting around the table in the kitchen when she went stealthily downstairs. Hidden from them by the darkness and a grillwork of mahogany, she searched their faces. Dieter was so earnest. Their interpreter, the planter Martin Becke, was explaining something to him. The trader, half French, half Spanish, silently watched them as did the last man — one of about sixty years of age, bald, gray-looking, with sweat that ran down his flaccid cheeks and eyes that bulged.

This one had a sense of humor that was driven to short bursts of dry, false laughter, as if sucking diamonds out of ignorant men were God's play and the baron were handling himself as expected.

Dieter hadn't made a fuss over the man's late arrival. Indeed, the small suitcase was still in the hall, and when she hefted it, she shut her eyes and clenched a fist, tried to hang on to herself.

The case wasn't heavy. It was all but empty.

Yet she knew the man would be staying in the area for a few days. He had that look about him, that look of so many back home. The Nazis, the SS...

Sickened by this, she thought to destroy the letter, then thought, No, she would not do such a thing.

Lying in the dark under the mosquito netting, she listened to the rain, to the bats as they clawed their way up under the eaves or tried to get in at the shutters. Would Richard love her just a little, knowing the terrible risk she was taking?

Dieter wasn't the same anymore.

The Mark Is and IIs were breaking down, those and half the other armored vehicles on the road. Hagen couldn't believe what he was seeing. From Berlin he and Krantz had flown to Munich, and from there had gone by car to Salzburg in the wake of an invading army.

The tanks were hopelessly mired in roadside mud and snow. Motorcycles lay on their sides or crushed beneath lugs. The half-tracks that pulled each Panzer division's artillery pieces had fared no better. At least seventy percent of everything they had passed had been strewn along the roadside, and this continued to the northeast as far as the eye could see.

If Austria should attack, the Nazis would be finished in less than five days. If she should have to fall, then at least he knew that one good winter would stop the Wehrmacht faster than anything.

Krantz irritably lit another cigarette. "You are quiet, Richard. Is it that you do not like what is happening?"

The Berliner had pull — he could order up airplanes and cars at will. He could chase after Heydrich whenever he wanted.

Hagen shook his head. "Your petrol gauge reads almost empty. I was just wondering where you'd get some. Every filling station we've passed has been drained by your army, and some of the stranded vehicles we've seen have simply run out of fuel."

With a scowl the Berliner leaned over the back of the front seat and spoke to their driver. "Walther, is this so?"

The driver acknowledged that it was. They managed to coast into the old town of Wels and to nudge the car out of the way behind a fifteen-centimeter gun.

The sleet had changed to wet snow but now, with the lowlands in the river valley, there was fog. Krantz hunched his shoulders against the cold and reached for the door handle. Hagen wondered how much pull the Gestapo would have when surrounded by an angry Wehrmacht.

Not a drop! Weiners, hot mustard, sauerkraut and coffee helped. The street vendors were out in force. German marks instead of Austrian schillings and groschen, grins and handshakes everywhere, Swastika flags, too. Would it be the same in Vienna?

Krantz got mustard on the lapel of his overcoat. Hagen found a napkin and helped to wipe it off. Then he did what no other spy would have done. "I think I can get us to Vienna."

The Berliner took a last bite before setting down his coffee on the hood of the car. In doubt, he sucked mustard from the flat of his thumb. "So, how is this, please?" Hagen was enjoying himself.

"Loan me our driver and let me have all the money you've got."

Krantz shook his head, but already the salesman and their driver were crossing the road. As he watched, they went into a pharmacy. An hour later they had cleaned out most of the others and their fuel tank had been filled with surgical benzene. Two cases of bottles were squeezed between them while another two were stacked on the front seat beside their driver. Hagen had rolled up his sleeves and had adjusted the carburetor. The engine sounded rough, but it ran.

"You impress me, my young friend. Is it that you wish to show me how wrong I am about you, or is it that you really do wish to watch the fireworks?"

The news broadcast ended. The radio began to cool. Arlette drew the shawl more tightly about herself. In the emptiness of her room she sat alone. Austria was gone — just like that. Absorbed into the greater German Reich. A province.

Neither Britain nor France had come to her aid. As of tonight, March 13, not only had Austria ceased to exist, but her army had been swiftly absorbed into the Wehrmacht without having fired a shot.

Some divisions had already been transferred to the north, to the borders of Holland and Belgium. The Jews had suffered; countless shops and homes had been looted. There had been arrests — the beginnings of a reign of terror. The anarchy that Hitler had used as an excuse to threaten an invasion of Austria had now become a reality. Along with the anti-Jewish riots had come the fanatical cheering of the people, the mass hysteria and shouts of, *"Ein Volk, ein Reich, ein Führer!"* One people, one state, one leader.

With the news of Austria had come that of a Czechoslovakia that was fast disintegrating. France backed the Czechs against Hitler. Britain said she wouldn't go to war, but with the chaotic state of French politics would the threat of France alone deter the Germans from invading Czechoslovakia?

So many armies, so many big and powerful men, and Richard still not home. No word at all since Berlin. No chance to tell him that she knew he was helping de Heer Klees. No chance to tell him that she was almost certain someone had tried to break into the office again.

They were drinking a Nussberger white out of air-twist goblets that were at least 150 years old. They ate — good God, how they ate! Black Forest ham, blue trout, pheasant, venison, pickled pork hocks, sausage, huge steaming bowls of sauerkraut, creamed potatoes, creamed leeks, creamed eggs...

The noise in Vienna's glittering Opera House was deafening. Goering, the loudest of all, swilled wine, smoked his cigar, laughed, chewed and filled his face. Resplendent in a white uniform with an Iron Cross First-Class pinned to his chest, he chided Heydrich, who sat on his left, and winked at his buyer, Herr Sigmund Menke, who sat on his right.

Menke had appraised the contents of the leather pouch Heydrich had dumped in front of the *Reichsmarschall*.

Himmler, bespectacled and fiercely intent, watched the pig eyes water as Goering gazed greedily at the loot. There were others seated about the table: Bormann, Hess, Rosenberg and Goebbels, about thirty men in Luftwaffe blue, the pilots Goering had chosen to join him. Eager young men with starched shirts, stiff backs and a fawning manner when it came to attending to the *Reichsmarschall* and his remarks.

There were also six actresses from Vienna and three from Prague —

tall, statuesquely beautiful women with ripe golden hair and blue eyes, one with jet-black hair and eyes whose pride made Hagen look a second time. Two brunettes. All but the raven-haired one flirted with the men, laughed at the ribald jokes and looked longingly at the gems. It was going to be quite a night.

Heydrich waited. Then he swept a leather riding crop over the stones to spread them out a little more. A soft and delicate shade of rose, two reds, some green, canary yellow and blue — Top Cape and Cape Fancies, white Jagers also. Against the damask tablecloth their facets caught the light from the chandeliers. None of the stones would weigh less than five carats; the largest, perhaps thirty-five. A truly superb collection.

The noise from the crowd Goering had invited to his dinner party ebbed and flowed about them. "One hundred thousand marks," offered the *Reichsmarschall*.

"For the largest of the blue stones?" asked Heydrich, leaning back from the table to let his gaze pass from the diamonds to the raven-haired actress, who stood uncomfortably beside him.

She was so like Dee Dee, Hagen had to wonder if she was present just to remind him of her.

"One hundred thousand for the lot," said Menke, taking his cue from the *Reichsmarschall*.

Heydrich grinned. "Richard, please, your valued opinion."

The stones could only have come from the Rothschild palace on the Ploesslgasse. The SS must have looted the place.

The noise of the cutlery fell off. In the hush, the waiters moved about, a *danse macabre*. One of the actresses touched the base of her throat.

Hagen picked up the largest of the blue diamonds. "What is it you want to know, Herr Gruppenführer?"

Gravy dribbled on Goering's lapel. There was a spot of plum sauce as well.

Himmler watched the two of them: Heydrich, who was so good at things; Hagen, the merchant of industrial diamonds who'd lost the third and fourth fingers of his left hand. Now how had that been?

"I wish to know if there are any flaws," said Heydrich. "I wouldn't want the *Reichsmarschall* to be cheated. Richard is an expert in such things."

In cheating? wondered Hagen. Just what had Heydrich in mind?

Fitting his loupe to his eye, Hagen examined the stone. The color was not nearly that of the diamond he'd given Arlette, but somehow Heydrich had learned of the stone and was using this as a warning.

It would be best to defer to him. The diamond, faceted into an emerald brilliant, would weigh a little over five carats.

He set it back and ran his fingers through the others. "Three hundred and fifty thousand marks for the collection. One hundred thousand for the larger of the blues, as the *Gruppenführer* has said."

"And the woman?" asked Heydrich.

Hagen looked steadily into her eyes. "I...I'm not sure that I understand you, Herr Gruppenführer. Is she really for sale?" He managed a grin.

The table erupted in laughter. Himmler snorted, *"The Office of Jewish Immigration*, Herr Hagen. We are going to let the pigs buy their way out!"

Scattering the stones, Heydrich said, "These are only a beginning. And these..." He held up a hand and snapped his fingers. An aide clicked his heels and passed him another pouch. "These are the solution to the Reich's little problem, Richard."

Once more he was forced to wait. Slowly, as if undressing a beautiful woman, Heydrich opened the pouch. He let him see the Abwehr insignia, let him know the diplomatic mails had been intercepted by an agent of the SD in the pay of the Abwehr.

Then he poured a stream of industrial diamonds among the gems. At once the granular, beaded, jet-black to gray carbonado was all too apparent, but there were octahedra, cubes and macles also, though many of these had the dirty light brown to light greenish brown coatings typical of Brazilian stones.

"Does Dieter Karl know you've got these?" he asked quietly.

Goering flicked his gaze from Heydrich to Himmler. Heydrich thirsted after the Abwehr. Everyone knew it, even the salesman.

The Jewess watched the American with hatred in her eyes.

Heydrich said, "The Abwehr, Richard. The admiral is far too cautious. The *Anschluss* has been an overwhelming success, has it not? Britain out of it, France out of it. Not a shot fired. And *that* is what I consistently advised the Führer. So, you must learn to back the right horse if you are to succeed, is that not correct?"

"Meaning?"

He ran the riding crop over the raven-haired woman's arm. "That now the Führer will let the Sicherheitsdienst have a more open hand in such matters. You'd do well to work for me instead of the admiral."

He poked at the blue stone, ferreted it out, and when it was at the edge of the table, gave it a final nudge.

A shriek went up from the actresses. Fascinated, Goering watched. Himmler pushed his glasses onto the bridge of his nose.

The Jewess stood back as the stone came to rest between her shoes.

"I don't work for the admiral, Herr Gruppenführer."

Heydrich ignored him. *"Bitte*, Fräulein Reismann. Pick it up."

"Why should I?"

"DO IT!"

She crouched, and when she was down, he laid the riding crop across her shoulders. "Richard, let me give you a piece of advice. The Jews or their friends can buy their freedom. Pay the price and there are no worries."

He lifted the riding crop. Sarah Reismann began to get up, but he laid it back down across her shoulders.

Krantz tried to interject something about the cables that had been sent from Hamburg. Heydrich waved a deprecatory hand. "Richard is free to leave whenever he wishes. Please, I must insist. He is a friend of the Reich and is always welcome.

"Richard, could I ask a small favor? The Fräulein Reismann wishes to go to Antwerp. Could you . . . ?"

"Of course, Herr Gruppenführer. I'd be glad of the company."

The wind off the Scheldt was cold, but in the lee of old stone buildings and leaded glass, the late-afternoon sun was warm.

Hagen went up another side street and came at last to the courtyard. Like an oasis of quiet in the heart of Antwerp, the house of Jacob Lietermann faced onto formal gardens where the yew and box had been carefully pruned and the lindens awaited their leaves.

Life-sized sculptures flanked the massive wrought-iron double door — Neptune to one side, Venus to the other, gorgeous things. Above the sculptures, the floor-to-ceiling windows of the main drawing room were arched and of leaded glass with stained glass panels in azure blue and ruby. High above these, on the third floor, Adonis and Cupid stood over stonework scenes of Rome with flanking urns.

The place was at once an expression of old Antwerp's love of art and beauty, and Lietermann's commitment to them.

"Richard, my boy, it's good of you to have come straight from the station."

"Mijnheer Lietermann, the times are such I would have done nothing else, but still I'm honored. In spite of our troubles, a visit here is always a pleasure."

In lesser men that would have been taken as flattery, but not with Hagen. "Come . . . please come then. Let us sit a moment in the sun. The others can wait."

Lietermann led him to a far corner of the courtyard where a fountain, nestled high in a rockery, fed water into a descending series of stone basins into which the goldfish had only just been placed. "I always sit here when I can. I like to look on my house and think it will be here long after I'm gone."

They avoided the gravity of Austria for as long as they could. Briefly they spoke of the house and the weather. Because of his age, the leader of the Antwerp Diamond Committee no longer did the heavy work, though he still found time to prune the hedges and liked to tidy things.

"Richard, knowing peace is farthest from Herr Hitler's mind, what would you do if you were me? Would you sell this place and run?"

There must be thousands of others thinking exactly the same thing. "You love the house too much, Mijnheer Lietermann. Why not lease a place in the English countryside and see what happens? At least then your collection of paintings would be safe."

"Unless destroyed by one of Goering's bombs or captured by some Panzer division. Hitler won't stop, will he?"

"No, sir, I don't think he will."

Lietermann tapped him on the arm. "But you'll preach calm to the Committee."

Hagen knew just how jittery they'd be, but still the request puzzled him. "If that's what you wish. Every day the danger grows, but to panic and run isn't the solution. The only thing the Nazis will understand is a force greater than their own. France still has far more divisions than Hitler. Combined with the British, ourselves, the Dutch, Czechs, Poles and the Russians, we could easily stop him from carrying out his plans."

"His *Lebensraum*, now that Austria is no more. His need for living space. You said 'ourselves,' Richard. I like that. You're adaptable — is that the reason, I wonder, or is it because you genuinely like our style and pace of living?"

For just a moment he hesitated, wondering what was behind the question. "I need roots just like everyone else, *mijnheer*."

"But are you working for the Nazis, Richard? That is the question you must answer."

It was all so futile, so impossible to outmaneuver Heydrich. "Sarah Reismann doesn't waste much time. I gather she telephoned you from her hotel."

Lietermann shook his head. "Not me, Richard. She called her uncle, de Heer Merensky."

The drawing room was sumptuous. Along with the Flemish tapestries and sculptures there were superb works by Peter Paul Rubens, others by Van Dyck, Jacob Jordaens, Teniers and Cornelis de Vos, all of them great Antwerp painters.

In the midst of this remarkable collection the Antwerp Committee sat in green baize armchairs around an antique inlaid table. Bernard Wunsch was chain-smoking. Isaac Hond, that thin, pale setter of prices, wore the harried look of the perpetually nervous, but to this had been added the wounded fierceness of the betrayed.

Abraham Merensky merely glowered.

"You're late!" This had come from Hond.

Lietermann gave the excuses. "Isaac, he is *not* the enemy."

"He is! You heard what Juffrouw Reismann has said!"

"So she is already a Belgian, Isaac? Come, come, please try to be calm. The woman is understandably upset, but there are perfectly logical explanations for her suspicions."

"Suspicions!" shouted Hond. "Accusations that are true!"

"Richard, what is this she says?" asked Bernard, madly stubbing out his cigarette only to take out another.

"Calm," said Lietermann. "Gentlemen, *please*! We are all here as friends."

"Friends!" spat Abraham Merensky. "Friends like him who needs? A traitor, if you ask me."

A harried Sarah Reismann chose that moment to come into the room. For an instant their eyes met and Hagen knew that no matter what he said, the woman would never believe him. She was like a fine painting superimposed on a tapestry, caught in that moment. Heydrich's unwitting Judas.

In silence he listened to her accusations of how the head of the Secret Service of the SS and their Gestapo had called him a friend and had allowed her to leave the country only because of this. "I had no money with which to *buy* my way out! That blue diamond wasn't mine!"

"What blue diamond?" asked Wunsch, but left the matter for she'd burst into tears.

Lietermann gently took her by the arm and led her from the room. Merensky called after him. "Jacob, she will wait for me. You can see how upset she is."

"But of course I can, Abraham. My Leah will take good care of her. Please, Fräulein Reismann, a little rest to calm yourself? You've had a very hard journey and are so extremely lucky. At least our Richard's being there has saved someone from their clutches."

They went at him then. Isaac Hond couldn't keep the bitterness from his voice. "Mijnheer Hagen, before we confide anything more in you, would you please tell us if the Reich has offered you a job?"

"Of course not. If they had, I would have refused."

The harried eyes watched him closely. "Then why is it Herr Heydrich has called you a friend? Why, please, were you taken to Vienna? It was not on your itinerary. Bernard has told us this."

"And what else has he told you?"

The softness of voice made the others turn to look at Wunsch, who shrugged and said, "Richard, these are difficult times. It is hard not to speculate. The telegrams...I ask you again, is it that the Gestapo and Herr Heydrich suspect you of spying for the British?"

Bernard could be so fussy when he wanted. There were things he would never leave alone.

Lietermann came to his rescue, but even so, his words carried dangers of their own. "Richard sent Sir Ernest a warning of the invasion. This I have learned as of late last night."

"A warning?" Merensky paused in lighting a cigar. "Why were we not given this, Jacob? Why were we not told that Austria would be invaded?"

That grand old man gave them a moment, then wisely said, "Because Sir Ernest couldn't have done so without compromising Richard. We would all have tried to contact our relatives and friends to warn them, isn't that so? Now look, no employee of the Reich would risk his life to send such a message."

"And the British?" asked Bernard. "Did you also warn them, Richard? Are you spying for them? Please, I ask you as a friend and one who admires and sympathizes with your task. Tell them, for God's sake. Stop this friction Heydrich has caused among us."

"May I sit down?"

Someone nodded — was it actually Merensky? "Look, I know it all appears suspicious but that's the way they want it. Of course I'm not spying for the British. I'd be a fool to do that. I was, however, hoping to use a line of escape out of the Reich for Ascher Levinski's daughter and son-in-law. If the Nazis are letting the Austrian Jews buy their way out, surely they'll extend the same rights to those of their own country. At the moment, though, all I can offer is that we must wait and see how things develop."

It was Bernard who told him what had happened to the young engineer.

"And Arlette?" asked Hagen anxiously.

Irritably Wunsch stubbed out his cigarette. "She has left a message that you are to meet her at the café of Cecile Verheyden. For me, I hope things are still all right between the two of you, though I must say I have my doubts."

Lietermann again interceded. "Since we still have no agreement from the British government, Richard, we have begun to make some plans to move the diamonds ourselves. Abraham, would you . . ."

Reluctantly Merensky nodded. "We have leased the *Megadan*, a freighter of fifteen hundred tons. She is no different than countless others. All the traders are to have their stocks ready to be placed in clearly identifiable strongboxes for shipment at a moment's notice. If we have to, Mijnheer Hagen, we will send the diamonds to London without the sanction of the British government."

Hond's voice began to rise. "The ship will be torpedoed! They'll sink it. Everything will be lost!"

Hagen waited a moment for things to settle down. As a plan, it was a start but... "Gentlemen, sailors talk. A freighter sits idle, perhaps for months, but is always kept in readiness. How sure are you of your security?"

"Meaning the Abwehr and the Sicherheitsdienst have their agents," said Merensky. "Yes, but you see there is also another problem. We would, of course, have liked to ask our navy to help us, but King Leopold still adamantly refuses to let us send the diamonds to London."

"So, in a sense our hands are tied," said Lietermann, "by our own people and by the British government."

"Whatever we do must be done in absolute secrecy, Richard. There can be no leaks," said Bernard.

"But there have been, and the policy of neutrality is utterly stupid. Look, the French swear by their Maginot Line but the Germans know every detail of it. Here in Belgium what did we do? To build Fort Eben Emael and the Albert Canal defenses, we hired Monnoyer, which in turn had a subcontracting arrangement with the Reich, who then compensated them for putting in the lowest bids on the construction. The Germans must know all about our defenses, even to having the drawings."

Merensky felt sick. Forgotten, his cigar dropped ash on the green baize of his chair. Wunsch leaped to brush it off.

Isaac Hond found his voice at last. "What you're saying then is that no matter whom we trust, the Germans will find out."

"In a sense, yes. Unfortunately there are Belgians who will help them, just as there are Frenchmen who do the same. Though the Germans might sink the *Megadan* by accident, Mijnheer Hond, more than likely they will seize her."

"What do you suggest?"

This had come from Lietermann. "That we stick with the *Megadan* — that you maintain the utmost secrecy on her — but that you agree to let me arrange something else that will be known only to the five of us. When and if war comes, we will then take dummy strongboxes to the *Megadan* and the diamonds to someplace else."

"Where?" asked Hond suspiciously.

"The Central Railway Station. Two sealed cars are all we'll need. These can then cross the channel at whichever port we feel is best."

Hagen had had it all worked out. "And if the Germans suspect a ruse? What if, instead of heading for the channel, the cars are rerouted to the Reich by you?"

"Isaac, please. What Richard says makes sense. Let us at least think about it," said Lietermann.

Merensky shook his head. "Enough is enough. We have to do something. Let's do as he says." Hagen had got his niece out of Austria.

Bernard Wunsch remained lost in troubled thought. On the death of the young engineer, Arlette Huysmans had wanted to tell him something but had then thought better of it. Had it been about Richard and de Heer Klees?

"All right," said Hond, "except that *I* will arrange for the railway cars and *we* will keep this and the time of shipment to ourselves." He'd use trucks. Never the railways!

Hagen got up to leave but turned suddenly back. "You've done what Heydrich wanted, Mijnheer Hond. You've got me out of it. He's not worried about any of you. Their agents have penetrated the bourses. They know the size of the diamond stocks. They know how vital they are to them."

Hond wasn't going to back down. "Why haven't you been able to convince your friends in London of the urgency? Why haven't they given their sanction to move the stocks before it is too late?"

"Because I don't have that kind of friends. Because if I did, Mijnheer Hond, I would probably be languishing in a German jail."

TO WINFIELD MRS LOIS ANNE INVERLIN COTTAGE BLACK DOWN HEATH PORTESHAM ROAD DORCHESTER ENGLAND

FROM HAGEN RICHARD DILLINGHAM AND COMPANY ANT-WERP

TELL FRANK TO BEAR UP AS I KNOW THE MADNESS WILL HAVE UPSET HIM STOP THOUGH THE SHADOW OF WAR HAS BEEN CAST THE DAYS OF SUMMER MAY YET PROVE US WRONG STOP LOVE HAGEN

When decoded, the message would read:

TO THE CARPENTER FROM ALICE

KLASS MURDERED / PLANS BEING MADE TO MOVE DIA-MONDS TO LONDON

An hour later an answer came back. Decoded, the message read:

TO ALICE FROM THE CARPENTER

URGENT WE MEET / WHITE RABBIT INSISTS YOU BRING HUYSMANS ARLETTE / GLAD TO HEAR YOU MADE IT

A light rain fell as he left the office. Hagen paused at the top of the stairs to pocket his keys. In many ways it was much like the night he and Arlette had first gone to Cecile's.

She'd be upset. To have seen a man die like that couldn't have been easy.

Worried about her and about what Dee Dee had told him Heydrich had said, he went down the steps. At the Central Railway Station there were several taxis waiting for the nine o'clock from Paris, and he thought then how nice it would be to take her to that city of light.

But the lights would be going out all over Europe. Hitler wouldn't stop. Czechoslovakia would be next and then Poland. There'd almost certainly be war.

Cecile had called her club Chez Vous, with you, her friends and ex-lovers. She'd been watching for him from near the bar. The sequins caught what light there was as she fluidly made her way through the haze of tobacco smoke and the tables.

"Cecile, it's good to see you."

"And you, if I understand things correctly. My God, Richard, what the hell are you up to?"

She kissed him on the cheek. "You smell good," he said. "I like your hair longer. It suits."

Though she smiled warmly, worry soon darkened the deep blue eyes. Fondly she ran a hand up and down his arm, as if to ask, Is it really you? Self-consciously she said, "So you're back. How was it?"

He wondered how much Arlette had told her. "Not bad — for me, that is. Vienna was a madhouse. The Nazis were beating people in the streets while the crowds cheered them on."

"The Jews." She tossed her head. "Did they really make them scrub out the latrines?"

"And the streets, but not just the Jews. Anyone who's been against them. By the time I got there Himmler and his boys had arrested something like seventy-six thousand people."

"Will the Nazis come here?" she asked.

He nodded and said, "Unless we're very lucky. Where's Arlette?"

Cecile blocked his way a moment longer. Richard had been so good in bed, and for a time they'd had such feelings for each other. "Is it that you really want to settle down? She's very upset — my God, she doesn't cry. What the hell have you done to her?"

"Let me past, Cecile. I couldn't get word out."

She didn't budge. "For me it doesn't matter, yes? But for her, she's so innocent, Richard. To hurt such a one, I wouldn't have believed it of you."

He caught her by the shoulders, but she stepped in on him swiftly and ran her fingers up the back of his neck. She pressed herself to him and found his lips. "Cecile, what the hell..."

"Now maybe she'll understand that for you there can be no roots."

Hagen followed her through the tables and when they came to where Arlette was sitting, Cecile dropped a comforting hand to Arlette's shoulder and gave it a gentle squeeze. "He's back. If I were you, I'd tell him to go to hell!"

As she left them, Arlette spread out the newspapers — pages from the *Völkischer Beobachter* and Berlin's evening *Der Angriff*. Two of the Brussels rags as well: *L'Ouest* and *Le Pays Réel*. The Committee hadn't said one damned thing about them! Bernard had left it to Arlette to tell him.

His photograph was plastered all over the pages, a bevy of buxom beauties in the background, Heydrich grinning, leering, Dee Dee very pale, the neckline of her dress plunging to reveal her breasts.

Arlette read from one of the captions. " 'The Gruppenführer Heydrich,' Richard. '*Relaxing* with his good friend, the American diamond trader from Antwerp.' The girl, she's pretty, Richard. A biologist who looks like a prostitute!"

He caught her by the arm and forced her to sit down. "Arlette, that happened over a month ago. It's not what you think!"

She wouldn't cry, wouldn't make a scene. "No, please. Allow me to explain. I have found these, Richard, in the snow where Guenther Klass had died. You are so lucky it was me who found them."

Hagen understood. The Jagers he'd given the engineer spilled from it when he uncrumpled the paper. Three clear, white diamonds.

"You, me and that young man who was murdered, Richard. *Murdered!* You are taking diamonds to England for de Heer Klees."

"Will you trust me a little?"

"Only if you tell me the truth."

"Arlette..."

"The diamonds, Richard, and de Heer Klees. Nothing else."

"Have you told Bernard?"

She shook her head. "Not yet. Not until I have heard this thing from you yourself."

He gave her the merest of nods. If Heydrich ever got to her, his work was finished. They'd kill her, too. "Guenther was to give these to one of the German customs guards at Emmerich. For some reason he didn't use the line. Did he say why? Arlette, you've got to tell me. It's an escape route, and yes, Klees is at the end of it, and yes, I've had to take his diamonds to London."

"How is it that he trusts you not to steal them?"

"Periodically the Dutchman goes to London and transfers the diamonds to another vault."

"Then he only needs you to carry then into Britain for him."

She'd thought it all out, had known he would have recovered the

Jagers and put them back. No need for signatures and dates, no record. Everything so secret.

"Arlette, I have to know exactly what Guenther said. Please, it's vital to others."

As she told him what had happened, Arlette found that the nearness of him was troubling in ways she hadn't thought possible.

He asked why the engineer hadn't used the line.

"Is it still safe, is that it, Richard?"

His smile was there as it used to be, but she couldn't look at him any longer. Lev's daughter and son-in-law were one thing, de Heer Klees another, and those Berlin women yet another!

"Arlette, I asked it only because others will ask it of me."

Others . . . the ones to whom he sent his secret messages. She shook her head. "There was nothing else. So, it is finished between us, Richard. I have helped you, and I will leave de Heer Wunsch's employ this time for good, hoping that you will have the courage to tell him the truth."

Out on the street he told her that Winston Churchill wanted him to bring her to England.

At 2:00 a.m. fog clung to the darkness of Amsterdam's canals. All along the Prinsengracht the bare branches of the lindens dripped moisture.

Up from the quays came the sounds of gently lapping waves. Two barges plied the eerie sargasso. Hagen could just see the faint glimmer of the running lights and hear the patient chugging of their engines.

He thought to use them as cover. Steps echoed from the cobblestones. Puddles lay in the hollows. The street lamps seemed so distant.

The steps came on, and when the man passed the doorway, the sour smell of the canal was mingled with that of stale tobacco smoke.

In time the other one passed him. Then this one, too, was gone, absorbed by the fog. Three . . . there had been three of them. Dutch fascists in the pay of the Sicherheitsdienst.

Hagen walked quickly back along the canal. When he found a lone taxi at a corner, he took it to the house Klees operated on the Achterburgwal.

The prostitute he chose had long dark hair and dark eyes. Just in case they had followed him here, he made her stand at the window as she undressed. He stood with his back to the bedside lamp so that they could see his shadow on the ceiling from the street below.

Then he drew the curtains but left the light on and went out the back door.

Again he headed for the shop on the Prinsengracht. This time the street was clear. A glimmer of lamplight revealed the puddles.

A child had lost her doll. It lay half in the water, half out of it. The china head had been smashed. The pieces were strewn about.

Klees's houseboat rocked gently at the quayside.

At a touch, the door to the shop opened, and Hagen closed it quickly behind himself and put the lock on.

"Mijnheer Klees . . . ?" he began. There was no answer. Had they killed the Dutchman? Was that it?

He felt his way forward and when he found the Dutchman in the darkness, Klees was breathing hard. The gun was in his hand. "Why are you so late? Why have you come like this?"

Seven

CHESIL BEACH was not that far from Black Down Heath. They'd come down in the car for a stroll, a quiet talk. In many ways Arlette felt so out of things. The obvious wealth of Inverlin "Cottage," the difference of class, the barriers of custom and language. Oh, for sure, her English it was good enough, but...

Lois Anne Winfield took the girl by the arm. The breeze tugged at the lovely hair, and for a moment she thought, Well, if Richard must settle down, this one would have been ideal for him. But then she shoved such nonsense from her. The girl would have to be told. "To Richard and Duncan you can lie, my dear, but to me you're still very much in love with him."

"Is it so evident?"

She gave the girl's arm a sympathetic squeeze and added a snort of wry laughter. "To me, of course. After all, I was young once, and Richard is so very like his father. Hell — absolute bloody hell — that man made my life a misery. You'd think taking a young wife and son into the jungle would be enough of a challenge for any man. Couple that with prospecting for diamonds in largely untracked ground and you've got yourself trouble. But oh no, take it all in your stride. Reach for the Beefeater's London Dry and top it up with Boodles. *Gin*, Arlette — please, I must call you that. If you still insist on trying to keep up with Richard, you'll need a shoulder to cry on.

"Bill Hagen regularly took along sixteen cases of Beefeater's and another eight of Boodles British. It 'beat' the malaria. It helped to 'cleanse' the pores, and after all, why God, you couldn't drink the bloody water anyway.

"At first I thought it a great adventure. He was handsome, so full of fun and such a damned good lover. My God, that man could send me crazy — but Richard's father didn't just have sex with me, Arlette. Oh my, no. In his cups that bastard was a roaring drunk and all female flesh was game, especially his precious Bantu to whom he was not above comparing me."

"Richard's...Richard's file does not say he is like this, Mrs. Winfield.

Please, I must tell you it says his affairs they are characterized by a deep sense of commitment. He is a man of responsibility."

The laughter was harsh. "My dear, you watch him. He'll go back to someone for old time's sake just like his father did."

They walked in silence, but now Arlette felt her arm gripped as if to prevent her from escaping.

"There was another woman, a Dutch one, or . . . oh, what is it you call them in Belgium?"

"A Fleming."

"Cecile . . . yes, a nightclub owner."

"A jazz club."

"Tall — an absolutely gorgeous figure. Richard loaned her money just like his father would have done. The poor boy was really quite smitten with her. They made a smashing couple, as the Brits are so fond of saying. There was a child, too — well, part of one, but she got rid of it."

Arlette shut her eyes and bit her lower lip. Why did the woman have to tell her this? "You do not think much of your son."

"And now you feel sick. My dear, I'm simply trying to warn you."

The light was almost gone. "If it was only this, I could understand your being upset. But you are worried, *madame*, and I know the reason why."

"Then tell him, please, to stop what he's doing before they kill him."

The gate house at Inverlin Cottage was crowded with artifacts from Maiden Castle and other archaeological digs. Bones, a skull, some hand axes, scrapers, arrowheads and spear points, bits of pottery.

Three cats and an old sheepdog lay about and didn't welcome intrusion.

Arlette tried to stir the fire to life. She felt like burning some of Duncan McPherson's papers! Oh, for sure, he could be kind, but this boyhood friend of Richard's viewed her with the utmost suspicion.

She was a threat to Richard's spying, and Duncan knew this. He doubted her abilities and was angry that Mr. Churchill had asked to see her. Secretly he blamed her for the loss of the engineer.

There were some papers in the wastebasket. Stuffing them beneath the coals, she added kindling and warmed her hands. Richard loved her. Richard was in danger all the time.

As the last of the papers caught, she read: *"The White Knight is sliding down the poker." White keyed to 7, 18, 3, 4 . . .*

Though she searched, there was no more of the code. Duncan had been so careless!

The passage was on page 22 of *Through the Looking Glass*. They had been working on another code. Instead of the poems, they would now use bits of the text. Perhaps both, so as to confuse the Germans.

"Arlette, what are you doing?"

She gave a yelp and spun around.

McPherson tugged the books from her fingers, knew then that he couldn't avoid things any longer. "Och, I'm no happy with your being here, and that's the truth of it, though in all honesty I wish things could be different."

"Where's Richard?"

"With his mother. Arlette, listen to me. We can't allow him to become mixed up with anyone. It's far too dangerous and far too important. He's our eyes and ears, for pity's sake!"

"And I am *not* mixed up with him! I did not ask to come here!"

"Then put him out of your mind. Listen to that mother of his."

"You ... you have told her to tell me those things! My God, I have thought ... "

McPherson shook his head. "I couldn't have told that woman to do a blessed thing, but no matter. Everything she said was true."

"Well, I am *not* interested in him any longer. For me he is finished!"

Angrily she turned back to the fire.

Picking up the dog, he sat down heavily in his favorite chair to gaze thoughtfully at her.

She was bonny — he'd give her that. She wore beige woolen knee socks, sensible brogues, had such an innocent look about her even when furious. "The Nazis will break you," he said. "If they should ever get their hands on you, Richard is as good as dead."

"Is it my fault that I am here?"

Anger shone in her cheeks. "How much do you know about his work?"

She shrugged. "Enough to matter, I guess."

"Then we're stuck with you, and I pray to God Mr. Churchill doesna see fit to send you back!"

Stung by this, Arlette hardened her voice. "You cannot keep me a prisoner. Not the British, or are you the same as the Nazis?"

She let him think about that, then said, "My parents would ask where I was. My employer, de Heer Wunsch, would — "

"Aye, he's another thorn we must deal with. Arlette, they mean business. You're being followed. The Nazis are on to you. Leave Dillingham's. Take another job. Go home if you must, but keep away from Antwerp and from Richard. Maybe then ... Och, it's a fool's notion to even think they'll leave you alone."

The Nazi takeover of Austria had a profound effect on Winston Churchill. He glowered, brooded, sat stonily by the fire in his study at Chartwell.

What had come to pass had in one bold stroke swept into the Nazi net the whole of Austria's industrial might plus her considerable stocks of weapons and modern, well-equipped army.

The road to war had been drastically shortened. Now, more than ever, the focus would be on the Antwerp diamond stocks and alternate sources should the Reich be cut off by a blockade.

God help the world if Czechoslovakia were next, which it would be! More industry then; a far greater need for diamonds and an increased threat.

He had listened in silence and with growing impatience to the salesman. The effects of winter weather on the Wehrmacht's Panzers had been vital information — absolutely critical. The Vienna business and Heydrich's use of Fräulein Reismann was, to say the least, exceedingly troublesome.

Hagen had handed him the blue diamond pendant that the Huysmans girl had returned. Impetuously Churchill spun the stone. It was such a pretty thing, but had Heydrich known the salesman had given it to the girl?

They'd been having her followed. They'd been playing on Hagen's sympathies, probing for weaknesses.

"Richard, does Heydrich think you corruptible yet?" he asked suddenly.

Hagen shook his head. "Canaris perhaps, but not him, though I'm almost certain Krantz knows about Klees and the escape route."

"Will Heydrich succeed in using this Schroeder woman against you?"

The lack of a ready answer angered Churchill and he caught the stone up in a fist. "Damn it, man, we are matching wits with infamy. Don't you become a mush of pulp in Heydrich's hands!"

"Dee Dee's in danger, Mr. Churchill."

"Danger is the staff of life! Cut yourself loose from her. Too much is at stake."

"I can't. She's a friend."

Churchill's voice leapt. "Heydrich's using her against you, is that it?"

"Yes, damn it, he is. But I'm not prepared to let him destroy her, not when I can get her out. There are others, too."

"Or else not live with yourself?" shouted Churchill. He knew it was. "Duncan, I'm off. Tell him to find someone else. I'll see myself out."

"Now wait. Let's not be hasty." Churchill raised a hand. "Duncan, stop him. Richard, you must understand the heart of infamy. Let us use the situation to our advantage and outwit Herr Heydrich."

The blue diamond was offered as a token of peace. Hagen pocketed it and reached for his hat and coat. "Neither you nor Duncan can possibly know what it's been like for me. The only thing I have is my friends. They've helped me in the past, and I'm not about to stand idly by and let that bastard destroy them."

"That is fair enough, and we will try to accommodate your wishes. Now put that coat and hat down."

Hagen hesitated. Duncan moved to block the nearest door. "Richard, please, for all our sakes. What Mr. Churchill has said may have seemed unkind but ... och, it's only too true. Heydrich's read your character. He knows he can use Dee Dee against you, and Irmgard or anyone else. Arlette as well."

Churchill went on as if things had been agreed, but altered his tone to one of reconciliation. "Richard, while you were in Vienna, Heydrich referred to the diamonds as the Reich's little problem. That suggests he thinks they have the solution well in hand."

Again it was Duncan who stepped in. "Richard, we must outmaneuver him. What the Reich needs most right now is a man of your experience. Dieter Karl canna match the years you've been at it. Och, you've said as much yourself. If they're to find sufficient diamonds they'll have to have you working for them."

"And that may well be what Heydrich ultimately wants," said Churchill. To think that they could have a man within the Reich! It was almost too good to hope for.

Hagen looked at the two of them. "Heydrich could well have another reason and another and another. For all I really know, he might simply have wanted me to take back to you the thought that he doesn't consider the diamonds to be much of a problem. Until I'm faced with what he has in mind. I can only speculate. Maybe Krantz will arrest me the next time I cross the border. Maybe Heydrich will let me continue to send information out if needed so long as he can trap me in the end."

"And if not a bit of blackmail with Dee Dee, Richard, then with Arlette. You know it as well as I," said Duncan.

Churchill waved the cigar to dismiss the thought and turned to other matters. "Will the traders in Antwerp agree to train the men the Reich will need to make their own diamond tools?"

"After what's happened to Austria, I doubt it. Far too many of them have relatives who are only going to be hurt."

"But you'll continue to tempt the Nazis with the prospect?"

Hagen nodded. "And the line through this Dutchman, Klees?" asked Churchill sharply.

"He's terrified of the Nazis. He suspects they may have discovered the line and that I might have brought them to this, but he isn't saying and

I'm not asking. Until I've made the run again I really won't know how to advise you. Klees is only the buyer. People on both sides of the frontier are involved. If they didn't use him, they'd simply find someone else."

Churchill took his time, and when the cigar left his lips, he carefully removed the ash. "Is there some Nazi bigwig behind that line? Is it a part of their 'Jewish immigration policy'?"

"I really don't know, nor do I see how I can find out without drawing attention to myself."

They returned to the Antwerp diamond stocks, and Hagen asked if Churchill couldn't convince the prime minister now of the urgency of moving them.

The pleading in the salesman's eyes was all too evident. "I can only try, Richard. Even if Ernest was to ask them himself, it still might not be possible. Whitehall views King Leopold's policy of neutrality with the utmost suspicion. They also cling stubbornly to the idea of establishing a cutting center in Brighton. They are determined to take over Antwerp's position, Richard — it's far too good an opportunity for some of them. They *want* to gamble, to stall, to do everything they can to thwart the move so long as they can win out in the end."

He tossed a hand. "Mr. Chamberlain also steadfastly refuses to rearm at a rate that is prudent. We are among fools."

"And the plan to move the stocks by rail instead of by sea?"

Churchill nodded to indicate that he had been puzzling over this. "Tell Heydrich you plan to use that rusty freighter. Keep the alternative of using the railway cars from him for as long as you possibly can — it's the price you will ultimately have to yield. But deal it off to Canaris. Make them jealous of each other. Then let Heydrich know they plan to send the diamonds by rail and not by ship."

"But . . ."

Churchill chuckled. "Be deceitful, Richard. Make Heydrich *think* you're hiding the truth! Make it so difficult for him to find out about the railway cars he will be forced into believing that is the way the Committee plans to send the diamonds. Mislead him, damn it! And Canaris!"

"And the Committee? What am I supposed to tell them?"

The cigar was savored, studied and savored again. The moment of truth had come. "Keep this little change of plan to ourselves until we absolutely have to tell them. Trust the sea and my judgment in this. Let us outwit Heydrich and Canaris so that if they should make a rush for the diamonds, we may yet see the expressions on their faces when those railway cars draw into Berlin with empty strongboxes!"

Was it all to be some sort of game? Were they to wait until the Germans invaded? "And Arlette Huysmans?" he asked quietly. "Can you not see that she stays in England?"

"That might be difficult, but I shall try. Leave the girl here to enjoy a day at Chartwell. We shall see that she's well looked after. Meet with Ernest in London, then take a flight from Croydon to Antwerp aboard one of Lufthansa's enviable box kites. Let the Nazis see that she is no longer with you, Richard. For her sake and for your own as well as ours. Oh, and by the way, on your next trip see if you can't get the Krupp to take you to the firing range at Meppen. I should like your views on their 88 millimeter cannon."

The man who had asked to see her wore a blue boiler suit, a straw hat and a white smock. Though the sun was not yet high, he worked at his easel beyond the ranks of brick walls enclosing a patchwork of rose gardens that tumbled to a series of ponds.

Timidly Arlette set out to meet him. Churchill continued to work. "Catching the light is so very important, Miss Huysmans. I see that you're up and refreshed. The breakfast to your liking?"

"Very much so but I . . ."

The chuckle he gave was gentle but it could only have made her feel more self-conscious. "Come, come, now. My daughters made you eat something to settle your stomach and bolster your courage. I'm sure they took the opportunity to press upon you the dire warning that I was like a bear in its den when at the brush. Pray tell me how you take us?"

The daffodils he was sketching were mingled with a rush of tulips and crocuses beneath which crept a ground cover of periwinkle. "Well?" he asked. "Do you feel at home, or have we put you off?"

This was the man who in 1914 had come to Antwerp to rally the Belgians to its defense and then, having been so successful, had asked to command the Allied armies there and had been refused and blamed for its later capture.

"A hero and then one who is tarred with the defeat of others," grumbled Churchill tartly. "You Belgians must not hold history against me, Miss Huysmans. The British Parliament and public are enough! Had I but been given the chance, we could have seized the moment and driven the Hun back! But enough. How do you take us?"

He was like a cherub in his crazy painter's clothes, and yet he had a most determined and commanding presence. "I have been treated as a guest, and this is most kind of you, Mr. Churchill, but I am worried. It is not just that Richard, he has gone, but that I do not know why you should wish to see me."

The girl was uncommonly pretty. The blush was there of a sudden and she found no words to counter his scrutiny.

"You know you are a danger to him."

"If I must, I will leave Dillingham's as Duncan has suggested. Perhaps

I will take the job in Liège at the Browning factory where they make the..."

"The Browning semiautomatic pistol. An excellent weapon, but I much prefer the Mauser of the Germans. Pray tell me, have you ever fired a gun?"

Doubt clouded her eyes, whose deep, rich shade reminded him of fully ripened chestnuts. "Well?" he asked. "A rifle perhaps?"

She was forced to shake her head, but now her expression was troubled. "Why is it, please, that you should wish to know this?"

She could be so useful to them. The gestures, the very look of her, the gift of languages. French, Dutch, German and English, Duncan had said...

He waved an uncaring hand. "Put it down to courtesy, to a love of knowing about one's guests. But come, I promised you a stroll. We shall go to the top of the hill to look back upon my house, so that you may see what sort of man has built it."

At the edge of a woods they turned to look at his house, and she said that though it was very grand, in some ways it reminded her of a canal house.

He would overcome his natural reservations about the French and remind himself that she was Belgian. "It's a hodgepodge of Kentish brick, and there is none finer in all Christendom! Now tell me, could you learn to use a gun? Not to kill someone, my dear. Simply for your own protection."

Surprise registered and then a slow and welcome smile. "Please, you will let me return to work at Dillingham's?"

Those pallid blue eyes looked steadfastly at her. "We could not have kept you from it, could we?"

Arlette hesitated, then grinned with relief. "Me, I have tried to tell Duncan that I could be so useful to Richard by being in the office."

"As a relay for his secret messages?"

"Yes, I..." He had caught her out!

Churchill took another moment to study her. She was like a fine painting, the Rockeby Venus perhaps, but did she have the mettle to stand up to the Nazis? Only time would tell. "Could you work with Hagen and not be in love with him? Such things will only get in the way and endanger the two of you."

Moisture rushed into her eyes, and to hide this from him, she turned away.

A point to consider. "What about this butcher's son? Could you become engaged to him?"

"To Willi? How is it, please, that you know of him?"

He drew on his cigar and looked steadily at her, and she knew then

that Duncan had had someone investigate her background. "Willi...
Willi would not wish to see me, Mr. Churchill, nor I him."

"But you will do so to help Richard in his work."

"Please, I do not understand?"

Was Duncan not correct in saying she was too innocent? "My dear, the
Nazis have already taken far too great an interest in your association with
Richard Hagen, but by allowing those press photographs of Richard and
himself, Reinhard Heydrich has given us a unique opportunity. If we
could show them that you and he were no longer lovers, they might well
leave you alone since they could not use you to blackmail him."

"And the gun?" she asked.

Duncan would object, but God only knew what the future might hold,
and there was still a slim chance the Nazis would leave her alone.

They went into the woods and he asked her to return to Dillingham's
via Ostend. "In August you must come back to us. By then Duncan will
have arranged a suitable place. If all goes well, we will teach you how to
shoot."

The meeting with Sir Ernest was at the Travellers' Club in St. James's,
London. The Dickensian atmosphere of many of the shops only served to
work against Hagen.

No matter how hard he tried, he couldn't get the thought of Arlette out
of his head.

Had Heydrich wanted to destroy their relationship, not knowing Klees
would do it for him?

If so, he had succeeded. But why destroy the relationship unless he'd
wanted him to find someone else?

Irmgard? he wondered, and knew that must be it.

As he stood at the curbside of Pall Mall, looking up toward the Roman
frieze of the Atheneum Club, a news vendor shouted the latest on the
Czech crisis.

Every newspaper, every newsreel and wireless broadcast said there'd
be war unless something was done to stop it. The tensions over Czechoslovakia were building. The long, hot summer was about to begin.

They'd been digging trenches in Hyde Park. Earnest young men with
single suitcases had made their way to the tube stations. The trains had
been crowded. People were on the move and collectively they'd had that
subdued, early-morning look of the resigned.

When he got to the Travellers' Club, he found that Sir Ernest had been
called away on business. The note of apology was sincere — he had no
reason to doubt it. They'd meet again soon.

There were sincere thanks for his warning about Austria, a suggestion that they use the blue diamond should there be the need for a warning over Czechoslovakia.

The situation is very grave indeed, Richard. Goering has demanded and received the Baron Rothschild's Austrian steel mills in exchange for the baron's release. Like others, we can but wait and wonder what will be next.

The blue diamond had a weight of 8.739 carats. Let us simply use this weight and attribute it to an old-miner.

The Chairman didn't know that Arlette had returned the diamond and had asked that he use it to buy the freedom of Lev's daughter and son-in-law.

Richard, the Central Selling Organization would be glad to train Miss Huysmans as a sorter here in London. You have only to send her to us.

Ostend was not the same. Though she had longed to be home for a visit, the place looked drab and depressing under leaden skies, and she realized then that she had outgrown it.

Arlette left the shop of her father and walked along the promenade.

Willi wasn't at the butcher shop. De Heer de Menten's "He's down at the garage" told her all she needed to know.

"Am I no longer welcome?" she asked. I have not sinned, if that is what you're thinking.

"I am busy, that is all. This talk of war. One has to figure out what to do."

She left him to his figuring. Willi had always been interested in fixing cars. Given half a chance he'd have escaped to work on his mechanic's papers. She was suddenly glad he'd done so. At least that was something.

But she remembered sailing the *Vega* that afternoon, remembered the military cemetery at Vlamertinge and the way Richard had said, "I think I must have met the man who shot him." His father . . .

The racket in the garage was followed by a curse. Sweat beaded the grease-streaked brow beneath the dirty cloth cap from which the red hairs sprouted.

De Menten blinked his sea-green eyes behind the wire-rimmed glasses that were always getting in the way. The coat, the look of her brought it all back in a rush, and he turned from her to the workbench. "What do you want?"

"To say hello. To see how you are."

"Has he left you? Is that it? That's it, isn't it, Arlette? He's buggered off."

He was just the same old Willi. Thinner even, and not taking care of himself.

The coveralls needed laundering. He smelled of oil, grease, gasoline and sweat but not of the butcher shop. "Can you take time off for coffee?" she asked. "My train leaves at five, but —" she heaved a sigh "— there is another at six-thirty that I could take."

Still he wouldn't look at her. "There's a dance down at the church hall tonight. You could stay over if you liked. It's Sunday tomorrow. They don't make you work on Sundays, do they? Or is he expecting you?"

So jealous it was still hurting him. "Let's have some coffee and see. Come on. Arni will let you have fifteen minutes to chat with an old friend."

They had their coffee not in the café across the street but in the little storeroom he and Arni used as a change room, catchall and kitchen. They talked and she agreed to go to the dance with him, though she knew it wasn't right of her.

"Richard and I are finished, Willi. It could never have worked."

"Now maybe you'll listen to sense. I'll soon have my mechanic's papers, Arlette. We can get married then."

"And the *Vega*?" she asked to hide her dismay.

"She's as good as the day we sailed her and you left me for him."

The strongboxes were heavy. As the men stacked the last of them in the vault, Bernard Wunsch worried about the load on the floor, the plaster, the count of the boxes, the thought of trusting his diamond stocks to some trucker, the channel ferries and the British.

Irritably he tugged at his shirtsleeves. The elastic bands were cutting off his circulation! "Juffrouw Huysmans, count the boxes, please. There are to be fifty-seven. I have only fifty-three."

He left her to it, and she ran her eyes over the cramped space that remained. There was hardly room to move, let alone take the diamonds from their drawers and place them in the boxes. A duplicate cataloging system would be required. Each paper and vial would have to be logged from drawer to box and there were hundreds and hundreds of them.

As she began to count the strongboxes, Arlette heard someone in the hall and knew that Richard had just got back from London. But then he went into de Heer Wunsch's office and closed the door.

Essen, Düsseldorf, Cologne and Frankfurt, then back down the Rhine to Emmerich and the Dutch border. Could it be that they would let him return this time?

She didn't know, knew only that she had to see him.

Bernard irritably stubbed out the cigarette he had just lighted. He reached for his coffee, tried it and grimaced. "Bah, it is cold! Can nothing go right around this place? Martine, she has insisted I get new elastics for my shirtsleeves."

He snapped one and then the other. "You see the state I'm in."

Hagen drew up a chair. "Isaac's not the only one with ulcers. You'd better try to calm down, Bernard. Things aren't going to get any better for a while."

Nodding grimly, Wunsch reached for his cigarettes, then tossed the package aside as if he smoked too much and knew it.

The time had come, and somehow he had to convince Richard that the Committee had settled on the railway cars. Trust Isaac to leave the dirty work to someone else!

"Richard, de Heer Lietermann and the others can think what they want, but will the British ever let us move our diamonds there?"

Even with the depressed market for gems, Dillingham's ran a stock of about £4,000,000 and another £1,500,000 worth of industrials.

"They'll have to, Bernard. It's simply a question of time."

Small comfort! "Do we need the Boches at our very doorstep? My God, Richard, what are we to do if..."

He couldn't say it. Hagen did. "If I don't come back and they invade."

"Yes, of course. Please, a moment." Bernard held up a silencing hand and went to check the foyer. Juffrouw Huysmans was still in the vault. Good.

When he returned, he didn't sit down but took to pacing back and forth. "Richard, what I am going to ask should have been settled long before this. Could you try, please, to let us know if you suspect trouble? A word tucked into a telephone message or a cable? Just so long as I have it to take to the Committee. De Heer Lietermann will then contact Sir Ernest and the British government. Isaac, he will organize the railway cars."

There, he'd said it. *The railway cars*, not the *trucks* that they would use.

He felt like Judas, but even if they trusted Richard, they couldn't take the chance of telling him the truth.

Hagen's tone was guarded. "What would you like me to send, Bernard?"

"Something from the little books, I think."

There, he'd said that, too.

Still, there was that guarded tone, that watchfulness. "What would you suggest?"

Wunsch searched among the papers on his desk and when he found the note, he paused to read it again. "It is from the last chapter of *Alice's Adventures in Wonderland*. There is a poem that contains many useful phrases that might pass unnoticed in a cable. We can choose anything you think suitable, yes? But I...I have thought of these two lines: 'An obstacle that came between / Him, and ourselves, and it.' "

How apt he'd been. "Which word? Choose one or two, Bernard. No more."

Then it was true that Richard was gathering intelligence for the British. "Obstacle."

"And the Nazis, Bernard? Their Fifth Column? What will you tell them if they should ask you about me?"

"Nothing. Absolutely nothing. This I swear."

Bernard was hedging, not telling him everything. No doubt the Committee no longer trusted him.

"Lev, would you do something for me and say nothing of it to anyone else?"

To Bernard? "Yes, of course. If that's what you want."

"My train leaves in a couple of hours. Will you go to de Heer Lietermann's house tonight and tell him that at all costs he must stick to the plan as we agreed?"

"Which plan?"

Was there more than one? "I can't tell you."

"Look, Richard, if it's about that rusty old freighter, you can tell me. The *Megadan*'s a piece of junk and she'll go to the bottom under her own steam, never mind the needle of a German U-boat. The Committee didn't lease what they should have, which was a destroyer. Even a fool of a diamond cutter knows that."

In spite of the seriousness of the matter, Hagen had to laugh. "How did you find out?"

"The telephone, how else? I was passing Arlette's desk to get to the vault. Bernard and Isaac... none of us are perfect, Richard. I had to find out if they were going to include the cutters and polishers in the plan."

"Lev, I know what you're saying, but for now we're dealing only with the diamonds. Did Bernard and Isaac discuss another plan?"

The scaife came to a stop. Lev swung the dop aside and reached for a cloth to clean his hands. Loyalty to Bernard and the Committee demanded one thing, honesty to Richard another.

"Isaac did say something about an alternative, but Arlette came back to her desk and I... I had to hang up."

Hagen gripped him by the arm. "Then go to Lietermann personally. Don't trust the telephones. Tell him what I said, and let him know what you overheard Bernard and Isaac discussing. It can only emphasize the need for caution."

"And Rachel?"

"Keep your fingers crossed. If the line is still working, we'll try to get them out as soon as possible. If not, I'll find some other way."

"Then do something for yourself. Speak to Arlette. She's very upset. Bernard and I can understand why you've broken off your engagement but a little kindness, a word or two, you understand."

Arlette pretended not to have heard him come into the vault, but then she tossed her head and said, "So, you're leaving us again?"

"For a little. Look, I wish you'd..." Quickly Hagen told her of Sir Ernest's offer. "It's a fantastic opportunity. You'd be good at it, Arlette. A natural. The first woman to become a sorter for the Central Selling Organization."

"And I'd be safer there, is that it? " she asked, pausing now to look steadily at him.

"Safer than anything Mr. Churchill might have asked."

As he handed her the blue diamond to put back in his trading drawer, their fingers touched and she thought how miserable she'd been at that dance with Willi. "Does Heydrich know everything about you?"

"Arlette, that doesn't matter. What does, is that he's been having you followed. I can't have that. I have to know you're safe."

"Why must you go back? Why must you do this thing?" She stamped a foot and clenched a fist. "It's stupid, Richard. It's criminal!"

He hoped Bernard hadn't heard her. He knew she was referring not just to the Reich but to Klees. "Because I have to. Because I've friends inside the Reich who need my help, and yes, because someone has to do it."

The spying... "I'm sorry. Forgive me. Of course you must."

The pendant went into a drawer, any drawer! She stood there with her back to him.

Hagen reached out, but she shrugged him off and turned swiftly to brush past him and close the heavy door of the vault.

Then she stood there, leaning against it, trying to catch her breath.

"I did love you. I did try to tell myself it was too good to be true.

It was no use. As Richard took a step toward her, Arlette came to meet him.

It felt so good to have him hold her again, to feel his arms around her. He kissed her lips, her chin, her cheeks and brow.

Suddenly shy and self-conscious, she used his handkerchief to wipe the lipstick from him. "I liked that. Any receptionist would. Please come back for more."

"Hey, listen, you take care of yourself. No late nights. These people mean business, Arlette. Go to London. Please, for my sake and for your own."

Fondly she touched his hair and laid a hand against his cheek, then stepped in again to find his lips. "Dear God, how I want you," she whispered. "My whole body cries out for you, Richard. Let's get married. Let's not wait."

When Wunsch found the two of them in the vault, Richard was busy writing down the telephone numbers of Sir Ernest and Duncan McPherson, should the girl need their help and change her mind.

April 17, 1938

Dear Richard,

I am giving this letter to an Indian who is to be sent for supplies and who understands the few words of Spanish I have learned.

I take this risk because, my darling — please let me call you that — because Dieter discovered my last letter to you. Heydrich had sent someone to him, a man whose name I never knew. That one questioned me. That one had me beaten. Dieter... Dieter was so angry, he stood by and watched.

Richard, I don't know what's happening to him. He's not the same. All day he works like a demon. At night he falls into his hammock. Since discovering the letter, he's hardly spoken to me. I'm a prisoner here. I think sometimes I may not be allowed to leave.

The deposit we are now working is on a tributary of the Jequitinhonha, about 220 kilometers to the northeast of Diamantina. There are no heaps of gravel, no huge, ocher-yellow holes in the ground where nothing will grow anymore. Just the jungle, the birds and snakes, the ragged cut of the river gully, our huts and those of the *garimpeiros* who have only grins and smiles and broken words for me. A new deposit, Richard. Something that was passed over in the early days.

The washing plant is a crazy thing on stilts that stretches drunkenly for a kilometer along the gully, going up and down and angling this way and that — you must know what it looks like. Sheet iron and whipsawed wood, a constant racket of boulders and water and sand that rushes along all day and night, while the pumps throb constantly.

There are some small tool diamonds, a little more of the boart — even some of the carbonado — and a few small gem diamonds. Seguras, the man who owns this deposit and who brought us here, insists there will be lots and lots of industrial diamonds if only more money and men can be made available. Understandably he wants to sell the deposit to Dieter or at least to lease it to him. He's a crook and not to be trusted, and I think, deep in his heart, my brother knows this.

Please take care of Dee Dee. The Indian is outside my window so I must stop. I hope you are safe and well.

All my love,
Irmgard

The head of the Abwehr let the ghost of a smile betray his elation. Hagen had sought him out in Berlin, at the Jagdschloss Tiergarten. "Please, a glass of wine, or would you prefer some coffee?"

They settled on the latter. Until the orderly left them, they talked of the *Anschluss* and of the Czech problem.

Then Canaris leaned forward. Somehow Heydrich's ambitions had to be curbed, and somehow he had to reinstate himself in the Führer's good graces. "First the details, Richard, then the terms."

"The official plan is to move the diamond stocks by freighter, Admiral, but there's an alternative plan, the one we'll really use."

"And what is this, please?"

"A little something Heydrich won't know about."

Hagen reached for the coffeepot and offered it. Canaris shook his head.

"The alternative plan, Richard?"

"The SS and Heydrich musn't know of it, Admiral. Herr Heydrich wouldn't take it kindly if you told him I was holding out on him."

The nod was there but just. So Hagen was working for the opposition as well.

"Two sealed railway cars. The diamonds in strongboxes, the cars to leave Antwerp's Central Station for one of the channel ports."

"Which one?"

"That hasn't been settled as yet."

The freighter would have been so much easier to intercept. Could he really trust Hagen? It seemed too good an opportunity to miss. "Richard, tell me something. Do you ever get to Paris? These *Treffs* of ours would be easier and more discreet if held outside the Reich."

"What do you suggest?"

"The Travellers' Club on the Champs-Élysées. Simply let the desk know when you'll be in town and where you'll be staying. Ask to leave that message for Dieter Karl. Our man will then get through to me, and I'll have someone reliable there to meet with you or I'll come myself."

"And Dieter?" he asked cautiously.

"Dieter is still in Brazil, but he won't mind us using his name."

He thought of telling Canaris that Heydrich had intercepted the sample of diamonds Dieter had sent from Brazil, then thought better of it. "I gather Dieter is working for the Abwehr."

"But of course. I thought you knew."

The moment was uncomfortable and Canaris let him suffer. "Now, please, the terms of your agreement with us?"

"I want Fräulein Schroeder out of Germany."

Irritably Canaris tossed a hand. "These things are difficult — delicate. Believe me, I'm doing all I can. It's not possible for me to force Herr Heydrich's hand just yet. Apparently he's still interested in the woman."

"That's not good enough, Admiral. In exchange for the diamond stocks I want her out."

"And the money? The mining company you wish to form, or is it that you no longer want this?"

"Dee Dee's a friend, Admiral. I try to look after my friends."

"Very well, I will see what I can do. Now, please. Dieter Karl wishes you to provide us with everything you can on the deposits in the Congo. As soon as he returns from Brazil, I must send him there."

Over lunch they discussed the deposits of Mbuji-Mayi, of how the diamonds were found in the gravels of old riverbeds. Because the terrain had been repeatedly uplifted, the ancient rivers had swung wide, thus scattering their diamonds over a huge area.

"One has to work hard for them, Admiral. One looks first for those places where the present rivers have cut down into the old deposits and reworked the ancient placers — the innermost bank of a bend, potholes, places where the water has swirled around and winnowed out all but the heaviest of minerals, coarse beds of gravel. The diamonds, being of a high specific gravity, like placer gold, will have found their way down to the bottom of the gravels. Sometimes a boulder twice the size of your dinner plate lies nestled beside a diamond no bigger than a pinhead. Once the old riverbed is exposed, we pick out the boulders and pan the sands in the crevices and hollows."

"Could it be done in secret — with sufficient men and materials?"

Hagen shook his head. "My father tried, though he was looking only for gem diamonds. If he couldn't get away with it, no one can. War will only tighten things further."

"Dieter Karl won't be much good on his own, will he?"

"I really don't know, Admiral. Some men are naturals when it comes to prospecting. But if there's a war, there'll be a blockade."

"Then what you wish is a mining company under the wing of De Beers so that you can secretly send us the diamonds."

"It won't be easy, Admiral. It'll take someone like myself whom they know and trust."

"And the money?"

"The fifty thousand to start. Put into this." He gave him the number of a bank account in Zurich, and again there was that nod.

The admiral got up from the table. It was all so civilized — the polite handshake, the concern in those dark blue eyes, the pleasure of a shared conspiracy, while all the time they planned to make war on the rest of the world.

TO WINFIELD MRS LOIS ANNE INVERLIN COTTAGE BLACK DOWN HEATH PORTESHAM ROAD DORCHESTER ENGLAND

FROM HAGEN RICHARD HOTEL ADLON BERLIN

HOPE THE SUN IS SHINING THERE STOP AM WATCHING FOR A LITTLE SOMETHING FOR YOUR BIRTHDAY IN CASE YOU ARE WONDERING AND YOUR FEELINGS ARE HURT STOP A BOOK WOULD DO BUT KNOW YOU CANNOT UNDERSTAND THE LANGUAGE STOP LOVE RICHARD

When decoded, the message would read:

TO THE CARPENTER FROM ALICE

RAILWAY BAIT TAKEN BY CANARIS/HUNT SHIFTING MBUJI-MAYI / SD-ABWEHR FRICTION CONTINUES / TRAVELLERS' CLUB PARIS HAS ABWEHR AGENT / CLARIFY IF SUSPECTED SD OPERATIVE / ALICE

In the late afternoon he took the train to Düsseldorf. Krantz had either been told to leave him alone or was being very good at things. Though he checked as often as he could, no one seemed to be following him.

The man was no longer in the street. Perhaps he had grown tired of watching the house.

Arlette waited a moment more. From the darkness of her bedroom at Madame Hausemer's she hunted the street below.

There was no one.

Reaching for her purse, she hesitated. Was it right of her to take the chance, knowing that they were watching the house? She wanted so much to see Richard again. The midnight train would soon be in from Amsterdam. He'd go straight to the office to leave the diamonds from de Heer Klees in the vault. Then he'd go to the club because of the message she'd left on his desk: *Chez Vous have requested that you pay your bill*.

The house was asleep. The locks were on and it took forever to withdraw the bolts as quietly as she could.

Keeping to the shadows, Arlette hurried along the street. When a car came slowly up behind her, she stepped into a doorway and waited.

The car crept past. Glad of her flat-soled shoes, she ran along the street and up a lane.

Sure enough, the car came back. Street by street they forced her toward the docks. No place for a woman at night. No place...

She kept to the shadows again. Dillingham's had their fabricating shop nearby. There was a shipping yard at the back, with a shed for the night watchman. She could hide there, could say she'd lost her house key or something. Anything!

When a taxi came along the quay after dropping a sailor off at his ship, Arlette stepped quickly out and raised a hand.

At the Club Chez Vous, she vowed she wouldn't tell Richard. He'd be so worried; he had worries enough of his own.

Hagen glanced over the cable he had written to the Dorchester address. When decoded, the message would read:

TO THE CARPENTER FROM ALICE

MEPPEN FIRING RANGE TESTING 88 MM ANTIAIRCRAFT GUNS AGAINST FRENCH TANK SOMUA-S / EFFECTS DEVASTATING / ARMOR PLATING BRITISH MARK III TANK ALSO TESTED WITH EQUAL RESULTS / GERMANS NOW USING ARMOR-PIERCING SHELLS TIPPED WITH TUNGSTEN CARBIDE / LINE THROUGH KLEES APPEARS TO BE STILL OPEN SUGGEST USE CAUTION / HUYSMANS ARLETTE BEING WATCHED ANTWERP OPERATIVES BELGIAN SD / ALICE

Coming into the city a little early, he'd seen them watching the house where Arlette lived. They'd followed her as far as the docks but then had suddenly left her alone.

When he got to the club, she was asleep on the couch in Cecile's sitting room and he hated to awaken her. Half in a dream, half awake, Arlette clung to him and when he lay on top of her, she wrapped her arms about him, couldn't stop the shaking, was terrified still.

Again and again they kissed. Faster now until nothing else mattered.

But then Cecile came into the room to tell them that it was getting late and she'd better drive them home.

In May he was gone again — to Prague this time, to Budapest and then to Warsaw and through the Polish Corridor to Danzig. And in May both Britain and France announced increased spending programs for arms. Plans were being drawn up to stockpile food. Britain told the Germans she might be forced into joining with France it there was a war.

Czechoslovakia, confronted by no fewer than ten German divisions on her borders, had ordered what the news broadcaster had called "a partial mobilization."

"The Skoda Works," muttered Bernard Wunsch. "Trucks, cars and tanks! High-temperature ceramics, Juffrouw Huysmans — insulators and the firing cones for rocket engines, if you ask me. Sawed by *our* diamonds! Guns! Glassware! Quartz crystals — ah, yes, I can see that you do not understand me. Quartz crystals for their secret wireless transmitters."

He touched the tip of his nose. "Wavelengths, Arlette. Me, I have some experience of such things. Each quartz crystal is sawed so as to give the exact thickness to emit only so many wavelengths. The Czechs have much that the Nazis must want."

All this had come in a momentary pause between bursts of "green bonding agents, copper rolling and sintering." The ways the diamonds were fixed into their respective tools.

The fabricating shop was running flat out.

"Train their technicians," he shouted above the racket. "It's a lot for you to learn, Arlette. Please, I understand this, but these are difficult times."

They retreated to the relative calm of the yard and began to check the latest shipment for the Krupp. "Train their technicians? How could we, knowing what we do?"

The order had been packed in labeled wooden crates for shipment by freighter to Hamburg. "Are we fools?" he asked. "Every ship they send carries their spies, and we both know that there are people of our own who work for them only too willingly. This I simply cannot understand."

"Please, you must try not to worry so much, Mijnheer Wunsch. Nor should you work so hard. Why not let me do this? Go home a little early. It's a lovely day for a walk. It would help you to relax."

Relax? he wanted to shout, but stopped himself. In spite of the continued crisis there was that fresh-faced vitality about her that told him more than words.

But then, pausing under his scrutiny, she said, "I will be going home to see Willi this Sunday," and he knew she had read his mind.

They worked at checking the shipment, she moving from crate to crate and reading the labels to him in her flawless German. She had a graceful way about her, a sureness now that she hadn't had when she'd first come to them. "Richard is a fool, my dear. If I were younger and unmarried . . . ah, I'd give this Willi trouble."

"And me?" she said, grinning at the compliment to hide the truth of what she was doing. "Me, I would welcome such a diversion from a man like you."

Wunsch found his heart racing. "Martine, she will be glad to see me home early," he said gruffly. "But first, a little walk."

Thrusting the clipboard into her hands, he went to find his briefcase. Such a sensitive man. Who would have thought . . . ?

Arlette left the shipping yard to watch him walk along the quays until at last his steps slowed and he began to take an interest in things.

For another hour and a half she stayed at the shop, using the change of shifts to go through the loft above and the watchman's shed. Memorizing the layout and the access points in case she should need to know of them. A broken window that could easily be opened if found in the dark. Lights above the loading bay and the back doors that would betray her.

The roof of the shed — was it low enough? Could she climb up there?

Later, she, too, walked along the quays until she came to the *Megadan*. Lev had said it was a rusty old freighter, and she had to agree with him. "A tramp steamer without a home port," he had called it. "A fifteen-hundred-ton bathtub with a leaky plug!"

Yet de Heer Wunsch, who should have been so worried about it, had strolled right past the freighter without a second glance.

"Willi, what will you do if there's a war?"

De Menten lay back in the blowout they'd found among the dunes. "Must you think of such things at a time like this?"

"But it is important, is it not? I wouldn't like to think of you in the army."

He snorted. "Then you needn't worry. With these eyes of mine they wouldn't dare give me a rifle. Besides, they'll stick me in one of the garages fixing their trucks and getting paid piss all!"

She *would* want to talk about the possibility of war.

Miffed, she said, "I was only asking."

The sound of the waves filled the air. Arlette climbed out of the blowout to stand on the crest of the dune, and shielded her eyes. The wind tugged at her dress. Richard . . . would he be thinking of her once in a while?

Of course he would, and Cecile's club was such a good place for them to meet. She just knew they'd use it again.

Shaking out her hair, Arlette shut her eyes and lifted her face to the sun, only to hear Willi say, "Don't you want to eat?"

"In a minute. I want to feel free, Willi. Just free like this." Dear God, but it would be heaven if Richard and she could be alone among these dunes, no fears, no worries, just the two of them in each other's arms.

There were several people on the beach, some hiking, some having picnics; a few even watched the birds.

When she noticed a man looking at her through binoculars, Arlette turned to face him. "Willi . . . Willi, come up here. It's . . . it's so beautiful. Come and see it. Please!"

He could be so impossible at times. Grumbling, he reached for his shirt and put it on. As he climbed to her, he fumbled with the buttons. You'd think he was going to church or something. "Please kiss me," she said. " A real embrace. Let's show everybody how much we love each other."

The kiss was wet, awkward and damned clumsy, the wind like ice! She hated herself!

They ran down into the hollow. De Menten tried to kiss her again, and at first she let him. Then he dragged something out of a pocket. It just had to be the right time.

The gold wedding band had been his grandmother's. "Try it on, Arlette. We can cut it if we have to. I can mend the break with the brazing torch and polish it up on the buffer."

He probably could. She kissed him lightly on the cheek and despised herself for betraying him. "I will ask Lev to fix it for us, and I will ask him to produce for me a diamond engagement ring."

They talked of the letters they had written to each other — Willi was not much use at it but he had tried. They talked of setting a date for the wedding, but she asked him to wait a little.

In August the Nazis called up an additional 750,000 men. Massive military maneuvers were being held near the Czech border. Everyone said the Czechs ought to be more accommodating, that the Sudetenland was not that important.

And in August Arlette waited until the last minute, then lied to Willi and said there could be no holidays for her as they'd planned.

"I must go to England for de Heer Wunsch. Yes, I know it isn't fair. Yes, I know everyone is taking their holidays. Willi, please try to understand."

She set down the receiver but stood there a moment. Even with the threat of war so close, the Belgians could still worry about their holidays. As did the French and everyone else. The world had gone mad.

Eight

FROM THE BROW of the hill the land spilled away in jade-green slopes to the cold, blue waters of Loch Assynt and the cloud-shrouded peaks of the Quinag Ridge beyond.

Arlette couldn't believe what she was seeing. The Highland light was so incredibly clear. In the near distance, the ruined tower of a lonely castle rose from a small promontory that jutted out into the lake. Waves rippled the surface of the loch, which stretched away into the hills and mountains. Cattle and sheep dotted the gorse and grass that lay before the white-stucco, slate-roofed, scattered cottages of the tiny crofting village of Inchnadamph.

"It's so very beautiful, Richard. Dear God, to think that I might never have seen or heard of this."

Amid a tracery of fields, a whitewashed, cut-stone manor house of thirty rooms or more stood alone. One line of beeches marked the road to the house. To the east there was what looked to be a playing field. To the west, where the fields sloped gently toward the loch, an inn, a shop of some sort and a house were clustered at the junction with the main road.

It was at once a land of mystery, of hopes for the future, yes, but of something else. Something almost indefinable. A great sadness that, in spite of the beauty, she felt only too deeply but could not understand.

Dwarfed by the landscape, the manor house commanded the eye, and she couldn't help but wonder why Duncan, a man of modest means, had leased such a place.

In spite of the anorak and heavy turtleneck sweater, she shivered. Duncan was watching them. She knew he wasn't happy to see her, knew he still didn't approve of Richard's loving her.

But this . . . this look of his was something else. A cold appraisal.

As they drove down into the valley, McPherson shouted the history of the place to her. The clan MacKenzie had owned the lands ever since the Restoration. They'd taken them by the sword from the MacLeods, whose chieftain had given succor to the fugitive James Graham, first marquis of Montrose, in late April of 1650.

"MacLeod broke the code of the Highlands. Och, he couldna resist the temptation and damned himself and his clan forever by turning Montrose in for silver."

It had been the gibbet for the one and the sword for the other. Ardvreck Castle had fallen into ruin. Kincalda House had been built a little more than one hundred years later, and ever since then it had been home to the MacKenzies.

Salmon rods, golf clubs, a butter churn full of walking sticks were set against the wall next the windows that flanked the open door. Arlette went on ahead, and they could hear her steps echoing in the halls.

"Well, Richard, what do you think?"

"It's a sight for sore eyes, Duncan. Has old MacKenzie passed away?"

"Och, no. He's as fit as a fiddle. I simply made him an offer he couldn't refuse."

"Those mountains ... you know how the weather socks in ... "

"The airfield will just have to do. Richard, we had to have a place to begin. Churchill was adamant."

A school for agents and infiltrators. "And Arlette?" he asked. "Duncan, just leave her be. Sir Ernest has a spot for her."

"Aye, that would be best." More he wouldn't say, but it was all too clear Richard was still very much in love with the girl, and equally clear that Churchill had plans for her.

They listened as Arlette's steps came to them from the hall above. She hesitated, then went on. Perhaps she was looking into each of the rooms, perhaps she was just getting the feel of the place.

The steps stopped and they heard her no more.

"Duncan, I won't have Arlette brought here for some sort of training, no matter what Mr. Churchill has asked."

"The lass is far too timid, Richard. The Nazis ... " He'd leave that unsaid, but Churchill, being Churchill, had wanted her evaluated. Indeed, he'd insisted on this. A first step for everyone.

Hagen went up the stairs after her, only to find Arlette had removed her shoes and had left them in the hall lest the noise give away the fact she'd come back to listen to them.

There were paintings on the walls, as he'd remembered — mostly eighteenth-century landscapes in gilt frames. Chandeliers hung in the stairwell. Above the open doorway to the west wing was a portrait of a Highland chief in full dress tartan with an unsheathed sword.

Arlette was looking curiously up at it. He chuckled at the worried frown. Without thinking, he said, "I never can remember if that's Kenneth a Bhlàir, Kenneth of the Battle, or his son, Kenneth Òg, the one who was murdered."

"Richard, what is this place?"

Though he wasn't to have told her, he did so anyway. Arlette placed her hands on his chest and looked steadily at him. "And now we both know one more thing we must keep from the Nazis."

It was all so like a well down which they had been thrown. There would be no escape, not even here.

The letter was open on the bedside table in her room. The writing was in German, the postmark and stamps from Brazil.

Arlette ran her eyes quickly down the thin, pale blue paper. Too few diamonds, an uncertain source... *a network of people* ...

They were to head for a river called the Jequitinhonha. The letter was signed, *All my love, Irmgard*.

The sister of the Baron Dieter Karl Hunter.

McPherson closed the door and came on into her room. "That letter was opened and then resealed, Arlette. The girl was crazy to have written Richard. Abwehr or SD agents know of it."

She would not look at him. "Arlette, listen to me. If I could, I would leave Richard and you to your loving, but I can't. Heydrich knows Richard's greatest weakness is his feeling of responsibility for others. I daren't show him this letter for fear he'll do something foolish."

"Yet if you don't, what then? And the Fräulein Schroeder, Duncan? Would you rob Richard of his sense of decency?"

"Please try to understand that these times aren't ordinary. We *have* to do things we wouldn't normally do."

"Like killing and murder?" she said, turning on him now. "Is that what you intend for this place?"

He crumpled the letter and threw it past her into the fire. "Richard is my friend. If you truly love him, you'll leave him. Now I'll say no more but that I think you weak and a danger to him."

At dawn, mist shrouded the upper slopes of the Quinag Ridge. High above the loch a light drizzle began.

Duncan was in the lead, then Richard and finally Arlette. None of them had said anything for some time. It was as if Richard had sensed things weren't right between them and had withdrawn.

As they picked their way across the screes, Arlette fell farther and farther behind.

Between the screes there were bare patches of lichen-encrusted bedrock. Out on the screes the boulders were sharp and angular. More than once she slipped and had to grab hold of the rocks.

More than once the slopes below her shot away to nothing, while those above were soon lost dizzily in the fog.

A smell of sulfur emanated from the rocks.

At last they came to a shelf on which stunted pine, gorse and peaty water enclosed the gray stone walls of a ruined cottage. Duncan didn't give the place a second glance. With dogged determination, he skirted the ruins and headed off up the barren slopes at a punishing pace.

Richard went after him. The mist drifted, became shredded by the ghost of a wind.

At the far end of the loch it began to rain.

When a boulder came tumbling down on her, she was caught halfway out on a scree. It bounced, went this way, that way from so far above she couldn't see it yet, couldn't seem to move...

With a crash it appeared out of the fog, bounced nearby and rolled away. A rush of rubble followed, a thunder of it as she hugged the scree and cried out, "*No!* Please, no!"

The sound of the rubble roared away until it was only a trickle. Terrified, Arlette picked herself up and stood there uncertainly. Richard and Duncan must have heard the rockfall.

Badly shaken, she began to retrace her steps, planning to wait for them at the ruins. She has almost reached the shelf, was just starting down to it, when the sound of a rifle shot came flat and hard on the cold, damp air. The echo rolled away to rumble in among the hills.

Panicking again — caught out on that slope — she froze. For ten seconds her heart raced madly. She began to run, to slip and slide on the boulders.

When she reached the shelf, Arlette dodged in among the pines and threw herself behind a wall.

A second shot rang out and then a third, but by then she knew for sure they had been meant for her.

Sheep droppings, a scattering of moldy straw and rusty ironwork, the wheel of a barrow and the weathered remains of a scythe lay among the stones and clumps of moss.

Caught on a bit of gorse behind the ruins was the bright yellow-and-black tartan scarf Duncan had handed Arlette that morning.

There was a trail, a bit of a path that climbed from the shelf to the crest of a low ridge, then disappeared beyond it. To the east of the ruins the land rose and fell in humps and hollows. Upon an endless carpet of moss, heather, gorse and bog water, lay a dotting of giant boulders. Ethereal in the clinging mist, they brought to the utter silence a harsh and unfeeling omnipotence.

Hagen hunted the terrain, then ran his eyes slowly along the distant line where mist and rock joined. There was scant cover. She had run out there and had left the scarf behind lest it give her away again.

Gradually the sun rose to break through the clouds and burn off the mist. Out over the moor nothing stirred. Behind him on the heights of the Quinag Ridge there was no sign of Duncan.

As if in defiance of the sun, it began to rain.

The cleft was not too steep. Where the burn fell over the edge of the moor, it plunged to a pool some thirty feet below her.

From there the woods — thin in places, thick in others — spread out toward the northeast, to a road and then more hills and moors beyond.

Arlette squinted over a shoulder at the afternoon sun. Once down in the cleft by the pool, she'd be out of sight. Once through the woods, she could follow the line of the road until she came to the village.

How she loathed this place, the feel of it, the endless silence, the hours of never knowing if he'd shoot at her again.

Easing herself forward on her seat, she began to make her way down into the cleft. Shadows hugged the inner wall, but on the opposite side of the burn she found a place to rest and bathe her blistered feet.

Pulling off her boots, she eased her feet into the icy water, then lay back on the ground and stared up at the sky. Everything in her said to leave while she could and seek the safety of the woods.

Exhaustion made her eyes close.

When Hagen found her, she was fast asleep but awoke at once. Motioning her to stay where she was, he searched the moor, then came down to her and spilled three empty brass cartridge casings from his hand.

"Did you get a look at him?" he asked.

She shook her head.

"Arlette, they didn't mean to hit you, only to see how well you'd respond."

Never for a moment would she forget the look in his eyes. One of defeat, of betrayal, of loss for the friend he'd once known. "How can you be so sure?"

"Because I found these on a rock up there at the top of the cleft. If he'd wanted to kill you, he could so easily have done so."

Hurriedly, she told him about the letter, of what it must mean.

He nodded and said, "I'll go back into Germany anyway. I'll do what I can to save them."

"Then I will go back to Antwerp and help you all I can."

It had been said so quickly, and yet in that moment he knew that no matter how hard he tried to dissuade her, she'd do as she'd said.

On Thursday the rain was gone. Across the sky gossamer clouds scudded, leaving patches of blue between.

The tower of Ardvreck Castle was really only three stories high, the remains of the other walls somewhat less. Moss clung to the gray stone blocks.

One curious thing set the tower apart. It was round at the base, but above the first story it was square and slotted so that it looked out on the world and the loch like a haunted gallows tree.

There was a cattle gate of peeled poles, a bit of a stone wall that ran on either side of the path to the water's edge. Beyond the castle, the land rose in a grassy mound to the low summit of the promontory.

Arlette let herself in at the gate. They had spent the days of the storm as prisoners of themselves. Nothing had seemed to work. She couldn't go to Richard and say, Let's just drive to Inverness to see the shops, to have tea someplace. Anything. He couldn't say to her, There's a film I'd like you to see.

Instead, he had worked with Duncan. Oh, for sure they had fought. Richard could never forgive his friend for what had happened. He'd threatened to quit, to take her to America, but he'd known only too well the reality of things. Dee Dee Schroeder and Irmgard Hunter were very much on his mind, and yes, Duncan had been ordered to "evaluate" her, and yes, she was still being seen as a threat to Richard's work.

More than once she had caught them talking about her. Twice she'd overheard Duncan saying, "They'll kill her, Richard. You canna continue to take up with the lass. She'll drag you down and then where will we be?"

Arlette knew that Richard felt he ought to break things off with her, that he was torn by guilt and was continually arguing with himself.

Willi would laugh at her if he knew how little she was enjoying herself. She'd have to go back to him, would have to continue with the lie, though she'd hate herself for doing so.

Exploring the ruins did no good. When Richard found her, she was sitting in the sun out of the wind.

"Where's Duncan?" she asked.

"Gone to Lochinver to meet his father. I said we'd like to have the day to ourselves."

"And would we? Richard, what's to become of us?"

In silence they walked back to Kincalda House, and when he had shut the door behind them, Arlette went through to the stairs and started hesitantly up.

She was a virgin and afraid, had all those nagging thoughts of an unmarried girl, all those worries, yet wanted him.

Hagen waited, not knowing what to do. When he reached the room, she was standing in front of the fire.

"So, it is only the two of us, Richard."

They kissed, she trembling with uncertainty. They touched. She said, "Here, let me. Please." A whisper.

As Richard watched, Arlette pulled off her sweater. She undid her blouse and slid the straps of her slip off her shoulders. Reaching up behind her back to unhook the brassiere, she gave him an embarrassed glance.

He took a step closer. She said, "No, please. Stand back a little."

Her breasts spilled into view, high, upturned, round and firm, the nipples seeming to strain at him, the nubby bumps around them in halos of rose.

Hagen held them. Tenderly he kissed her on the lips, then lowered his head to brush his lips across each nipple. Waves of pleasure ran through her, ripples of it. Repeatedly he kissed each breast, then found her throat, her lips, her hair, his arms enfolding her at last as she ran her hands up over his shoulders.

Arlette pulled off the rest of her things. It felt so good to be naked in his arms. Not wrong, not evil, not a sin.

Hagen slid his hands down over the soft, smooth arch of her back. He held her by the seat and drew her closer. She fought for air and tilted back her head, pressed her middle against him. Now his kisses came lightly on her throat, her breasts, and she gave a soft laugh, a gentle chuckle of rapture and whispered, "My love. Oh, my love."

Naked, Hagen stood there looking down at her as she lay on the hearth rug. The copper tones in her hair were burnished by the flickering light. The slim, flat tummy, the tangled clutch of auburn curls in the soft V of her slightly parted legs drew his gaze. She held her breasts and nervously parted her lips...

He said, "You're so very beautiful."

Self-consciously, Arlette kept on looking up at him. His shoulders were fine and strong, the muscles corded at his waist. The curly hairs of sand began at his chest.

Lowering her eyes, she found the maleness of him hung below a thatch of sandy curls. She had never seen a naked man before, a penis only in paintings and sculptures and but briefly.

Tenderly, Hagen began to explore her body. He kissed her on the lips several times, resisted the pull of her arms.

Trembling, she felt his lips against each breast, he sucking the nipples now and running his tongue around them until rushes of warmth had spread again to her loins. He stroked her tummy, stroked each breast. Now her tummy, now a breast, now her throat, her lips. He kept himself there as she felt his hand between her legs, moistening her, parting her, touching, touching...Dear God, what was he doing? "Richard..."

Desperate now, she clung to him, but it went on and on, his fingers...

his fingers...the rushes of pleasure building, building until the ache within her became unbearable and she parted from him with a gasp, gave a cry — and kissed him harder, harder!

Crying out, she arched her body and came. Every part of her went mad with joy. For ages she throbbed within, then caught a breath and caught it again. Realized at last that he was inside her.

Her knees were raised on either side of him. Sweat dampened her brow and clung to her upper lip. There was moisture in her eyes, a film of it.

It felt so good to have him inside her.

Even as she lay there in wonder still, a part of her glowed. Never for a moment had she imagined it would be like this. Arlette thrust her hips up at him and then it started all over again, the thrusting of his penis, the smoothness of it, the thickness, the depth...

Richard came, and she felt him throbbing deeply inside her, warm, so warm.

Wrapping her legs about him, she held him tightly to her. It was done. Done at last! And, dear God, how well it had been done.

On September 13, in a speech at Nuremberg, Hitler ranted at the Czechs, accusing them of murder and oppression. Chamberlain hurried to Berchtesgaden on the fifteenth, and while he was there, the Russians began massing troops in the Ukraine.

On September 22 the government of Czechoslovakia fell, while Polish troops gathered to invade that strife-torn country and take back territory Poland claimed as its own.

The British navy mobilized. French and German troops tensely faced each other across the narrow strip of no-man's-land that lay between the Maginot and Siegfried lines.

Munich came on September 29 and 30. According to Neville Chamberlain there would be "Peace in our time," as the leaders of Britain, France, Germany and Italy settled the fate of Czechoslovakia without a shot having been fired or a Czech having been present.

On October 1 the Germans marched into the Sudetenland and the next day Poland occupied that part of Czechoslovakia known as the Teschen.

This left only the Hungarian demands to be settled. What had once existed was no more.

TO HAGEN RICHARD DILLINGHAM AND COMPANY ANTWERP FROM WINFIELD FRANK ALBERT 10B THE MEWS MAGPIE LANE OXFORD ENGLAND

Apprehensively Arlette glanced over the cable. Going through to Richard's office, she found him still on the telephone to Berlin. Patiently she waited. Richard wanted clearance to go back to Augsburg, to the Man diesel-engine factory. The Ministry of the Interior was refusing.

At last he gave up and said harshly, "Then I can't be responsible for what happens, Herr Dekker. The heads on those threading machines just won't get replaced."

Reluctantly Dekker gave in but insisted Richard must check the clearance with a higher authority when in Berlin.

Grimly Hagen hung up, then seeing her worried frown, gave her a comforting smile. "So, what's new?"

"Another cable from Duncan. This one from the Oxford address."

"You look a picture."

"Richard, please!"

"I thought all girls liked to be complimented. How's Willi these days?"

"Fine, he's just fine." Damn him for teasing her. "Now will you be serious?"

"I like it when you get mad at me."

"I'm not mad. I'm worried. Richard, why won't you and Duncan funnel the messages through me? It would be so much safer. My shorthand's good. I could take them down. You could fit things into orders for the shop or things you want to discuss with de Heer Wunsch."

"The telephone lines are being tapped — we're almost certain of it. Besides, Duncan can't give you things for the shop."

She swept her eyes anxiously over him. She knew that night after night he'd been watching her place and trying to pin down who had been following her.

"Will you come to the club tonight?" she asked. "Cecile says it's okay for us to use her place. She's a little jealous — who wouldn't be — but..." Arlette gave him a shrug and fell silent.

Hagen reached out to take the cable from her. "I have to work late. It's..."

"It's not wise of us. Yes, I know it isn't, but I *want* to see you, Richard. I want... Oh, you know what I want."

Her eyes had found the desk — she couldn't look at him. She was still so very shy.

"Don't be afraid to say you want to make love."

"Cecile won't mind."

"Cecile *will* mind, and that's one reason I don't think it's such a good idea for us to use her place."

"And the other reasons?" she asked sharply.

"You know very well what I mean."

"There's a ten o'clock mass at the cathedral. If I were to... Richard, you could be there. I could..."

"Let them follow you there?"

"Yes."

"Arlette..."

"Be there, and then I will go straight home afterward. I won't see you tonight! You can follow them and find out who they are."

When decoded, the message read:

TO ALICE FROM THE CARPENTER

CANARIS ABWEHR CONTACT TRAVELLERS' CLUB LINKED TO INSPECTOR LAFLEUR PAUL PARIS SÛRETÉ / LAFLEUR IN PAY OF HEYDRICH'S SD / EVIDENCE OF WELL-ORGANIZED NAZI FIFTH COLUMNS IN FRANCE BELGIUM AND HOLLAND SUGGESTS WAR IMMINENT / WHITE RABBIT REQUESTS SIGNAL DIAMOND STOCKS MEGADAN ROUTE EARLIEST POSSIBLE DATE / AS YET NO OFFICIAL SANCTION CAN BE GIVEN CONVINCE ANTWERP COMMITTEE TO SHIP WHILE TIME STILL AVAILABLE / REALIZE LACK OF GUARANTEES MAY BE A PROBLEM / URGE UTMOST CAUTION IF RETURNING TO REICH

Working after hours, Hagen wrote out a reply.

TO THE CARPENTER FROM ALICE

BELGIUM STEADFASTLY MAINTAINS NEUTRALITY IN FACE OF MOUNTING TENSIONS / KING LEOPOLD STILL REFUSES TO LET DIAMONDS LEAVE / TRADERS WILL NOT I REPEAT NOT SHIP WITHOUT FIRM GUARANTEES RECEIVED BRITISH GOVERNMENT IN WRITING / FLYING TO BERLIN 3 NOVEMBER / REQUEST YOU TAKE HUYSMANS ARLETTE TO ENGLAND FIRST SIGN OF TROUBLE / ALICE

It was all so stupid. In the face of the inevitable the diamond stocks still languished in Antwerp.

To be on the safe side he took the cable down to the Central Railway Station rather than phone it in.

Then he waited in a call box.

Sure enough, someone went up to the wicket and a copy of his cable was passed over. Within hours the message would be in Otto Krantz's hands or in someone's from the Abwehr.

They'd make of it what they could. To try to stop the man would only tell them that he knew.

Damas saw Hagen leave the Central Station, and when the diamond salesman was crossing the square, he picked up his trail. Others would watch the girl's place. She could be taken at any time. Berlin's interest was very much in Hagen — his activities while in Antwerp, where he went, whom he saw — dates, times, places. Even which restaurants he favored.

The girl was simply the mayonnaise that might or might not have gone sour.

When Hagen went into the cathedral, Damas was surprised, for Hagen wasn't what one could call religious. Nor was he of any particular faith.

Uncertain how to handle things, the schoolmaster waited in the shadows beneath the awnings of a perfume shop. Could he chance a cigarette? Tailing Hagen always keyed him up. One had to be so careful.

Sliding his left hand into the pocket of his trench coat, he closed his fingers over the pistol. Why had the diamond salesman gone in there if not to meet the girl?

The cathedral was crowded. These days so many people were worried there'd be war. Arlette hurriedly crossed herself and, squeezing between the rows, knelt to bow her head. Would Richard come? Would he see her? Would he find the two men who had followed her from Madame Hausemer's? They'd kept right after her. She'd run — they'd forced her to do this, forced her to give away the fact that she'd known they were there.

And now? she wondered anxiously.

Framed by Corinthian columns, Rubens's masterpiece, *The Elevation of the Cross*, soared above everything. All the candles had been lit. The gold of the cross behind the altar served only to make one focus on the painting.

Richard, she whispered silently. Richard, please be careful. I don't like this. Something isn't right.

Not three rows in front of her and a little to one side and across the center aisle, a man had turned to look at her. Laughing, grinning, a week's growth of stubble on the fleshy cheeks and double chin. In a flash she remembered him in the street outside the Café Lindenbos, remembered the young engineer, the screech of brakes and then...and then...

Quickly she bowed her head. Richard...Richard, my darling, please forgive me for suggesting this.

Across the square and along from the man who had followed him, Hagen waited in the darkness, and when the service was over and Arlette would have turned for home, he started out. Joining a group of people, he used them as cover, but they went off toward the Grote Markt to find a brightly lit café in the shadow of the cathedral.

Alone for a few moments, he felt exposed. Antwerp's gas lanterns had long since been electrified, but here they still jutted out from the walls.

The man paused at a corner to light a cigarette — a good sign. Irritably waving out the match, he drew in deeply before flipping up the collar of his coat and sliding his hands into its pockets.

Then he started out again but headed for the docks.

Four hours later and back at the office, Hagen encoded another message, this time typing it out using two sheets of carbon paper and the Magpie Lane address.

Each of the copies would go into widely separated mailboxes.

TO THE CARPENTER FROM ALICE

SD KEY OPERATIVE ANTWERP DAMAS KARL CHRISTIAN NUMBER 239 THE WAALSEKAAI APARTMENT THREE FOURTH FLOOR AT BACK / SCHOOLMASTER AGE ABOUT 40-45 TALL THIN LEFT-HANDED SMOKES CIGARETTES A HARD MAN TO TAIL / ARLETTE A SECONDARY ASSIGNMENT BUT STILL DEFINITELY BEING WATCHED / URGENT YOU GET HER TO LONDON AS SOON AS POSSIBLE THEN NOTIFY BERNARD / ALICE

It was nearly 4:00 a.m. when he slipped into the Club Chez Vous via the back door that led to the kitchens. Cecile was still up, the place all but empty. Though there were two glasses on the table in front of her, one hadn't been used.

"Richard, just what the hell do you and that girl you've got up there think you're doing?"

"Is Arlette here? I thought..."

"You *thought*! You didn't think. She was followed on her way home but lost them. The poor kid was terrified. Berke found her crying on the back steps and brought her in. I've had to telephone that landlady of hers six times just to calm the woman down."

Hagen ran an exasperated hand through his hair. Had Damas purposely drawn him off so as to find out what was up?

"Look, I told her I didn't want us coming here. It's too dangerous for us and for you."

"Just what the hell are you involved in?"

"Nothing. It's all a mistake."

"That's some mistake! Are you screwing that kid upstairs in my place?"

"Cecile..."

"My God, I hope you wear a sock for her sake!"

"Please try to understand."

"Why? What's it got to do with me?"

"I thought this was a place for your friends to meet."

"It is. Now tell me honestly, does this business have anything to do with Dieter Karl and his sister?"

"Exactly how much did Arlette tell you?"

"Enough for me to know you're working for the British and that Dieter and you can no longer be friends."

Cecile had met Dieter in Berlin in 1936. Dieter had been quite envious. Anyone with an eye for beautiful women would have been.

"Things are piling up on you, Richard. Look, I don't want to know but I do think you'd better get her out of this if not for your sake, then for hers. Now go on up to my bedroom — I'm sure you still remember where it is — and tell her you're safe."

She reached for the bottle and Hagen took it from her to refill her glass.

Strains of a recording of "Begin the Beguine" filtered up from the club below. Unable to sleep, Arlette lay in the darkness on her side. It was all so unfair! Why couldn't they simply have had a life of their own?

She heard the door softly open and close. Anxiously she sat up. "Cecile..." she began.

"Arlette, it's me."

They came together in a rush, she bouncing out of bed, he stepping quickly toward her. They fell back onto the bed, Arlette softly crying, "Richard... Oh, Richard..."; Hagen saying, "It's okay. It's okay. Everything's okay."

Still in her slip and stockings, she lay beneath him, his hands under her, her arms wrapped tightly around him. "Love me, Richard. Love me, please!"

Nothing seemed to matter but that they have each other. Richard's hands slid under her slip and up over the tops of her stockings. His lips were parted. She could feel the tip of his tongue, felt his fingers as they touched the skin above her stockings. Caressing it now, softly so softly as she drew in a breath and found his lips again.

"I want you," she said, her breath coming in a rush.

When she heard him hurrying to undo his belt, Arlette yanked off the rest of her things. "Hurry... please hurry. Richard, I *have* to have you."

In a rush he touched her thighs, her hips, her breasts and wrists as he slid himself up over her to stretch her arms above her head and press his lips to hers. Parting them, he slid his tongue inside her mouth as his penis nudged her, she lifting up, arching hard, splitting her body apart to receive him, always thrusting... thrusting. Ripples of pleasure all over again, waves of it. No thought of the men who had followed her. No thought.

Arlette felt him coming, felt every muscle of him throbbing deeply inside her. Then it was done and she was crying, was kissing him again. Longer now. Murmuring sweet urgent things, then lifting a breast to his lips, running her hand through his hair.

As they lay in the darkness she heard him say, "I've arranged a code with Bernard. If you hear me use the word *obstacle* in the course of some instructions for the shop, Bernard is to insist that de Heer Lietermann and the Committee send the diamond stocks to England right away, and they're to be sent only by ship."

"In the *Megadan*."

She felt him nod his head. "If you don't hear from Duncan, you're to contact him and get out yourself — the sooner the better. Go to Ostend and cross over there. With luck, he'll have sent someone to accompany you."

"And the ones who followed us tonight?"

"You leave them to Duncan."

This was a Richard she hadn't known. "Why must you go back into the Reich? Why must you do this thing?"

"You know the answers."

"Then take the diamond this time. Give it to the Nazis, Richard. Get Lev's daughter and son-in-law out. Do this for us."

His flight left at six in the morning. At six-thirty Arlette was waiting outside the office. November's wind was cruel, the street so utterly desolate she had to wonder how it would look if the Nazis were to invade.

Empty like this — the whole city without a soul to walk its streets or stand as she did, with her back to the wind. It was all so unfair — criminal of them!

At seven o'clock Lev came along to find her. The tears were very real, and as she wiped them away, he said, "So, he's gone again, and you who are engaged to the son of a butcher in Ostend must broadcast a different love to the world at large. Come on, I think we both need some coffee. Would you like a piece of honey cake with it?"

They took the lift up to the fourth floor. As the thing stopped, she felt Lev's arms about her. "The risks, Arlette. The chances he must take."

"He's taken the pendant with him."

"It's hidden in one of the drill bits. I fixed a metal plug to hold it in and made him a key to get it out."

"They'll find it, Lev. I know they will. I have this feeling."

Lev clucked his tongue. There was about the building that same inevitability of emptiness. It made her shiver. Their steps sounded loudly.

He got her to make the coffee, and when he unwrapped the honey cake Anna had included with his lunch, he cut the slice in two. "Let's each of us eat it slowly so as to think of the past and hope for the future."

All along the Friedrichstrasse the shops were busy. Throngs of people sought the pavements as if the euphoria over Austria and the Sudeten-land could never end.

Berlin was all aglitter. Munich had been a triumph for Hitler.

On the Leipzigerstrasse — a far better shopping street — the action was even more frenzied. Couples strolled arm in arm. The uniforms were everywhere, the gray-green of the Wehrmacht, the blue of the Kriegsma-rine, that of the Luftwaffe.

The black of the SS, the Schutz Staffel.

In a nation of uniforms, all were proudly accepted.

The taxi headed west along the Unter den Linden. An early snow, whose wet flakes all but refused to melt, did nothing to dampen the enthusiasm. Floodlights lit the museums and government buildings. Lovers stood, policemen walked.

No one had bothered him at the frontier. He'd been allowed in without a raised eyebrow. From Essen he'd gone to Frankfurt — still had a folded copy of the *Frankfurter Zeitung*.

Hagen set it on the seat beside him. When he'd rung Dee Dee's flat there'd been no answer.

They turned onto the Kurfürstendamm. Soon the bright lights of the film theaters were everywhere, clashing with those of the bars and cafés. A giant billboard recommended Berliner Kindl. Another defied it by recommending Dortmunder Union.

The burned-out bulbs of a nude cabaret signaled that streak of false purity the Nazis had brought to the city. No naked maidens riding white stallions as at the Munich torch-lit fetes, no orgies as in Hitler's new artists' center there. None save in the sleazy bars Heydrich knew.

The lights were out in Dee Dee's flat. "Wait for me, will you?" he said.

When he rang the buzzer there was no answer. When he stood looking up at her windows, he felt a renewed and growing sense of uneasiness.

Aschinger's was cheap and good, a place to stand and eat or sit, and he went there to wait, knowing that he'd been followed.

A beaming Otto Krantz soon pushed his way through to the counter. "Richard, how've you been? Glad to see you're back."

Krantz took in the half-eaten bowl of pea soup with ham, the plate of little sausages, the stein of beer and the cheese on rye with sauerkraut.

"You're one of us, my friend. Hah, this weather, Richard." He tossed his fedora onto the counter, used a stumpy forefinger to order the same. "So, how've you been?"

Guardedly the salesman chose to discuss the weather and the international situation. Krantz broke a fistful of rusks into his soup and added salt and pepper. "Herr Heydrich wishes us to have a little talk, but first, a question or two of my own."

Hagen tossed off the last of his beer. Krantz ordered another for him. "Fräulein Schroeder, Richard. Did she have friends or relatives in the country perhaps?"

"*Did* she . . . ?"

"*Gott in Himmel*, I'm sorry. You thought . . . but of course. No, she's fine — at least as far as we know."

"But she's not at her flat."

The policeman's expression was bland. Slowly Krantz shook his head. "I was rather hoping you might tell us where she is."

Had Canaris made good his promise? Had the admiral managed to get her out of the country?

"The *Gruppenführer* ..." said Krantz, savoring his soup as one would a juicy piece of gossip. "He's really quite fond of the woman. If you could ... as a favor." The Berliner shrugged.

"Herr Krantz, I don't know where she is. I was hoping you'd tell me."

The spoon went into the soup again. The Berliner puddled the rusks and drowned them in the gray-green. Bits of ham floated up. "When I find out, I'll be sure to let you know. So, now let us come to business. Whatever you and the admiral have agreed to, the *Gruppenführer* wishes you to extend the same to us."

Hagen reached for his coffee. He thought to say, I don't know what you're talking about. Grinning, he set down his mug. "Perhaps we'd better talk outside."

Krantz lit up. Were they putting rat shit in the tobacco? "*Gott in Himmel.*" He coughed and wheezed in.

They'd take a little stroll but first he'd finish his meal.

TO WINFIELD MRS LOIS ANNE INVERLIN COTTAGE BLACK DOWN HEATH PORTESHAM ROAD DORCHESTER ENGLAND

FROM HAGEN RICHARD HOTEL ADLON BERLIN

CHAMBERLAIN HAILED AS A SAINT STOP EVERYONE SAYS HE DID HIS VERY BEST AND SUCCEEDED IN OVERCOMING AN ALMOST IMPOSSIBLE TASK STOP HITLER DIDN'T YIELD ONE BIT BUT SHOWED HOW SHREWD HE WAS AND GAINED ALL MANNER OF CONCESSIONS STOP THE GENERAL FEELINGS ARE OF PEACE BUT EVERYONE IS STILL WATCHING IN CASE THERE IS A TURN FOR THE WORSE STOP MY FEELINGS ARE THAT YOU SHOULD RELAX STOP DON'T BE ANXIOUS ABOUT ME STOP LOVE HAGEN

SD Antwerp had again entered the offices of Dillingham and Company. Karl Christian Damas had sent word of two books in English he'd found in the director's desk but hadn't removed.

Through the Looking Glass and *Alice's Adventures in Wonderland.*

The Belgian had said some passages had been lightly marked and that Wunsch had left a bookmark at one poem. "The Walrus and the Carpenter."

Krantz read the cable over again. Lost in thought, he fingered the cigarette case. Where would it all lead? What would Heydrich really do?

Hagen and he had walked and talked for nearly an hour. They'd finished up with a coffee at the Cafe des Westens and had watched the nightlife stroll up and down the Damm.

Then the bastard had gone back to his hotel and at 4:00 a.m. had sent this wire.

He did his very best had come from verse one, line three of "The Walrus and the Carpenter." The rest of the quotes had come from page 21 of *Through the Looking Glass*.

Unknown as yet, the message when decoded would read:

TO THE CARPENTER FROM ALICE

OFFER MEGADAN ROUTE EXTENDED SD VIA KRANTZ £50,000 PAYABLE ZURICH ACCOUNT / RAILWAY ROUTE HELD BACK / IMPERATIVE DIAMOND STOCKS BE MOVED / BELIEVE PLANS IN PLACE TO SEIZE THEM / ALICE

Hamburg was shrouded in gray. Around the harbor the forest of cranes swung eerily back and forth in the mist. Day and night the offloading and loading went on. Ships from all over the world came here.

Hagen stood in the director's office of Blohm and Voss, Germany's largest shipbuilding yard. The skeleton of another cruiser funneled his view down into the harbor. Motor torpedo boats, landing barges — they had several of these as well as submarines. The din of the riveting hammers intruded, as did the flash of acetylene torches.

The office had been put at their disposal. Unknown to him, Dieter Karl and Irmgard had arrived back from Brazil, Dieter tanned and fit but cautious and demanding.

A meeting here — ostensibly in secret. Dieter and the Abwehr had chased after him. Very worried about Dee Dee and Irmgard, Hagen found he could barely control his anger.

"Dieter, you'll never get diamonds out of the Congo unless you work through the cartel, buying on the open market. If Canaris thinks the Abwehr and the SS have the best security systems in the world, he'd better think again. Each washing and concentrating plant — each mine if need be — is enclosed by barbed, electrified wire fences. There are patrols with dogs that are no less fierce than those of the SS. The Bantu who work there sign on for periods of three months and they don't come out until someone says they can.

"When they pass through the gates, they go into a shed to strip off and leave their clothes and anything else they might have brought — even a pipe and tobacco pouch. Then they pass through the showers, are disinfected and given a suit of work clothes."

Dieter grinned. "You're making it sound like one of the camps."

Hagen didn't react. "They live and work within that compound until their tour of duty is up. *But* —" he paused "— they never know exactly when they'll be told to leave — what day, what hour — so they can't plan ahead. On the way out they leave their work clothes, shower and are body-searched — and I mean searched.

"Sometimes a fellow will swallow a diamond or two. The fear in his eyes nearly always gives him away. Castor oil, an enema or a fist in the guts — whichever way, he's forced to get rid of it. And again, he never knows if he'll be selected, for there are always random checks as well."

Was Richard afraid they might try without his help? "But you have said the deposits at Mbuji-Mayi are almost totally industrials? Surely the security is not so tight for those?"

"About two percent are gems. One stone, even at today's prices, is a lifetime's work for several men. Some still try to steal, and I feel sorry for them because they're nearly always caught."

"And the tool diamonds?"

"About three percent. Look, doing it illegally just isn't worth the try."

"But some do get by. This security of La Forminière's is not so good as you say."

Dieter would never understand. "Only a white man could accomplish what you're thinking of, and even he couldn't get enough diamonds past the mine security to keep the whole of your war machine going."

"We are not at war, and we do not plan to be." A white man...a Belgian...

"When it comes, we both know there'll be a blockade."

"The British will still need diamonds to run their industries. They won't close those mines, Richard. They wouldn't be able to."

"Mbuji-Mayi's production is almost totally of crushing boart. Sure you need it, but how are you going to get it out of the mines, and if you should manage that, how will you get it past the blockade?"

"There must be ways. We will see."

"And the tool diamonds you'll need?"

"You told Canaris it might be possible — from Tshikapa, I presume, with your help."

"With my help, Dieter. Mine! A company of my own so that you can work through the official channels even if there is a blockade."

"I must have my assurances that you really have our interests at heart."

"And I want to know what's happened to Dee Dee. Just where is she, Dieter? The admiral promised me he'd get her out."

Richard could be such a fool at times. "Steps are being taken to find out. Believe me, I'm just as upset by her disappearance as are you and Irmgard."

"But are you upset by what's happened to her? Heydrich, Dieter. Heydrich!"

"You know I am. Now, please. The Antwerp stocks? The admiral wishes to know if there have been any new developments? Which of the channel ports will they use to send the railway cars across?"

"I'd like to see Irmgard, Dieter. I'd like to know that she's okay."

"You'll see her soon enough."

Hagen clenched a fist and turned away to the windows. "I want the fifty thousand first, Dieter. It should have been deposited to my account by now."

"The channel port they'll use, Richard?"

"I don't know which one. Not yet. But I can't see them sending the diamonds through France. They'd be afraid the French might seize them."

No love lost among such allies, the truth at last. "Then it has to be Zeebrugge or Ostend."

"That's correct."

"And this freighter, the *Megadan*? Is it really to be a ploy or do the traders intend to use it?"

Dealing with Canaris had been one thing, Dieter quite another. "I can only repeat what I know to be the case. Look, I want something for myself, Dieter. I can't be forever shuttling back and forth across Europe. Besides, if war comes and they do manage to move the diamonds to London, you'll need me in the Congo. With my own production and those I'll buy on the open market, I can see that you get all the diamonds you'll ever need."

"You'll be subject to the blockade just like everyone else."

"I'll get around it by setting up a dummy company in the States. Orders from there go to the mine, and I ship to a third and neutral country. Only you and I know what's really going on. You fly in and out, or you use a submarine."

Hunter took his time. Studying Richard had become an obsession of Heydrich's. The admiral wanted absolute proof he'd work for them.

There was a Dutchman in Amsterdam, a crook named Klees. Word had it that Richard was making a little money on the side.

Knowing what he did of him, it simply wouldn't wash.

There was also Irmgard and the letters she had written to him; Richard's cables, too — not just suspicions of a code but almost the proof.

Yet Richard could help them so much.

"All right. I'll tell the admiral to authorize the funds." He grinned then and got up, felt Richard's firm handshake. "So, we are partners at last."

But partners with whom? wondered Hagen.

The headquarters of the Berlin Municipal Police was in a massive gray stone building on the Alexanderplatz. From the roof terrace there was a superb view of the inner city's bustling life. Krantz waved away the choice of meeting place. "Old haunts die hard, Richard. I still have occasion to work closely with these boys."

The Berliner flipped up the collar of his overcoat. "It's a bitch of a wind but private up here."

Hagen waited. The police radio tower was directly behind Krantz. Ice clung to its iron crosspieces. A swastika flag flapped mercilessly from its top.

"The Fräulein Schroeder, Richard. Word has come to me that she's in the concentration camp at Ravensbrück. Me, I thought you'd like to know."

Hagen felt sick. Ravensbrück... "Can nothing be done to get her out?"

Krantz found his cigarette case and lit up. "Herr Heydrich must have had his reasons. An argument, a bun in the oven — *Gott in Himmel*, how should I know? *But*, to get her out? Yes, I think there is a possibility."

They knew, then, of his meeting in Hamburg with Dieter.

The Berliner rubbed a thumb over the tarnished head of the kaiser. "A deal, I think. Yes, that would be best. Everything you give to the admiral you will give to me and some."

"What guarantees have I got that you'll let her out of that place?"

The snort of laughter was there, the quick drag on the cigarette. "None. *But*, she can be whisked away at a word. Switzerland, Zurich, if you like. All Herr Heydrich has to do is wave his magic wand."

What could be easier? Hagen told him about the alternate plan to use the railway cars. "The *Megadan* is just a ploy."

Krantz nodded. A rusty shit box of a freighter, SD Antwerp had said.

"And the money?" asked Hagen.

The Berliner grinned. "We will let the admiral pay you. It wouldn't be right of us to do so twice. Not for the same thing."

They went indoors and along a corridor to one of the offices. Krantz tossed his cigarette case onto the desk and asked to be excused. "I'll only be a moment, then I can give you a lift back to your hotel."

Krantz had left his cigarette case on top of a clipboard. Hagen nudged the case aside and read the memo.

TOP SECRET

THE FOLLOWING MESSAGE WILL BE ISSUED AT 11:55 P.M. NOV. 9, FROM GESTAPO HEADQUARTERS.

BERLIN NO. 234404 9.11.2355

TO ALL GESTAPO STATIONS AND GESTAPO DISTRICT STATIONS

TO OFFICER OR DEPUTY

THIS TELEPRINTER MESSAGE IS TO BE SUBMITTED WITHOUT DELAY:

AT VERY SHORT NOTICE, AKTIONEN AGAINST JEWS, ESPE-CIALLY AGAINST THEIR SYNAGOGUES, WILL TAKE PLACE THROUGHOUT THE WHOLE OF GERMANY. THEY ARE NOT TO BE HINDERED. IN CONJUNCTION WITH THE POLICE, HOWEVER, IT IS TO BE ENSURED THAT LOOTING AND OTHER PARTICULAR EXCESSES CAN BE PREVENTED*

Between twenty thousand and thirty thousand Jews were to be arrested, the wealthy in particular.

He'd have to wait — have to carry on as if nothing were to happen. He couldn't try to send anything out right away, no matter how much he wanted to. Nor could he attempt to warn anyone yet.

Krantz had left him with the temptation, but Heydrich had been behind it. Now they would wait to see what he'd do. Key phrases — the date, an action against the Jews. They'd hope to use these to help them decode what he'd sent.

The diamond was clear, a cushion-shaped macle whose top and bottom had been ground perfectly flat. A viewing window had been cut and polished in one side and through this, with the microscope, he could see inside the stone.

As always, he was impressed and humbled by Lev's skill, more so now because of what he knew would happen and the need to get a warning out.

The diamond was one of a sequence of twenty-two such stones in one of the wire drawing machines of a small factory on the outskirts of Berlin. Copper wire of 1.8 mm in diameter entered the first diamond in the sequence and was then reduced in twenty-two stages to wire of 0.21 mm.

The hole through its center had been drilled using steel sewing machine needles, grades of diamond dust of varying sizes and very high speeds of rotation. From top to bottom the hole looked like a funnel whose spout opened slightly into a small cone.

The walls of the hole had been carefully polished; the stone was of far better quality than most gem diamonds simply because die stones had to be that way or else they would break.

There were pressure rings around the top of the hole, the first signs of wear. They'd have to do.

Leaning back from the microscope, Hagen patiently explained the problem to the foreman and asked to call Antwerp. The blitz call took a

* directive from Gestapo II Müller.

good ten minutes to get through, and when he heard Arlette on the line, he hoped she'd understand and do the right thing.

"Mijnheer Hagen, is that you?" she asked.

The line cleared. "Arlette, have you a pencil handy?" She said she had, but he found his throat had suddenly gone dry and he was shaking.

Frantically Arlette searched for something to say. "Richard..." God forgive her for saying his name like that! "Mijnheer Hagen, I...I have broken my pencil. A moment, please."

He waited, seeing her at her desk. "Arlette..."

"Please continue now, Mijnheer Hagen." I love you very much.

"It seems a shame to have to ask it but could you get the shop to send me a set of replacement die stones for the Metz und Langbehen plant in Berlin?"

There were some other things, and she took down everything he said. Then he was saying goodbye, and she was sitting there, staring at her notepad.

Bernard Wunsch nervously took the pad from her. The word *obstacles* hadn't been mentioned.

"It seems a shame" had come from "The Walrus and the Carpenter." The girl was softly crying.

"Are you working for the British too?" he asked.

She gave a nod. "I must relay this to England but not let the Germans know I've done so."

Then it was true.

Arlette wiped her eyes and blew her nose. "I will go to a place I know of this evening. That will be okay, I think."

What kind of a world was it becoming? "The club of Cecile Verheyden?" he asked.

She gripped her stomach, wanted suddenly to throw up. "Yes."

Unknown to them, the message read:

TO THE CARPENTER FROM ALICE

MOST URGENT YOU WARN JEWS IN GERMANY OF SS POGROM THE NIGHT OF 9 – 10 NOVEMBER / DIRECTIVE SENT TO ALL SS UNITS READS 2355 HOURS / SORRY BUT I HAVE TO DO WHAT I CAN / ALICE

At 3:30 on the morning of November 8 the Motzstrasse was clothed in darkness. From the direction of the Nottendorfplatz, a car crept up the street.

It reached number 87 and for a while sat there. Then the window of the passenger door was rolled down and the beam of a flashlight shone up the steps before fleeing to a nearby entrance.

Out of the darkness two men hurried over to the car. Hagen cursed his luck. Krantz was having the place watched around the clock.

The two men got into the car and it was driven slowly away.

For almost an hour he searched the frigid darkness for the third man, only to find the street deserted.

Waking Lev's daughter and son-in-law was like waking the dead! The echoes of his first hammered in the hall. No time... "Goddamn it, open up in the name of the Führer!"

Moses, terrified and blinking at the unaccustomed light, timidly opened the door. "Herr Hagen..."

He shoved past him in a rush and nudged the door closed. Rachel hurried into the hall only to stop suddenly at the sight of him.

As calmly as he could, Hagen told them what was going to happen. "You mustn't tell anyone. Just get dressed and leave while you can. Use the morning rush hour to cover yourselves. Take a little food and water, a blanket perhaps — so little, no one will notice."

"And where shall we go?" asked Tannenbaum bitterly.

"Haven't you any relatives in the countryside? Isn't there someone, some Gentile who'll take you in for a few days until things blow over?"

The bookseller snorted at this. "Her grandparents perhaps."

"Good." He realized then that the husband had meant the cemetery. "Could you stand it there for a day or two? Look, I need time to work something out."

The cemetery... "It's at Weissensee, in the northeastern suburbs. So far the Nazis have left it alone. There are crypts, Moses. Perhaps we could...?" Rachel left it unsaid.

They'd never leave the flat and he knew it! "Get dressed and I'll go there with you."

The tramcar ride was the loneliest he'd ever made. At four-thirty the city was just beginning to awaken. At five-thirty the dawn had not yet broken. At six-fifteen the beam of their flashlight revealed that the cemetery had been left untended for some time. Ivy covered many of the stones that lay flat on the ground. The grass was thick and soaked with dew, the air damp and cold. Weeds had grown up everywhere and their bare, dead stalks protruded from among the standing stones.

Rachel took the lead. Soon their shoes were soaked through. Hagen wondered if the couple would be all right, if Krantz had had them followed. He cursed Heydrich for the bastard he was. He was grateful for the size of the place.

When they came to a small white oval set in an upright slab of black marble, he saw the photograph of Lev's mother. There was a passage in Hebrew; above this, the star of David.

"I never knew her," said Rachel, "yet I come here often for my father's sake."

"There's a crypt just over the hill, Herr Hagen. Perhaps it will do."

The light fled away to angels, blue-green with verdigris, that guarded the door. Hagen broke the rusty padlock with a stone.

"I'll be back, don't worry. But for now you must stay here and keep out of sight."

"And how do we know you'll be back?"

"Moses, please. Herr Hagen has risked his life to do this."

Hagen glanced over his shoulder. "Look, if I'm not back within four days you'll know I'm in trouble. Wait at least until then — longer if you can."

Quickly he told them of the route through the border crossing at Emmerich and handed Rachel the pendant.

They couldn't help but see the worth of it.

Shaking hands very formally, they said goodbye. He hated to leave them. Even with the pendant they stood so little chance.

Horcher's was crowded as usual. From the far side of the dining room came the strains of a waltz, from the tables whose occupants were nearly all in uniform, the sounds of cutlery and talk, broken now and then by sudden bursts of laughter.

Seated at a table for four, not far from the central buffet, Hagen waited.

Already he'd been waiting for some time.

Two tables from him Goering and Heydrich were earnestly discussing something, while Goebbels smirked and Himmler remained fastidiously remote.

At another table the generals Guderian, Jodl and von Brauchitsch added wineglasses to their maneuvers.

Heydrich had simply ignored him. There was no sign of Canaris.

When a hand touched his shoulder, Hagen turned suddenly to look up and saw the warning and the fear in Irmgard's eyes.

She was wearing navy blue, with a stark white blouse and dark tie. The crispness of the uniform suited her. "Aren't you glad to see me?" she asked, her voice despondent.

"I didn't know you were working for the Abwehr."

"Dieter," she whispered, leaning over to kiss him on the cheek. "Didn't he tell you?"

Hagen refused to answer. What was she playing at? She looked well-tanned and fit, her hair lightened by the sun. But had Canaris sanctioned the meeting under Heydrich's watchful gaze? Just what the bloody hell was going on?

Picking at the tablecloth, she said, "Tell me how things are. It's been so long. Dieter sends his regrets. As you can see, he and Herr Piekenbrock were to have joined us. Business . . . always it is business these days."

Hans Piekenbrock was the Abwehr's second in command.

Fortunately the waiter came. Hardly glancing at the menu, she ordered something, he the same. He thought of Rachel and her husband and decided that no matter how much he might need Irmgard's help, he couldn't risk asking for it.

When she said, "I'm to drive you to Munich this evening," he knew that the admiral wanted him out of Berlin.

The street was strangely silent, while all around them the sound of breaking glass came harshly.

Gripping the steering wheel, Irmgard eased her foot back down on the accelerator. As the Daimler began to move slowly forward, she glanced tearfully into the rearview mirror, then at Richard, who was grim and silent.

In each town and village it had been the same, but here — here in Munich at two o'clock in the morning when people should have been asleep? Dear God, no!

The wail of another fire engine came, but it was over on the Brienner-strasse where the shops were so expensive and fashionable.

Street after street had been littered with broken glass. Each time they had tried to get through some place it had been the same. All the windows of the Jewish shops had been smashed. Roving jackbooted gangs of drunken SS and storm troopers had run howling from street to street. What they hadn't looted, they had set afire either intentionally or by accident.

"Richard, pray for us. I don't like this."

"Just get down the street. Maybe we can work our way around them."

Again she glanced into the rearview mirror. They passed a department store whose mannequins wore the furs and suits of winter. They passed an antique shop, a jeweler's.

Halfway down the block, he told her to back up.

"I can't. They're behind us."

Time stopped. The mob of fifty — a hundred perhaps — paused. Their torches seemed to waver.

Then, with a shout of rage, the carnage began. As the mob surged past each shop, the windows shattered and showers of glass spilled onto the walks and the street beyond.

Unable to take her eyes from the rearview mirror, Irmgard clung to the steering wheel. Unable to take his gaze from the street in front of them, Hagen gritted his teeth in anger.

All too soon the order banning looting was forgotten. As blood ran down their fingers, they fought their brothers for the choicest things.

Those who objected to the looting and the damage were dragged into the street and savagely beaten. Now and then a Gentile shop was left like an island in the storm. When they reached the car, the mob surged around it, then began to rock the Daimler violently. Hagen tried to stop them. Someone smashed the windshield. Irmgard was grabbed and dragged kicking and screaming from the car. He forced his door open and went down in a welter of blows as she shrieked, "I work for the Abwehr, damn you! The *Abwehr*! He is Admiral Canaris's friend!"

Someone must have heard her, for they backed away as if threatened by the plague. As she clutched her torn coat, Irmgard stood in the light from the headlamps defying them. "The Abwehr," she said. "The Abwehr."

Grinning, leering now, they backed away a little more, but to prove their worth, to make up for things, they dragged a young Jewish woman into the lights.

As Irmgard's screams joined those of their victim, they tore the nightclothes from the woman. Not content with raping her, four of them seized the woman by the arms and legs and pitched her through the window of her father's shop. Then they tossed a torch in after her and ran.

The bedroom of the Villa Hunter overlooked the gardens far from the carnage and the smoke that still hung over parts of the city. As the dawn came up, Hagen turned away from the window. The pogrom had been far too extensive. It wouldn't be over for weeks. The arrests would go on and on. The borders would be closely watched.

The young Jewish woman who had been raped had died in his arms. "Irmgard, I need your help. There's something I'd better tell you."

Her gaze moved over the bandages, the gash in his forehead, the blackened eyes and battered chin. "I work for the Abwehr, Richard. Remember? If Canaris had had his way I would have slept with you last night. That was the order — get Richard Hagen out of Berlin and into your arms."

"Or else?"

She didn't answer. He said, "Brazil...there was trouble, Irmgard. Why not tell me about it?"

She answered, "I tried to send some letters to you and found out the truth about my brother."

And yet Canaris had given her a job? That could only mean the admiral hadn't been aware of the letters.

"What will you do?" he asked.

"Does it matter? Yes, I can see that it does. You're such a good person, Richard. Me, I'll carry on until they take my head. Now, please, what is it you need?"

They were on their way back to Berlin that morning in a van, borrowed from one of her father's factories, that was full of new uniforms for the Wehrmacht. When they arrived at the cemetery in the late afternoon, the synagogue nearby was a blackened ruin. Only the outer walls still stood. Apart from an old woman and a gaping child, there wasn't another soul about.

"Wait for me, will you?"

"No. I'm coming with you. You might need me, Richard."

"Stay with the van. That way you won't have to park it and draw attention to us. Come back in half an hour. Please."

"Tell them I'll hide them in Munich at the house. Tell them they'll be safe."

Ask for forgiveness — it was written in her eyes.

Hagen stood at the side of the road while she drove away. Then he headed into the cemetery. Just when he began to run, he'd never know. Just when he had torn open the heavy doors of the crypt, he wouldn't remember.

Sunlight filtered into the depths. There wasn't a sign of anyone.

Irmgard and he hadn't spoken in hours. The night had come down long ago, yet still she drove the van with the same desperateness, though Berlin was now far behind them.

Another convoy of SS trucks appeared ahead of them, and she started out to pass it without a thought for the approaching headlamps. There was a screech of brakes — theirs, someone else's, he didn't know.

Some eighteen kilometers outside of Munich she turned off the autobahn to the west and followed more of the trucks until, at another turning, they had finally left them.

"The concentration camp at Dachau is not far, yes? So I thought this would be best for us. The greatness of the Germanic peoples, Richard. It is possible for us to build such things."

The van slowed to a stop before the gates of Schloss Schleissheim, one of Munich's loveliest castles.

"Dachau, and this, Richard. Ravensbrück — oh, yes, I know about Dee Dee. For me, I would have preferred that we could have walked together in the Nymphenburg's Hall of Mirrors. Then we could have seen each other's secrets, isn't that right? Me, you, naked among the mirrors. Heydrich there, Canaris there, Hitler, Goering... all of them watching us."

She switched off the headlamps. They would sit here in the darkness and she would let the cold and the damp seep into him.

Her voice was harsh. "You know you cannot say one damn thing about what has happened. You cannot object, cannot cry out. To do so is to admit that you tried, Richard, and for them that will be enough. As for me, I am simply your accomplice."

"I couldn't just let it happen."

She hit the steering wheel. "Oh, for Christ's sake, do you not see what they're trying to do to you? Those two Jews were nothing. Nothing!

"And now...and now you have been forced to understand that Heydrich knows everything about you. Don't try to fool them anymore. That's the message he wants you to get."

One of the night watchmen tried the entrance doors to the castle. No guns, no dogs, just an old man in the distance with a hand-held biscuit tin of a torch.

"Richard, we can never get Dee Dee out of Ravensbrück unless you cooperate. For you, for me, there is only one solution and that is to give them the Antwerp diamond stocks and to work for them to secure their diamond needs for the foreseeable future."

She ran her hands around the steering wheel and stiffened her arms as if coming to a decision.

"You are caught in a power struggle between two monstrous organizations. The Abwehr are no better, no more decent, no less cruel than the SS and their Sicherheitsdienst. But Heydrich has the Gestapo. He's Himmler's boy, Richard. Canaris may think he has the ear of the Führer but Himmler kisses it always, and Heydrich knows this better than anyone. Those who choose to work for the right side will survive and prosper. Those who don't, will join the Jews and others in the camps or the grave."

Hagen heard himself asking, "What happened to you in Brazil?"

"As I said last night, I found out the truth about my brother."

"Is Dieter working for Heydrich as well as for Canaris?"

"That is what I've been trying to tell you. Canaris still thinks Dieter is loyal to him. That is why he has asked him to meet with you, but that is also why Heydrich chose to ignore you at Horcher's. For now Dieter will be excused the sister who is an enemy of the Reich. Besides, I can be useful to them with you. You're still far too important to them, Richard. It would not be right to kill you yet, but always this must be the question in Heydrich's mind. How useful are you to him and when must he have you killed?"

"Has Dieter been able to hire any diamond cutters and polishers?"

"Not yet, but they have a Dutchman who knows the industry and they have been able to persuade him to help them. They are also looking to set up a central fabricating shop. This will take time, so Dieter has some others to assist him, but I don't know who they are."

A Dutchman . . . Klees. "When will your brother leave for the Congo?"

Her brother. Not Dieter anymore. "In another week."

Dieter had said there was someone else. A Belgian girl . . . Arlette. They'd kill her, too, if Richard wasn't careful. They'd try to get to her . . .

"What about the cables I send?"

"They know you must be gathering intelligence for the British, but they still do not have your code. At least, I do not think they have."

"Arlette, it's Hagen here. How are things?"

"Fine . . . they are fine, *mijnheer*. I . . . I am so glad you've called. The flawless Ds you requested for your trading account have come in, and I have given de Heer Dunkelsbuhler your thanks."

D for Duncan. She had sent the message over, but flawless Ds would only make the Scharführer Helmut Langer suspicious and the Gestapo would be listening in.

"Clear blue-white diamonds, Herr Scharführer. Gem diamonds of the highest grade."

"Mijnheer Hagen, is there someone with you?"

He told her not to worry, that it was only the chief of security at the Messerschmitt factory in Augsburg. "We need a few grinding wheels and some other things, Arlette. A rush order. If you'll take down a message for the shop, I'll do my very best not to go too fast."

When he rang off, Arlette felt lost and empty. She had wanted so much to tell him Lev's daughter and son-in-law had arrived safely in Antwerp, that the man he'd sent to the crypt had reached them in time and had driven them to a railway station outside of Berlin.

That night, after eleven, she went to the club of Cecile Verheyden and telephoned Inverlin Cottage. The butler said that Mrs. Winfield was not available but that he would take down the message. So many grinding wheels, so many glass cutters.

When decoded, it would read:

TO THE CARPENTER FROM ALICE

ESCAPE LINE DEAD REPEAT DEAD / NOTIFY DE BEERS SECURITY HUNTER DIETER KARL WILL ATTEMPT CONTACT SMUGGLERS MBUJI-MAYI AND TSHIKAPA REGIONS CONGO / HUNTER IN PAY OF ABWEHR AND SD REPEAT SD / HUNTER SAILING 3 DECEMBER NORTH GERMAN LLOYD STEAMER ILSBERG OUT OF BREMERHAVEN / ATTEMPTS BEING MADE RECRUIT SKILLED WORKMEN DIAMOND TRADE AMSTERDAM SUSPECT KLEES ADVISE ACCORDINGLY / PRODUCTION ME 109

FIGHTERS AUGSBURG PLANT 120 UNITS PER MONTH MESSER-
SCHMITT FACTORY BEING GIVEN PRIORITY OVER DORNIER AND
HEINKEL BOMBERS FOR DAIMLER-BENZ ENGINES / ENTRY TO
MAN DIESEL-ENGINE FACTORY REFUSED / ALICE

The night was cold and the streets were lonely. At first Arlette was
certain she was being followed, but then the steps faded away and she
was left alone.

Damas watched as the girl went up the stairs to find the key in her
purse and unlock the door. Light from the hall threw her silhouette at
him, she pausing tensely, uncertain still.

Then she closed the door, had words with her landlady probably, and
finally went up to her room to undress in the dark.

Berlin had urged the utmost caution. Something was not right. Krantz
hadn't been happy. Hagen had pulled a switch on them — Damas was
certain of this and smiled at the thought.

When she parted the curtains to look down at the street and search its
places of deeper darkness, Arlette found it empty.

Nine

T HE DUNES TO THE WEST of Ostend were white with snow, the sea was dark and where it met the land there was a broken rampart of ice. Arlette leaned her bicycle against a picket fence, then made her way through to the beach. Richard was in England again. He'd come back from Germany, had come down with malaria right away and had been ill for weeks.

"It's the strain of what he's doing," de Heer Wunsch had said and had shaken his head. "It can only end in disaster for him."

To think that the Nazis had arrested so many Jews and yet had let Lev's daughter and son-in-law go. To think that they still expected to be supplied with diamonds after such a thing or that Dillingham's and the others would continue to sell to them.

Richard had smiled sadly at this and had said, "Do you know where the tires come from that are on the Heinkel 111 bombers?"

Tires from England, French guns, armor plate and aluminum ingots, so much, so many things to sell the Germans.

Pulling up the collar of her coat, she began to walk along the shore. Something would have to be done. She couldn't risk staying in Belgium much longer. They'd have to work out some other system.

And Willi? she asked. Willi suspected the truth. Somehow she would have to tell him how it really was. He'd never understand, never believe her for a minute. She couldn't afford to take that chance in any case.

Since November, since Crystal Night, the Nazis' agents in Antwerp had left her alone. No one followed her anymore. She was certain of this. Nor did they watch the house or the office.

Yet it was strange to have them pay so much attention to her and then to suddenly stop. Richard had been troubled by this — upset, too. "I specifically asked Duncan to get you out, Arlette. I warned him of the danger. The man's name is Karl Christian Damas. He's a schoolmaster — tall, thin, about forty-two years of age and left-handed."

When the girl reached a dead herring gull, Otto Krantz watched as she stood there looking sadly down at it. What should he do with her? Take her now and break her, or give Hagen a little more rope as the Gruppenführer Heydrich had suggested?

The things she'd have to tell them.

Damas removed his glasses and cleaned the condensation from them. "Hagen could not possibly have found out who I was, Herr Krantz. I swear we've been far too careful for that."

"And if you haven't?" asked the Berliner sharply.

There was no answer, so Krantz said it for him. "If you have, my friend, you've jeopardized our chance to take the diamond stocks. Now put on your priest's collar and go have a talk with her. Let's see if she knows who you are. Ask her if she's been to confession."

The Berliner snorted harshly at his little joke; the Belgian waited stiffly for the outburst to pass. "And if she knows me?"

Krantz took a moment to study this schoolmaster who had been so useful to them. Unmarried, a bitter, lonely man — why no wife? he wondered. Dark thoughts about women, was that it? Being a Berlin detective had hardened him to everything. "Then I will leave her to you for a while, but you will not kill her until she and I have had a little talk. Now go."

The Belgian went along to the car, which they'd left in the lee of a farmer's shed. It being Sunday, and between church services, there was sporadic traffic. The road stretched away from them on either side to scattered farmsteads, distant church spires and a bleakness that reminded Krantz only too well of the Great War but was eminently suitable for their purposes.

The Huysmans girl was again gazing out to sea.

Dressed in a black overcoat, hat, scarf, suit, tie and shoes, Damas looked the part. The Belgian made his way down to the beach and waved a polite hello to the girl.

She smiled at him when they stood talking. No fear, only innocence in her eyes, the delight of unexpected companionship, the security of a priest.

Krantz gave a satisfied grunt and turned his back to search the surrounding terrain.

"Do you come here often?" asked the priest.

He had seen her from the road and had come to join her because she had looked so sad. "Ah no. I have a job in Antwerp and am just home for the day to see my fiancé and my parents."

Damas gave a solicitous nod. "Myself, I am here to visit an old friend and mentor, Father René Roosan in Middlekerke. Perhaps you know of him."

"Father René, but of course! Who doesn't? So he is an old friend of yours."

"It's such a small world."

They talked of the priest, who in his younger days had been a missionary in darkest Africa. "It must have been something, all those natives who couldn't speak a word of his language nor he of theirs."

Arlette thought of saying, I know someone who could, but left it unsaid. There was something odd about this priest. Something...

"Your fiancé, Juffrouw Huysmans, why is he not with you?"

"Oh, Willi... Willi is working on his sailboat."

"You've had a disagreement. My dear, it's not hard to tell. Come, come, let me know what's wrong. Perhaps I can offer a suggestion or two."

He was really being very kind, a little shy perhaps.

Anxiously Damas wondered why she hadn't answered. "Some little disagreement?" he asked, a reminder.

She gave a shy smile and then a shrug. "The usual, I think, Father. Willi likes to dance, and I was very tired when my train got in last night."

They picked their way around an open space where frozen kelp and rusty tin cans lay with bits of netting.

"It's a long ride. The trains are not as good as they used to be. It's all this talk of war," he said.

"Yes, I suppose it is."

"He'll be called up, won't he? If... if there's war? I know how you must feel. Tell me, when is the wedding? Perhaps Father René and I... You'll be asking him, won't you?"

She shook her head and found herself blushing under his scrutiny. His gaze seemed so intense. "I do not know Father René that well, only because others speak so highly of him."

The priest tossed a hand. "That is so. And the wedding? In the spring perhaps?"

"More likely the end of summer. Willi wants to get married right away. I... for myself, I want to be sure." What was it about him?

"A little time. Yes, that is wisest. But a pretty girl like you? If I were this Willi, I'd not leave you to walk alone on the beach. It's far too cold in any case. Brr! What would you say to a cup of coffee with a priest who at times is lonely, too?"

He'd wait to offer her a ride back to Antwerp. He'd give her all the time she needed.

When he saw the two of them approaching, Krantz stepped into the shed. The car started up, and he was left with a bicycle the girl had padlocked.

No sooner were they gone, but who should turn up to find the bicycle but the boy, the fiancé, the son of a butcher, whose van looked as if it needed new springs.

The boy put the bicycle in the back and drove after them.

All well and good, or had the boy seen him go into the shed and figured things weren't right?

The terrain was so flat the boy couldn't have hidden anywhere. Hectares of tall, frozen grass lay about the shed, the dunes in the distance low and tumbling down to the wide apron of the beach.

Only when a van of similar size came along the road from Ostend, did he notice that there was a slight bend behind which the boy could well have stopped.

He'd have had a clear view of the shed, the car, the dunes and the beach.

The three of them were having coffee in a seaside café when Krantz stepped down from the lift he had thumbed in a truck. They were sitting over by the windows, seen through a screen of people in their Sunday best. The Huysmans girl had removed her hat, coat and gloves; the boy had simply unbuttoned his leather jacket and had put his beret on the table beside him.

Damas played the benevolent host. Krantz had to credit the Belgian with a coolness that was impressive. "A coffee with sugar and cream," he said, not looking up at the waitress. "Make it two and a shot of brandy."

In fluent German, the waitress reminded him that he could buy all the booze he wanted in their shops, but he couldn't get a drop of the hard stuff in their cafés and bars. Too cold for beer, too early for a glass of wine. She suggested the layered cream cake and he grunted, "Of course."

Arlette Huysmans was even better looking than her photograph. She had about her, though, a wariness that troubled him. Perhaps it was simply the embarrassment of her and the boy's sitting down with a priest they didn't know. Perhaps it was the way the boy seemed jealous of the attention Damas paid to the girl.

When her hand closed over the boy's, Krantz saw her smile briefly and say something reassuring. In turn, the boy simply stared at her hand. Love? Was there love? A girl like that and a clod like him? Family ties? The hometown boy? It didn't make any sense when the boy was stacked up against Hagen.

Arlette felt the trembling in Willi's fingers. "Willi, please don't be angry with me. I know I was to take the eight o'clock train tonight, but if I can get a lift with Father Lannay, it would save us the money, isn't that right? I will help with the gas, Father. Please, it wouldn't be right of me otherwise."

Damas held up a protesting hand and shook his head. "You must allow me. The pleasure of your company will be sufficient."

The boy was insanely jealous of every spare moment the girl had, while she was trying to be so much more mature about things.

"You said we'd have supper with your parents, remember?"

"Ah, so I did." Arlette gave the priest a rueful look.

Damas said, "A few hours won't make much difference. Perhaps I could stay here a little longer."

He gave her the look of someone wanting to be invited.

It was the boy who said, "Arlette, why can't you take the early-morning train? We could go to the concert then. I've got two tickets I'll just have to give away."

"The 4:00 a.m. train? It is so early. Ah . . ." She grinned and squeezed his hand, then nudged Willi's shoulder playfully. "Of course I could. Do you mind, Father Lannay? He is so lonely without me, this one. I must tell myself to be more kind."

They didn't see much of each other. A six-day work week left little time.

Damas acknowledged defeat with a smile. He took off his glasses to clean them. The boy was too intense, the girl — what could he say about her?

Trapped perhaps, or relieved? "Another time then. No, please, stay and have some more coffee. I'll settle the bill on my way out."

They both got up to politely shake hands with him, the girl all smiles now, the boy glad that he was buggering off.

Krantz waited a good half hour. In all that time the two of them sat there, not saying much, not looking around but only at each other now and then. That they were self-conscious with each other was evident. That they quarreled — was it a quarrel? he wondered — seemed possible.

The boy urged the Huysmans girl to do something. She twisted and untwisted the engagement ring on her finger and ran her thumb over it, as a girl in trouble would.

Krantz reached for his hat and left the café. Damas had driven out of sight up the nearest side street.

When he found the Belgian, the Berliner got into the car. "Well, what did you make of it?"

Damas didn't smile. "It's so very hard to tell if she knew me."

"And the boy?"

"A typical butcher's son. Jealous as hell and resenting my little intrusion into their affairs."

"Then what's the problem?"

"They may have played a little game with me. First dinner at her parents and then a concert and the early-morning train for her. I'm wondering if there is such a concert in Ostend this evening."

"We'll check."

"And the girl?" asked the Belgian.

Had the nearness of her excited the schoolmaster? "For now we leave it. If there is a concert, we'll have a look for them. If not . . . "

They drove out of town along the coast road toward Ostend. Arlette watched them until their car had disappeared from view and she was left alone with Willi.

"Arlette, what the hell's going on? I thought you were coming to see the *Vega*. I had everything ready for us. The coffee, some gingerbread cookies, a surprise. Instead of this, you go to the beach of all places, to where that bastard Hagen first came to see you."

"Willi, don't. I didn't mean to hurt you."

"That priest didn't blink, Arlette. People always do when they take off their glasses."

"Yes, I know. I noticed that, too."

"He had a friend."

What could she say? "Willi, let's go home. Let's go and see the *Vega*."

"You're still in love with Hagen. Those guys are mixed up with him. You bitch, Arlette. You let me think we were engaged. You . . . "

She walked away, and when she reached the van, climbed in and sat there waiting for him.

"Willi, don't hate me. I couldn't do anything else."

He smashed a fist against the door; he very nearly broke the window. He grabbed her by the hand and she fought with him until he bent her fingers back and she had to let him wrench the ring away.

Then he threw it at her and tried to push her out of the van. Arlette shrieked and ducked her head, shoved against him and braced her feet. "Willi, no! Please, you *don't* understand. They may be waiting down the road to see what we do."

De Menten sucked in a breath and flicked a stinging blow at her cheek.

She didn't duck. "Do that again. Be just like them!"

They were both crying. Fog misted the windows. Willi clenched the steering wheel and bowed his head. "I loved you. I really did! I thought we'd be happy. I was saving all my money. I had a good job. Arni was going to sell me a half interest in the garage. I . . . "

Like a stone Arlette sat there. "If you love me, then help me. Those two are working for the Nazis. Richard Hagen is spying for the British, and I've been helping him."

"You're crazy. Do you know that? Those guys'll kill you."

"And you, Willi, if you ever say a thing about this. Believe me, I'm telling you for your own good as well as for myself and Richard. It would be best for us to remain engaged, but for now I must leave that decision to you."

The ring Lev had made for them lay between her shoes. The diamond was a soft rose color, and when she handed it to Willi, all he could say was "Why? Why did this have to happen to us?"

"Why to anyone?"

The Kentish wold lay in the grip of winter. Depressed by the news coming out of Europe, Churchill scowled at the land he loved.

Down from him the road ran through scattered woodlands to rolling hills and valleys. From the nearest woods came the sound of dogs.

"Richard, what is your considered estimate of the diamond stocks the Nazis now hold?"

"Sufficient for a year and a half — more perhaps of the crushing boart and the lower grades of tool diamonds, less of the higher-quality stones."

"Is it so much?"

Hagen said that it was. "Without the Antwerp stocks, should they have them?" demanded Churchill.

"Without them, sir."

"Damn it! We could cripple their industry if we could stop the flow of diamonds. Why can't you people stop selling to them?"

"If it were left to me..."

Churchill tossed an apologetic hand. "Of course you'd cut them off, but will the Belgians keep selling to them if there's war over Poland? Britain will have to act then. She'll not be able to back out of that."

In spite of the heightened international tensions, King Leopold and his government steadfastly adhered to their policy of neutrality, as did the Dutch. "Convince the British government to act now, Mr. Churchill. Let the traders bring their diamonds to London without Leopold's sanction."

"And the skilled personnel the Nazis will need?"

"Don't let them be captured."

"Tell me about the Congo. If there's war, will Ernest keep those mines running?"

"It's not his decision, Mr. Churchill. It's La Forminière's and the Belgian government's."

"Yes...yes, but will the Congo mines remain open?"

"With the rapidly expanding use of boart and tungsten carbide, definitely. The States will have to be supplied, so, too, Britain and France, and anyone else engaged in heavy industry."

"There'll be a naval blockade, an embargo. We'll not let them through to the Reich. We'll *throttle* their industry! We'll cut them off from the diamonds just as we did in the Great War."

Churchill's anger obviously stemmed from being ineffectual at a time of continued crisis.

"Richard, I greatly fear that in a few short months I shall be asked back into the cabinet as First Lord of the Admiralty. Should this be the case, I will personally see that the diamonds are escorted to safety."

"And the Congo, Mr. Churchill? The blockade?"

Ruefully Churchill admitted they had a problem. "Blockades can never be what we want them to be. Pray tell me, will your friend not find a way around us?"

"Dieter's clever and determined. I think also he's been told he must succeed."

Churchill fixed him with a piercing look. "And are there people at those mines who could arrange things, given the right incentives — assuming, of course, we have plucked the Antwerp stocks from the clutches of the Nazis?"

Hagen knew he was referring to the corruptibility of certain Belgians, and to men like Damas.

"Richard, we need to know. God willing we shall save the Antwerp diamond stocks, but if your friend should arrange alternate sources..."

"Sir Ernest wouldn't sanction such a thing any more than would the management of La Forminière. Besides, their security's far too tight."

It had been spoken like a loyal company man, but had there been a touch of naiveté? "Then we shall hope that is the case. You've been a bloody fool. You know that, don't you? Heydrich's read your mind and character to a tee. Saving the Tannenbaums can only lead to trouble for us!"

"I thought they'd killed them."

"Precisely! You let Heydrich fool you completely! You've made him pay a pittance. He's got you right where he wants. He *knows*, Richard. Damn it, man, use your head. Cut your ties with Irmgard Hunter and this... this friend of hers Heydrich has had thrown into Ravensbrück. Do so publicly. The Hunter woman is far too great a threat to you."

"She's also helped us, as has Dee Dee."

"Don't try to save them, Richard. That's what Heydrich wants."

"And Arlette? Can't you insist Duncan bring her over?"

"She's too essential. Mislead the Nazis for as long as you can. Never fear but that we shall be forever in your debt and that when the right time comes, we shall pluck the girl from their clutches."

Churchill crammed his gloved hands into the pockets of his overcoat. "The Scheldt, Richard. Fifty miles of estuary lie between Antwerp and the sea. If we should manage to get the diamonds on board that freighter, she'll be as naked as a dockside harlot under the loading lights. Pray tell me, are there any plans to arm her? A token perhaps, just to fool the Nazi agents?"

"None that I know of."

"Then we must see that a company of Royal Marines is dispatched to seize the ship while she's still in Antwerp."

Hagen laid the safety deposit box on the cubicle's counter and opened it. Two pouches held the gleanings of several months. He added a third, then on impulse, opened them all and emptied their contents into the box.

Spread loosely, Klees had a small fortune's worth of stones. Heydrich had to be aware of what had been going on.

There was nothing like the blue diamond, nothing even approaching its quality. He was glad of the loss, glad Heydrich had let Lev's daughter and son-in-law leave the Reich, but why had he done it?

And what were Duncan and he going to do about the Dutchman?

Idly he trailed a finger through the glitter. Most of the stones were of far less than a quarter of a carat. He could picture Klees prying them out of their mountings, surrounded by his warren of junk and his wall of broken dolls.

The Dutchman would know enough diamond cutters and polishers in Amsterdam to get the Germans started. Once Dieter got back from the Congo, they'd have them in place.

Out on the street, the pigeons were busy.

Everywhere in London there were signs of a coming war: a magnified grimness among the people, Anderson shelters in the tiny back gardens, larger shelters in Hyde Park, a line of toddlers practicing the art of walking in their gas masks. Antiaircraft batteries springing up all over the city. Hurricanes and Spitfires flying overhead, but still far too few of them.

When it came, the carnage would be terrible.

Duncan was waiting for him at the Red Lion in St. James's. Right away Hagen broached the subject of getting Arlette out before it was too late.

McPherson gripped his pint. Would it be the last time they'd see each other? "The girl's no longer being followed. Dillingham's is definitely not being watched. Our sources —"

"Your sources won't be good enough, Duncan. Damas is far too sharp, and if not him, then Otto Krantz."

"Richard, I wish it weren't this way. We'll do everything we can — you have my word on it. I've assigned Collin Forbes to see that she gets out when the time comes. He's been on to Damas and the others. Collin's good, one of the best."

"But he'll be working alone?"

McPherson knew he couldn't tell Richard that the British Secret Service had been having trouble with its people in the Hague, that there'd been a scandalous misappropriation of funds there and that none of the bastards could be trusted until cleared.

"Collin's not known to the Nazis. Until the past few weeks he's been in the Far East."

"From one fire to another, is that it?" Hagen had the sinking feeling it wasn't going to work.

"The Abwehr might know of him but the Sicherheitsdienst won't. Besides, Collin has an aunt who lives in Bruges. It's ideal cover. He's been staying with her, having a bit of a rest."

"And how will Arlette know him? How will she even know he's not one of Heydrich's people?"

McPherson let his gaze pass over his friend. Everything in him wanted to stop this business, but he knew he couldn't. "Collin will use 'the Carpenter' as his code word."

It was a bitch of a night. Bernard Wunsch struck a match and tried to light the pipe his doctor had told him would be better than so many cigarettes. The tobacco had been tamped down too hard! He wasn't drawing on the damned thing well enough.

In anger, he slammed the thing down and broke the stem quite by accident. Martine had bought him the pipe! "My dear, I'm sorry. It's Richard. He can't possibly cross the channel in this. Croydon airfield will be socked in, and if not there, then here."

That good and ample woman set her knitting aside. "Oh, do try to relax. You know your ulcers will only act up."

"I can't! That renegade Dutchman, Klees, has had the effrontery to call the office and demand to see Richard. Have you any idea what this means? De Heer Klees will discredit Richard, and all his work will have been for nothing."

"Bernard, Bernard, I really don't know what I'm going to do with you. Is it the hospital you want at such a time? Have some sense and try to calm down. Here, I will make us some tea."

"Tea! I want coffee...My dear, forgive me. Richard has been to London. The Committee...we're all anxious to hear what he has to say."

She clucked her tongue. "Perhaps if you'd talk to me about things. Be more open with me, Bernard."

"The matter is far too secret."

"Then I will make the tea."

Wunsch followed her into the kitchen and ran an apologetic hand over her shoulders. They'd had no children since the death of their daughter at the age of three. In all those years there'd been just the two of them. "It's this continued stubbornness of the king, my dear. Neutrality can only make the British suspicious of us. Hence they still refuse to give us the written guarantees, and without those the Committee's hands are tied."

"Won't King Leopold talk to de Heer Lietermann?"

Irritably Wunsch finished his cigarette and shook his head. "He adamantly refuses to meet with us. It's as if our desire to save the diamonds is unpatriotic! He's afraid the Germans will see such a move as weakness of resolve on his part."

"Then there is no hope?"

He shrugged. What else could he do? "Richard may have news. I only hope he hasn't tried to cross the channel in this weather."

They settled down by the fire. Wunsch tried to fit the pipe together. It might be possible to glue it. She offered him the cigarettes and he took another immediately and lit up. "Ah, that's better! We may not have that long to live in any case."

She told him not to talk like that. He fussed about the Dutchman. He said, "Richard should never have seen him in the first place."

At 11:00 p.m. they listened to the news. Poland still refused to grant the Nazis transit rights across the corridor. The German Foreign Minister, von Ribbentrop, swore that Germany would never come to an understanding with the Bolsheviks of Russia.

In the South China Sea the Japanese had taken some island of strategic importance. Italy had eyes on the Suez Canal, so the British and French navies had begun maneuvers in the Mediterranean as a show of force and solidarity. Albania was very much on Il Duce's mind. The premier of Hungary had been forced to resign because of his Jewish ancestry.

Finally, in a Reichstag speech, Hitler shrieked that the frontiers of what remained of Czechoslovakia could no longer be guaranteed because of internal strife within that country.

Wunsch snorted. "Martine, it's as though the Czech problem is over. They've relegated it to the end of the news instead of the beginning!"

He switched off the wireless and sat there brooding. He'd have to tell her something. "Because of the work Richard does ..."

"Because of the spying."

"Yes, damn it! God help us if the Germans should ever be in a position to ask you that.

"My dear, forgive me. Because of his work, I suspect that Richard has had to enter into a sort of business arrangement with de Heer Klees. Now this Dutchman is claiming that he must see Richard on a matter of great urgency. Arlette, she has taken the telephone call, as I was out of the office at the time. She says that Klees sounded very agitated and afraid for his life. He wouldn't tell her what the matter was. She couldn't tell him that our lines could well have been tapped."

What was the world coming to?

He took a sip of tea and grimaced. "This Dutchman must want to get out of Armsterdam before it's too late. The Nazis may also have put the squeeze on him. So, a panic call to Richard, a little blackmail perhaps. Who knows? I have the feeling he will want residence papers for England, and for that the British will have to excuse his criminal record."

He waited a moment, then said, "So you see how anxious I am about Richard."

The knitting was taken up and concentrated on to the point of irritability. She stopped suddenly, had to ask it of him now because there was more to this. "Is Richard still in love with Arlette?"

Those sad brown eyes met hers. "My dear, it is a love affair that must go on in secret but cannot be hidden forever."

The dress was of silk, a rich brown paisley with such a sheen. It had a broad and floppy collar, a neckline that plunged a little but not too much. Buttons down the front, a fullness to the skirt that was divine.

Arlette ran a smoothing hand down the front, turned sideways to look at herself in Cecile's mirror, then went through to the sitting room.

"Well?" she asked.

Hagen grinned up at her from his chair. Cecile exclaimed, "My God, he's speechless! To think you could choose such a thing, Richard. Arlette, it matches the color of your eyes."

Arlette stood primly before him. He reached out to take her by the hand. Neither said a thing. They just looked at each other, Richard pleased, Arlette delighted, her legs touching his knees . . .

Cecile couldn't keep the brittleness from her voice. The sight of them together like that still made her jealous! "I'll leave you two, I think." She went downstairs to the club, only to find an agitated Bernard Wunsch waiting for her in the kitchens.

"My God, it's a night for travellers. Let me get us a bottle and two glasses, *mijnheer*. We will drink to their health and continued happiness, and we will have us a little talk."

Arlette felt Richard's arms slide around her. The dress was so soft. He drew her against him and she laid a trembling hand on the back of his neck.

When she found his lips, they kissed each other longingly. That quickness came to them both, that nervousness. Her hair spilled forward as she drew away a little. "I want you," she whispered. "Richard, I have to have you in me."

Hagen cradled her in his lap and they kissed again, each time a little longer, each time a little more urgently.

Then Cecile came back, and with her was Bernard.

Across the canal the Dutchman's shop was in darkness, but a single light had been left on in his second-floor apartment as agreed.

Hagen anxiously glanced at his watch. The meeting had been arranged for as close to 3:00 a.m. as possible. The Dutchman had been afraid.

There was no one about, not even a drunk.

Arlette had pleaded with him not to go; Bernard had insisted that he must for all their sakes.

Satisfied that he hadn't been followed, he stepped out from the doorway and went quickly along to the nearest bridge. Again he waited, hidden from view. Again the street remained empty.

The Dutchman's houseboat was still moored to the quay- side.

The door to the shop opened and he stepped quickly inside and closed it behind him. At once the clutter, the mildew, that stuffy, musty feel and smell of things old and discarded came to him.

Cupping a hand over the beam of his flashlight, he swung it up past the knives and rings to a tuba whose brass gleamed dully. The counter was there, the shelves behind it holding clocks, clocks and more of them. He didn't call out to the Dutchman. Cautiously he made his way over to the counter.

With a forefinger, he eased open the drawer and found the pistol but didn't take it out. So far so good.

Behind the shop there was less need for caution from the street. The flashlight swept over a nail keg full of rusty swords and pikes. It passed china piled high on sideboards, tables and bureaus; porcelains; a stoneware jug and basin.

It settled on the brick wall with its broken dolls.

He switched off the light and stood there in the darkness. Everything in him said to leave.

When the beam of the light found a child of ten or twelve, she was lying on the floor naked. Her pale little seat was rucked up, her thin arms were clasped beneath her. Blood had pooled on the floor where her throat had been cut. The blue eyes were glazed, the silky blond hair in disarray. Things had fallen over everywhere about her — chairs, a table, the shattered remains of a demijohn. She'd run from Klees, had tried to escape, tried to hide, and he'd . . .

Hagen's stomach heaved. Suddenly he found himself moving swiftly away from her. More things began to fall — a copper washtub, a stoneware crock, the curtain that had been across the entrance to the Dutchman's office . . .

Cut gem diamonds and their mountings were scattered on the floor. The door to the safe was wide open. Klees was slumped against the far wall, gray slabs of flesh hanging from him in rolls to fall to the hairy pubis and flaccid penis that drooped between his chubby legs.

They'd shot him. A trickle of blood had congealed on his forehead. The pale gray eyes were unfeeling.

Blinking, Hagen switched off the torch and tried to think, tried to figure out what to do. *Heydrich!* It had to have been done on his orders, but why? To pin the murder on him? To rock the Antwerp diamond world with the scandal? Child Murdered. American Spy Helps Dutch Sex Killer. What to do? What the hell to do?

The Belgian government would be in an uproar, the British government all the more suspicious of them, Germany the only safe haven for him. A diamond trader on the run.

"Well, Richard, it looks as if you've got a problem on your hands."

Hagen swung around and shone the light into Krantz's face.

"Please." The Berliner winced. "It's too bright for my eyes. A little agreement, Richard, that's all Herr Heydrich wants. No more lies. Save yourself a lot of trouble, and we'll tidy this up for you. No questions, not one word. Just that Herr Klees has gone for a little trip in his houseboat and the sea . . ." He gave a shrug. "Who can trust such a thing in this weather?"

"What did he do? Refuse to work for you?"

"Let's just say he wanted out, and we saved you the trouble of trying to get him a visa."

"And the child? Did you bastards have to kill her?"

"*Bastards*, Richard? Please. The honey pot got broken. He couldn't let her scream."

"I'll never work for you people."

"Then tidy this up yourself and see what happens, but remember, my young friend, that the Dutch have stamped your passport at entry and Herr Klees has left us a record of your dealings with him."

The Berliner walked away into the darkness and the clutter. Hagen shone the light after him, shadows on the walls and ceiling, a nest of Roman lances, the image of a bass violin, a stack of plates, a pair of skis, a wall of broken dolls.

The Villa Laumannfeld was on the Prinzregentenstrasse in Munich's center near the park. Stark and alone amid neglected grounds, it brooded in the rain and snow.

Irmgard swung the Daimler in at the drive, and they came to a stop before the Moorish gates of the iron fence that surrounded the estate.

Winged statues of naked nymphs and warlike gods lined the eaves.

There'd been the parties, the gala balls in 1934, 1935 and 1936, Dee Dee and Irmgard in stunning dresses . . . so long ago it seemed. Dieter and he in tuxedos and black ties.

"Irmgard, what did they do to you?"

She had said so little, didn't look well at all. The flight had been over an hour late. As the plane had touched down at Oberwiesenfeld, he'd seen her standing beside the car.

They'd driven past Landsberg Prison, past Gestapo Headquarters on the Briennerstrasse, and come straight here.

"Irmgard . . ."

"It doesn't matter."

"But it does."

She couldn't look at him. She got out of the car to open the gate. Shards of glass littered the barren patches among the rapidly vanishing snow. As she hurried ahead of him, the glass ground beneath her shoes. It seemed everywhere, yet the windows had all been replaced.

Hagen caught up with her. "What's happened to the family?"

That was just like Richard! "Dachau, Ravensbrück and the grave. What did you think? One doesn't talk about such things. The villa simply became 'available,' that's all. Would you rather someone had put a torch to it?"

"No, of course not."

"Then for Christ's sake, shut up!"

Built at the turn of the century by a master of the classical and art nouveau, the place had been a Munich landmark until Crystal Night.

Beyond the grinning jaws of a bronze Medusa letter box, the entrance foyer was huge, of black, white and gold marble. A mosaic of tiny white tiles covered the floor. In black, an uncoiled cobra appeared as if moving across the center of the foyer.

In one wall niche there was a glossy black copy of a Florentine male nude. Against the opposite wall, a superb female nude in black dared her chosen lover to cross the floor between them.

Stripped of its paintings — gutted by Goering's thugs — there still remained the many frescoes and bas-reliefs, the sumptuously decadent scenes of Pompeian brothels on some of the ceilings.

Far from the range of most bombers, Dieter Karl would use the villa as a center for the cutting and polishing of industrial diamonds. They'd build a factory in the suburbs for making the grinding wheels and cutting tools.

At a turning, Irmgard went ahead of him to unlock a room that was octagonal and lined with steel cabinets whose drawers were flat and so like those he knew.

On the dome of the ceiling the azure-blue dust of the heavens held a golden tracery of stars. On the walls were ghostlike scenes of Eden in soft pastel. Tall windows faced northward, giving reasonable viewing light. On the benches beside the nests of stainless-steel sorting screens, were two white canvas sacks.

From the throat of one of them came a cascade of diamond rough. Some Congo cubes, a lot of carbonado, stones from Brazil and Venezuela, glassies from South and South-West Africa. A hodgepodge gleaned from several forays to the digs and buying wherever they could.

Yanking open the other sack, he spilled a stream of cut gem diamonds onto the bench. All of them were small and of little value, a point or two. Salvaged from the jewelry of "emigrating" Jews and other refugees.

Not stopping, he went to the cabinets and began to open the drawers at random. Most were empty, others held a little more. They had no ready source of diamonds as yet. They were desperate.

In a basement that had once held thousands of bottles of wine, there were now the settling tanks full of olive oil to separate the ground boart into its various grades of diamond powders.

"Dieter will never do it, Irmgard."

"Not without your help."

They were waiting for him in the sun room at the Villa Hunter. Long before he reached them Hagen heard the baby. She made noises over everything, played with the spoons and tried to grab Dee Dee's teacup.

"Richard, it's good to see you."

She searched his face for answers but gave no explanation. "Erika's beautiful, Dee Dee. How've you been?"

It seemed so stupid to ask such a thing. The child played strange. Hagen took hold of Dee Dee's outstretched hand. Was it all to be so awkward and formal?

Richard was everything she had remembered, only there were changes. He had grown a little older, had been hurt by things, not just by the news of them. She could see this in his eyes, in the way he no longer smiled so easily. "We have lived — survived. Let's not talk about it. Please, for me this is . . . what can I say? Such a relief."

"You're not going back!" This had come from Irmgard. "She's staying here with us, isn't she, Richard?"

He took the baby from her. Erika tugged at his ear. Suddenly he felt the warmth of the child's lips on his cheek, the silkiness of her ash-blond curls. He kissed her forehead, held her high above him and chuckled. She was just a child, a person all her own.

Heydrich's child. The bastard had raped Dee Dee repeatedly. When she could no longer hide the fact she was pregnant, he had become enraged, had had her thrown into Ravensbrück and her property stolen.

Afraid for her life, she'd had the child there and Heydrich had made her keep it.

Not a word as to who the father was, not even to Irmgard.

"She will come to love you quickly, Richard. Even the worst of the SS guards are a little afraid of her magic. We're special, did you know this? We have a small hut to ourselves — just a room, a bed, two chairs and a stove. That is so rare a privilege the others who line up every day think I'm the commandant's whore and don't speak to me for fear I will betray them."

From not wanting to talk about it, she couldn't help but tell him.

Irmgard tried to reassure her. "Heydrich's said you'll be allowed to stay here with me for the summer. Richard's free to come and see us whenever he can."

Hagen sat down at the table and bounced the child gently on his knee. Her little feet and hands were perfect. She seemed at home with him already.

When he tried to say something, Dee Dee reached across the table and put a finger against his lips. "You're so kind and good, Richard. In a world where kindness has all but left us, you and Irmgard are the only ones who care."

"Don't give up hope. Day and night you're both on my mind."

"On your conscience."

"Yes."

"Then don't let us interfere with what you have to do."

Irmgard hit the table and shouted at her. "I told you not to say that!"

Dee Dee had a depth of serenity that surprised him. "Irmgard, I'll say what has to be said."

Tears rushed into Irmgard's eyes. "And I'll be forced to repeat it, damn you! Don't you understand they'll make me tell them everything?" She went to pieces before their eyes, felt so ashamed for the things she'd had to say.

"The bathtub," she said cruelly, her voice climbing. "Again and again, Richard. Naked in their hands. Naked! Them tearing at the roots of my hair and shoving me under. *Under*, Richard! Gagging. Crying out. Gasping for air. I need air. Air! Dear God . . . air. I had to fill my lungs. I had to.

"I vomited underwater. I gagged. I sucked in another breath and another. I had to. So many times. So helpless. Don't you see, my darling, I had to tell them everything?"

Her head was bowed. Exhausted, she stood before them, he and Dee Dee so stunned by what had just happened, they couldn't seem to move.

At last Hagen took her gently in his arms. He kissed her cheek; he tried to wipe the tears away. There were no words to say what he felt, yet he had to tell her he understood. "Let's just try to be ourselves and spend what time we have together."

Gestapo Headquarters in Munich was in a somber brownstone building.

Garages out the back held the limousines and Black Marias. The cellars held the detention cells.

Hagen went up the front steps between black-uniformed SS sentries and in under the ever-present flags. The duty sergeant examined his briefcase. More guards stood at attention just inside the doors and at the entrances to each of the halls.

Emptying his pockets, Hagen hid the fear and outrage he felt. "I'm a man of few possessions, Herr Scharführer. Murdering the Gruppenführer Heydrich would be the farthest thing from my mind."

There was no humor in the sergeant. With a curt nod, the visit was cleared.

The marble halls were the loneliest he'd ever walked. A hive of activity, telephones rang; typewriters hammered; secretaries, both male and female, went to and fro with telexes, documents, photographs and maps.

Would it do any good to try to memorize the layout of the halls, the positions of all the guards? Could he kidnap Heydrich and free Irmgard and Dee Dee that way? It was a futile thought.

Heydrich wasn't in his office on the second floor. He was shown in anyway and left to sit in one of the leather armchairs within sight of the adjutant in an adjoining room.

The office was a mirror of the one Heydrich had in Berlin. All the Nazi leaders had these exact duplicates. Should Berlin ever be threatened, they could move here at a moment's notice and still govern the country.

The antique desk was spacious and fastidiously tidy. There were photographs of Frau Heydrich and their children. Maps on the walls concentrated on both the west and the east. So many pins and tiny swastika flags, so many notations.

There were batteries of gray filing cabinets and card indexes. Heydrich was rumored to keep tabs on the more than one hundred thousand leaders of the Nazi hierarchy. There'd be files on those who were collaborating with them in other countries, dossiers on those who'd resist.

The men who'd followed Arlette. Her "priest," Karl Christian Damas.

Heydrich's black leather trench coat with its swastika armband hung in a corner with his cap, holster and pistol. There'd be spare uniforms, spare jackboots. Heydrich and he were of about the same height. Would it be possible to . . .

"Richard, my apologies. Things are so busy these days."

Heydrich didn't bother with the Heil Hitler or even with a handshake. He moved in swiftly and sat down behind the desk.

Then he sat there building church spires with his fingertips and studying Hagen.

The fingertips impatiently tapped together. Should he confront Hagen with everything or simply ask, "Have we an understanding, I wonder?"

The salesman's gaze gave nothing away.

"I think so, Herr Gruppenführer."

"Good. So, first, the new diamond center. Dieter Karl has left lists of the equipment that is needed. My adjutant will provide you with copies and you will go over them. Add what is missing, delete what is unnecessary. Suggest the best available suppliers."

He nodded. They'd get to things soon enough. "Anything else?"

Heydrich brushed the tips of three fingers over the front of his hair. "I'm glad you asked, but please forgive me if I haven't much time. The Polish question is very much on our minds."

"Will there be war?"

Startled by the effrontery, Heydrich paused. Had Hagen thought to anger him? "That depends entirely on the Poles, but the question does not concern you and me."

"With all due respect, Herr Heydrich, we both know it does. If Germany declares war on Poland, the traders in Antwerp will transfer their stocks."

"Unless Belgian neutrality interferes."

"Even if it does. They're not fools, Herr Gruppenführer. Sure, it looks as if they're wringing their hands in despair and unable to decide, but stop for a moment. The threat you people pose is breaking up what it took five hundred years to build. Some of the traders have already gone to Israel to start up a center there, others to Buenos Aires and still others to New York."

"They are fleeing like rats."

Hagen shook his head. "They are realists. They'll ship those diamonds even if they don't receive the written guarantees they want. They'll gamble, Herr Heydrich, because you'll have forced them to do so."

"Then let us agree that you work to our benefit and that you remember Herr Klees. We've a man in Antwerp we want you to contact. You'll work through him when not in the Reich."

Hagen couldn't believe they'd let him leave the country. There had to be something — Arlette? he wondered. Arlette . . . "That might be hard for me, Herr Gruppenführer. As it is, the Committee aren't all that happy with my being so involved."

Heydrich brushed this aside. "He'll be discreet. Now first, Dieter Karl has another request. Through our sources he has compiled lists of suitable tradesmen in the diamond industries of both Antwerp and

Amsterdam. You will go over the lists and circle those you feel are absolutely essential to our needs."

Lev's name would be on one of the lists... "I'll do my best, but you mustn't think it possible for me to know them all."

Again the matter was brushed aside. "There are those in the sintering factories of the Diamant Boart that we will need. Dillingham's can provide others. You will find out, Richard."

Heydrich swung his chair away from the desk to cross his legs and stare across the room. Quickly he came to a decision. "Richard, the admiral and I have reached an agreement about you. From now on you will be considered an agent of the Sicherheitsdienst. We'll provide you with the necessary documents but will keep them on file here — signed, of course, by yourself in case you should ever think of trying to double-cross us again. There will be no more need for these little *Treffs*, these little games you've been playing with Canaris."

Heydrich asked about the railway cars. "Are they really the means by which the diamonds will be shipped? Doesn't the Jew Isaac Hond plan to use trucks, Richard? The trucks of the Mercantile Company?"

So that was what Bernard had been hiding all this time. "I didn't know of them. You can see how well you've managed to discredit me in their eyes."

The salesman's look of dismay was genuine. "Now that you know, you will find out for us all the details. Trucks will be so much easier for us to intercept."

Had they a team of ten, twenty or thirty men in place already? "If I can, I will, but it may not be so easy."

"Your director, Herr Wunsch, knows all about the plan."

Heydrich made no mention of Hagen's having gathered intelligence for the British, none whatsoever of alternate sources or of Dieter's efforts in the Congo.

It was only as Hagen got up to leave that the *Gruppenführer* asked him which factories he'd be visiting this time.

"None, I'm afraid. Herr Krantz left me no time to prepare. But since I'm so close, maybe I should take a run down to the quarries near Landeck. Last fall they were having a problem with the grinding wheels they use to sharpen the new tungsten carbide drill bits. They also use our saw blades for trimming the rock."

Hagen had made his first move under the new order. And so soon? "The Fräulein Hunter can drive you. Stay over in Innsbruck — a little holiday, Richard. Please, I insist."

There'd been no mention of Dee Dee and Erika, none at all of Arlette.

The adjutant had him sign the papers, then swore him in as a member of the SS. They even took his photograph downstairs in the basement.

Out on the street a light snow was falling, the last perhaps before the world would descend into war.

"Richard, don't try to do anything foolish. Just get the hell out of Germany and don't come back."

"Dee Dee —"

"Look, I'm not expecting anything for myself."

"But Erika..."

Dee Dee pulled off a glove and felt the snow, the leaves of the boxwood hedge, such simple things. She ran her eyes over the gardens at the Villa Hunter. Erika was sitting with Irmgard at the edge of one of the fish ponds. Irmgard was telling her about what big fish there'd be come summer.

"Erika, yes. If you could get them to let you take her to Belgium, I'd give her to you, Richard. I'd be so happy. It's not her fault what happened. I've had to tell myself that so many times, and I've come to love her all the more."

Hagen reached for her. "Trust me, will you? I need a bit of time."

"He'll kill us and then he'll kill you."

"Maybe, but for now not a word."

She turned quickly away, couldn't look at him. "What makes you think they won't make me tell them what you've just said?"

He laid a comforting hand on her shoulder, was surprised at how thin she was. "It's a chance I'll just have to take, Dee Dee. You're both my friends. I can't leave you to face this alone."

She flung her arms about his neck and kissed his cheek, burst suddenly into tears and whispered, "The Hunter factories have been asked to supply the SS with 150 Polish uniforms."

It could only mean that Heydrich planned a little diversion, an "intrusion of German territory." An excuse, then, to start the war.

In the afternoon a note came from Heydrich. It was dated April 7, 1939, and bore the official stamp of the SS.

Richard, we have seen the Belgian lists of strategic materials they will not supply to any of the belligerents in time of war. Diamonds are not included, nor are the tools you people make. In spite of this, we will still proceed as if cut off from all supplies. Heil Hitler.

"Arlette, it's Hagen. Can you hear me okay?"

"Just. Could you talk a little louder, please?"

"That better?" he asked, almost shouting.

"Yes ... Yes. De Heer Wunsch, he is on the other line, Mijnheer Hagen. I will take down the order, if you like. Then you can speak with him."

"Richard, it's Bernard here. How are things?"

"Bernard, good of you to come on the line. I want to take a few days to go down to the Freisen und Milhausen quarry near Landeck."

"Those blasted experimental drill bits. Their breaking has *nothing* to do with us!"

Good for Bernard. "And the saw blades."

"It's always the case with granite. Obstacles get in the road of progress."

Wunsch covered the receiver and nodded grimly to Lev, who'd been having a worried cup of coffee with him.

"No real problems yet, Bernard. If there are, I'll let you know."

"What, no obstacles?" Ruefully he looked at Lev and shrugged.

Richard tried to ease his mind. They talked, then Wunsch listened in as he gave Arlette the message.

Unknown to them, it read:

TO THE CARPENTER FROM ALICE

RED ALERT / 150 POLISH UNIFORMS ORDERED SS HUNTER FACTORIES MUNICH / MOST URGENT YOU ORGANIZE TRANSFER ANTWERP DIAMOND STOCKS MEGADAN NOTIFY DE BEERS / COURIER HUYSMANS ARLETTE ENGLAND IMMEDIATELY / DIAMONDS NOT INCLUDED BELGIAN LISTS STRATEGIC MATERIALS / ALICE

The mountains were all around them, breathtaking under snow and ice. From Innsbruck the road ran west to Landeck.

Hagen then turned southward. The snow was soon piled high beside the road as the car climbed into the wooded heights.

At a bend, a recent avalanche had cleared a swath down the mountainside, and they could see the gorge and valley below them. Irmgard got out of the car to take in a deep breath and stand with her back to him. "It's almost like the time we had before things went to hell."

"Why not wait here for me?"

"That quarry's full of snow, and you know it!"

"Isn't the watchman still there?"

"How much dynamite do you want and for what purpose, please?"

He looked steadily at her. "Enough to do a little job. Enough to ask you to keep that from them until you can no longer do so."

He wasn't asking her not to tell them. He was giving her the excuse she needed.

By a stroke of good fortune the watchman wasn't there. The alpine hut and barn were on a ledge right at the top of the road. The plow the old man used to clear the snow lay to one side next a frozen heap of horse dung.

From there the road, unplowed but showing a track, ran into the gaping canyon of the quarry. Towering cliffs of gray granite were cut by ledges, some so high above them they looked like eagles' roosts. The wire saws, the boom hoists, donkey engines and drills were all silent in their winter.

A trickle of snow fell from a precipice where, in summer, men pounded wedges into holes they had drilled to feather out the giant blocks of stone.

Dynamite wasn't a large part of their operation — its use would only shatter the rock and spoil the tombstone quality. But now and then it had to be used to remove the knots of waste rock. There'd be blasting caps and fuse enough. Hagen ran his eyes over the snow-covered expanse of the quarry floor, and when he found the tiny tar-papered shed of the magazine, it looked forlorn.

A well-trampled trail led right to it.

Irmgard wouldn't meet his gaze. Hands jammed into the pockets of her coat, she just stared across the quarry floor.

He started out. The silence came to him. After hours it was always like nothing else on earth. All quarries were the same in this regard, though some more than others.

When he neared the shed, he found he couldn't go any farther. His hands shook. He knew he might have trouble using dynamite again, but the shaking wasn't from this.

Irmgard took the key from him. The padlock was frozen. Blowing on it, banging it against the door, she finally got the thing to open.

The shed was empty.

"What did you want the dynamite for?"

"To keep in case I'd need it later on — I don't know. It was just an idea."

"To destroy Dieter's diamond center? Admit it, Richard. If there'd been explosives, you'd have taken them back to Munich and wired that place. You'd have come back in a few weeks, months — who knows — and you'd have destroyed it all and Dieter, too."

She'd tell them everything.

"Or Heydrich or both? Was that it?" she asked.

"Irmgard, why don't you leave it be?"

This angered her. "You can't fool with them. You are to give them all the information they need to take the Antwerp diamond stocks. You are to help Dieter establish a cutting center second to none, and you are to give them the codes you've been using. They have to have them, Richard. There's no getting away from it. They need to know exactly what you've told the British. Dee Dee, Erika and I will be allowed to live only so long as you do exactly as Heydrich asks."

"Did you know they'd empty that shed?"

"Did I betray you?" She shook her head. Turning from him, she lit the candles on the table in front of the fire. The ski resort was on the outskirts of Innsbruck. They'd have their supper. She wished for another time, another place, but that could never be. She asked about Arlette and was he in love with her? Was she very pretty?

He asked, "What will you tell them?"

"That we made love and that I slept with you. Richard, wait! The Gestapo will ask for every little detail, how many times we kissed, where we did it, what it felt like for me, for you, did we both come madly with joy? How could we? But I must try and so must you because that's what Heydrich wants."

"And if I don't?"

"Then he will know you're in love with this Belgian girl. She's been helping you, Richard. They are certain of this. They will try to kidnap her and there's nothing you can do about it now."

"Kidnap . . . ? Why haven't you warned me?" It was a cry that had been ripped from him.

"Because I couldn't! Because I have done as they asked. Richard, the lines will be down, the roads sealed off."

She began to pull at the buttons of her sweater, to undress in front of him, but she knew he'd not touch her now, not even look at her.

When he started for the door, Irmgard shouted after him, "There's nothing you can do, Richard. *Nothing!* The plan to take her will already be in motion. That's why Heydrich let us come down here. He *knew*, Richard. He *knew!*"

Bernard Wunsch gripped his sopping mackintosh by the collar. Already his fedora hung from its peg in the hall of the apartment. "Arlette's what?" he shouted.

"Gone. The one from England came here not more than an hour ago. Ah, he was such a nice young man, still a boy and so very English."

Wunsch tried to still the rising panic within him. "But he was to come to the office. He was to say, 'The Carpenter has sent me.' Ascher and I —"

That ample woman clucked her tongue and shook her head. "Bernard, Bernard, when will you learn not to worry so? Arlette would have checked him out most thoroughly."

"My dear, how did this courier know she was staying with us?"

Martine shrugged. "I went shopping as I always do. There were three nice lamb chops at the butcher's. I know meat is so expensive but lamb like that —"

"Three!" His voice was like an alarm.

"But . . . but of course. Arlette must eat as well as you and I. Bernard, I have done this now for several days, ever since she has come to stay with us."

The sinking feeling in the pit of his stomach deepened. With it came the sudden knife of the ulcers.

As the spasm passed, his voice leaped. "And at the grocer's? A few more potatoes, a little more endive? Martine, how could you? These men are not fools. Arlette lives within a very small circle. All they had to do was follow you and ask a few questions of one of the shopkeepers."

Pushing past her, he grabbed the telephone. Were they tapping this one, too? Well, damn it, let them listen!

"Ascher, the worst has happened. Go at once to the Central Station. I will take the car and try the airfield."

"And the roads? Bernard, what will we do about the roads?"

"I will notify the police. I will say that some diamonds are missing from the vault."

An hour . . . Arlette and the "courier" had left the house nearly an hour ago.

Rain streaked the windows of their compartment. At Ghent there would be a ten-minute stopover, at Bruges another. With luck, they should arrive in Ostend at about eight o'clock in the evening.

Everything seemed to be all right. The very fact that they were heading for Ostend should have banished any doubts she might still have had. Yet there it was, that lingering hesitation in her mind. There was something not quite right about him.

Collin Forbes uncrossed his long legs and gave her another smile. With the absolute surety of a young man of twenty-eight, he said, "Now you're not to worry, Miss Huysmans. Believe me, everything's been laid on. Relax. We'll soon have you over to England."

Duncan could well have sent someone else. This one could be a German agent.

"Do you like working with diamonds?" he asked, brushing a hand over the smooth brown hair that was so neatly trimmed.

"Yes, very much. It's really quite interesting."

"So, you'll be given a job in the same line, I suppose?"

He pulled out a package of Gold Flakes, shook it open and held it out to her.

She shook her head, watched as he lit up and blew smoke nonchalantly toward the luggage rack above him. Evasively she said, "I don't know what I'll be doing. And you? What do you do — usually?"

He gave a toss of his head. "Oh, a bit of this and that. Things are heating up, so I expect they'll soon have us all in uniform."

At Ghent he got off the train and she could see him through the window, hurrying into the station to find a call box. Again she felt uneasy.

When a woman with two young children entered one compartment, Arlette got up to make room for them. Folding Forbes's coat, she went to put it up into the luggage rack, then thought better of doing so.

The knife was in the right-hand pocket. Sitting there, with the little girls watching her and the woman prattling on about how late the trains were and why was it they could never seem to run on time, Arlette drew out the knife but managed to hide it from them.

Its handle was black. A stainless-steel thumb catch released the blade. All this was fine and as it should have been, except for the double rune of the SS.

Damas moved along the car. Lootvens was in the one ahead of them, Van der Velsen in the one behind. Jurgens was their contact man, and Jurgens was good. One of the best.

Three cars back of them a disgruntled Otto Krantz would be impatiently waiting for it all to be over. At Ostend they'd take the girl off by fishing boat and put her on a freighter that would be lying in wait at the rendezvous some ten kilometers out to sea.

Everything was going like clockwork. Now the Nazis would really see how well his team functioned. There'd be other assignments, far more responsibility with the Antwerp diamonds.

The girl left her compartment, but only to walk away from him along the aisle toward the lavatory. Nerves perhaps. The door was locked, the Occupied sign all too clear.

Dismayed, she turned to retrace her steps as he ducked into the nearest compartment and sat down.

She was terrified. Pretty — yes! Those eyes of hers betrayed so much.

Damas felt his hands encircling that neck of hers, felt her struggling beneath him, felt the softness of her skin, her breasts and thighs...

Some of his special students had been like that. In for private tutoring, late, too, and in tears afterward, but too afraid to tell their parents. It had been a way of getting back at the rich, the Jews who'd soon be taught how it really was.

Arlette walked the length of the car, afraid to glance into each of the other compartments, yet knowing she must.

Later — how much later was it? — Forbes's coat began to slip off the luggage rack. Glancing up at it, Arlette turned quickly away. The coat haunted her, slipping a little more each time. The knife would fall out of the pocket. It would clatter on the floor between her and Forbes. The knife...

Since returning to the train, he'd been preoccupied, no longer so confident.

As if he sensed her thoughts, his grin came swiftly. "Steady on, old girl. We're going to get through this."

Oh he was so good, so very good. An actor.

When the coat slid dangerously, Arlette leaped to take it down and fold it over her lap. He got up to take it from her, but she said, "No, it's all right, please. I'm cold. It will warm my knees."

As his eyes settled suspiciously on her hands, she smoothed them over the coat. After a moment he looked away.

"There's a new station at Bruges. Have you seen it?" she asked.

What was she on about? "Of course I've seen it. My aunt lives in Bruges." They could see the factories in the distance.

The knife was warm and smooth. Sliding it under the coat, Arlette tried to fix her eyes on the man who had called himself Collin Forbes. There must be no hesitation. As the train came to a stop, she must leap up, shove the coat into his arms and drive the knife straight into him.

And the little girls? she asked. Could she murder someone in front of them?

The train began to slow. As it drew into the station, the woman spoke firmly to the girls and put her knitting away.

Forbes pulled his gaze from the corridor to the platform but soon returned it to the corridor.

The woman from Bruges got up to put on her coat. As the brakes were applied, she stumbled. "*Mon Dieu*, these trains, *mademoiselle!*"

Arlette threw the coat in Forbes's face. Shoving past the woman, she hit the side of the door, then bounced through and raced down the corridor only to collide with someone. Tearing past him, she fought to reach the exit at the far end of the car, but people were everywhere. Someone shouted, "Hey, you!" Someone else cried out. Suddenly there was a shriek, the sound of fighting...

With a leap, she hit the platform and began to run.

There were tracks, tracks, tracks, and in the early-evening light, brand-new warehouses and sheds in the distance.

The lights came on to shine in loneliness outside the warehouse. For some time now the place had been quiet. Still she waited, straining to hear again the sound of their footsteps.

Satisfied, Arlette began to climb down. Splinters snagged her silk stockings. She no longer wore shoes, had lost those out on the tracks when she first fell.

Each crate had offered narrow toe- and handholds. It had been good that the stack was high; good, too, that the opposite door of the warehouse had been open. Even as she climbed, they had run past her — first a harried Collin Forbes, and then three others who had fanned out among the crates and had gone to ground like her.

Straining, she lowered herself stealthily to the floor but clung to the crates.

The concrete was cold, the air damp. There'd be a fog.

When she reached the heavy sliding door, she found that it had been left slightly open. There was just room enough to squeeze through.

The light was dim, shrouded by the mist that all too soon crept through her clothes. Pressing her back to the wall of the warehouse, she moved cautiously into the shadows and then into a wedge of darkness.

One of the men came to stand under the light. Another soon joined him. A train came in and they waited for it to pass. The ground vibrated. There was a hiss of steam, the smell of soot.

When she stumbled into someone, the scream lifted from her in silence.

The man who had called himself Collin Forbes lay dead at her feet, and when she ran a trembling hand up over the jacket, she felt the blood-soaked shirt.

The men looked her way. Unconscious of what she was doing, Arlette began to clean off her hands on Forbes's trousers.

One of the men spoke to the other and pointed her way. At a nod, they parted. As she got hesitantly to her feet, Arlette wished with all her heart she had kept the knife.

He struck a match and held it over the body. In death, Collin Forbes looked pale and shabby. The man was German, a Berliner. Grim, brutal, short, squat and muscular, about fifty-five or sixty years of age . . . The one who had been with the "priest." The one Richard had called Otto Krantz.

He found Forbes's passport, wallet and keys. Putting these away in a pocket, he struck another match and searched for the pistol. It was not far from the body.

Then he sensed that she was near and came after her. Arlette backed away until once again she was among the piles of crates.

Damas could hear her breathing. The British agent had surprised them all by killing Lootvens in the car ahead of them and leaving the body slumped against the compartment wall as if asleep.

He'd paid for it, and now the girl would, too.

Arlette heard something — the soft rustle of clothing, the muted scrape of a shoe. Richard, she began. Richard . . .

Fingers touched the right sleeve of her coat. In panic, she lunged away. Damas made a grab for her. She cried out and ran blindly into a stack of crates, banged her knees, her hands, fought him off, was being smothered...smothered...

Panting, she lay tensely under him. He had a knife. Its point was pressed against the underside of her chin. "Don't move," he whispered.

A voice rang out. "Damas, you leave that girl alone!"

It was the German, the one called Krantz. "Remember, my friend, we've a boat to meet."

A boat...The Belgian lay so still. His breath hardly came at all as he slid the fingers of his other hand around the base of her throat and felt the skin there, the strand of pearls.

The top of her sweater was gripped. A button popped. Arlette got ready to lunge, to scream, to fight back.

The knife pricked her skin, a warning.

"Damas?"

"Over here."

With all her might, Arlette swung a fist, hitting him on the side of the head and in the eye. Damas shrieked at her. She brought her head up hard, hitting him in the face. She fought with him, hit his eyes, struck out blindly at them until in agony he shrieked again and let go of her.

Bolting up, she ran from them, ran until she could run no more.

Then she began to climb, and when the iron ladder reached the beams high above, she left its security to crawl out on one of them and find the overhead crane.

Not content, she pulled herself up onto its roof to lie there on her side, curled into a ball.

To the west of Ostend the road was bright with sunshine but lonely in the early morning. As the wind rushed in from the sea, it dried her clothes and went on to pass a rippling hand over the lush green meadow grass that stretched away.

The first of the church bells came faintly. From the nearest farmhouse, a woman appeared with her children. Arlette rode past them, they watching her with curiosity, she concentrating on the road ahead.

From time to time she chanced a look behind. She was exhausted, her clothes in ruins. She had stolen the bicycle from a garage near the railway station on the outskirts of Bruges. A piece of luck, a slim, slim chance.

They'd have a car. They'd know where to look for her. She couldn't go to her parents, couldn't ask for their help, hoped they'd be safe and left alone.

Willi might be waiting for her with the *Vega*. His mother had answered the telephone with a halting voice, the stranger. Yes, Willi was in the army. No, he wasn't there at the moment. Yes, he might come on Sunday. Mechanics did get leave since there hadn't been a full call-up of reservists.

But could Willi bring the *Vega*? "Please, Mevrouw de Menten, it's urgent! You must call the base and tell Willi I'm being followed. He'll understand and know what to do."

Dear God, she hoped he'd be there. If only Krantz and the schoolmaster would leave her alone for just a little longer.

Gulls cried in the gusting air. Below her, on the right, the marram grass bent among the dunes. Waves broke. Endlessly they called to her, and all around her now there was the sound of them.

The car was black, shiny and distant. As it sped toward her, Arlette began to pedal faster and faster. She knew it was no use. He'd get her again. He'd lie on top of her like that. The one called Krantz would want answers — answers about Richard. She couldn't let them get her. She couldn't!

When the bicycle pitched off the road and disappeared among the dunes, the car came to a screeching stop.

Arlette heard the doors being flung open, heard their shouts as they raced after her.

When she hit the water, she saw the sail and heard their laughter but didn't stop, couldn't stop — ran out into the freezing waves until they had dragged her down.

"Willi . . . Willi, over here!"

She tried to wave, went under again only to come up and cry out to him. The waves were pushing her back toward the shore. No matter how hard she swam, she could make so little headway. "Willi! . . ."

It was a fishing boat, a small trawler with a faded brick-red sail. Not the *Vega*. Not the *Vega*.

Arlette knew it wasn't Willi. Repeatedly she let the waves suck her under. "Willi . . ." she began again. "Willi, why didn't you come?"

As she sank below the waves, her dark brown trench coat floated up and then her sweater. She'd be tearing at her things, trying to get free of them, until her arms and legs no longer of any use, the sea had taken her.

"You fool!" seethed Krantz, swinging so hard he knocked Damas to the ground, opening the schoolmaster's lips and breaking his nose. Not content, the Berliner gave the Belgian's ribs a savage kick.

The girl . . . the Huysmans girl. They'd been so close, the boat so near. She'd have had so much to tell them.

Krantz flung a last desperate look out to sea, as a seaman signaled that it was all over.

Richard was in her arms, warm, so warm and close to her. As Arlette sank, her hair floated out and she felt his kisses in it, felt his lips on hers and saw him smile, knew again how much he loved her.

Richard . . . Richard . . . She wrapped her arms about him and sank.

TO HAGEN RICHARD VILLA HUNTER MUNICH GERMANY

FROM WINFIELD MRS LOIS ANNE INVERLIN COTTAGE BLACK DOWN HEATH PORTESHAM ROAD DORCHESTER ENGLAND

DARLING IT WAS SO KIND OF YOU TO WRITE STOP CAN YOU MANAGE THIS SUMMER I WONDER STOP FRANK IS ALWAYS PLEASED WHEN YOU JOIN US STOP DO TAKE CARE STOP LOVE MOTHER

Decoded, the message read:

TO ALICE FROM THE CARPENTER

OPERATION A FAILURE / WHITE RABBIT SENDS REGRETS

Ten

THE HOUR WAS LATE, the music hauntingly mellow. A few couples still clung to one another on the postage-stamp dance floor. Tobacco smoke hung in the air, and the talk, as if by mutual consent, was sporadic and muted.

Cecile Verheyden made her way among the tables of her all but empty club. When she came to Richard's table, she reached out to touch the evening shadow. "Why not come upstairs and tell me? Sometimes it helps."

"There's nothing to tell."

"Look, I read about the drowning in the papers. Would it do any good to say I'm sorry? Arlette was lucky, you know. So lucky."

"Why? They killed her."

Her slender throat constricted. As she sat down opposite him, Cecile ran an uncertain caress over the table. Von Ribbentrop had been shuttling back and forth to Moscow at an alarming rate. Molotov had gone to Berlin. If the two of them should make an accord, there'd be war.

"Cecile, I could use a little help."

"Are you asking me to take sides? If so, then I... What a stupid thing for me to say. Of course, I must choose, mustn't I?"

There was no warmth in Richard's gaze, no memory of the good times they'd had together.

"Let's go upstairs then, to the office. We can talk better there."

Hagen shook his head. "I was followed, as I am everywhere I let them. When you close up, leave the lock off the back door."

When he returned, Cecile was waiting in the darkness of the kitchens. Hagen could hear the gentle swish of her nightgown as she led him through to the club and up the stairs. On the landing, she paused and felt the breath of him on her shoulder.

"I don't like what's happening to you, Richard. You act as if you were in the jungle and it was your father speaking to you."

"He is, and I am."

She opened the door to the office, felt for the light switch, only to feel his hand close over hers. "What is it you want?" she asked.

He moved away, and when she heard him opening a drawer, she understood.

The gun had been her husband's, a Browning FN 9 mm Parabellum pistol with a thirteen-shot magazine. Richard slid the breech back, removed the clip and made certain the thing was loaded.

"Can I use your telephone?"

"Richard, what the hell is this? Some kind of death wish?"

He moved to her and she felt the chill of the gun in his hand. "Only that I don't want you hurt. You've done enough already."

They sat in the darkness, and when he got through to England, she heard him saying, "Mother, this is Richard. I'm sorry to be so late but could you . . ."

When decoded, the message would read:

TO THE CARPENTER FROM ALICE

CONTACT MADE ANTWERP SD CELL DAMAS KARL CHRISTIAN SCHOOLMASTER ÉCOLE DE MAAGDENHUIS ANTWERP / DAMAS USES ALIAS FATHER LANNAY ADRIAN / HAS LOCATIONS SIZE ALL ANTWERP DIAMOND STOCKS QUESTIONS MEGADAN ROUTE RELAYS DIRECTLY TO KRANTZ THROUGH BRUSSELS EMBASSY ASKS DETAILS FINAL PLAN / REQUEST PERMISSION BRING KRANTZ OUT SILENCE ALL BEFORE TOO LATE / ALICE

"So, what was that all about? Since when did you ever talk to that mother of yours about 'oysters,' Richard, and 'quantities of sand'? My God, are you crazy? The Nazis —"

"Cecile, I met one of the men who caused Arlette to drown herself. London can help me put an end to them."

"London . . . Is Duncan involved in this, too?"

"Yes."

"Then I don't think I'd better hear anymore. Would you like a drink before you go? Oh, I'm not tossing you out, Richard. We're like lost lovers, you and I, cast adrift at a time of what could well be war."

They'd have that drink. Hagen followed her and when they were in the sitting room, he found the whisky and let her drink from his glass. "Get out now, Cecile. Run while there's still time. Go to the States. You'd make a fortune. New York, Chicago . . ."

"Not Antwerp and Chez Vous? No, I couldn't do that. For me, each day I'm getting a little older. Besides, a man has come back into my life and I would like to seduce him for old times' sake but know he would only think of the love he has lost."

She took the glass from him and finished the whisky.

"Cecile . . ."

"Come to bed. Just lie there with me. Nothing more. Look, I don't expect anything. We've had all that and it was finished for us. But you need to be with someone, Richard, and I think I need to be with you."

He let her lead him by the hand. She lay down beside him. "Tell me about Dieter Karl."

Tell me, Richard. Tell me.

They were choosing sides. Denmark, of course, had agreed to a nonaggression treaty with the Nazis. Danish eggs, butter and cheese in exchange for Hitler's smiles. Norway, Finland and Sweden had turned the bastards down flat. Latvia, of course, and Estonia hated the Communists, so what could you expect but that they'd sweetheart Hitler.

The Russians, though, were such a problem. If they agreed to an alliance with the democracies of the West there still might be some hope.

"Ascher, it is like watching a traffic accident develop. One knows people will be maimed and killed. One sees it, ah, with such clarity, and yet one is powerless to stop it."

Lev squeezed the last of the lemon into his tea. Normally he didn't take sugar but today . . . just the pleasure of being able to choose was enough.

He set down the spoon and left the sugar untouched.

Wunsch lit up, took in a drag and nodded grimly. "Yes, yes, I know what you're going to say. Ship the stocks to London. Give those Belgians the letters of guarantee they want. Bah! You'd think the British would have the sense to agree. You'd think the king would insist we move the diamonds. But what do we find? They distrust each other and the king still tries to appease the Nazis. We'll be caught with our trousers down, Lev. I know we will."

Lev asked the question they'd both avoided. "When will Richard go back?"

Wunsch loosened his tie and tugged at the elastic bands that held his shirtsleeves up. Cigarette ash was all over the place. "Arlette . . . we miss her, Lev."

"I asked —"

"Yes, yes, I know, but I am still the director here, and I have said he is not to go."

"Then I can drink my tea with pleasure, Bernard, and offer you a slice of my Rachel's honey cake."

Wunsch tossed his head. "I'm getting to think your daughter can't bake anything else! Ah, Ascher, forgive me. I just don't know what the hell to do with our diamonds if the Nazis come. Toss them in the sea, I suppose."

He snatched up the latest batch of orders. The August Thyssen Hütte in Duisburg was Germany's largest steel mill. Hamburg, Bremen, Kiel held the major shipbuilding firms. All up and down the Ruhr and the

Rhine, the industrial heartland of the Third Reich poured out its smoke. Siemens-Martin steel, ball bearings — Lorenz and Heliawatt, mammoth engineering works.

Where hadn't Richard been?

"They are raising a hue and cry for him, Lev, and the Nazis are beginning to think he won't be coming back."

"If I were him I'd go fishing in Scotland."

Bernard's eyebrows lifted.

Lev gave a brief smile. "Arlette . . . she had never been there before. Did she tell you that? We used to talk a little. That girl, Bernard. In many ways she was so like my Rachel."

"Lev, listen to me. If the worst should come, we will take the diamonds we have here and leave."

"The Belgian police would only impound them at the border. We're trapped, Bernard. Why not just walk out the door and leave everything?"

When Hagen joined them, Lev had just finished making a fresh pot of tea and Bernard had switched to coffee. The wireless set was on and Hitler was screaming invective at the Poles.

"It's his lungs," said Lev. "I think he's got a cold."

The moths seemed not to care about themselves. If on the first fall they didn't hit the water in the fish pond, they would struggle back up through the air to scurry madly about the glowing paper lantern. It was as though, in seeking the light, they had become drunk with its power and would throw their lives away.

Irmgard watched them for a while. No telephone calls could get through to Antwerp. No civilian cables were being allowed out. In the warmth of June 1939, the Wehrmacht had closed all the filling stations in Munich even though there were tourists everywhere. Poland was very much on everyone's mind. Daily there were great flights of fighter planes and bombers, and at night they had heard them, too.

She couldn't warn Richard not to come back, not to try to save them.

Dipping a hand into the fish pond, she rescued a moth and took it toward the house where she set it in the branches of a cedar.

She could, of course, extinguish the paper lanterns — there was no reason why she couldn't do so. The party was over for them. Soon there'd be no light at all.

When Irmgard went upstairs, Dee Dee heard her scream. Naked and shivering in the bathroom at the far end of the hall, she was staring at the tub.

Rushing past her, Dee Dee turned off the tap.

Irmgard couldn't look at her. Aware of what had happened, she hung her head in shame, and when Dee Dee threw a towel over her shoulders and hugged her tightly, Irmgard's voice was empty. "Don't let Richard tell me anything. Don't ever let him trust me again. They will ask me what he's said, and I will have to tell them everything. They'll drown me if I don't."

She had gone upstairs to have a bath — such a simple thing — but had filled the tub with ice-cold water.

"Will you come with me to the mountains?"

"Heydrich has said I can't."

They were above the tree line now, and as they threaded their way along the crest of the moraine, Dee Dee no longer had any doubts as to what Heydrich intended.

At Bludenz, just before the border with tiny Liechtenstein, they had turned off onto a side road to leave the car and begin to climb. Three Wehrmacht corporals, with rucksacks and slung rifles, were ahead of her, then the sergeant and the colonel. The men carried her suitcases and Erika, the *Feldwebel* a Schmeisser and rucksack, the *Oberst* his pistol in its holster. All of them were from the army. There hadn't been a sign of the SS, but who could tell where loyalties lay?

High above the valley, caught in a small amphitheater, they stood out against sky and earth. To the east, at their backs, an ice-capped crag gave veils of meltwater that dropped some three hundred meters to angular talus. Then the water disappeared among the rocks and issued far down the slope as a rushing brook.

All around the shelf the moraine curved in a steep horseshoe-shaped embankment. Somehow she would have to warn Richard. Somehow she would have to stop him from trying to save them.

Beyond the moraine a scree slope rose to a tiny patch of alpine meadow, which culminated in a naked spur and ridge. The *Feldwebel*, an experienced mountain guide, indicated that they were to go over the ridge. From time to time the colonel looked back at her. Impatiently he pointed to the clouds and shouted, "We must have time to return to base before dark," as if it was the only important thing and he was as fearful of the place as she.

The echo of his voice rang in the silence. A boulder clattered away, and when the sound of it had finally faded to nothing, Dee Dee started up the final slope. Richard would try to bring the rocks down on the men. He'd take a look at that talus and think, It wants to fall.

But he wouldn't know Irmgard wasn't with her.

The moment passed. She began to climb again. The ache in her chest was now making her pause every second step. Hooking her thumbs into the straps of her rucksack, she tried to get her breath.

The scree was too steep. Behind them it fell away to the ledge on which the moraine huddled. From there, the valley's amphitheater opened outward to drop down into the forest far below.

At last she reached the crest of the ridge. Now the land before her fell away in a meadow bright with sky-blue lupines, cotton grass, the tiny yellow flowers of the mountain avens and the soft pink bells of the heath.

With its steeply pitched roof and darkly timbered eaves, the alpine hut clung to the shores of a tiny ice-fed tarn. From the hut, a trail wound past the woodshed and down the mountainside.

Switzerland lay before her, and Dee Dee knew she would have to look at freedom each day knowing she would never be allowed to reach it.

"Mijnheer Lietermann, it's kind of you to see us."

"Not at all, Richard. Please come in. Bernard, it's good to see you. Ascher, you should come to work for me. How many times must I ask? Loyalty, Bernard. Such loyalty."

They went upstairs to the main drawing room. "The walls, gentlemen. I apologize but I've taken Richard's advice and leased a modest country house in the Lake District of England."

The place looked positively barren. An uncomfortable silence settled on them. Lietermann offered coffee, which was politely refused.

"So, we will sit the four of us and talk. And you, Lev, will not think, There I told you so, Bernard. The brass always save their own asses first."

Lev's eyes were watering. He had difficulty swallowing.

"Ascher, I'm not — I repeat — not pulling out on you or anyone else. My wife and I will stay to see it through. The paintings... My God, they are priceless. Now, please, what have you come to tell me? Is it about Isaac and his secret plan to use the trucks of the Mercantile Company?"

Wunsch reached for his cigarettes, then thought better of it. "Jacob, Richard is..."

Hagen took over. "What Bernard wants to say, Mijnheer Lietermann, is that although I'm not guilty of it, the SS are blackmailing me over the death of de Heer Klees. I've had to tell them certain things but not the plan you and I agreed to. What is essential is that we stick to the *Megadan* and that you tell me exactly what de Heer Hond has in mind for those trucks. Believe me, *mijnheer*, the SS know everything about it, but if I'm to mislead them, then I must know everything, too."

A sadness came to Lietermann's dark eyes. "Is it that you intend to go back into the Reich in spite of everything?" This could not be.

It was Lev who said, "What else has he to lose but his life?"

Lietermann acknowledged the loss of Arlette and briefly sketched the plan for him. Hagen told him about Irmgard and Dee Dee. Though the risk was there, he had no other choice.

"Will you try to save them?"

"If I can, though not at the expense of the diamonds. What I need is your absolute guarantee we'll use the *Megadan*. Mr. Churchill will take care of things from his end. The dummy strongboxes must be placed in those trucks, and I'd go so far as to suggest some of them be filled with diamonds. Sacrifice if we must, for the greater objective of keeping the stocks out of their hands."

"There are collaborators, Belgians who will help the Nazis seize those trucks," said Bernard gruffly. "For me, I wish we could mine them somehow, Richard. A simple switch — the ignition perhaps — explosives in among the boxes."

"Bernard, Bernard, these new American films..." began Lev. "*Gone with the Wind*...Gone with the Blast! It sounds as if you want to go to war."

"It sounds as if I am angry, Lev."

"Then leave the thinking to Richard. He's the spy."

The tension in Berlin was everywhere — in the news vendors around the Potsdamer Platz, in the man who had sold Irmgard a handful of roasted chestnuts, which she had bought not to eat but to feel the warmth of them.

All the headlines were the same: Berlin-Moscow Nonaggression Pact Signed.

For days — weeks — the crisis over Poland had intensified. Every wireless broadcast had poured out the invective. Every newspaper had shrieked the same. The Poles would not listen. They would not peacefully settle their differences with the Reich. Peace could only be bought at the price of blood.

As the car pulled in to the curb in front of the Hotel Adlon, Irmgard looked down at the newspaper packet of chestnuts. Their warmth had all but gone.

Leaving the bag on the seat of the car, she took a moment to compose herself, then got out and walked steadily up the steps and into the hotel.

Here, too, especially, there was tension. The bar was crowded with foreign correspondents who clamored for news.

She stood alone before the lift.

Richard was waiting for her in his room. Suddenly nothing else mattered but that she be held by him.

He felt her tears, felt her lips pressed against his cheek.

Shaking, she clung to him and bit a knuckle to stop herself from breaking down completely. They'd drown her if she didn't tell him what they wanted. "Richard...Richard, you *must* get us out! Please! Before they kill us. Dieter won't do anything! Dee Dee's got tuberculosis. Heydrich's sent her to the mountains. I'm to go there, too."

He held her from him and dried her eyes. He took her out into the hall and closed the door behind them. "You know it's a trap."

Irmgard shook her head. "No . . . no, it isn't!"

In fragments, she came apart, couldn't stop herself, saw the water in the tub, felt their hands on her body. Panicked! Cried out and felt him cover her mouth, fought for air . . . rolled up her eyes.

Hagen slapped her gently. "Irmgard . . . Irmgard, it's me."

She shut her eyes and tried to get her breath. "Richard, *please*! I . . . I can't take it any longer. *Get us out!*"

"Where will you be? The mountains, Irmgard? Where?"

She pressed her forehead against his chest. He wrapped his arms about her. "It's a *trap*. A *trap*! Don't . . . don't even try."

"What's Heydrich really after? Irmgard, he could have me arrested now."

She shook her head, was so afraid. "The Wehrmacht — Dieter says they're guarding Dee Dee. Heydrich . . . Heydrich must want to use you to show them up and reinforce his demands for more of the SS to be in fighting units. You're an American, too. Perhaps it's better if an American spy does something like that. Then he really can arrest you and embarrass Mr. Roosevelt and his government into remaining neutral."

God only knew what Heydrich really wanted. So many things, the diamonds, Arlette, himself . . . Dee Dee and Irmgard.

Hagen gently lifted her chin and kissed her tenderly on the lips. "Now tell me where you'll be."

Dawn on August 25 was gray and cold. Across the skies of Berlin squadrons of Stukas and Heinkel 111 bombers headed east to chase the last wings of peace.

Richard wouldn't know the date of the invasion. There would be no news of it on the mountain.

Like others in the city, Irmgard made her way through the streets to slip silently into the cathedral.

Only a scattering of the faithful remained — the Nazis had purged that sort of thing just as they had everything else. But those who came, came every day.

When Dieter found her, the razor was in her hand. Gently he shook it from her and it clattered at her feet. "The invasion has been canceled. Mussolini has sent a directive to the Führer saying the Italians cannot possibly go along with things. They aren't ready for war on such a scale.

"Irmgard, listen to me. For my sake, and that of our family, I hope you do not think of trying to kill yourself again."

She would concentrate on the altar. "There'll be a trial, won't there?

The sister who once loved you and her country, the man she still must love in her own way."

"Forget about Dee Dee and the child. Forget about everything else. Offer to come forward to testify."

"You speak as if Richard was already a prisoner."

"Irmgard, forget about him! He doesn't love you."

"Was she pretty, this Belgian girl?"

"Very."

The noise of the water filled the narrow gorge. Mist rose from the plunge pool. At a place just above the falls, where two ledges jutted out, a covered bridge with shingled roof and open timbers spanned the frontier.

Hagen lowered the glasses, was lost in thought. Lev quietly chewed on a stem of meadow grass. "There are four of them, Ascher."

Guards. There were always guards. Since when would anyone *want* to get into the Reich? And at a place like this? Shepherds! Smugglers! "Why not climb higher? Perhaps there are boulders across the bed."

All around them the mountains soared. They had left the bottomlands, the valley of the Rhine long ago. Schloss Vaduz had clung to its forested slopes. Beyond the castle there had been the rising peaks of the Austrian Alps. The road had seemed to lead nowhere, had dwindled into a stony track. Then they had heard the waterfall against the tinkling of sheep bells and had climbed through the forest to an eagle's nest above the bridge.

One of the guards dried off the barrel of his rifle. Another was sitting on a stump, methodically slicing bread with a bayonet. They looked like decent types. "Ascher, I'll have to wait until nightfall. Then I'll go across underneath the bridge."

Lev bit off the end of the piece of grass and spit it to one side. "That's a hundred-meter drop over the falls. Are you crazy or something?"

Hagen gave his arm a friendly jab. "This is where we part, old friend. Wait three days and if I don't show up, go back to Switzerland and home as fast as you can."

Never mind the diamonds, never mind the British, who had refused to help him.

The French and Swiss frontiers had not been so bad for Richard, who had carried the guns across, but here . . . "I will wait five days, maybe six in case there are complications."

"If you do, you'll be dead by then."

Always they had had this argument. It had seemed far too hasty a plan — Richard supposedly into a private clinic because of a severe attack of malaria. Out of sight, of course, but . . . One used diamond cutter and a salesman whose worth in the eyes of the Reich must be fast dwindling.

"Richard, I'm not doing this to pay you back for saving Rachel. I'll stay in a different pension every night and make a big thing of having a quiet holiday in Liechtenstein. But when you reach that bridge I'll be here with the car to help you get back across it. You can watch for me from that spur. I'll shoot as many of them as I can and draw their fire."

There was no use arguing with him anymore. "All right. Shalom."

Lev reached out to grip him by the hand. Would they ever see each other again? "Shalom aleichem."

The moon broke through the drifting clouds to wash its light across the valley floor. The dog barked, and somewhere up on the mountain an answer was given.

They would go at it now, those two, until one or the other was clubbed into silence.

Out of the darkness, the farmhouse and barns grew steadily until he could see them quite clearly. Down over the fields, in the hollows, the gray gossamer of frost hung low.

Rubbing his hands together, Hagen started out on the trail. In the early morning the woman would expect one of the soldiers to come down for the milk and eggs. He would have to be near their hut well before dawn. The killing, if killing there must be, could not start until after the guard had come back. Otherwise the woman or her husband would sound the alarm. Then, too, there was bound to be radio communication with headquarters in Bludenz or Feldkirch — twice a day perhaps, morning and evening. Damn!

Alpine troops were stationed at both places.

There'd been no sign of the Daimler or of a staff car — just one of the Wehrmacht's trucks with a canvas tarp over the back and half a tank of gasoline.

It would be enough to give them the head start they needed. It would have to do, but what if the guards received three radio checks a day? What if there was a transmission schedule he couldn't determine?

The warning would be out, and then what? Lev would have to drive home alone.

The sound of the stream came to him as the trail entered the forest. The smell of the pines was sweet and close and the air cold. Only now and then did the moon break free. The slope steepened, then steepened again and again until the trees provided handholds and resting places, and footbridges crossed and recrossed the stream.

The water was never silent. The air seeped down from the mountainside, bringing the faint trace of wood smoke. Rain was in the offing and if not rain, then snow on the upper slopes to make their descent all the more obvious and hazardous.

Two women and a child who could cry out from fear perhaps to give them all away.

When he came to the hut, he came upon it suddenly. One minute his legs were aching from the climb, the next he had stopped on a ledge not a stone's throw from the guard post. The back of the hut lay against a rocky cliff beyond which the crown of the roof rose slightly.

The dog was chained to a tree, and for a moment neither of them moved or made a sound. Then Hagen drew the pistol and the dog heard him cock it.

The night awoke, shattered by the barking that echoed in the cirque above and rolled down the mountainside to irritate the guardian of the farm. Back and forth the two dogs barked. Splashing among the boulders, Hagen crossed the stream and scrambled up the slope to climb out onto the roof of the hut and lie along its crown.

The dog's barking increased. Tugging at its chain, it lunged this way and that. The moon came out to bathe the place in an eerie light. The guards came stumbling into the night to stand there hunting the darkness, then shouted at the dog in anger.

There were three of them. Would there be one, two or three others inside the hut?

A spill of lantern light gave echo to his thoughts. It broke from one of the windows below him. It flooded from the porch.

"Heini, what the hell is it this time?"

"One of the sheep perhaps, Herr Hauptmann."

"Take the lights and have a look about. Don't let the dog run loose. Keep the bastard on his chain or he'll bugger off on us again. That bitch must be in heat."

"*Jawohl*, Herr Hauptmann."

As the sound of them faded, that of the radio transmitter beneath him grew. Regardless of the cause of the disturbance, the alert was being sent. Only if he waited now would he hear if the all clear would be given.

Stretching a little more, he flattened himself against the roof. The moon came out, then disappeared as the rain began to fall.

Two of them brought the milk at eleven o'clock and climbed to the ridge beyond the hut to stand in the rain high above the tarn.

Scanning the slopes through binoculars, they took no chances. When they returned to the hut to collect the empty canister, Dee Dee brought them coffee in tin mugs, and they thanked her.

There was no sign of Irmgard.

Both men shared a cigarette on the porch, leaning their rifles against the wall. Every now and then they would look down the trail toward the guard post. Like soldiers everywhere, they took what few luxuries they could get, but did so on stolen time.

When the coffee was done, one of them left the porch and came toward the woodshed. Hagen waited for him.

The smell of saddle soap and wet leather, the sour odor of sweat, wet clothing and stale cigarette smoke were mingled with the resin of split pine logs. The man was no more than a boy of twenty with flaxen hair and sky-blue eyes.

His arms were full of firewood when Hagen pressed the pistol to the back of his closely shaved head. "Don't move. Don't even think of crying out. How many are there of you?"

The boy tensed. The sound of the shot would bring the others. Hagen said, "Why die for two women and a child?"

Two women . . . It would be best not to tell him, to talk, though, and stall for time. "There are six of us. Four in the hut — the *Hauptmann*, the radio operator and two others. Munk and I are the only ones up here, but if I do not come back with the wood he will know something is wrong, and if we don't report back to the *Hauptmann*, the others will soon be here. So, you are stuck. There is nothing you can do."

"Except shoot you."

Hagen let that sink in. He stood back a little. "How many times a day do you fellows have to check in with base?"

"Only the *Hauptmann* knows that. Sometimes it is three times, sometimes five. The schedule varies. We patrol. We do as we're told. Twice a day the Oberst Steiner brings a bunch in from the other way to sweep that valley clean."

His right hand edged toward a piece of firewood. Hagen wished he would try something because then it would be so much easier to kill him. "Walk in front of me. Don't try anything."

The boy snorted. "Munk will only shoot me and then you. If you should manage to get away, he has orders to kill them."

"Then I'm sorry for you."

Prepared for the blow of the pistol butt, the boy turned swiftly aside only to feel the knife plunge into him.

Stunned by it, he choked in confusion and staggered back as the firewood showered down around him.

He was staring up in disbelief when Hagen hit him between the eyes.

By his dialect, the kid had been from the north, from around Bremen or Oldenburg. "Hey, Munk, come here. Look what I've found."

Munk was older, taller, tougher, smarter. As Hagen watched him through a crack between the boards, the corporal picked up the rifles and slung one of them over a shoulder. With the other rifle, he rammed a shell into the breech and took the safety catch off.

When he reached the woodshed, he used the muzzle of the rifle to give the door a nudge. Then he kicked the door open and stepped back a pace.

The rain fell steadily. It ran from the slicker, streamed down the field-gray oilcloth to puddle on the ground beside his boots. The door swung back and he nudged it open again.

"Stefan...Stefan, what the hell are you after? You know the *Hauptmann* won't like it if we're late."

As he stepped cautiously into the woodshed, Hagen gently teased the rifle from his hands. "Now the other one. Lean it against the wall or you'll join your friend."

Munk smelled of the Limberger and sausage he kept in his pockets.

The guard post was quiet. The dog lay curled in the sun, drying out and catching a bit of sleep. Warm air from the valley below lifted up the slopes, and all around Hagen now there was only the sound of the stream.

Then he saw the *Feldwebel* — the one called Heini. Heavy-set, with an all but shaved head, he was sitting on a board, leaning back against the trunk of a tree not far from the dog.

There was a Schmeisser across his lap. The dog would sound the alarm.

One of the others came out of the hut — kitchen duty. Above the boots and drab olive-gray dungarees, he wore an undershirt that exposed the dark curly hairs on the backs of his shoulders and arms. Heini took no notice of him. The man went over to a line of washing to feel the socks and shirts.

The distance to the sergeant was about 100 meters, that to the cook, a little more. Shoot the one, the other, and then put the rest into the hut.

Hagen wished he could have the Schmeisser.

When the reports of the shots came, they rang like cannon on the mountain. The sergeant toppled over. The cook threw up his arms and took the line of washing down. The dog barked but Hagen didn't run, didn't listen.

Methodically he cut an arc across the hut, splintering the boards at waist level with first one of the Mausers and then the other.

Inside the hut the *Hauptmann* lay badly wounded on the floor, trying desperately to reach the shattered radio, whose operator had been flung against the wall.

The transmission key was up. Cursing their luck, Hagen pushed the *Hauptmann*'s arm away and shot him with the pistol. Then he silenced the dog.

He was racing now — leaving the hut with a Schmeisser, three stick grenades and a satchel of ammunition — when Dee Dee came running into the clearing to stop and stand there in shock.

Erika was in her arms. For perhaps five seconds they looked at each other. No sign of Irmgard...

When the cry came, it was torn from her. "Richard, no! No! She isn't here!"

Hagen shouted to stop her from screaming. "The truck. Come on. Run!"

The roots, the stones, the rocks came up fast. Down, down they pitched, sliding, falling, crying out, then running blindly.

When they missed a bridge, they stumbled across the stream and he dragged them up the slippery bank.

No time... No time... "Dee Dee, try. Please."

"Heydrich knows you're going to do this. Please leave us..." She slid and gave a gasp, then dragged herself up and ran on again.

Throwing her words over her shoulder, she shouted at him in anger, "He wants you to do this! The more you kill the better. Escape... escape while you can."

The fields were empty. Cattle grazed. The rooster crowed, and from the barn he heard the sound of the farmer forking dung. The woman was working in her garden and half rose among the dill to pause and stare at them.

As they ran to the truck, she went back to her weeding. Better not to see. Better not to watch.

Hagen tried the ignition, then tried it again and again before scrambling out to open the hood.

The fields were empty. From the farm, the dirt road ran down into the valley to gravel flats, gray-white in the sun. There were puddles in the ruts, silence... It was so silent and peaceful. Woods lay on either side. The woods... the stream...

At a point some one thousand five hundred meters from them to the south, the land rose out of the fields a little. From there it climbed into the forest. There would be height. Perhaps...

The truck started. He slammed down the hood and shouted, "Hang on!"

They made it to the main road and bumped up onto it. Jostled, Dee Dee cried out in panic and clung to Erika, clung to the door, the dash — anything to stop herself from being thrown about.

Richard put his foot down to the floor. Faster, faster... They were heading down a long incline now, crossing the valley flats, coming to a bridge, another road... trucks... trucks... men leaping out... men throwing themselves on the ground...the shattering of glass...a scream...her own...her own...

Krantz watched in dismay as Hagen drove like the damned. The truck reached the hills and began to climb.

He tore a rifle from the nearest man and threw himself on the ground. Kill...kill...kill...

The truck came to the first of the bends. Krantz lined up the sights and fired.

Glass shattered at Dee Dee's shoulder. Blood, scraps of skin and fair, fair hair spattered over the windshield.

She screamed again and flung the baby from her, went crazy then. Hagen tried to stop her, tried to control the truck.

Krantz hit the front right tire, and they pitched off the road.

Trees...trees...try...try...

The truck rolled over. Dazed and bleeding badly, Hagen fought to drag Dee Dee out. "Run...got to run!"

Stumbling, they started for the woods, only to find themselves hemmed in by the river.

They ran back toward the road. The wheels of the truck were still turning.

As they scrambled up over the rocks, Krantz waited, held himself. The woman reached the road and he shot her first. She threw up her hands — wouldn't even have cried out or anything.

Just died as so many had. The fields of Flanders, the last advance on Ypres, and never mind the diamonds, never mind what Heydrich wanted. Just kill or be killed.

Hagen held the woman in his arms and waited for it. Krantz lowered the rifle and buried his face in the earth. All his energy had suddenly left him. Drained, he lay there, knowing he should have killed Hagen while he'd had the chance.

Part Three

Fall 1939 – Spring 1941

The little fishes' answer was
"We cannot do it, sir, because ⸺"

Eleven

T HE HUSH OF THE OFFICE was the hush of the times. In the wake of the appallingly savage destruction of Poland a quiet disbelief had settled over Western Europe and the British Isles. The world had changed and yet it had not changed. It held its breath. There had been no real fighting in the West.

People had begun to think the unthinkable would not happen.

Bernard Wunsch lit yet another cigarette, the fourth since arriving for work at 7:00 a.m. Richard's office continued to haunt him as did Arlette's vacant desk.

The vault was all the more perplexing since it held the whole of Dillingham's diamond stocks, even though both England and France had gone to war and there had been an immediate naval blockade of the Reich.

The sound of the lift came to him, then the opening of its cage door. He gave it a few more moments, didn't turn from the windows.

"Ascher, I still cannot understand it. To all intents and purposes we are at war with the Nazis and yet we aren't at war. In France they call it *la drôle de guerre*, in England the phony war, in Germany the *Sitzkrieg*. And here? What do we call it but neutrality!"

"Bernard, Bernard, try to calm yourself."

"How can I? We stand like bewildered ducks before a dried-up pond awaiting the butcher's knife."

Belgium had moved into its third stage of readiness. This was not a full mobilization but the call-up of some more reservists. The defenses of the Albert Canal and Fort Eben Emael were being manned. Antwerp was gradually becoming a fortress city — tank traps, bridges to be mined, areas in the countryside to be flooded, et cetera, et cetera.

While the French General Gamelin, the commander in chief of the Allied armies, told his soldiers not to fire on German working parties for fear the enemy would fire on theirs, 158,000 soldiers of the British Expeditionary Force languished along the French border with Belgium. The soldiers, both French and English, fought boredom. Drunkenness was not uncommon, apathy legion. Like moths, their fighter planes ventured out only at night.

King Leopold had denied the Allies transit rights across Belgium, though there were now some fifty German divisions on the borders of southern Holland and Belgium.

It was suicide and they both knew it.

"Has your visa come through from England?" asked Lev.

Wunsch swung away from the window. "What visa? Do you think I could leave here at a time like this?"

Lev ducked his head. "I was only asking. Some coffee? While we still have it."

"Coffee...yes, yes, that would be good. Ascher, our hands are tied. The export of diamonds is not strategic to Belgium's needs, not like some vegetables and perhaps a little butter. Under article 9 of the Hague Convention neutral states must not deny the belligerents equal rights to whatever else they might need. So we ship to them and that stinking freighter sits in the port of Antwerp or out in the middle of the Scheldt. Churchill, he is Britain's First Lord of the Admiralty, but what does he do? Where are the destroyers Richard said they'd send? Where are the letters of guarantee from the British government?"

"Churchill has other things on his mind."

"Ah, yes, but of course. On the high seas ships are being sunk, but in isolated battles. By mines, too, that have been sewn from the skies or by the silent arrows of their tin fish!"

Lev clucked his tongue and shook his head. "You get better every day, Bernard. I swear this business will make a poet of you. Tin fish, seeds from the skies..."

Wunsch slammed a fist down on his desk. "The ghost of war hovers over us while we wait for the grim reaper to sharpen his scythe!"

"What's got you into such a stew this morning?"

Wunsch shrugged. "Our diamond stocks, what else? Belgium is fast becoming a haven for spies. The French kick Otto Abetz out of Paris, and where does he go but to Brussels? And what do we find but a German 'economic' mission wanting to have a look at our fabricating shop."

Bernard's wastebasket had overflowed. Cigarette ashes were strewn about the floor. "A 'trade' mission?" asked Lev.

The nod was there, the letter, too. "Richard's former friend, the Baron Dieter Karl Hunter, wishes to see what we have."

Lev found it hard to speak. "Perhaps he will give us news of him?"

Wunsch stubbed the cigarette out and crushed the butt. "Perhaps, perhaps, but I very much doubt it. As we are still under contract to supply the Krupp, he will, no doubt, bitch about the continued tardiness of our deliveries."

"Just don't ask me to talk to him, Bernard. Let me have the day off. I'll be too sick to work in any case."

"I will give him that new apprentice who knows nothing. I, too, will be otherwise engaged. Of course, if he should have news for us of Richard, we would not receive it."

"Then you'd better lock up that revolver of yours. I wouldn't want to go to jail for killing a Nazi, not at a time like this."

Steep, heavily wooded hills clothed the ruined walls that surrounded the picturesque medieval town of Landsberg in Bavaria. Behind the turrets and broken ramparts of its fortress Hitler had been imprisoned for nearly nine months after the Munich putsch of 1923. It was here that he had dictated *Mein Kampf*.

Otto Krantz was glad to be back in the Reich. Poland had given him a bad taste. The things he'd seen; the things they'd done.

After Poland, dealing with Hagen would be a pleasure. And to think that Heydrich had locked him up here.

So far he'd told the schmucks who'd been dealing with him sweet bugger all.

As he drove up to the gates, the Berliner leaned on the horn and flashed his Gestapo badge. As always, the badge worked wonders. The iron-studded gates swung open and he was waved on.

Hagen was in the cellars. Krantz didn't like the room. The white-washed walls were spattered with blood and too reminiscent of Poland. The dirt floor around the execution posts smelled of feces and mold. Behind the wooden posts, the stone wall of the dungeon was pock-marked with bullet holes.

They'd beaten the shit out of Hagen more than once. The bugger was hardly recognizable.

To steady his nerves, Krantz took out his cigarette case. Thumbing the dent that had saved his life, he asked about the prisoner.

"He still refuses to talk, Herr Krantz."

You sadist, thought Krantz scornfully. "Take him back to his cell. Feed and water him. Turn the light off. Give him extra blankets and all the sleep he needs. He has to talk."

The four-door Cord sedan was forest green with big, handsome tires and lots of chrome. Twelve cylinders under the hood, and by God, she loved the throb of that engine.

Cecile Verheyden stood in the laneway behind the club. She'd thrown the garage doors wide open. She'd told herself she had to come to some decisions. The car, the club, her flat above it and everything else she owned — the farm, for God's sake. What the hell was she to do?

Things could only get worse. Richard had made her choose sides, but Richard was gone, Arlette was gone. Each time she went upstairs, she thought of the two of them. Arlette lying in her bed. Richard making love to the girl. Fucking her, for God's sake. Fucking her in a bed that had meant so much to them!

Richard saying, "Cecile, why don't you get out while you can?"

New York, Chicago... London. Shit!

Even in the gray light of a blustery afternoon, the car's paintwork gleamed.

Richard and she had made love in the back seat of that car several times. They'd driven out into the country time and again, for a picnic, a swim, weekends at the farm. Shacked up and drunk on love.

And now? What the hell was she to do now? What were any of them to do?

Sell the car? Sell up and get out? The car would have fetched a good price if gasoline hadn't been so hard to get, but by God, the thing drank it!

And the club? No one would buy it. Not now. Not with the way things were.

She closed the garage doors. She ran her eyes up over the cut stone walls to high gables and the dormers in the loft. She'd loved this laneway, had loved the old Antwerp feel of it. The bas-relief panels that gave a tracery all round, the leaded octagonal window above what was now the door to the kitchens.

Nicolaas Van der Meer had once run a bookshop from here and had left a bust of himself, knowing art and beauty surrounded him because he and others like him had made sure it would be there for all to see.

The stable and her car — to think that such places of beauty had once held horses.

The Plantin-Moretus Museum was one of the private-house museums of Antwerp. Not open to the public, it allowed access only to the chosen few. The inner courtyard, like her back lane, was an exquisite example of Flemish architecture — something to be preserved, guarded, saved.

Cobblestones, columned walkways, yew and boxwood hedges, a sundial in the middle, vines that climbed the lovely old stone walls, barren now but in early summer full of the delicate hyacinth blue and the perfume of wisteria.

Decisions, decisions. One had always to make decisions. Richard had forced it on her. Richard...

"Dieter, it's good to see you. My God, you look well, but it's been such a long, long time."

A thin black smoke drifted from the *Megadan*'s funnel. Stern down, the freighter rode at anchor out in the Scheldt.

Hunter scanned the decks, but there was no sign of any armament. The rust was everywhere, the black hull looking more like a derelict. Her forward cargo booms hadn't been used in years.

Waves lifted the bow. The wind tore at her flag. What was there about that ship? "The pumps have stopped working."

Damas looked at the man Otto Krantz had sent. A Bavarian, but of the upper class. A baron no less, with dark hair, dark eyes and a superior manner that grated. Krantz had been angry over the loss of the Huysmans girl; the Berliner no longer trusted his competence, though he had continued to use him and his men. But this one . . .

Damas had the idea the baron would kill him if things went wrong.

"The pumps are often down for repairs. First the starboard one, as you can see, then the larboard. Believe me, Baron, there can be no thought of their using that freighter. The Jew Isaac Hond and the others of the Antwerp Diamond Committee have been to see the management of the Mercantile Company far too many times. Besides, they talk, and this we have heard."

Something wasn't right. "See if you can't get someone aboard her. I want that ship scuttled the moment we give you the signal."

"I will try, of course, Baron, but believe what I say about the Mercantile Company. I have five of my best men working there as drivers. They report that trucks are being kept in readiness at all times. My drivers and three others have been placed on call twenty-fours hours a day."

"Have they been told why?"

"No, of course not. But there is the normal shop talk. The manager of the company has received a letter of instruction, but as yet I haven't been able to get a copy of the route they intend to use."

"Get one. Get more men into that place."

Or pay the consequences? "Baron, this might not be wise, as we had to provide 'accidents' for two of the drivers my men replaced." You'd think it had been easy.

"Could one of your men stay behind to let me into that warehouse?"

The Germans wanted the diamonds very badly, but did the anxiety stem from knowing the invasion would soon come? "Have we the time to arrange such a thing?"

"Time enough. I give you three days."

Hunter took up the glasses again and concentrated on the freighter. "What has happened with the railway cars?"

The Belgian turned away to search the quays. In spite of the grayness of the weather, there were still far too many people about for his liking. "We have plans to wreck the lines. Those are our general orders. Should the traders try to use the railways, they'll find them in a shambles."

"And the airfields? Could they be planning to send the trucks to one of them?"

Damas forced himself to smile. "The Luftwaffe, Baron. Have you forgotten? We are counting on them to stop all such traffic while it is still on the ground. Besides, we have organized major disruptions. As soon as the invasion starts, we will be out in force. First the telephones and radio towers, then the landing fields and railway tunnels, then the rest, all other things. They couldn't possibly fly those diamonds out."

The Belgian had been thorough — no more mistakes — but Heydrich had given an ultimatum. Take the Antwerp diamonds or else. "Two Whitley bombers are all that would be required. Get men into every airfield within a sixty-kilometer radius of Antwerp. I want them watched."

"Ascher, this is the Baron Dieter Karl Hunter from Munich."

"Richard's friend. Has he news of the boy?"

Lev found himself shaking the hand of one of those who had been responsible for Arlette's death and the loss of Richard. Forever afterward he would look at that hand and wonder why it had gone out so readily. Had it been impulse, something conditioned since childhood, a need to be polite, or something commanding in the baron's youthful presence?

"So you are the cutter whose skill Richard swears by."

The Jew was seventy, if a day. Those ancient eyes couldn't be much good.

"Have you news of him for us?"

Hunter laughed good-naturedly. "But of course. He is well and very busy with our new diamond center. He's married now to my sister. They have a child, a son. Yes, he's turned into a family man at last. Who could have believed it?"

"And eating well, is he?" asked Lev.

Standing a little to one side and behind the baron, Wunsch shook his head to stop Lev, whose hand was still gripped by the German.

"Very," said Hunter. "Don't believe all the stories you hear about the Reich, Herr Levinski. There's plenty to eat."

"With Poland in the bag?" Lev shrugged. "I suppose there is. So, Bernard, what would you like me to do with this fellow? Show him around the shop or take him down to the Scheldt?"

And drown him. Wunsch found the will to smile and play the good host. "Lev, please . . ."

"Let him go, Herr Wunsch. For us he is of no consequence. Now, please, the shop, if you would be so kind? Richard went over our lists of equipment and we have modeled our center on your operations. He's in the SS. Did I tell you that? Ah, I can see that I didn't."

Richard in the SS? Wunsch felt himself trembling. "That cannot be, Baron. Not Richard. Never him."

Only the fussy would be convinced by papers and signatures. Dieter took out the forms and showed him. "Here is his membership card."

Somehow the day passed. Somehow Wunsch got through it, and when the inquisitor of industrial diamond processes had finally gone, he sat alone at his desk. Richard a member of the SS? How could that be? Had he fooled them all completely? Of course not.

Then either the Nazis had forged his signature, or he had signed those papers under duress. In either case, it would be best to tell de Heer Lietermann.

Getting his coat and hat, he went through to the shop to tell Lev where he was going. The diamond cutter's bench was empty. Back in the office, Wunsch gazed out over the street below. What the hell was happening to them? Lev had never left the place early in all the years he'd known him.

"Don't do it, my friend. Me, I know what you are up to but I would ask you to reconsider. They are experts at this, we but novices."

Lev pursed his lips in thought. The man who had come to ask about making diamond tools had now gone to the Red Cross depot, whose warehouse was along the docks and not far from the fabricating shop. Now why would a baron concern himself with such things?

It was a puzzle, but then Belgians, like everyone else who cared, had been trying to send relief parcels to the thousands and thousands of Polish POWs in German camps. Perhaps the baron had something to do with that. Another little duty to perform.

Ordering a cup of coffee, Lev pretended to read his newspaper. A second cup was called for. Finally the baron left the warehouse. Lev waited another twenty minutes — he'd have to give it that — then walked across the street. It was nearly closing time.

Still blushing, the girl looked up at him from behind the information desk. "The Baron Dieter Karl von Hunter is an honorary director of the German Red Cross, *mijnheer*. He has come to inquire about the shipment of relief parcels from the Congo. And yourself? What can I do for you?"

Relief parcels from the Congo. "A small donation. A hundred francs, that's all the wife and I can spare at the moment. More next week, of course. Could I bring it here just to save on the postage?"

He could. He paid up and thanked her. "We all like to do our bit, not just the German barons."

The Obersturmbannführer Ernst Laubach had the perpetual smile of a benevolent vintner with his glass raised. A native of Bernkastel, ruddy faced, tanned — a man of fifty or so — they had talked of the slaty schists beneath the Doktor vineyard high on the bank of the Moselle, of how the slate helped to create such superb wines.

The Frau Ilse Dietsch, a stern, matronly woman of sixty who looked more pious and stern than SS or Gestapo, had come from a farm near Raisling in Upper Bavaria.

Krantz, of course, had come from Berlin.

Each day this battery of three spent two hours with Hagen. Just what specialties Laubach and Dietsch held he didn't know. But there'd been no brutality, no sadism, simply a series of questions over coffee sometimes or, because Frau Dietsch preferred it, green blackberry tea with mint. For the health.

Rose hips, too. Sometimes a beef broth flavored with dill.

He could never forgive Krantz for having caused Arlette's death and for having shot Dee Dee and her child, but then, they couldn't forgive him either.

"Richard, just before you discovered we'd taken care of Herr Klees for you, you met with your director at the club of Cecile Verheyden."

Krantz offered Frau Dietsch a cigarette and held the light for her. "Did you often meet there?"

Was Cecile to be the theme for today? "No. Bernard didn't care for jazz."

"But the occasion necessitated his finding you on short notice?"

This had come from the vintner. Hagen wondered how they could possibly have known of the meeting. He explained why Bernard had come to the club.

"But, please," asked Krantz, "was the Verheyden woman present when you discussed Herr Klees with him?"

Frau Dietsch watched him as she'd watch a rebellious hen.

"Cecile was downstairs in the club."

"Then you met upstairs?" said Laubach.

"Yes. Yes, I met him in her office."

"Her sitting room, I think."

Trapped, he glanced at each of them, receiving their individual expressions: one smile, one bland mask, one stern gaze of suspicion of certain sin.

Magnanimously, Krantz spread his meaty hands on the table. "Why the sitting room, Richard? It's a club, isn't it? Why not a table downstairs?"

"I asked Cecile if we could use her sitting room. Bernard didn't want anyone to overhear us."

The three of them exchanged glances. The farm wife said, "That is not so, Herr Hagen. The Fräulein Huysmans and you were already upstairs in the sitting room."

Krantz leaned forward. "Richard, it's time for us to tell you a little something. Arlette Huysmans didn't drown. We have her in a cell here. Must Frau Dietsch disclose to you just what you and that girl did in that flat? Not once, I gather, but several times. The most intimate details."

How could they possibly have found out? Damas? Cecile? Had someone got to Cecile and made her tell them?

"You can't possibly have Arlette. She drowned in the sea off Ostend."

Ignoring this, they began their questioning in earnest. Always softly, always turning, turning. First the Antwerp diamond stocks. Why was he so certain the trucks would be used? Why not the freighter? Of course he had said the freighter would be used. Not the railway cars, but these, of course, would be so much more convenient, wasn't that so?

Then the code. "These things, they are unpleasant, yes?" said Frau Dietsch. "But necessary. The Huysmans girl, you understand? She has said — and this can be confirmed, Herr Hagen, by analysis of your cables and telephone conversations — that you used phrases from the poems of *Alice's Adventures in Wonderland* and *Through the Looking Glass*."

They were lying about Arlette. Lying! "My mother and I sent those back and forth. We quoted them to each other so as to remind us of the past."

"Your father and the jungle, prospecting," said the vintner.

"Yes. My mother read those poems to me as a child. We had little else with us, so I came to love and know them well."

Frau Dietsch pinched her nose in thought. "But you do not get along with your mother?"

Irmgard would have told them this. "Not well. Not since my mother married Frank Winfield within a week of my father's death."

"In the war," said Krantz. "Ypres." Did Hagen realize what had happened?

"In the war, yes, Herr Krantz. But we still quote the poems back and forth to remind each other of the good times. I was once very close to the two to them. My mother wishes me to remember this and I, her."

"And your father-in-law. The Magpie Lane address, Richard. Did you also quote passages with him?"

Hagen refused to answer. His cup was refilled. Frau Dietsch passed him the last of the poppyseed cakes, flat, biscuitlike things, not too sweet. He had gorged upon them and managed to hide — he hoped — two of them in the folds of his smock.

The woman said, "Please, Herr Hagen, you must understand that the cases of the fräuleins Huysmans and Hunter are out of our hands. If I could stop what they are doing to them, I would."

"So, please, Richard, the code," said Krantz. "Tell us and I assure you, nothing more will happen to them."

"You haven't got Arlette, Herr Krantz. Quit trying to tell me you have."

The Berliner shook his head and said that he was sorry. "Your friend, Duncan McPherson, didn't tell you everything. He wanted you to be angry, Richard. He wanted you to go back into the Reich. Karl Christian Damas and I kidnapped the girl and made it look as if she'd drowned."

The late-autumn sky was gray and streaked with rain. On the horizon, the setting sun broke beneath the lead-lined clouds and the wind came in gusts to wash across the marshes, bending the reeds.

The Verheyden farm possessed the best of everything. Absolute privacy, sand hills to the rear of the house, expansive views to the front and side.

Canals, of course, with distant windmills turning. A place for a wireless set, if needed. A place to cache men and arms — the house and barns, built in the traditional style of a square, surrounding a cobbled courtyard, were perfect.

From the east of the Scheldt to the Dutch border, the landscape was one of lonely moors and sand plains upon whose desolate expanses the farm buildings, as here, stood out starkly against the sky. Now and then clumps of sand hills marked the positions of old coastal dunes. Those behind the house and barns would give the wireless aerial height. Cecile need never know.

They had passed several defensive works, and at each of these she had displayed a disarming charm that could be useful to them. Even the most stubborn of Belgian colonels had let them through. It would be easy to get around them. A squad of thirty men — would it take more to seize the diamonds? Not with Damas and his group.

The shooting had been good — ducks on the marshes as she'd promised, grouse and snipe among the sand hills ...

"So, Dieter, you like my little nest? Who would have thought my parents had been farmers? My father had this place from his father, who had it from his. Me, I lease the land to a neighbor but have the house and the rest for myself. It's good to keep one's roots, don't you think?"

Hunter took the cigarette from her and set it in the ashtray. For a moment they looked steadily at each other, then he drew her to him and felt again the litheness of her splendid body.

They kissed ... the kiss lingered. Hesitantly she pressed her hands against his chest. He said, "Go on. You first. I'd like to watch."

She shook her head. "There's room for two. That way we'll get to know each other even better."

The copper tub had a high back, flared sides and the patina of long use.

Hunter brought the champagne, she the soap and towels. Neither of them said a thing as they undressed.

Cecile stepped into the tub but stood there, tall and statuesque, her breasts high and firm. He lit the candles and blew out the lanterns. He watched her as she watched him.

Damas and his men mustn't know that he planned to use this place. He must keep that from them until the very last.

The triangle of blond curls beneath the soft and gentle swell of her stomach drew his gaze. Her fingers spread over the pubis, over her breasts. The mock modesty, the laughter was there. The candlelight gave her skin the glow of crushed velvet, her hair the sheen of corn silk.

Then her hands gripped the cheeks of her rump. The stance became one of impudence, of "Oh, what the hell do you think you're up to?"

She gave a laugh, let him know she was only too well aware of what he was doing.

He opened the antique dressing mirror that had been her grand-mother's most private possession, and set it to one side. She could see herself and the candle on the table. Her back was to the stove.

Dieter Karl's shoulders were not as broad as Richard's. He had neither the gentleness nor the will to laugh at himself. There weren't the scars. No, the frame of him was good, but not as strong, not as at ease with himself.

The maleness of him drew her hands. They stood and kissed. She cupped his testicles and stroked him to erection. Together, they sank into the water, facing each other. "It's best this way," she said, still gripping him.

She could kneel and he could kneel. One had to sit with knees upraised.

Again they kissed, lightly this time. Again he wondered about her. How much could he trust her? Had she known Duncan McPherson? Had Richard not introduced them when he and Cecile had been engaged to be married?

Cecile didn't shut her eyes. Glancing in the mirror, she wondered if Dieter had placed it there for some other purpose? "Mmm," she said. "I like it when you soap my breasts. Your cock is big and strong."

"Your shoulders, your neck . . . " He nibbled an earlobe and wondered if she was working for the British.

He did her back, ran his fingers firmly up and down the length of her, touching each vertebra. As she bent to kiss the maleness of him, Hunter slid his hands around to soap her breasts again, to caress her flanks, her buttocks.

Cecile leaned back. He filled their glasses and held hers out.

"You're not to worry about Richard. He's a realist, Cecile. He's helping us with our new diamond center in Munich. I'm hoping to send him to the Congo in the not too distant future."

"Must we talk about him?"

"You were once his lover."

The acid all too clear, she said, "Before Arlette. Before that bitch."

He set his glass aside on the floor and refilled it. She said, "Is your sister really like her?"

"Arlette? Me, I never met the girl. Were they very much in love?"

"I think Richard wanted to get her pregnant. My God, Dieter, the stupid cow took no precautions, nor did he. It was just like him."

Hunter ran a hand between her legs and began to wash her. She eased herself well down in the tub and parted her knees as far as possible, then dangled her legs over the sides and took a sip of champagne.

"Weren't you just a little bit jealous?" he asked.

He felt her stiffen, heard her scoff, "Me? Why should I have been? For us it was finished. She said she was being followed all the time and that they needed someplace private. I said okay."

"Did they ever talk about the Antwerp diamond stocks?"

"Only once that I overheard, but Arlette had to telephone things to England for him."

Hunter chuckled. "You listened in. You *were* jealous."

"What if I was? Richard . . . Richard and I . . . "

He flattened a hand against her stomach and began to touch her clitoris, said, "Forget it, please. Of course you two were once in love."

Again she sat up but this time turned and asked him to do her back properly. The long journey up her spine began. She sighed when he reached the base of her neck. Now she let her arms and head hang over the end of the tub. Through the half-open draft of the firebox door she could see the flames.

Dieter began to do her seat, his hands going round and round, the thumbs now up to the base of her spine, then to her neck, now her seat again, massaging her, now the spine again.

Taking the sponge, he repeatedly squeezed water over her back, and she felt it falling on her skin, her seat, her neck. Richard had done that. Richard . . . They'd spent a fortnight here, the two of them — he'd been such a fantastic lover. They'd done it so many times.

Hunter kissed each buttock. Cecile murmured softly and shut her eyes, let the warmth of the stove bathe her face and arms.

"Did they ever mention the Congo as a source of diamonds?" he asked.

Dripping, she stood up suddenly and turned to face him. Was there anger now? he wondered. Had he tried to gain too much?

"Will there be war in the West?" she asked. "Look, I know you can't answer that. It was stupid of me, but the club, this place, I . . ."

Suddenly she was very afraid.

He smiled up at her and shook his head. "Nothing could be further from the Führer's mind."

"Then why not ask Richard all these things you want to know?"

Hunter reached out and took hold of her by her hips.

"Arlette is in prison. We kidnapped her. That is why Richard has married my sister, and that is why he still hesitates to tell us everything."

A grin broke out on her face. She drew him to her and felt the warmth, the roughness of his tongue as it probed among the hairs and found the nubby bump of her clitoris.

Standing there, she watched his hands as they molded and gripped the cheeks of her seat. The jet-black hair, the shoulders, the hands . . . now the tongue again, flicking, probing, encircling. It didn't stop. It went on and on. She couldn't draw away. God, oh God . . .

Her voice broke. "Come to bed. Please, I . . . I'd like to . . ."

Hunter didn't stop. He drove her to orgasm and when she came, Cecile shut her eyes and fiercely gripped his head and held his mouth against her, held it until he had run his hands up to her breasts and pulled her down.

Hungrily she kissed him. Shutting out all else, she gripped his cock and began to stroke it.

Kneeling on the rug before the fire, she felt him push himself inside her. She was tight, dry; he too big, too hard. He used his thumbs. She caught a breath, swallowed and shoved herself against him.

"Look up. Look at yourself," he said.

Her breasts were pendulous, the nipples red and taut. Dieter caressed them constantly as he drove himself inside her. Faster now . . . faster. The dark eyes watching her, misting as her own eyes misted, the mask of him twisting as he withdrew one last time and she gasped, "Don't! Please don't," only to feel him drive himself deeply into her again.

Lifting her up, he came. No sound. Nothing. Not a cry of ecstasy, a moan of joy to join her own. Just the silence of his ejaculation.

Afterward, she told him a little more about Richard and Arlette, just enough to tease him, just enough to make him return.

Cold, it was so cold and damp in the cell. Freezing! Involuntarily the shivers came, but when they passed the sweating started.

Hagen sat up and clutched his shoulders. They had cut his rations back to nothing. Sleep, then no sleep. Water, then no water. For weeks they'd kept it up. Did he even know what date it was?

They'd told him that the trial would take place in the old Munich Infantry School on the Blutenburgerstrasse. There'd be the testimony first, then further interrogation and the final speeches by the defense and the prosecution. A tribunal would decide how swiftly they should die, and the foreign press, especially those from the States, would be witness to the executions.

The iron-studded gates of the prison would open once more. The drive back from Munich would take two hours. Would they blindfold him? Would he be allowed to see Irmgard before she died?

At nine o'clock that evening an impatient Otto Krantz came into the cell. The shaking had passed. The fever had now climbed until Hagen was delirious. Tossing and turning on the bunk, he mumbled snatches of nothing, only to cry out every now and then, "Duncan, they say they've got Arlette! Kill Heydrich. Kill him for me."

Krantz gave a curt nod to the man who had come with him. He moved aside. The man leaned over Hagen and took hold of him by the shoulders. "Richard...? Och, it's me, Duncan, laddie. Can you no hear me?"

"Duncan..." he gasped.

"Aye, I'm here, Ritchie. Here."

"Water. Give me water and quinine. Sulfa! I've got to get back to Antwerp. The diamonds, Duncan. They're after the diamonds!"

"Richard, did Churchill say he'd send a squad of men to help?"

"Rabbit...White Rabbit..."

He drifted off, mumbling things about fighter planes and guns.

"He'll die, Herr Krantz."

"Ask him about the code. We *have* to know what he told the British. Hunter must know if they're sending in a team of men."

"Richard, listen to me. Use the code. Send a message. 'The sun was shining...'"

Hagen sat up and stared blankly at them. The sweat poured through the stubble. Slowly a smile grew and he gave a childlike laugh.

"He's back in the jungle now, Herr Krantz. We'll get nothing further from him."

"'A loaf of bread,' the Walrus said, / Is what we chiefly need...'"

"Take him to the prison hospital. Give him the quinine and sulfa. Don't let him die."

Damas finished his cigarette before quietly getting out of the car, which he'd parked some distance down the road from the Verheyden farm. Krantz had been definite. Have a look. Find out everything.

Had the Baron Dieter Karl Hunter fallen in love with the Verheyden woman? Was she working for the British?

The stars were brittle, the moon bright. Lights shone from the house.

Fortunately, though there were dogs on the neighboring farms, the woman had not the time or the patience for them.

When he came to the house, he found the couple in the sitting room. The Verheyden woman held a map of the surrounding countryside. She was pointing out things to the baron in answer to his questions. She looked ... what could he say about that look? Afraid? Anxious? What ... what was there in those blue eyes, that pretty face?

The couple had their coffee, the baron laughing now and trying to ease her mind.

As Damas watched through the lace of the curtains, they set their cups aside and began to kiss, the baron clasping the woman's left breast, she sliding a hand up his leg.

Momentarily they parted, each studying the lips of the other. Then the Verheyden woman began to pluck at the buttons of her blouse as the baron's fingers caressed the soft skin of her neck before burying themselves in her hair.

When the woman slid to the floor, pulling him with her, the baron resisted and ran his hands under the blouse and over her shoulders.

She gripped his thighs. He spread his knees. Laughing, she undid his trousers and began to play with him as he continued to caress her neck and back, pulling at the clothing, plucking at it until both sweater and blouse were free of the skirt and he was unhooking her brassiere.

The nubby bumps of her spine, the slender waist and flared hips were soon exposed. The woman stood to remove the rest of her things. The baron, not satisfied, pulled her down to her knees again and she stroked his penis, laughingly ran her tongue up it before taking it into her mouth.

The baron drew her head forward. Now back, now forward. Now back...

Damas watched, and when it was done, the blood pounded in his veins. Had the Berliner known what effect the sight of such a thing would have on him?

Had he known that now he'd find out all he could about the woman and watch her as never before?

There was snow in the courtyard of Landsberg Prison. The guards stamped their feet and swung their arms. Those that manned the machine guns got the full sweep of the wind. Bundled in their greatcoats, they watched the platform that had been set up.

At a sound Hagen turned from the infirmary window. Otto Krantz came in with a formidable sheaf of papers under one arm and a bulging briefcase.

Setting these on the table, he rubbed the circulation back into his fingers. "Richard, be reasonable. You know we have Arlette Huysmans.

She's confessed that you were an agent of the British Secret Service, and that you routinely sent information by coded cable, telephone — even by postcard, or simply took it with you to Britain. Yet you still deny this and claim the words and passages from those poems were meant only to remind your mother of how close you'd once been?''

"That's correct. If my mother hadn't left my father, he wouldn't have gone off to war. He'd still be alive."

More of the same bullshit! Krantz studied the nicotine stains on his fingers. Increasingly he had come to believe that the only way to break Hagen was to offer the bastard freedom. They'd done it in Poland. For most, the shock of recapture had been too much and they'd broken down and wept like babies before spilling everything. One or two had had to be shot — there were always the tough ones. None escaped because, of course, there had been no escape. It was the elation of freedom one encouraged before suddenly taking it away.

Quickly he came to a decision. "Because of your illness, the Reichsführer Himmler decided that the woman Irmgard Hunter was to be tried in your absence. You are to be allowed ten minutes with her. The death sentence can be commuted, Richard. It's in your power to save her."

"And Arlette?" asked Hagen.

"She will die the same way if you continue to refuse to cooperate."

On the way, Krantz stopped to chat with one of the guards. As Hagen listened, he got his first real news of the war. Poland had fallen in less than fifteen days, in eight her army had been smashed. But now the Russians were fighting the Finns in what must be the bitterest winter in over sixty years.

The Finns had invented the Molotov cocktail. Vodka bottles filled with a mixture of gasoline, kerosene and tar.

He tried to think. If Russia and Finland were at war, then Germany was still waiting, but for how long?

And the diamonds...had the traders in Antwerp finally got them safely away? Was there nothing he could do?

"Come on, my young friend. You've got a date to keep. If you're wondering how things are at home, then let me tell you it's business as usual. Leopold's policy of neutrality forbids the Jews to jump. Britain's distrust prevents them from giving the necessary guarantees. Seven... eight tons of diamonds just sitting there, Richard. All this time. Can you believe it? And Baron Dieter Karl has found himself a new lover, something really gorgeous. Fucks like a mink, or so I hear."

"Cecile?"

"Who else? Happy to be working with us, Richard. A sensible woman."

Irmgard's cell was near the far end of the courtyard. She didn't turn to look at them when the door was opened, but sat on the edge of her cot, staring up at the tiny window.

Krantz motioned the guard to stand outside the door. The turnkey brought them two plain wooden chairs and they crowded into the cell.

Hagen begged to be left alone with her, but the Berliner wouldn't hear of it.

She was very thin. They'd shaved her head. The plain gray-blue smock was loose, and when he went to sit opposite her, the welts and broken pus-filled sores were all too evident. "Irmgard, it's me, Richard."

Still she wouldn't look at him. Hagen reached out to touch her. She flinched, then absently asked how he was.

"All right. Alive. Actually, I've managed to escape for a while."

Not catching the humor, she turned suddenly in alarm. "Escape?"

She saw the grin — the same old Richard. The cuts and bruises were healing. The nose had been badly broken.

Hagen took her hands in his. She felt his tears, said, "It's all right, Richard. It doesn't matter."

At a nod from Krantz her voice lost its steadiness. "Arlette... they really have her, Richard. You mustn't let them do this to her anymore. Tell them what they want to know. Give them the Antwerp diamonds. She loves you very much, but nothing could have stopped them from making her betray you. Even the best of us break down and confess."

Fear haunted her eyes. Furtively she ducked them away lest he see this. "Tell them the code. It's absolutely essential to the security of the Reich that you give them the content of every one of those messages you sent. Work for Dieter. Please, I beg it of you!"

All down the side of her neck there was a burn. When he tried to comfort her, she cried out, "Don't be such a fool! They'll win in the end, and then what?"

The Berliner was gruff. "That's enough, Fräulein Hunter. Your time together is up."

"May I give him my Bible?"

What did it matter? Toilet paper when needed. "All right. Yes, yes, you may do so."

Hagen held her a moment. "Think of the good times, Irmgard. Remember the mountains. Remember me as I will remember you."

"Don't watch me die. Please, I'm so afraid."

Snow fell. Swirling, the big flakes were caught in the wind to eddy in the far corners of the courtyard and play dust devils across the intervening space. Krantz and two guards walked him to the center, to stand before the platform on which, as yet, there was no one. Just a guillotine, a raised sheet of weighted, sharpened steel that stood tall and bleak.

"Richard, I don't like this anymore than you. Confess, for Christ's sake. Agree to work for us and the woman will be spared."

Hagen turned on him. "Give me a rifle, damn you. Let her die with dignity!"

Krantz backed away and let the guards restrain him. "It's Gruppenführer Heydrich's command that you be a witness to this. They will force you to keep your eyes open, Richard, and when we go up on the platform afterward, you are to remember that the Fräulein Huysmans faces exactly the same fate."

The whole thing wouldn't break Hagen's resolve. It would only strengthen his will to resist. Escape was the only thing. They had to lead him to believe it possible. Then they must close the iron fist around him.

They had to have the diamonds.

Irmgard was led out onto the platform. Each step faltered. As she neared the guillotine, her guards had to drag her toward it.

They forced her to her knees. Her lips began to move, but what she said, Hagen couldn't hear. Her wrists were fastened to the rings with ropes, then her ankles. They made her rest her neck in the slot.

One of them yanked her head back so that she could look out at him. "Richard . . . Richard, please don't watch! I beg it of you!"

Hagen tried to get away, tried to get a rifle. They ripped the smock open and it fell off her back to hang there. The snow thickened. It began to swirl faster and faster. The guards nearly broke his arms. Someone else seized him by the head. Krantz — was it Krantz?

Fingers pried his eyes open.

"Save her, Richard. Say the right thing!"

"I can't, damn you!"

The blade fell. A cry of agony lifted from him. Blood spurted from her severed neck.

Her head rolled across the platform. Her body jerked, bucking up several times to strain at the ropes.

Then one of the SS guards kicked her head toward him, and it came to rest in the snow at his feet. "Irmgard . . . Irmgard . . ."

It was only later, much later, that he was able to turn the pages of her Bible. He read a line here, another there. When he came to the Psalms he took more time. When he came to Psalm 56, he found the message. Using a bit of graphite, stolen from the end of a broken pencil, she had written in the margin, *Richard, be of good cheer. They do not have Arlette*.

"Name?"

"Odette Latour."

"Age?"

"Twenty-six."

"Place of birth?"

"Brussels."

"Occupation?"

"Red Cross nursing assistant."

"How long have you been doing this?"

"About a year and a half."

When asked, she told them readily that her brother and father had been killed in the 1914 – 18 war. "My mother died when I was fifteen."

"No others? Not an aunt or an uncle, a cousin perhaps?"

The interrogator spoke excellent French. "They are living abroad, *monsieur.*"

"Where, please?"

"In America."

"Then who brought you up after your mother died?"

"Her sister, my aunt."

"Address?"

"My aunt's, or mine?"

"Yours," he said.

"Number 47 Boulevard Anspach, apartment 5, Brussels."

"Occupation?"

"But I have already told you this, *monsieur.* A nursing assistant for the Red Cross."

"What, please, is Euflavine?"

"It is an antiseptic, very good and nonirritating. One can even inject it into veins — in dilute form, of course."

"Hypoglycemia?"

"Insulin shock — the loss of blood sugar below normal."

"Symptoms?"

"Sweating, pallor, a feeling of sickness, tremors — all these often follow a state of confusion, but I am not a nurse, *monsieur,* only a nursing assistant. When I have passed my examinations —"

He shrieked, "*Simple fractures? What does one do?*"

Quickly she rattled off the steps: "Make sure the patient is comfortable. Support the injured part. Do not attempt to remove clothing..."

"Fräulein?"

"Yes?"

"You understand German. You were speaking in German."

He had switched from using French. "But of course I speak your language. My mother came from Düsseldorf."

"And your mother's sister, Fräulein Latour? Where is she now?"

"In America, as I have already told you. They have a shop in Brooklyn. It is a suburb of New York."

"And what is the address of this *aunt* and *uncle*?"

"You do not trust me, and this I cannot understand."

"The address, *fräulein*. The address."

"One hundred and ninety-seven Montague Street. Upstairs. On the top floor. The house is near the East River and the Brooklyn Bridge. There is a letter in my purse. It is . . . it is the last one I have received, so I have kept it with me to remember them."

The Gestapo man motioned to one of the SS guards. The purse was dumped onto the table. His hand went out, and she sat there tensely, waiting for him to pick up the letter. He shrieked, "*Hagen!*"

She jumped, cried out, "Please, what is it? Is this some person?"

He tossed the letter aside. "Richard Hagen. You knew him, Mademoiselle Huysmans. Look, it's no use your lying to us. We know who you are. We have photographs. You used to work in Antwerp for the firm of Dillingham and Company."

"I know of no such person or firm. I am Odette Latour, and if you will check with the Red Cross, you will see that this is so."

"Your hands."

"*Pardon, monsieur?*"

"Your hands! Put them on the desk."

The touch of him was cold. He held her life by a thread, felt the palms, the fingertips, examined the nails, then took a pair of pliers and laid them on the desk. Oh God . . .

"Your hands are not those of a nursing assistant."

"Then you know nothing, *monsieur*! Nothing! That is the whitening that is caused by too much carbolic! The redness, it is . . . it is caused by . . ." She wiped her eyes and bit a knuckle. "I . . . I must scrub out the toilets and do the floors each day. It . . . it is not so very nice to have to do such things."

He smiled and spoke finally in English. "What a waste of talent. Care to come dancing with me some evening when we're free of this wretched place?"

The whitewashed walls of the root cellar were low and stained by the peat. Outside, the night would be clear and very cold. The stars over Kincalda House and the frozen wastes of Loch Assynt would be bright.

Duncan McPherson got up from the observer's chair. She had panicked but had handled herself well. Still, he had reservations. Weakness couldn't be tolerated.

Word had come again from Bernard Wunsch that Dieter Karl Hunter was showing an uncommon interest in Antwerp's Red Cross depot. Only someone working from the inside could get them the answer they needed, but the girl mustn't know of her assignment until the last possible moment.

The diamond stocks were still in Antwerp, but now there was a much stronger Fifth Column than ever before. The German Fourth, Sixth, Twelfth, Sixteenth and Eighteenth armies were all poised near the borders of Holland, Belgium and Luxembourg. The First and Seventh armies waited behind the Siegfried Line in case of a French counteradvance across the Maginot Line. So many things would interfere.

"I hate you, Duncan. I think I hate you more than I have ever hated anyone."

"Captain. You are to address me by my rank."

"Captain, then, but I still hate you — hate all this, the Nazi trappings, the flags, the jackboots, the uniforms..."

He managed a smile, for the interrogation room had been a work of painstaking research designed to express the harshness one might have to face. "Hate away, but you'll love me for it when the time comes."

The others were gathered around the wireless in the school's common room. Arlette knew them only by fictitious names that wouldn't be used elsewhere. There were two women and seven men from Poland, all of them eager to return to their country. The women were wireless operators, the men, saboteurs and intelligence agents.

As well, there was a motley collection of Czechs, British, French, Dutch and yes, one token Belgian. She, too, had worked with the wireless, both receiving and sending in code. Nights in secret out in the hills and mountains, freezing at times and gray with fatigue because... why because Duncan nearly always had them chased and one never knew if he would do so.

The man who had interrogated her offered an ale and a cigarette. He was nice and she liked his smile, but that was as far as such things could go.

She asked about the news.

"Not good, I'm afraid. The Germans have invaded Norway and Denmark. The Danish were finished in four hours. Apparently there's a jolly good row going on off the coast near Narvik."

"Have the Germans landed?" To think that it had happened at last, and in Norway.

He held the match for her and she leaned close to light her cigarette. "In force apparently. They've taken the Norwegians completely by surprise. Had their chaps hidden in their merchant ships. That new Nazi cruiser, the *Blucher*, has been sent to the bottom though."

Arlette had to leave the room. Outside the night was cold. It was April 9, 1940, and the phony war had suddenly come to an end.

When McPherson found her she was looking up at the stars. For a time he said nothing. What could one say in any case? But he knew she'd be thinking of home. He'd cheated her, of course. He'd had to lie to Richard.

It had been touch and go getting her off the shore at Ostend. Krantz had been bloody close to taking her. Then the lads had come along and plucked her from the sea. Thank God she'd put through a call to Willi de Menten. Thank God she'd asked for the boy's help, and the message had been relayed. They'd prevented the Belgian crew of the fishing boat from leaving Ostend's harbor; they'd sailed in their stead, but it had been far too close a thing.

McPherson knew he'd have to work her hard for the next few days. He'd send her on a cross-country run with her wireless set and her Browning. Yes, that would be best, that and live ammunition for the lads.

The Nazis would crush Belgium. They'd race for Antwerp and the diamonds.

Hagen concentrated on the man who sat directly before him. Reinhard Heydrich now wore the collar pips and flashes of an SS general.

Müller, head of the Gestapo, and Schellenberg, head of Counterespionage, flanked the *Oberstgruppenführer* but had said so little the trial had been a farce.

A van had brought him to Munich, to Gestapo Headquarters on the Briennerstrasse. For one brief moment he had seen the light of day and had felt the breath of spring. The tulips had been in bloom.

"The prisoner will rise."

Why did they insist on this charade? "I'd prefer not to stand, Herr Oberstgruppenführer. My legs are still not my own."

"The malaria. Yes, that is correct, but you will stand all the same." To kill or not to kill Hagen, that had always been the question.

The prisoner dragged himself to his feet. The clothes he had worn in the mountains now hung on a frame that had lost a good fifteen kilos. A loose tooth kept bothering him, and like a tramp, he unconsciously sucked on it or pushed at it with his tongue.

"Do you still deny that you were an agent of the British Secret Intelligence Service?"

"I will always deny it."

"And you refuse to reveal the code you used?"

"If I'm not a spy, how can I give you a code that doesn't exist?"

The fact that Hagen hadn't been broken infuriated Heydrich, but the time had come to end it all. "Very well. It is the decision of this court that you be taken to the place of execution, there to await your time of death. Heil Hitler."

"Herr Oberstgruppenführer, if I might have a word . . ."

Heydrich turned, and for just a second paused to coldly study Otto Krantz, the man who had failed him so miserably. "Well, what is it?"

The Berliner made a suggestion. Heydrich shook his head. Krantz was bold enough to argue. Schellenberg added a word or two in support.

Rumors had fled through the cells by tappings, by chance whispers. Norway and Denmark had fallen. Sweden was cooperating with the Nazis. Finland had settled with the Russians. For days the skies over Landsberg had been empty of airplanes, the sound of them gone, like the sound of northward flying geese.

Heydrich got up from his chair and came to stand in front of him. Hagen smiled, infuriating the bastard so much that he swung away and angrily shouted, "You'll get nothing out of this one. Have him shot!"

"But...but..." The Berliner gave a shrug. "As you wish, Herr Oberstgruppenführer."

Dead, Hagen could tell them nothing. Alive, there might just have been a chance.

As Heydrich returned to his chair, Krantz heard him softly say, "Arrange it then, but lose him and pay the price."

"Richard, I'm here to help you."

"Go away, damn you! Haven't you done enough? Irmgard was your sister, Dieter! She was my friend."

"She was an enemy of the Reich."

Hagen refused to look at him. "What the hell do you want with me? I've been sentenced to death."

"A word, that's all. We would appreciate your help at the diamond center. If you agree, there will be a stay of execution. Who knows, you might yet prove your worth to the fatherland."

"You sound like a parrot."

"Even a parrot has the good sense to perch on its master's shoulder when they're out hunting."

Dieter sat down on the bench beside him. Richard would never agree to what he'd been told to ask him, but they did need to know if the British would send in a squad of marines to take the diamonds off. "Don't be so stubborn. To die is senseless. I can use you."

"How?"

"Let's leave that for the moment. If you give me your word not to try to escape, I think I can get them to take us to the center. There are some things I'd like to show you."

"And then?"

"A few questions, that's all."

Krantz...it had to be because of Krantz. "Will I be handcuffed?"

"Of course. The guards must accompany us, as will Herr Krantz, but once we're there perhaps the handcuffs can be removed. What would you like to eat?"

"Coffee. I haven't had a decent cup of coffee in a long, long time."

It was strange to see Munich in the dark of night. Because of the blackout regulations the headlights on the cars were hooded to emit only pinpricks of light. Occasionally small blue flames at the curbside replaced the once-glowing street lamps. There was none of the glare, none of the excitement of a once-bustling city.

Outlined against the night sky, antiaircraft batteries surmounted some of the taller buildings. There were others in the squares.

They drove by the cathedral and then the Hofbräuhaus. They took a little detour of the place, and the sound of the Daimler's engine was soft on the still night air.

"Dieter, it's good of you to take me for a spin, but isn't there a much shorter way? If I remember it, the Villa Laumannfeld is only a few blocks from Gestapo Headquarters."

"I thought you'd like a drive."

They came to the banks of the Isar and drove along it until turning onto the Prinzregentenstrasse. Even in the blackout the city awakened memories. There was still much beauty, a generous nature hidden. Maybe someday these would triumph.

As they pulled up to the gates of the Villa Laumannfeld, two armed SS guards shone flashlights into the car, while others patrolled the grounds with guard dogs on the leash.

Dieter got out and spoke quietly to the guards. One of them went quickly through the duty roster. Krantz came to join them from the car that had been following. There was a nod, a grimace. "Well, if that's what Heydrich wants, then the prisoner is all yours, my friend, but I'm leaving some of my boys just in case he tries to get smart."

The car door opened. The Berliner grabbed him by the arms, and in one brutal lift, he was on his feet and slammed against the side of the car. A key was jammed into the handcuffs. As they came away, Hagen rubbed his wrists and drank in the air.

Krantz lit a cigarette, took time in waving out the match. "So, Richard, a test of your good behavior. Baron Dieter Karl gives you a reprieve. You have two days to make up your mind." He stabbed a finger against Hagen's chest. "My advice is to do what he wants or else you'll be back with us."

Stuffing the handcuffs into a pocket, the Gestapo strode away into the night. The gates opened and they drove on through with the car full of guards behind them.

There were some changes to the villa. A duty clerk manned the desk in the foyer. The statues were gone. Only the tiles and the cobra in the floor remained.

The cutting and polishing rooms were full of the latest equipment, now silent but well used during the day. Guard dogs prowled loose but made so little sound the sudden appearance of them was startling.

Upstairs, the whole of the second floor was occupied by Dieter's apartment. An adjutant, butler, maid and cook all lived in.

Hagen asked for a bath. Dieter clapped a hand on his shoulder and gave a laugh. "If you hadn't asked, I would have insisted. Do you want another shirt, a better pair of shoes?"

After months of prison even the simplest things brought an agony of guilt. A bar of soap caused utter consternation, a towel drove him to the brink of despair, the feeling of hot water gave up the ache of its loss but made him hate himself for having such luxury.

When the butler, graying, thin and tall, brought in a complete change of clothes, a nondescript suit, shirt, tie and heavy brogues, Hagen had to force himself not to think of escape. He would fit into the crowd. He might just get away...

Later, from the balcony, there was a view of the sky, the darkness of the gardens behind the villa, and the woods of the park beyond.

The taste of the coffee was bitter. Sweetened with saccharine, it clung to the back of his throat.

Krantz had figured out how to make him talk. Freedom — give him a chance of freedom, let him feel it and then take it suddenly away.

"Richard, we still need cutters and polishers. I want you to pick out for me the best of them in Antwerp."

"So you can have them taken prisoner and brought here?"

"Far better here than a concentration camp and certain death. Things can still be overlooked. Jews can be made honorary Aryans if necessary. No one need know."

"I won't do it."

"Why must you continue to be so difficult? I'm giving you a chance to save your life."

"And when the list is done, what then, Dieter?"

"We're going to win, Richard. As in Poland, so in the West. The British haven't got an army in France and the French haven't the spine.

"And you don't have the diamonds, do you?"

"The Antwerp stocks? They're as good as ours."

"Is Cecile helping you? Will you use her farm as a staging point?" Richard had figured it out. Krantz must have told him about Cecile.

"She's very beautiful, Richard. So good in bed. Far better than Dee Dee could ever have been."

So it was true that she was helping them. This he couldn't understand. Not Cecile. Never Cecile.

"Don't look so betrayed, Richard. She's being a realist. Now tell me, will the British send men in to take the diamonds off at the first sign of an invasion?"

"I really wouldn't know, Dieter, but if they should succeed, what then? With the blockade that must surely be in place, you people haven't got a chance. You'll never get enough diamonds to run Germany's industries."

Hunter grinned and shook his head. "As with your former lover, Richard, so with the Congo. I have arranged a little something no one will ever think possible. Diamonds we have, and will have regardless of the Antwerp stocks although, of course, we will have those, too."

"And Cecile?"

"Will be waiting for me, Richard, and only too willing to spread those lovely legs of hers."

Twelve

T HE POSTER was an advertisement for Chicorée-Pacha. The turbaned Turkish sultan with the golden slippers sat among his harem of beaded beauties sipping a steaming cup of coffee substitute. The smile on his face was not the grin of a lecher but that of a wholly satisfied man.

"With all those girls," clucked Lev. "Bernard, if that's how the other half live..."

Wunsch had no patience. "Lev, I did not ask you to see that, but this!"

He tore the poster from the wall and turned it over. "Look...look at these."

Route signs, arrows, faint shields that could only be the shoulder badges of German parachutists.

The roads leading toward Antwerp. The defenses of the Albert Canal and the ways to cross it safely.

Lev let his gaze hunger over the land. They'd come out here to find the Verheyden woman, who had sent a farmer to them with a message. Three Spartan words: "Please contact me." Nothing else.

Her club had been closed and boarded up. The notice on the door had read: Under renovation.

It was May 3, 1940, a Friday. The weather had never been better, the spring more beautiful. In Holland there was a full military alert; in Belgium the army had reestablished the five-day leave.

Rachel and Moses had reached Brazil and were wanting him and Anna to join them...

Wunsch indicated the back of the sign. "I only heard about these yesterday. I didn't believe it was true."

"And the Verheyden woman?" asked Lev. "Does she know of these too?"

It was absolutely crazy, but the diamonds were still in Antwerp. The stall, the wait-and-see had continued, the it's-all-being-taken-care-of and, finally, the cold shoulder as other events, or the lack of them, and the terrible waiting had taken precedence.

Churchill hadn't sent the promised escort. King Leopold and his government still clung to their policy of neutrality.

"Come on, my friend, we'd best find out what she has to say."

Parachutists . . . butterflies floating down in the early-morning light.

The moors were ideally suited, Antwerp not that far.

Wunsch longed for a cigarette, but with the coming of spring his doctor had cut him off completely. Chewing gum was of no use, but he tried it anyway.

The farmhouse, with its square of buildings, looked deserted. It sat well back from the road, with stunted oak, marram grass and brush among the dunes behind it. Canals cut the land on either side. A windmill turned slowly on the marshes, and when he drew the car to a stop, Wunsch heard the sails creaking in the distance.

"Lev. I don't think she's here."

They knocked but there was no answer. The curtains were all drawn. No smoke issued from the chimney, and in the cobbled courtyard of the square there was an emptiness they felt.

Her car was in one of the barns — up on blocks and under canvas, all shiny and new looking but without its tires.

They found the tires secreted in the loft beneath a mound of hay. What the hell . . .

Lev glanced anxiously at Bernard and held his breath before saying quietly, "Does she know something we don't?"

"My thoughts exactly," grunted Wunsch. "Lev, we must have a little look around but do so carefully."

There were bootprints in the sand among the dunes behind the place — not many of them. As a matter of fact, only a few.

The spent cartridge of a Very light lay just beneath the sand. Brass against the buff brown grains.

"Bernard, what has happened here?"

"Someone came in last night."

"Perhaps a day or two ago," said Lev.

"Perhaps."

"At least a squad, Bernard. Twenty or thirty men. There were tire marks in the laneway. Trucks."

They turned to look toward the house and barns, wondering if they'd be allowed to leave. "We must not show we are aware of anything, Lev. Let met pick Martine a small bouquet of daffodils. Mevrouw Verheyden won't mind."

"Not if she's dead."

As they reached the house, Lev was certain an upstairs curtain had moved.

Bernard gathered flowers as a squirrel would acorns, passing up most only to decide at last on the perfect bloom.

Damas watched the two of them. So much was at stake. Berlin had sent thirty parachutists of the armed SS, the *Verfügungstruppe*,* with orders to take and hold the Antwerp diamonds at all costs until the invasion

---

* Later to be called the Waffen SS

overran the city. As yet Baron Dieter Karl Hunter hadn't arrived to command his men, but the invasion must be coming soon, at any hour. Could he let Wunsch and his diamond cutter go? Should he kill them now?

Cecile Verheyden tensely waited. Would he kill her? Would he terrorize her first? She'd been such a silly fool not to have realized others would be watching her.

With a sharp intake of breath, Damas eased the Luger's hammer closed. He turned away from the window and, with a smile, came toward her.

"They've gone," he said. "Now perhaps you will tell me why they came out here to see you?"

Her eyes darted over him. Angrily she said, "How should I know? Perhaps they wanted news of Richard, perhaps they thought I could . . . "

Using the muzzle of the gun, Damas forced her to face him. Her frantic eyes were very blue.

"Could *what*, Mevrouw Verheyden?"

"Could tell them if Richard was really alive. Look, I *don't* know! Ask Dieter."

"The baron, yes." Damas touched the soft skin of her throat with the muzzle of the pistol. He ran it under the line of her jaw until, pressing it behind her right ear, he had cocked the gun again.

Her eyes hardened. A stillness came to her. "If you harm me, Dieter will kill you."

"The baron, yes."

Reaching up, he undid the top two buttons of her blouse. He'd seen her talking to the farmer, had had the man followed to Antwerp, to Wunsch. She'd been waiting for them. Waiting . . .

Cecile couldn't face him. Momentarily she shut her eyes, wished she could make a run for it — knew she'd have to.

Damas fingered the frilly lace of her brassiere. "You told them to come here. You said, 'There's something I must tell you. A squad of men came in two nights ago.' "

"I didn't! How could I have done such a thing when I'm working for Dieter?"

He hit her then. As her head jerked away, he grabbed her. She began to fight back, to kick, to struggle.

When she made a lunge for the door, he threw her back across the bed, began to hit her again and again, not too hard but just enough.

When she was naked, he forced the muzzle of the Luger into her mouth. "Now talk or else."

The Browning semiautomatic kicked a little but when she held it steadily with two hands, Arlette could let it rise and fall of its own accord and bang all thirteen rounds into the target with no trouble.

The Lee Enfield .303 rifle and the Mauser were all right, the tommy gun far too jolting. It terrified her. The Schmeisser . . . now there was a slightly better weapon.

Arlette reloaded the pistol. This time she would have to fire as she ran at the target.

The Scottish Highlands seemed so far from what was happening in Europe. Belgium and Holland were still free and neutral. Perhaps the war would never come. Perhaps they'd let her go home one day.

She mustn't think of Richard — he was dead. She was certain of this. She mustn't think of what might have been. She was Odette Latour now. Another person.

The instructors never told her much, Duncan least of all. But she'd seen him leave the school in great haste, had known something must be up.

"Och, you've done very well t'day, miss. It's grand t'see a lass shoot like that."

Sandy McIntyre was in his sixties, a retired drill sergeant who'd seen too much of war but knew that the only hope for others lay in teaching it to them. The lass was bonny. The blush of youth and the Highlands were all about her.

She breathed in easily and grinned at him. The compliments were few but well deserved when given. "They'll never send me over in any case. I flunked out with my jumps. I'm to go back and try again, but I don't think I'll ever get the hang of it."

Parachuting! This ever-changing war. The Nazis had used them in Poland and Scandinavia. "Lass, the thing is to empty your mind of everything."

While plummeting through the darkness! To what? Some marsh? With a forty-five-pound wireless set dropped with its own chute just for you or the Nazis to find! And anyway, Belgium hadn't been invaded. Not yet.

McIntyre indicated the target. Arlette dug the toes of her boots into the springy turf and launched herself at it.

The holes made a pattern about the heart and lungs. Two had, however, gone into the German soldier's face.

She slid the breech open and removed the clip. As she handed the gun to him, McIntyre shook his head. "From now on it's yours. Keep it by you in readiness. I greatly fear you're about to need it."

At evening they played the pipes in the glens, and from across the loch Arlette heard them. "Murdo MacKenzie of Torridon," "Farewell to the Creeks," "Scotland the Brave with Wings" . . .

"The Battle of Waterloo."

A curlew called and was answered by its mate.

Damas leaned the bicycle against the wall. Dressed as a priest, he approached the two men who stood in the laneway looking curiously up at the windows above the Club Chez Vous.

So worried were they, neither heard him until he was almost upon them. Then Wunsch leaped; the diamond cutter froze.

The priest smiled and indicated the club. "She's gone to the country. I was just about to see if the carpenters had started work."

Somehow Lev found his voice. "Do you know her then?"

"But of course. Cecile, she is an old friend of my family. Me, I am also her priest, so" — he gave a priest's shrug "— she and I share a few things. A cup of coffee now and then. She has asked me to keep an eye on the place while she's away."

Crossing the lane, he went up to the back door and inserted the key. "Is there a message you'd like to leave? Was there something . . . "

Wunsch shook his head. "No. No, there is nothing, Father. My firm was asked to quote on the roof. The eaves, you understand."

"The eaves? But she hasn't mentioned this to me."

Worried now, he came back and stood there staring up at the roof. "The eaves look well enough."

"That's what I was going to tell her but —" Wunsch asked for a cigarette "— one can't really tell without the ladders, Father. These old places . . . always it's the same thing. Lift a bit of flashing and . . . ah! a thousand francs' worth of work."

"Would you like to see inside the place? I'm sure she wouldn't mind. The attic's easy enough to get at."

"No. No, that wouldn't be proper. When will she be back?"

Wunsch drew on the cigarette and filled his lungs. To hell with doctors. To hell with everything. They'd stop this "priest"!

Lev heard the man say, "In two weeks. She always goes to her farm at this time of year, but usually leaves the club in Berke's hands."

Berke was the woman who ran it for her. The padlock was on the garage.

The "priest" slid a hand into the left pocket of his jacket. Lev said, "Bernard, there's that other job we have to look at. Perhaps we should come back on Monday with the ladders?"

"Monday . . . yes, yes, that would be best. Father, do you think that would be all right?"

Damas glanced from one to the other and allowed himself a faint smile. "But of course. Monday would be perfect. I'll tell her you were by."

The diamond, an octahedron from South Africa, was shot through with specks of ilmenite but ice clear otherwise and of about two carats in weight. One corner of the crystal had been broken off to create an extremely sharp edge.

Hagen held the stone under the bedside lamp before slipping it away in a pocket of his jacket. Dieter Karl hadn't seen him palm it. He was certain of this.

There was only one way he could possibly escape. For a night, a day and on into the following night he had thought of little else. Somehow he had to get a warning out that they intended to seize the diamonds, that Dieter now had a squad of men in place and that he was in contact with them by wireless. Dieter was so anxious to get back to Antwerp, he could barely disguise his impatience.

The only thing in his favor was that from the cook, the butler and Dieter's adjutant right to Krantz and the SS guards, everyone expected him to try to escape. They were all watching for it.

Again he glanced at the clock. The workers had left the villa at 7:00 p.m. At eight the guards had been changed. At eight-fifteen they had begun yet another patrol — forty-five minutes, no more. Twice around the building and then out into the grounds to the very edge of the park for a final sweep.

Once done, they had returned to the guardhouse, which was just inside the gates. There they'd had a chat with the sergeant, a smoke perhaps or a cup of coffee. At nine-fifteen they had begun it all again, and at ten-fifteen.

The dogs would be on the leash. Both of the guards would carry their rifles over a shoulder. Both would have flashlights they wouldn't use unless necessary. But would they stop by the fountains and the fish ponds as they had before? Would they let the dogs drink?

Hagen pulled off his shoes and socks. Stuffing the socks into the toes, he tied the laces together with a slipknot, then left the shoes on the bed.

Easing the heavy chest of drawers against the door took time. Adding everything else he could to stop them from entering the room as long as possible took a little more.

Again he watched the clock and practiced counting so as to time himself. Switching off the light, he slung his shoes around his neck and stood there in the darkness.

At twenty minutes past midnight he crawled out of the window and clung to the narrow stone ledge high above the driveway.

Krantz would be watching for him through binoculars. There'd be shades of darkness. The Berliner would be sure to see him climbing down the drainpipe and running out across the lawns to hide in the gardens. He'd give him a chance to get away and then close in.

From the last of the fish ponds a tiny stream ran on to join one of those in the park. Irmgard and he had once followed it. He knew he had to reach that stream. There were footbridges and paths, even a small lake in the park, surrounded by roads except where a branch of the stream rejoined the Isar.

Talking softly, the guards passed below him.

He began to count. When he judged the guards had turned the corner, he worked his way along the ledge until he reached the balcony.

Clinging to the corner by the drainpipe, Hagen hid his shoes between the bars of the railing. The guards came back and headed out into the gardens. They would now go from pond to pond, from clump of cedar, boxwood hedge and arbor to beech, linden and fir. They would make a careful circuit of the edge of the park where it adjoined the garden, and then they'd come back.

He was lying in the last of the ponds, all but submerged behind its central fountain, when the guards returned and paused to let the dogs drink.

"We are not to shoot him, Bruno. He is to be caught."

"And if he gets away?"

"The Oberstgruppenführer Heydrich will have our balls and if not him, the Gestapo Krantz."

The one called Bruno broke wind. The dogs threw up their snouts. "He won't escape. The searchlights will pin him down."

Their voices faded. From pond to pond the guards cut across the lawns and gardens, heading for the far corner of the villa.

Staying well clear of the stream, Hagen ran at a crouch for the edge of the park. He was in among some trees when he smelled stale cigarette smoke.

Krantz had men everywhere. Time . . . there was so little time.

Stealthily crawling away from the man, he forced himself not to bolt and run. When he reached the edge of a broad grassy swale, he went cautiously down into it and quickly up the other side.

More shrubs and trees followed, then more open grassland. The stream would be off to the right. Making for it, he stopped suddenly.

When he found the man, he was so close to him he could hear him breathing.

The man moved off. Hagen stepped into his place. There was a path. Stone chips were underfoot.

Reluctantly he followed.

The path wound down through a scattering of trees to a footbridge. Beyond this there was a narrow strip of parkland and then a road.

The man reached the bridge and spoke quietly to someone. Hagen turned away downstream of them and crossed, recrossed and again crossed the stream.

When he waded back upstream to the bridge, the men were still there.

How much time was left? A minute? Five minutes? Could he really do it?

Crawling under the bridge, hearing the sound of their boots softly scuffing the boards above him, he moved silently away.

When a light rain began to fall, he had reached the first of the fish ponds. Then he went from pond to pond across the gardens, picked out as best he could the route he had taken on leaving the villa.

The shoes were there where he had left them. Pausing only long enough to slip them about his neck, he tugged on the drainpipe once more and looked up at the eaves.

He was on the roof of the villa when the searchlights came on and the dogs began to bark.

The building in which Dillingham's had their offices and shop was in darkness, as indeed were all the buildings on the street.

Damas signaled to the two men who had come with him. One would watch the street, while the other came into the building with him.

Bernard Wunsch was working late — very late. The heavy drapes had been pulled across the windows of his office. The city was quiet.

Using the keys he'd had made, Damas unlocked the outer door and reached in to switch off the alarm system. Walking quickly, they went along to the stairs. The musty odor of closed rooms, dust, ink, carbon paper and stale coffee and tobacco smoke came to them, and at last the sound of muffled voices behind the dim and rippled glass of the office door.

Wunsch had someone with him.

Troubled at the thought, Damas strained to listen, then slid the key into the lock and softly opened that door as well.

Turning to the man who'd come with him, he said "Wait here. Shoot only if you have to."

The door to Wunsch's office was partly closed, the green of the lampshade showing at once the worried frown, the cigarette and the back of the man who sat before him.

"Cecile wouldn't work for the Nazis, Mr. Wunsch. Och, I met the woman when she and Richard were engaged."

"But I am telling you something has happened. Lev and I went to the army for help. We tried to get them to believe us — my God, won't you? That empty cartridge for a Very light — isn't that evidence enough?"

Damn the Belgian army for not listening. "How many men do you think they have?"

That was better. "Thirty — at least that many. Lev and I believe they are hiding in the club of this woman and that they know we are to use the *Megadan*."

"The Club Chez Vous."

"Yes, yes, that is the name of the place. This priest —"

"Karl Christian Damas."

"Yes, yes, that's the name. This man, he has so many others. We know they have infiltrated the premises of the Mercantile Company. Five of his men have jobs there as drivers. Five, Mr. McPherson. Hence, it was so easy for them to find the trucks to move these parachutists from the farm."

"And Cecile?" asked McPherson.

Wunsch drew on his cigarette. The woman had obviously had a change of heart and had shown her true colors. "Working for them. In bed with the baron. Of this we are certain."

McPherson couldn't tell him that Cecile had taken it upon herself to contact him through Richard's mother. He couldn't say, You're wrong. She's one of us.

Instead he said, "What's happened to her?"

"Gone to Munich, I should think. Left the country perhaps."

Wunsch kept glancing at the shade of his lamp and then flicking a quick look past him to the door of the office.

"Another cigarette?" said McPherson, offering the package he'd brought over. Their fingers touched, the Belgian quickly tapping out an SOS.

McPherson reached for the telephone. Wunsch grimaced and madly shook his head.

The Scotsman glanced at his wristwatch. "The men I brought with me should have been here by now, Mr. Wunsch. It's gone half two already."

When they went to check the building, they found it empty.

"I thought someone was listening to us," said Wunsch. "I must have been mistaken. Nerves . . . it was just my nerves."

As darkness came again, Hagen stretched out on the slates. For the remainder of the previous night and throughout the day armed SS and Gestapo men had come and gone and never once had they thought to look for him on the roof of the Villa Laumannfeld.

Coiled into the base of one of the statues that lined the eaves, he had kept out of sight and had tried to ease his cramped limbs.

The slates were treacherous. More than once he slipped. When he reached the main part of the roof, he lay there too exhausted to move.

The cars and trucks of the SS and the Gestapo still lined the Prinzregentenstrasse. Across the way there was a row of tall houses; beyond these, a maze of old and fashionable streets. If only his luck would hold. They must have already done a house-to-house search of those streets.

The crown of the roof was flat. Hagen wormed his way across it and went down the far side. A pigeon flew off, startling him. Then the sound of the rain came to him and he felt it on his hands and face.

Clinging to the wall, he reached the window at last and took out the diamond. First he'd need a small hole up in one corner...

The glass cut easily. He pressed a thumb against the corner and the piece broke free.

Now he cut the pane, outlining a large enough area so that he could lift the glass away and open the window.

The blackout curtains were heavy. The room was off one of the bedrooms. By degrees he picked out a sewing machine, basket of mending, some cloth — material for a dress perhaps — a pair of scissors.

Frau Gerda Meyer, the cook, was reading in bed. The satin nightgown was pink and frilly, her shoulders rounded, the tired blond hair unpinned.

She adjusted her glasses and looked up and across the bedroom toward him. Hagen didn't move from the crack in the door. She shivered once, twice, plucked at the nightgown and settled down.

None of them would sleep until this business was over. For once she'd managed a decent situation and now some pig of an Englishman or was he a Belgian? — no, he was an American, *ja* — had come to spoil things for her.

This war was no good. Now more and more the Gestapo and the Sicherheitsdienst were asking things about the baron, and she was having to make them up just to show she was loyal to the fatherland.

Far better one should read detective novels and let the world go by.

She turned a page and heaved a sigh, but the cold, damp air had gotten to her. Hagen knew it had. She'd give him away. She'd cry out and sound the alarm.

From the sitting room windows of Bernard Wunsch's comfortable flat, McPherson looked out over the lights of Antwerp. The Club Chez Vous hadn't contained a soul, the farmhouse had been empty.

Had Damas murdered Cecile Verheyden?

Somehow the schoolmaster had managed to get his men away. The Belgian army had done the searches, including a warehouse-to-warehouse scrutiny that had, for the available time and men, been quite thorough.

Yet still, there were so many warehouses in the port of Antwerp. It hadn't been easy convincing the powers that be to sidestep their own government and do the necessary.

Still gazing out over the city, he said, "We'll be ready for them. Just you see that your army holds them off long enough for us to get up the estuary."

The Belgians would throw an armed guard around the *Megadan* and the diamonds if — and this was the fly in the ointment — if, for bloody sakes, there was the need!

An invasion...

"There'll be planes — fighters and bombers," said a grim-faced Bernard Wunsch. "Tin fish, hawks in the sky and eighty kilometers of estuary to negotiate."

"Small arms and grenades before that. Mortars," said McPherson.

"We will do what we can. Me, I have my revolver."

Damas hadn't been picked up, though the police and the Belgian security service had a countrywide bulletin out on him. McPherson wished he had someone in Antwerp to replace Cecile, someone to keep a watch on things independent of Wunsch and his diamond cutter.

Arlette? he wondered. With his eye steadfastly on the future, Churchill had said the girl was to stay in Scotland.

Yet could they not use her now? Could they not send her over? The girl could handle herself well enough, could shoot with the best, knew Damas, knew the ropes, the city.

Would only be killed, as she would in any case if the worst came as it surely would, and the Germans overran the country.

As yet he'd not told Wunsch and his wife the girl was alive, though he now knew how much the news would mean to them.

Reaching for his coat, he gruffly said, "We'll keep in touch. Do what you can to hold them off and I'll be here with the destroyers as soon as I can."

Frau Gerda Meyer had read for a good hour. Now her snoring came softly. Hagen eased the sewing room door shut behind him. She stirred, murmured in her sleep and turned over with a sigh.

Feeling his way cautiously across the room, he soon came to the bed and felt for something to cover her face. But did she really have to die? Was it right of him?

He left her alone and went out into the hall. Dieter was still up. The voice of a young woman came and then that of Dieter. "I should be in Antwerp, Hilde. Heydrich should never have agreed to let Krantz release Richard to me. Now the Gestapo will hold me responsible for his escape, and we may well lose the Antwerp diamond stocks."

The girl spoke soothingly to him. "Don't worry so much. My God, they'll catch him, those guys. Darling, come to bed."

"In a while. Richard knows we're getting diamonds through from the Congo, Hilde. It won't take him long to figure out how. This we cannot have."

"Come back to bed. *Bitte*, Dieter. I'm ready for it."

"Go to sleep. My men are all in place, but I'm not there to be with them."

Dieter went into the sitting room to switch on the wireless, but all he could get from the Propaganda Ministry was an interlude of Bach.

Along the hall from him Hagen clutched the brandy decanter and a box of matches. The lift was just big enough for the laundry or a breakfast tray, but it ran from the second floor down into the cellars.

Easing himself into the thing, he tried the switch but nothing happened. The girl came along and went into the washroom. The music grew louder. Hagen tried the switch again.

Dieter... Dieter was so close.

The water closet flushed. The girl began to run a bath. Hagen slid the lift door closed, and at once the thing began to move. Would Dieter hear the sound of it? There were dogs loose on the first floor. Did they have the run of the cellars as well?

Hilde Meissner tossed her nightgown into the sink and turned on the taps. Heydrich had ordered her to get to know the Baron Dieter Karl Hunter. At twenty-one years of age she had the body of a goddess, had ridden naked at some of the Munich festivals. The startling blue eyes and blond, blond hair were those of a pure Aryan. The baron had money and power but not so much of the latter as she would have liked. And he had a mistress in Antwerp that the *Oberstgruppenführer* of the SS wished to know more about.

She bathed her neck and let the water run down between her splendid breasts. They would catch this Hagen and they would kill him.

Tossing a bar of scented soap into the sink, she left the laundry for Frau Gerda Meyer. "Dieter, come and join me, yes? Come, come. Let me wash that lovely thing of yours and see if I can't awaken it."

The lift reached the cellars. Above him, Hagen could hear the nervous padding of the dogs as they went through the cutting and polishing rooms.

Silently he moved away.

There was a technician in the room where the diamond powders were separated by settling in olive oil. The man was dozing in a chair.

Blackout screens covered the windows. The stone walls had been whitewashed. The rows of stainless-steel settling tanks were up on wooden stands.

Beyond the tanks there was a door through which he could just see the gray iron cylinders of the ball mills they used to grind the boart. For some reason the mills had been shut down, and he realized then that Dieter hadn't wanted him to hear them.

From a nail beside the furnace Hagen took a coil of old electrical wire. He broke off a length, then went back through to the settling room. The light coming from it seemed brilliant. There'd be no shadows, no place to hide.

The technician stirred and gave a yawn. Sitting up, the man stretched to ease his cramped limbs and looked at the clock. It was almost time to decant the number-threes.

The wire cut into his throat! Gagging, struggling to get free of it, he slammed Hagen into the wall. One of the dogs barked. The man hooked his fingers under the wire. Desperately he fought for air and fought to escape.

Hagen rammed the man's head against the wall and twisted the wire. The dogs began to whine. Restlessly they prowled the room above them.

At last he was able to lower the body to the floor.

One after another he opened the valves that allowed each size of diamond dust to be drawn off. As the oil and sludge poured onto the floor, he brought kindling and papers from the furnace room.

Splashing brandy onto the papers, he went to see if there was any kerosene in the furnace room. The oil and sludge soon followed him. The caretaker was a fussy sort. Everything was there as it should be to light the furnace on the coldest of nights.

Everything including the brown paper wrappings from several parcels. Address after address showed the names of prisoner-of-war camps in Germany, the return addresses of Leopoldville in the Congo.

Struck by what he'd found, Hagen quickly folded a few of the things and put them in a pocket, then stuffed the lift with papers and kindling, and splashed kerosene over them.

From the furnace he took a shovelful of glowing coals.

The blazing lift started on its way. The dogs began to bark. As the oil ignited, tongues of flame spread throughout the cellar. Soon the cook began to scream. "Fire! There is fire in the cellars, Baron!"

Guards poured in the front door and raced for the cellar stairs. He'd have to get out, have to get away!

Hagen found the coal chute and went up it and out into the grounds. He was lost among the houses on the other side of the Prinzregentenstrasse when the first trucks of the fire brigade careered around a corner.

There was only one place the Gestapo wouldn't think to look for him.

The darkened streets led him to the gardens, these to the Residenz, the palaces of the kings of Bavaria. From there it wasn't far to Gestapo Headquarters on the Briennerstrasse.

Krantz fingered the cigarette case. Had he misjudged Hagen? In spite of everything one did, luck still played a part in so many things. The father had been a real hunter but it had been against him then.

Where would the son go? To hide in the diamond center had been one thing — good and certainly enough to have tricked them all.

But here? he wondered as he stood in the courtyard behind the headquarters and looked at the garages. To lie down with the lions? Hagen couldn't possibly have done it. There were far too many guards.

"So, where would he go, Baron?" he asked. "The Villa Hunter?"

Badly burned about the face and hands, Dieter Karl found it painful to speak. "It's already been searched."

"Then search again. You're the one who let him go."

"If you'd had any sense..."

The diamond center had been completely destroyed. The floors had fallen in. They'd have to build again. "We must find him, Baron. You and I share in this, more so yourself, I think, than I. Is it that you let him go on purpose?"

Hunter cursed him. "Why should I have?"

The Berliner budgeted a smile. "Perhaps it's only that you were busy with other things and neglected your duty to be watchful."

Damn him anyway! "I should be in Antwerp. The diamond stocks... My men are waiting to attack."

"They won't wait long. They've been given their orders. So, a little more looking, I think. You to the Villa Hunter, me to have a few words with the boys."

"He'll get word out about the Congo diamonds."

"Not if we stop him, Baron."

The garages were empty save for one disgruntled mechanic in greasy coveralls, who was busy fixing something at one of the workbenches.

Krantz walked through the place without a word and went up into the garage loft. The loot was everywhere and he had to wonder at the greed of the SS. The place had been turned into a sort of Aladdin's cave. Rolled tapestries, crates of silver and fine china, pieces of sculpture enough to stock a small museum but no sign of Hagen. Of this he was certain.

Even so, he called in some help and gave the place a fine-tooth combing.

The offices of Britain's First Lord of the Admiralty were a hive of activity, no matter the lateness of the hour. Dragged out of bed and put on a plane at Kincalda's field in Scotland, Arlette was shown in.

Churchill nodded grimly as he ran his eyes over the latest telex. "Intelligence reports are in deluge, my dear. Pray do forgive me. I seem to have so little time. Do have a look at that mosaic of aerial photographs Duncan is perusing. Find us the warehouse wherein this schoolmaster Karl Christian Damas hides his squad of Nazis."

Briefly Duncan outlined things for her. Arlette, nervous under their combined scrutiny, began to search the mosaic. Everything was so tiny, the houses, the streets. She found the Meir, Antwerp's great thorough-fare, found the Cathedral of Our Lady, the Grote Markt, the town hall, even the house of Madame Hausemer.

Locating the Club Chez Vous without much difficulty, she soon found places where she'd window-shopped, strolled along the quays, done so many things.

"Try," said McPherson. "Damas knew where to take them on very short notice."

Dismayed by the problem, Arlette turned to face them. "There are nearly two hundred hectares of warehouses in the port of Antwerp, some fifty kilometers of landing quays and over eight hundred kilometers of railway lines. It's huge, whole towns and villages . . . "

"But you will try to find the one place this schoolmaster has used, my dear, because we absolutely must know of it."

"Try to put yourself into Damas's shoes, Arlette," urged Duncan.

How could she? Arlette remembered the closeness of him, the point of his knife, the way he'd lain on top of her.

"Duncan, give me that file on him," said Churchill gruffly. "I seem to remember that before he went to teach at the École de Maagdenhuis, he taught in Ste. Anne at . . . "

"Ste. Anne is across the river," said Arlette. "There is a tunnel — two tunnels. One for pedestrians, the other for cars and trucks."

"Neither of which is far from the harbor. Am I right?" demanded Churchill.

Yes, of course he was right. She pointed them out to him. "But the school in Ste. Anne, if it's the École de Sanderhuis Watermael, has been closed and empty for some years."

"Would you be able to take a good look at it for us?"

"Yes . . . yes, I could do such a thing."

The cigar was clenched. "Duncan, see that she is dropped into Belgium so that no one knows she is there but ourselves. Brief her and cut her loose. At all costs we must stop them from getting the diamonds.

"My dear, forgive me. I cannot trust your compatriots — no, not Wunsch of course, and the others, but this Damas . . . you do understand? When you've located them, simply contact Duncan and we'll take care of it from here. Oh and try to do a little something else I had in mind for you should Belgium be overrun. The Nazis may well be getting diamonds out of the Congo via the International Red Cross in parcels that are slated for Polish POW camps in the Reich. Get us one of those parcels, my dear. Get me the proof so that, if need be, I can take the Diamond Corporation to court for violating international law and our naval blockade of the Reich."

Churchill tossed an indifferent hand. "Of course, it might simply be the work of some corrupt Belgian official at the mines. But I must have the proof, and you —" he fixed her with the intensity of his gaze "— must never let what I have just revealed pass your lips."

He hated to see her go; she'd have been so useful to them later, could easily have formed the nucleus of a resistance. But war was ever-shifting. One had to take the offensive no matter how small the advantage.

"My dear, would you do something else for me?" he asked more kindly. "Kill this schoolmaster. Put an end to him."

The loft above Munich's Gestapo headquarters was in darkness. For hours now there had been only the infrequent comings and goings in the garage below him. At last Hagen could stand the waiting no longer.

One man was changing a tire, another was replacing a head lamp. There were three cars in the garage, but all were some distance from the stairs to the loft.

The third man was underneath a black Mercedes, changing the oil or searching for possible trouble. It was the car that Heydrich used when in the city.

The man crawled out from under the Mercedes. Wiping his hands on a rag, he put a cloth over the driver's seat and gave the engine a try.

Leaving it running, he went back to adjust the carburetor. As he worked, one of the others let out a curse and opened the door to vent the exhaust.

Hagen went down the rest of the stairs and turned the corner into the lunchroom. Behind this there was the change room. He ran into the lavatory only to hear a water closet flush.

There were no doors on the cubicles. The man was not far from him. Back in the loft, he waited again.

At about 4:00 a.m. the place was dead quiet. There seemed to be only two men on duty, and both were having something to eat in the lunchroom.

It was now or never. He went down the stairs and through the garage. Not stopping, he entered Gestapo Headquarters and went straight up to the second floor and along to Heydrich's office, which was locked.

Far down the corridor the lonely sound of a typewriter drifted from somewhere below, that of a telephone, and from below this in the cellars, a single scream.

He tried the door to the adjutant's office and found it open. From a desk drawer he took a bunch of keys. Some opened the filing cabinets, one switched off the alarm system, another unlocked Heydrich's door.

Pulling the rug over to the bottom of the door, he turned on the desk lamp. Everything was as it had been before.

There were two spare uniforms in the closet, a leather trench coat with an SS armband. Two Walther P-38s hung side by side in their holsters.

Worrying over the boots, he went into the washroom and silently filled the basin, had a wash, a shave and a look at himself.

Even though he'd seen himself at the Villa Laumannfeld, still the sight was a shock. Not only was he haggard and old looking, his nose was still swollen and crooked. One eye was partly closed and still bore shades of purple. There were cuts and scars he hadn't owned before.

In the filing cabinets he came across Heydrich's personal dossiers. Choosing the top generals, he filled a briefcase, then found a file marked Antwerp. Page after page held the names of Belgians, of contacts, possible contacts and outright collaborators.

Stuffing the file into the briefcase, he left the office dressed as an SS *Oberstgruppenführer*. Though he forced himself to walk steadily, he fortunately met no one.

The Mercedes was parked in the lot beside two others. The keys were on the board in the garage. The men were busy with brooms, getting the place ready for the day shift.

At 4:15 a.m. one of them went to change. At 4:20 the other two followed him.

Hagen drove out of the yard past sleepy guards too startled to do anything but stand to attention. The Mercedes awoke to the road but there was still a long way to go.

Otto Krantz was impressed. Hagen had not only got into Gestapo Headquarters, he'd got into Heydrich's office and had stolen a few things.

But that car wasn't going far. They'd rigged the fuel gauges of all three of them to read full and had virtually emptied the tanks. Hagen must have hidden on the roof.

Would he break down and tell them everything when captured? Would he sing as so many had?

A momentary feeling of sadness came to Krantz. The chase had been good, the hunt far better than average. In many ways Hagen had been a lot like his father. Difficult.

Every nut and bolt seemed to rattle in the twin-engined Whitley bomber as it banked to the west and began to reduce altitude. The wind whipped at her boots and tucked-in trousers. Below her, the land was black as ink and then dusted with tiny lights — the farms, villages and towns just to the south of the Scheldt and to the north of Brussels.

The Whitley leveled off at an altitude of about eight hundred feet. The light came on. The flight lieutenant gave her the thumbs-up sign, and she dropped through the hole into the night.

At once there was incomparable panic and terror. The chute wouldn't open! She'd hit the ground and...

The static line snapped. The relief of floating freely swept in on her, an elation that was like no other.

Instinctively Arlette bent her knees and rolled over as she hit the ground. Immediately she began to gather in the chute.

As the sound of the Whitley faded, the wind came cool on her cheek. Then suddenly she was cold, lonely and terrified all over again. Worse still, she didn't know where she was. Worse even than this, the wireless transceiver could be miles away. Hung up in a tree someplace, out in one of the canals or in the river.

There was no reception committee, no one waiting for her.

Routine took over. She bundled the silk canopy into a tighter ball and went in search of the wireless set.

The ground grew wetter. Soon she was wading through shallows, parting the reeds.

The canopy had floated out into the river — but was it really the Scheldt?

There was no moon.

Gingerly, Arlette went down the bank and tried to pull the heavy pack in with a stick. The sound of the reeds came back to her, then the barking of a dog. For an instant she listened, trying to determine the direction of the barking.

Pulling off her things, she went out into the icy water. Mud squished between her toes. Marsh gas welled up. Loaded with water, the canopy dragged. More than once she slipped and fell. More than once the dog barked.

Then she saw the farmhouse — just the outline of it against the sky. It was off to her left, across the river.

The dog was quieted. A door was closed. Slowly, cautiously, she gathered in the last of the canopy and carried it up the bank. Then she went back for the bulky pack that held the forty-five-pound, short-wave WT transceiver in its plain brown suitcase.

Shivering, her teeth chattering, Arlette removed the packing and carried the set up to her clothes. The temptation to shove the packing out into the river was almost more than she could resist, but she buried it and the chute some distance downstream of the dog.

After another dunking to wash off the mud, she dried herself with a handkerchief — that was all she had to spare. Ops hadn't thought of her getting wet! Ops seldom thought of things like that!

Quickly she got dressed. She was freezing, wanted desperately to head for Ostend to see her family, to get news of them and perhaps even tell them she was alive and back in Belgium.

Instead, she picked up the suitcase and headed across the fields away from the dog.

Krantz surveyed the scene before him. The jackboots were mired in cow shit. Heydrich's brand-new trousers hung from a cow's tail, and the thing had passed water on them.

The jacket, cap, belt and holster lay on the floor in a puddle of milk that had now gone sour.

The milkmaid was bawling her eyes out! Hagen had buggered off on them! He hadn't done the obvious. He'd taken the car only a few short blocks to the Karlsplatz, the traffic hub of Munich. There he'd ditched the thing and hopped a tramcar, only to leave it almost immediately.

They'd seen him run into a lane. They'd blown the whistle on him and had fanned out but he'd commandeered the bicycle of a news vendor. Two blocks later it had been a passing car of the Uniformed Municipal Police who had swallowed hook, line and sinker his story about trying to get to Berlin with important documents.

The lift with the police had ended on the outskirts of the city with two dead cops and the engine still running.

He'd taken a farmer's cart, then yet another bicycle. A horse...had he used one and gone across the fields? "*Gott in Himmel*, you stupid slut, shut up and tell us what happened!"

The girl was incoherent. When she was slapped, her braids got in the way. "He has...He has...the clothes of my father..."

The farmer had gone off to war like everyone else and had left the place to the women. Krantz kicked the pail across the shed, startling the cows and bringing a fresh well of tears to the girl.

"Issue an all-points. I want every road from here to the borders checked."

When asked which borders, he shrieked, "*All of them!*"

A harried Dieter Karl was thrust into the shed. In spite of the burns, the Gestapo had handcuffed him. Krantz didn't waste time. "Gone! That bastard's gone!"

Hunter ducked. The Berliner swung again and lifted the bandages. "So, you're to blame. Dachau for him. Bugger the diamonds, Baron. Bugger you! When Heydrich finds Hagen has flown the coop with his files, he'll cut your heart out!"

Blood trickled from a split lip. Hunter straightened himself. "Then use your head. Richard will try to reach Antwerp."

The abandoned school was back from the river up a narrow street whose cobblestones glistened in the early-morning rain. People were about — housewives at their shopping, seamen coming from ships that had docked in the harbor, others going off to work. Children...always there were children, the boys scruffy in their school uniforms, the girls often tidy but so sleepy-eyed.

There was the usual pub and on the corner, a tobacconist's, a café, a greengrocer's, a milliner's...the village was self-contained, the street itself.

Arlette paused to look in the window of the tobacconist's. She longed for a cigarette, a thing she had never done before Ostend. She'd come to date everything in her new life from that awful day she had had to run into the sea and had so very nearly drowned.

And now she was back, and the city...the Central Station, the Pelikaanstraat and the diamond district, the Meir and its tramcars, the Cathedral of Our Lady, the Grote Markt...all had brought so many memories. Richard had been in each of them. She mustn't think of him. He was gone from her. Gone, and she had a job to do.

Nicholas Pijner looked up from the cash drawer where he'd been ruefully puzzling over a handful of crisp new German marks. The girl had finally made up her mind and had came into the shop. Pretty, with short-cut deep chestnut hair whose wisps stuck out from beneath a dark brown beret. About twenty-five years of age, he thought, giving her a generous smile and forgetting all about the marks, which hadn't had the look of real currency about them.

"Good morning," he said, the accent thick. "Can I help you?"

Arlette set the faded brown leather briefcase she'd bought in a second-hand shop in Brussels on the edge of the counter between them. "Yes. Have you any English cigarettes? Everything in your window is Dutch, and I...I'm not yet used to anything other than the English ones."

"Tobacco is tobacco, and these —" he reached for a package "— are extra mild."

She had the money ready, knew exactly how much they'd be.

"That school at the end of the street..." she began. "Is it still in use? Someone has said it..."

"Is it that you're in search of a position?" he asked. The young — she was so earnest.

The blush the girl gave was emphasized by the shyness of incredible bedroom eyes that ducked away, then came back to gaze quite frankly at him. "I had hoped there'd be something for me in the fall perhaps. Languages...I have my certificates. Girls...I would prefer to teach only girls."

The languages would explain the English cigarettes. Pijner hated to tell her the truth. "That old place has been closed for years."

"Is there a watchman?" she asked, dismayed by the news.

"A watchman? No...no, the place went bust and they simply bolted the doors and left. But the boys...the drunks..." he gave a shrug. "It's not a place I'd go if I were you."

Arlette broke open the package of cigarettes. Offering them, she took one herself and he lit it for her, watched as she gratefully sucked the smoke into her lungs like a trooper. My God, had she been playing around with him?

"That school...has anyone been interested in it lately?" she asked.

Within the past two days, perhaps?

Pijner thought of the fistful of German marks the priest had given him. He thought to tell the girl that the bills could quite possibly be counterfeit.

The priest had bought more than enough cigarettes for one man. Mevrouw Oudkirk had said that her youngest son had thought he'd seen someone in the place.

Gruffly Pijner said, "The school's closed, Juffrouw. It's no place for you."

Again she filled her lungs before stubbing out her cigarette in the cup of the sawed-off mortar shell he used as an ashtray.

Keeping to the inner side of the street, Arlette went along until she saw a chance to cross over to a bakery. From there, using the windows as a mirror, she could see the school well enough. Steps led up to the front door. Windows, high and streaked with grime or broken, gave out onto the street.

A gabled crown would be above it all. There were four floors and they'd be in the top one. From there, the roofs offered not only a means of escape but also of defense.

The bakeshop was busy. Waiting at the counter to be served brought no comfort. Somehow she'd have to get into the school. She had to be certain they were there.

"An almond croissant and a coffee, please. No cream. Just black."

She found a table in the window where she could watch the place.

No one paid it the slightest attention. It simply looked what it was supposed to be, a derelict. The front door would be bolted. There must be a lane behind the school. A window...? Another door? A fire escape? Would such a thing be required by law? It would be so much better if there was a fire escape, so much easier for her.

The back door opened at a hesitant touch. At once the smell of the place came to her, that of the damp, the dust, the chalk, the drains that were plugged...so many things. Rags lay about — bundles of them, heaps, one of which stirred in its drunken stupor, too tired and sodden to open his eyes.

Still clutching the briefcase, Arlette picked her way through to the front entrance. The rooms were huge, the ceilings high. The staircase that led up to her left was wide.

She slid a hand in over the butt of the Browning in her coat pocket and released the safety catch. Clumps of dust filled the corners of the steps, whose brown linoleum runners were torn in places and worn through in others. Rubbish was everywhere, graffiti on the walls whose plaster had been broken open in fist-sized holes.

Upstairs, in the first of the classrooms she came to, someone had cleared a place for sleeping. The blackboard was a mass of scribblings, some of which had been carved by nails that had been pulled out of baseboards and moldings that had been removed.

She drew the gun and, still clutching the briefcase, which contained nothing but two newspapers, made her way through into the next room only to stop suddenly at some sound.

A scraping...? Yes...yes, that's what it was. A boot against the floor? A haversack?

No, neither of these.

Anxiously Arlette gazed up at the ceiling above her. Had she heard enough? Could she be sure?

Would Damas recognize her? And why should he be here at all? Why wouldn't he have gone out to watch the place as she'd watched it, knowing someone might come?

She wished Mr. Churchill had said she could call in help. To do this alone...it was crazy of her.

Routine took over, and she slid the gun away, willing herself to be calm.

She was studying one of the blackboards when the scraping started up again. Concentrating on the writing, she waited but no steps came.

And soon the scraping stopped.

When she found the cause, Arlette turned quickly away, then bravely stepped forward into the room to put her foot down hard on the thing.

It was a rat whose hind legs and tail had been cut off, and whose right front leg had also been removed. The poor creature had gone round and round in agony, leaving a thin trail of blood wherever it went.

There was no other evidence of anyone having been on the second floor, none at all on the third floor. Then on the fourth and last floor she found the butt of a cigarillo in the chalk tray of one of the blackboards.

The smell of sweat and men, close on the air, was added to the others.

Arlette went over to the windows to look down at the street. A squad of thirty men...a schoolmaster. Where would they have gone?

Back to the port of Antwerp, now that it had been searched?

Determined to quit the place, Arlette crossed the floor only to stop suddenly as she passed the blackboard.

Though hastily erased, there were traces of something...of the river...? Yes...yes, there was the Steen Castle, and upstream of it the pedestrian tunnel she'd taken, the Tunnel voor Voetgangers.

Downstream a kilometer from the tunnel, at the head of the old port of Antwerp, there was the outline of the Tunnel voor Voertuigen, the one for cars and trucks that was so much longer. The Willemdok Oude showed vaguely, the outlines of the Kempischdok and the Kattendijksluis, the maze of the modern port opening to the north and east of these.

Where had they gone? Time...would there still be time?

From a vent in the roof of the warehouse loft there was an excellent view of the Kattendijkdok, which here ran straight away at a right angle to the north from the Willemdok Oude. The freighter *Megadan* was still moored to its quay halfway along the dock. The tracks of the electrical railway that serviced the docks ran past the freighter as did the cobbled surface of the access road.

Damas studied the maze of cranes and ships before him, picking out the movement of a trawler that had been in for repairs. As always, the port of Antwerp never stopped, always there was something moving.

The overhead sheet-iron roofs of the quays would offer places for sniper fire, but better still, the roofs of the warehouses themselves.

It had been good to have overheard Wunsch say they'd be using the *Megadan*.

Squeezing aside, he let the SS Untersturmführer Gerhard Theissen join him. Blond, blue-eyed, rawboned and incredibly fit, Theissen had about him a decisive air of command. No matter that the Baron Dieter Karl Hunter had not yet been able to join them. He had his orders.

Theissen noted the rooftops of the warehouses, in particular one that lay close to the much smaller Kempischdok which ran parallel to the Kattendijkdok and lay just to the east of it. "That one," he said, his voice a whisper, "has a small shed on top to house its lift machinery. Two of my men up there would do nicely."

The shed was almost in line with the freighter. An iron access ladder ran up the near side of the warehouse. "The trucks? Can they approach from the far end of the dock?" he asked.

Two Belgian army trucks had been stolen and were being kept in readiness at a warehouse across the river.

Damas nodded. Had they thought of everything? The steel girders that supported the roofs over the quays left the areas beneath open and exposed. The *Megadan* lay on the other side of its quay. That, too, was good. Three freighters were berthed beyond her, then a passenger ship of the Norden Line that had found haven here.

A tugboat entered the Kattendijkdok and began to make for one of the other freighters. The boom of a hydraulic crane swung near another, unloading lumber.

"For now we must wait," he whispered tensely, cursing the delays, cursing the continual need to move the men.

No one spoke. All talking in the loft was forbidden. They weren't even allowed cigarettes until after hours when the shop below them finally closed and the men on the evening shift went home.

As so many times since their arrival in the dead of night at the farm, Cecile Verheyden anxiously swept her eyes over the assembled men. They were tough and well disciplined, wore Belgian army uniforms over their own.

They all had their weapons — Schmeissers, she'd heard one say at the farm, Bergmanns another. Two machine guns, even an 80 mm mortar, lots of stick grenades and boxes of explosives and ammunition.

A short-wave transmitter whose operator had definite times for making contact with Berlin or wherever. These times were late at night, in the small hours, but still the wireless operator stood by on the hour during the day.

Damas looked at the woman. Always watched by one or two of the men, she had not as yet tried to give them away. He should have killed her at the farm, but Krantz would want to question her. And the baron? he asked himself.

The baron might also wish to do this.

One of the men tugged at his trouser leg. Turning, Damas saw Theissen motioning him to the vent.

A girl was walking along the Kattendijkdok toward the *Megadan*. Stevedores paused, seamen paused to whistle, to grin and to leer at her. She fought off their stares, carried a briefcase and walked more quickly.

Theissen raised questioning eyebrows. It was not usual for a girl to walk along the docks.

She passed the freighter, and when she reached the warehouse of the Norden Line, turned in at their office.

The girl soon reappeared, the manager pointing eastward and indicating that she was to go two docks over. "The Asiadok," breathed Damas. "Help me onto the roof. I must see what she's after."

"Is that wise?" asked Theissen.

Damas knew there was a good chance he'd be seen. "That girl... there's something about the way she walks."

"Like a soldier, *ja*," said Theissen, grinning.

"A soldier?" blurted Damas. "No... no, as if she knew someone might be following her."

Arlette reached the railway line that would lead her to the Asiadok.

The dikes along the riverbank were not far to the west of her, perhaps a little more than a kilometer of warehouses, channels and quays.

Dillingham's fabricating shop was to her right, down the long length of the dock. She thought of de Heer Wunsch and how worried he'd been that time they'd checked the shipments for the Krupp. She thought of how he had strolled along the Kattendijkdok and hadn't even given the freighter a glance. But that had been a long time ago, and now things were so very different.

She wished she could have used the loft above the fabricating shop. It would have been ideal for her purposes. No problem with stringing the wireless aerial. No one need ever have known.

Not the distance to Brussels — at least a good hour and ten minutes by train. A loss of valuable time. Oh for sure, it was far better security for her, but here was where the problem lay, and it was going to take her days to find Damas and his men. Days!

That night she sent the briefest possible message from the flat on the Boulevard Anspach in Brussels. GROUP HAS MOVED FROM SCHOOL / AM SEARCHING PORT OF ANTWERP

The night watchman at the fabricating shop was a creature of habit. As soon as the evening shift had given their last shouts of departure, he would lock all the doors, then walk to the foot of the loft stairs to switch on the lights above and sit down on the lower steps to have a cigarette.

Outside the building, he made a circuit of the place, only to reenter to switch off all the lights and scare the hell out of them each time, for they never did know if he'd take a notion to check the loft.

Then this crusty old Fleming would retire to his shed in the shipping yard behind the place, to read his newspaper yet again perhaps, to have his coffee and another smoke.

When he was certain the man had left, Damas stepped out into the night and went quickly along the Willemdok Oude and across the tracks that separated it from the Kattendijkdok. Fog had rolled up the estuary. Lights above the warehouse doors glowed dimly, those of the ships, dimmer still.

The girl had continued to haunt him. Why a briefcase, why here today, why now? Was she an assistant of some kind? Had she merely been sent to deliver some papers?

East, along the Kempischdok, there were warehouses for steel girders, bearings, rubber and bananas... more of the same along the Asiadok.

None of them would have been interesting to a girl of that age. Tall and with such a good figure. Where... where had he seen her before?

When he found the warehouse Theissen had pointed out, he found the iron ladder that ran up the side of the building. From the roof of its lift shed there'd be excellent views of the *Megadan*. Two snipers could easily pin everyone down, letting the trucks get closer.

But still he'd have to use the suitcase. They'd need that, too. Thirty kilos of high explosive and a timer.

The ever-present sounds of the harbor came to him, the winching of cargo, the distant shouts of stevedores. Hammers on a sheet-iron hull, the trains as they rumbled alongside the docks.

Chancing a cigarette, Damas stood motionless on the roof of the lift shed, feeling how close they were to the diamonds and yet how far.

He'd have to watch for the girl with the briefcase. If she came back tomorrow, he'd have to kill her.

Thirteen

THE SHATTERING CRUMP of the bomb threw stones and plaster dust into the street. The mournful wail of air-raid sirens and the steady thump of antiaircraft guns were broken by the cries of a child.

Bernard Wunsch didn't know what to do. The child was standing in the middle of the street beside the body of its mother. Behind it, the walls of the house were ready to collapse. Flames leaped from the roof and poured from the windows.

He ran. The pain in his chest hit him like a sledgehammer. Baffled, he dropped to his knees to frantically claw at his chest.

Lev caught him up and grabbed the child. Somehow they got across but not without the scream of another Stuka.

At dawn on May 10 the greatest army the world had ever seen had invaded Holland, Belgium and tiny Luxembourg. A mass of over 2,500,000 fighting men, legions of motorized armor.

Not content with bombing and strafing all of the airfields, the Germans had turned on the cities and towns. People were fleeing from homes they'd known for years. The roads were clogged, both hampering the rush of reinforcements to the front and leading to the air of general panic.

Lev propped Wunsch against a wall and tried to stop the child's crying. Was it a heart attack? Must it happen at a time like this?

The eyes rolled up. Lev slapped him gently. "Don't panic, Bernard. We must get through. They're bombing the docks. We may have to use the trucks."

"Never! The message from Duncan McPherson has said . . ." Wunsch gasped and held his chest. "Lev, listen to me. The British are sending two destroyers. We are to take the diamonds to the *Megadan*."

"And that squad of men?" asked Lev.

"The Belgian army are to provide a guard. It's been okayed, Lev. Just tell the others." Wunsch winced.

"Lev, leave the child with me. I'll be all right in a moment. Don't let any of them use the trucks of the Mercantile Company. Remember what I told you. Infiltrated, Lev. That place has been infiltrated."

Lev didn't have the heart to tell him they'd be lucky to use anything.

When he reached the Central Railway Station, he found the streets milling with people, all wanting to escape the city.

At the Beurs voor Diamanthandel, the largest of the four Antwerp bourses, the windows had been shattered. Glass littered the street, the floor and the tables inside.

Jacob Lietermann, Isaac Hond, Abraham Merensky and some others were arguing. In the heat of chaos they had time to bang their fists and shout at one another. Merensky thought the railways might be better. Isaac Hond kept mentioning the squad of Nazis that had still to be found.

"The British...where are they?" shouted someone.

Another bomb fell wide of its mark in the docks, and for a moment no one knew just where it would hit.

When the dust had settled, they picked themselves up. Ashen, they looked at one another.

In all the years he had worked in the industry, Lev had never been inside any of the bourses. Now, of all times, he had been granted that privilege. As he walked among them, they stepped aside. It was Lietermann who asked, "Ascher, what's happened to Bernard?"

"A minor indisposition. Bernard has received word from England that two destroyers are on their way. You are to take the diamonds to the *Megadan* but under no circumstances are you to use trucks of the Mercantile Company."

"How long will it take the destroyers to get here?" asked Merensky. "A day...two days? Are they somewhere at sea, Mijnheer Levinski, or are they still in their home ports?"

With a sinking feeling in the pit of his stomach, Lev said he really didn't know.

Merensky clenched a fist. Hond said it would be best to wait. Lietermann advised against this. "We will just have to take our chances. The army will surround the diamonds and see that we get them loaded onto the freighter."

The village was deserted — completely destroyed. Only a few shattered walls remained.

Splintered timbers; wrecked, charred and uncharred cars; trucks; vehicles of all manner were strewn about the road. Among the fallen bricks and bodies, a child lay dead.

Hagen looked at the boy. No more than ten years old, he had run from the family car and been hit by cannon shells, the 20 mm exploding shells from an ME-109.

The father was slumped over the steering wheel. The mother, her stomach ripped open, lay half in, half out of the car. Her black leather purse and gloves were still clutched. The little red pillbox hat had rolled away. What the hell had she thought she was doing? Going to church?

The baby was a congealed pulp on which the blowflies still feasted. Maggots crawled from its eye sockets and nose. They squirmed in the gaping mouth and trickled from the tiny lips.

All along the road as far as he could see it was like this. Here and there horses lay on their backs with stiffened legs and bloated bellies.

The sun was high, the silence eerie. Mingled with the smell of plaster dust and cordite, the stench of death was everywhere.

In a daze he walked on. The village square had received a direct hit from a Stuka. Some twenty — or was it thirty? — refugees had been fighting one another for water. Some had managed to crawl away. One man, completely naked, his back badly burned by the blast, had lost both legs below the knees and yet had managed to drag himself almost to a side street.

From the shattered bell tower of the church the lonely trickle of cascading mortar stirred. Then the silence crept back in.

Hagen wore the uniform of a Wehrmacht lieutenant whom he'd shot behind a barn. Taking off the haversack, he moved into the shade of a ruined wall to wipe the sweat from his face and ease his blistered feet.

Vast sections of southern and eastern Belgium had been just left — abandoned, destroyed. Who would bury the dead and rebuild the houses and the factories? Where would he meet up with the battle and try to slip through the lines?

When a dispatch rider came by with an empty sidecar, he waved him down.

The cries of a wounded horse, the incoherent babbling of dazed and bleeding men broke the silence of yet another village. Among the horrible faces that had come to surround them in the square was that of a woman in tatters whose lower jaw had been blown away. In her arms she carried a dead boy. Hiccuping, coughing blood, she tried to speak.

Hagen attempted to take the child from her, but she refused to give it up. Repeatedly she drove herself to speak.

At last he understood.

Their uniforms didn't matter. It was help she wanted, not for herself but for others. From the shattered remains of a house came cries of agony.

Trapped, they were peering through gaps in the rubble of a cellar. There was nothing he could do for them.

"Herr Leutnant, it would be best for us to leave."

"Yes, yes, of course, *Gefreiter*."

"Shoot her, Herr Leutnant. Please."

The woman was dying. How had she carried on this long? In French he asked if anyone could tell them the name of the village. No one seemed to want to understand. They all gaped at him.

The whole second floor of the house suddenly collapsed. Dust, noise and rubble filled the square. Everyone ran except for the woman. Enveloped in the cloud, she stood there looking toward what had once been her home. The dust blew into her eyes. The wind of it tore at her, and when the cloud had passed, she was gray.

Blood seeped from the cavity in her face. Hagen cocked the gun. She blinked. Perhaps she understood. "Forgive me," he said.

The square echoed with the shot. She fell without a sound, and the dead child tumbled from her arms.

"It was for the best, Herr Leutnant. Jesus, this is a mess!" The dispatcher turned suddenly away and threw up.

That night they were camped in an abandoned farmhouse when the dry whip-crack of 88 mm guns awakened them. Far to the north toward Antwerp, lightning flashes lit the horizon while overhead a pale moon hung.

Millions had fled and thousands had died. Every bridge they had come to had been destroyed. Every railway line had been torn up.

For an hour they watched the battle. Then, safe from it, they settled down again only to be awakened suddenly. Around and around them the noise circled, clanging, throwing sparks, until at last the sound of the guns came back.

Two plow horses stood in the moonlight by the flattened ruins of the barn. Trailing behind them was the tongue, the front axle and a few boards from the wagon they'd once pulled.

Patiently they waited for the harness to be removed, content in the knowledge the farmer would feed them.

Blood, scraps of flesh — the remains of an arm — still clung to the reins, all of it clear under the ghostly light.

The flat on the Boulevard Anspach in Brussels was not far from the Central Station and the Gare du Nord. Arlette knew it was hopeless to try to get back to Antwerp. It was as if the whole of Belgium had suddenly been set afire. News traveled like flames leaping from roof to roof. The crowds would surge at the least hint of hope, then surge back to wickets that had long since been closed. Every means of transport had been used. Bicycles, baby carriages, wheelbarrows...

The roads from Brussels were jammed with cars and trucks, all honking, all trying to head northwest to one of the channel ports.

Somehow she had to get back to Antwerp; somehow she had to find Damas and his men before it was too late.

Lugging the forty-five-pound wireless tranceiver in its plain brown leather suitcase, Arlette started out. If only she could steal a bicycle. If only she could thumb a lift with the army, but they wouldn't take her, a civilian, and anyway they were heading south and east toward the front.

When she saw a train of three cars and an engine parked along the tracks from the Gare du Nord, she started for it. Others followed — they'd caught sight of her. The train began to move. Arlette reached out to grab its handrail. Damn the suitcase! Damn the thing for moving!

It was like running with an anchor.

Giving the suitcase a heave, she flung it up onto the platform and grabbed again for the handrail, hit her knees, tore her stockings and dragged herself up into the car.

"You'll have to get off."

It was the conductor. "How?" she asked, trying to catch her breath. The coach was empty but for the two of them.

He indicated the suitcase and the rapidly receding tracks.

She shook her head and grinned at him. He reached for the suitcase and she said sharply, "You touch that and you're dead."

The girl meant it, too. There was a pistol in her hand.

"Let's have a cigarette," she said. "Is this thing going to Antwerp?"

It was. It had been waiting for King Leopold, who had decided to go elsewhere.

An eerie glow bathed Antwerp's harbor. High above the docks the night sky was filled with the drone of heavy bombers and the stiletto whine of Messerschmitt fighters.

Searchlights sought the planes. Bursting antiaircraft shells reached out with fists of shattering phosphorus.

Suddenly the wing of a bomber was illuminated, now the fuselage. The great plane lurched, seemed to hang in the sky. The scream of its engines began to grow as it passed over the docks to fall somewhere in the city.

The explosion rocked them. People milled about the docks — the old, the young, the terrified and those whose job it was to maintain order. The clanging of the fire engines and the shrill warnings of the ambulances only added to the din of bombs, the AA guns and the air-raid sirens that wailed when everyone knew exactly what the hell was going on.

Trapped in the harbor, the ships were sitting ducks, and that was the trouble, the whole damned trouble.

As another of the trucks arrived at the *Megadan*'s wharf, a harried Bernard Wunsch turned to the Belgian army captain whose men had thrown a guard around the place. "I think I will have that cigarette after all. I've just spent the day in hospital. A minor heart attack, they say, perhaps the first of several, but...ah, what can one do at a time like this?"

The truck backed onto the quay. Immediately men began to unload the strongboxes and stack them with the others onto the waiting cargo nets.

Would there be time? Would they get the diamonds off? Would this blasted air raid never end?

Two more trucks arrived, then of all things, a horse-drawn wagon whose canvas tarpaulin was soon pulled away to reveal yet more of the strongboxes.

With the diamonds had come their owners or those chosen to represent them. At first they hung about the strongboxes, then gathered into a tight little knot for mutual consolation.

More trucks arrived but none of these was from the Mercantile Company. Now the cargo booms were being swung out over the quay, and the men were working like crazy to get the boxes onto the nets. The sounds of the air raid dwindled to last bursts from the antiaircraft guns. Soon the all-clear broke over the harbor.

Wunsch wiped the sweat from his brow. Dillingham's diamonds had finally arrived. But would the *Megadan* get safely away, would the British destroyers come?

Would the blasted things even get loaded? The winches...had they been sabotaged?

"Lev..." he began, only to glance up at the nearest cargo boom. Jammed! The thing was jammed! "Lev, where is that 'priest,' that schoolmaster?"

It was then just a little after 3:00 a.m., and all the winches had been sabotaged. The diamonds...eight tons of strongboxes — God alone knew their exact value. One hundred million British pounds worth of gems? Two hundred? Five, ten, twenty millions' worth of industrials...?

Simultaneously at 3:07, two shattering explosions ripped the stern right out of the freighter. She began to list at once. Men leaped into the water.

Satisfied, Damas walked away into the night.

Richard Hagen had escaped from Germany and was attempting to do the impossible. The salesman was carrying a briefcase full of top-secret documents as well as information that couldn't be allowed to leak out.

They'd get Hagen, too, should he make it to the city.

From all reports the invasion was proceeding rapidly. As soon as the German army was within sight, they'd seize the diamonds and hold them until reinforcements arrived and finally Antwerp was overrun.

Dillingham's watchman shook his head in wonder. Arlette Huysmans was caught in the beam of his flashlight. He knew it was her, yet couldn't believe it.

"Dagg, I have to get up into the loft. London must know they've sunk the freighter."

But how could she possibly let London know?

"I have a wireless set. I'm working for them."

When he still refused to believe her, Arlette set down the suitcase and opened the catches. "Now are you satisfied?" she demanded.

Lijnbach saw the Bakelite dials and switches, the heavy oak cabinet. "What are you? Some sort of spy?"

"Dagg, please!" She stamped a foot. "At least have sense enough to switch off your light."

Fussy, he said he didn't know about letting her into the building. Perhaps she should go and talk to de Heer Wunsch. "He's along the docks, at the freighter."

God save her from stubborn Belgians! "I am not to let him know I'm here. Each moment you waste is one we must have. There's a force of Nazi parachutists just waiting to steal the diamonds."

Lijnbach hesitated. Everyone had said the girl had drowned in the sea off Ostend, and now here she was. De Heer Wunsch and de Heer Levinski would be pleased, yet...should he let her into the building?

"All right, but I'll go first. I've been hearing things in there," he grumbled.

"What sort of things?"

"Funny noises. Like the sound of someone closing the breech on a rifle. It's only been since the men stopped coming to work and de Heer Wunsch had to lock the place up during the day."

Arlette waited while he opened the side door. She hesitated, then said, "Look, check the loft for me, will you, Dagg? I think I will go and speak to de Heer Wunsch after all."

When he didn't come back, she knew they must have killed him.

An oily black smoke trailed over the city from the burning fuel tanks in the harbor and the Shell depot, which was just upstream. Some of the debris had been cleared but many of the streets were still impassable. And as for the roads, forget them! Every road from Antwerp to the sea and the French border was clogged with refugees.

Fort Eben Emael had fallen in thirty-six hours, some said less. All along the defenses of the Albert Canal and the Meuse the troops were falling back. Of one dozen Belgian planes that had escaped the dawn raids of May 10 to bomb the bridge at Vroenhoven, only one had returned.

And now there was alarming news from the French front. The Germans had seized Sedan and made a gap into which they had poured a formidable mass of armor.

They'd head for the coast to cut off and encircle the British and the French armies. Would it be at Calais or Dunkirk that a last stand would be made?

Bernard Wunsch went through the office. Apart from destroying a few confidential memos and the personnel files, what else could he do?

Down at the docks the oil slick from the sunken freighter glistened. The *Megadan* lay on her side.

He spoke to the Belgian captain who commanded the men guarding the diamonds. To think that so many millions were concentrated in such a small space.

There was still no sign of the promised destroyers. At any moment the planes would start coming over again.

"You've not seen a priest hanging about? Tall and thin, and with spectacles?"

No, he hadn't seen a priest.

De Heer Lietermann joined him for a quiet word. "Bernard, we are leaving the city. Come with us while there's still time."

Was it to be that they should all flee like rats from a burning ship? "Jacob, my doctors have ordered me to stay in bed. Can you believe it?"

They shook hands. Lietermann signed for two of his strongboxes and had these loaded into the trunk of his car. "Then it's goodbye, Bernard. Take care of things for us and may we meet again some day."

At noon Wunsch saw the priest, and at noon the planes started coming over again. They would bomb the harbor so as to prevent all ships from entering or leaving.

Panzers fought at points of least resistance. Reconnaissance units, often on motorcycle or in armored cars, used the roads to locate those pockets, and if not them, low-flying Storch and Folke-Wulf aircraft. It wasn't always so beautifully coordinated, but with the main roads ahead cleared of refugees by ME-109s and soon clogged with long lines or armored vehicles and men, complete mastery of the skies was essential. Supply lines were kept open, bivouacs laid out in advance, artillery swung into position and the tanks and other armor held back until the points of least resistance had been pinned down.

Seldom did they cut across country — that would only have slowed the advance. Instead, they tended to stick to the roads until meeting resistance. Then the heavy guns would start up.

Later the tanks would move ahead in echelon waves of five, with infantry in their lee. Flamethrowers, mortars and grenades — some hand-to-hand fighting — took out the pillboxes, the farmhouses or railway sheds that offered resistance. MG-42s raked the battlefield.

So often there were short bursts of fighting, then none at all. Usually it was simply the unstoppable advance of armor, the sound of tracked vehicles, the squeak of thousands of tank lugs even in the dark of night, the steady drone of their engines.

Disheveled, still in the uniform of the German lieutenant, Hagen tore open the dead dispatch rider's satchel.

St. Trond had been devastated. It was now May 13, and the Allies had fallen back to the Namur-Antwerp Line. Tirlemont and Haelen faced the full brunt of the assault.

He'd have to go around the battlefield, go east and north. Somehow he'd have to ditch the uniform and cross the lines.

As he kicked the motorcycle's starter to life, he gave the dispatch rider's body a last glance.

They'd become quite friendly, the two of them. Harald . . . the boy's name had been Harald.

Damas knew they were living on borrowed time. Wunsch would soon discover that his night watchman hadn't gone home at the break of day.

Angered by the thought of having to wait, he asked Theissen to contact the Baron Dieter Karl Hunter.

The *Untersturmführer* nodded grimly to his wireless operator. There was so much military traffic, the airwaves would be jammed. Hen scratchings were coming in from everywhere, but then Berlin was replying.

The operator whipped off the earphones. "Eindhoven, Herr Untersturmführer. The baron and the Gestapo Krantz left for there at dawn."

The Dornier tipped its wings and raced its engines. Not one to panic easily, Krantz sat in the pitch-dark belly of the plane with his feet and back braced against the struts. The whole fuselage shook. Rivets rattled. The aluminum was freezing. Air leaked in through the bomb doors, mercilessly flapping the legs of his trousers. One mistake, that was all it would take, and it was goodbye Berlin, goodbye Heydrich and every-thing else as the pilot, more used to bombing runs, opened the doors.

Silent like himself, Hunter sat opposite him. Heydrich hadn't been kind to the baron. *Gott in Himmel*, no! Far from it. Himself as well.

Suddenly a shrill voice came over the intercom. "Two o'clock and high." Jesus Christ, what the hell was going on out there?

Holes pierced the fuselage. The staccato chatter of the MG-15s began.

The engines labored, screamed, faltered and screamed again as the wings dipped and shreds of metal were sprayed all over the place.

The Dornier lurched, lifted, then dropped like a stone, only to rise suddenly as the gun in the lower part of the cockpit began to fire.

Again the enemy fighter came at them. Was it Dutch, British, French or Belgian?

The thing cut a swath across the fuselage, killing the lower gunner to the shrieks of the others and opening a fist-sized hole not far from Hunter's foot.

The nose of the Dornier pitched downward. The engines raced. There was more firing, thicker, heavier. Krantz ducked, cringed, ducked again, only to hear the crew cheering as the nose came up and he was flung back, had to hang on for dear life as the engines roared and the aircraft threatened to shake itself to pieces.

Then someone was shouting, "Rotterdam! Jesus, you guys should see it!" and he knew they'd made a small detour from their flight plan.

The Dornier banked away from the city and began rapidly to lose altitude.

At the airfield outside of Eindhoven a lone Stuka headed west toward Antwerp and the Scheldt. Grateful for the ground underfoot, Krantz found his cigarettes but didn't dare light one. The smell of high-octane fuel was far too overpowering.

"Well, Baron, what now? So Holland has fallen. Just how the hell do you propose to get to Antwerp?"

Hunter's dark eyes followed the rapidly disappearing Stuka. "We will do the impossible because we must."

Richard could be out there for all he knew. The diamonds were still on the docks. No British destroyers had been sighted as yet.

Heydrich had thrown himself into a violent rage at the news of Richard's escape and had threatened to have them both shot.

When their wireless operator got through to Theissen, Hunter told him to ask them to watch for the Stuka. "If it makes a pass directly over the fabricating shop, then they are to attack at once. Otherwise, they are to wait until the city is about to fall. We will be there by then with reinforcements."

For an hour now the birds had been singing. Wunsch found the experience both touching and profound. The haze that hung over the city had taken on the tint of old gray paint to which long threads of ugly black smoke still gave their contribution. On the horizon to the east the sun was rimmed with fire, yet it couldn't break through the haze. Miraculously a flight of gulls circled on a hidden eddy, looking more like phantoms bent on urgent business but uncertain of which direction to take.

Then the songbirds all shut up — just like that, and he craned his neck out of the apartment window, anxious now, robbed by the loss of their songs.

The high-pitched whine of a single Stuka came to him from out over the harbor. The thing made a run of the estuary, disappearing swiftly to the northwest before returning to bank eastward and climb back into the sky.

It hadn't dropped its bombs. Was it a pathfinder, a reconnaissance flight — the precursor of things to come?

After so much, it was eerie to hear the birds begin to sing again. It reminded him of the shelling during the last war. Dead silence after the bombardment of heavy guns, and then, miraculously, the sound of birds.

"Martine, it's too quiet. Something is wrong. The city appears deserted."

Had it come to pass so suddenly? One moment British and French troops side by side with their own at last, the next, a general evacuation.

"I must find Lev and go down to the harbor. Perhaps something will turn up."

A last desperate measure.

She came through from the kitchen. "Have your breakfast first, Bernard. Please, at least a cup of coffee. They are bombing Rotterdam. It is savage what they are doing to that city."

"Then we have gained but a moment's peace at the expense of others."

From the vent in the roof of the fabricating shop, Damas watched the Stuka disappear on the horizon and knew they must somehow get through another day. The watchman's family were bound to come looking for him, but with the confusion, anything could have happened to the man.

Theissen had had the body dumped in the river, but why had the watchman suddenly decided to check the loft? Had that girl they'd seen had anything to do with it? So like Arlette Huysmans, and yet that could not be possible. Or could it?

It was an uneasy thought that lingered. The detail guarding the diamonds were having their morning coffee. The sergeant was discussing things with his captain. A few stragglers, portents of the throngs to come, roamed the quays in search of passage. The sergeant pointed down the length of the dock toward the fabricating shop, then swung his arm in a loop to pick out the highest of the rooftops.

Damas climbed down from the vent to make his way silently among the men. When he reached their wireless operator, he wrote something on a pad and Cecile Verheyden saw him do this. Asking for a cigarette, she filled her lungs with smoke and waited. The wireless operator looked to Theissen for the okay — always there was this chain of command that had to be obeyed.

"Arlette Huysmans," whispered Damas. "It's just a thought. Perhaps Krantz or the baron know something we don't."

Arlette alive? Had Duncan lied to Richard? Sickened by the thought, Cecile found her eyes moistening. She mustn't betray herself. She must be brave. Richard had been the one great reason she'd contacted Duncan McPherson, not feelings for her country, her home, though those had been a part of it.

They'd kill Arlette if she was alive and back in the city. They'd kill Richard, too.

Halfway between her and Damas, their explosives expert had just put the finishing touches to the suitcase bomb that contained a good thirty kilos of explosives and a timer.

It was all to be so simple. Damas and she would take the suitcase and join the throngs of milling refugees. Theissen and his men, in two stolen Belgian army trucks, would make a rush for the diamonds after the suitcase bomb had gone off.

They'd load the diamonds onto the trucks and cross under the river to the other side. The traffic tunnel was being kept open and free of refugees by the army. They'd be waved on through, would hide the trucks and the diamonds in some warehouse and wait for the city to fall.

Damas noticed her watching them. Somehow the woman had managed to keep herself reasonably tidy in spite of the days of captivity. He wondered what the baron would do to her if she survived the next twenty-four hours. He wondered what she'd say to Hunter about what had happened to her at the farm.

The Stuka had landed at Eindhoven, the baron and the Gestapo Krantz had set up a temporary command post there.

Damas had the idea that the Verheyden woman would keep that little episode to herself.

And Arlette Huysmans? he asked. Krantz had ordered him to check the girl's former contacts. The Club Chez Vous could be ruled out for the present. The offices of Dillingham and Company would have to be looked into; he still had a set of keys, but unfortunately they were at his flat and probably by now in the hands of the Belgian police.

That would leave the flats of Bernard Wunsch — the girl could easily have stayed with them again, but surely Wunsch would have shown signs of this?

And the Jew, Levinski? he asked himself.

A possibility, as was the girl's former landlady.

Dismayed by what lay ahead of her, Arlette packed the wireless set away.

London had replied that the promised destroyers were elsewhere engaged but that they would do all they could to reach the diamonds.

Somehow she had to warn de Heer Wunsch and the Belgian captain that Damas had a squad of men hiding in the loft of the fabricating shop.

The schoolmaster would be watching for just such a thing. He'd try to stop her.

As she went up to the roof to take down the aerial, Arlette thought back to the brief hours before dawn and the expression on Madame Hausemer's face.

Standing under the glare of that good woman's hall light, she had said, "*Madame*, you must forgive me, but I have nowhere else to turn."

She mustn't stay any longer than she absolutely had to. If the city should fall, the Germans would want to question the woman.

Duncan would come — he must! Damas might have moved his men again. The watchman's body? she wondered. Would that have caused them to leave?

A faint hope she knew she couldn't count on.

Then she must go to the diamonds at once and ask the Belgian captain to let her have some men. She would kill Damas — stop them before they left the loft.

Richard . . . Richard would have wanted her to do this. Dear God, why could he not have lived?

The *Sielbex* was a tour boat that had seen better days. Moored to two barges, she lay along the bank of the Scheldt near the lighthouse beacon at the tiny village of Bath.

Hagen couldn't believe his luck. He'd been to Cecile's farm, had changed his clothes — found things of Dieter's — and had hidden Heydrich's dossiers and the Red Cross labels from the parcels.

Armed with a Schmeisser in his rucksack and a pistol, he had crossed and recrossed the Albert Canal at night, had gone through first the German lines and then the Belgian.

And now here he was, fifteen or so kilometers downstream of the port of Antwerp.

It was early in the morning of May 15. With skies that could be filled with German planes at any moment, it would be suicidal to attempt to move the diamonds in broad daylight. But were they still in Antwerp? Would there still be time to wait until darkness? Would that possibility even occur?

The boat rocked gently as he stepped aboard. The aroma of coffee came to him as he quietly opened the wheelhouse door.

"So, my friend, have you come to steal my boat?"

Hagen felt the muzzle of a single-barreled shotgun as it was pressed into the small of his back.

Leo Ooms was normally a humble giant, a man in his late sixties with drooping jowls and sad, baggy eyes, little hair and often a grin. A Zeelander who was used to people trying to steal his boat.

Walter Vreeken — the man who held the coffeepot in one hand and a shotgun in the other — was his second in command. Thin, tall, glazed by a life on the river and in its brothels and pubs, it was Vreeken who said, "The rucksack, my friend. Gently."

"Interesting," snorted Ooms when the Schmeisser was exposed, along with spare clips of ammunition and a half dozen stick grenades. "Just who are you?"

They'd heard all about the Nazi Fifth Column in Belgium, all about German parachutists in the guise of priests and nuns. They were glad they'd caught one of them.

"Look, my name's Hagen. I'm a diamond salesman who escaped from Germany."

Vreeken lifted the thin arch of his eyebrows in mock surprise before displaying in a wolfish grin the set of false teeth that had given him trouble for years. "Next thing you know, Leo, he'll be telling us he's Hitler."

His hands held high, Hagen said, "Why not make a telephone call for me? You do the talking."

"The lines are down. You bastards cut them."

As calmly as he could, Hagen began to tell them of the diamonds.

No, they hadn't seen any British destroyers. Yes, they'd seen lots of German airplanes. "They can bomb hell out of the diamonds for all we care, Mijnheer Hagen. We're taking you in."

But it meant leaving the boat, and that, neither of them was prepared to do. When Vreeken's grandson appeared with a wicker basket, they decided to have their breakfast and think about it. "War can't be fought on an empty stomach," commented Ooms dryly. "We will send young Rudi here with a message for the constable, yes?"

Yes, that was what they'd do. Never mind the invasion, never mind the diamonds. First the herrings and hard-boiled eggs, the bread and black-berry jam, and then another mug of coffee with lots of sugar and cream.

"But you must listen to me. I have a wireless set. I've been in contact with London. The destroyers *will* come, but they are being engaged elsewhere. Off Rotterdam perhaps. I . . . I don't really know."

"And this supposed squad of men?" asked the Belgian captain in charge of the detail guarding the diamonds.

"Waiting down there." She pointed angrily. "In the loft of Dillingham's fabricating shop."

"She could be right, sir," said the sergeant. He didn't like it one bit. The crowds of civilians, the rooftops of the warehouses . . .

"I can't spare the men. You'll just have to wait until I've contacted HQ and asked for reinforcements."

Arlette knew it was useless to try. Turning from him, she looked along the quays toward the fabricating shop, which was all but lost among the distant warehouses. "They will come for the diamonds. They will have seen me talking to you."

As the sergeant watched, the girl with the lovely brown eyes quickly lost herself in the crowd.

Lieutenant Gort Kloostermann had had just about enough. Assigned with far too few men to guard the electrical power facility at Merksem and the Kruisschans Lock, which together controlled the port of Antwerp, he didn't want to hear about two bumboat captains who had caught a Nazi infiltrator. But when the village cop from Bath mentioned the Antwerp diamond stocks, he changed his mind.

"Hagen . . . he says his name is Richard Hagen."

HQ Antwerp got through to the captain of the detail guarding the diamonds.

There'd been no sign of the promised destroyers. No hope of getting the diamonds out of Antwerp by sea.

They were going to load them onto trucks. If the army could let them have the use of two of them, they'd take what they could and try to make for one of the channel ports.

"Hagen?" said the captain, shouting to be heard. The docks were being inundated again. Streams of people.

"Hagen?" asked a harried Bernard Wunsch, who had only just arrived. "Not Richard Hagen?"

The captain thrust the field telephone at Wunsch and told him to take care of it.

The offices of Dillingham and Company were empty. Dismayed by the futility of trying to get anyone to listen to her, Arlette made her way through to the cutting shop.

Lev was tidying up, fussing over the relics of a lifetime's work. There was no one else around.

"Lev . . . Lev, it's me."

Tears sprang into the diamond cutter's eyes. With difficulty, he tried to find his voice.

"The diamonds, Lev. There's a Nazi raiding party hiding in the loft of our fabricating shop."

"Arlette...?" He couldn't seem to move. She stood in the doorway looking at him as she'd so often done in the past and yet... "Arlette, is it really you?"

They came together, he throwing his arms about the girl and holding her tightly, she saying, "Lev...Lev, where is de Heer Wunsch? I must speak to him."

"The docks, where else?"

Both of them ran from the building to catch an already crowded tramcar and join the throngs that were heading for the docks.

At 1147 hours Damas noticed activity on the quay beside the *Megadan*. A dark blue, half-ton Ford truck with an open back was being hurriedly loaded with strongboxes.

Men were clearing the road of refugees. People were being forced back. The road ran from the diamonds toward him along the quays before turning out of sight toward the river.

Two sets of docks lay between them and the Scheldt. Perhaps a distance of a kilometer. No more.

They would have to attack. "Notify Eindhoven that the diamonds are being moved. The British must have sent a ship to take them off."

When he reached for the suitcase, Cecile Verheyden knew she'd have to accompany him. Was she about to die? Five minutes, ten...would it be ten the timer would allow? Or seconds?

Piles of possessions of every imaginable kind were heaped among the thousands of refugees who milled about the docks. There were cars with mattresses tied on top, baby carriages stuffed to the limit.

Damas clutched the handle of the suitcase. Her arm was gripped at the elbow. He'd kill her if she said anything, kill her if she tried to run away.

Bernard Wunsch saw them detach themselves from some refugees but then the crowd closed about them again.

When next he saw them, the Verheyden woman was between the priest and the sandbags. The priest set his suitcase down beside one of the machine guns and reached inside his suit jacket for his papers. The Verheyden woman started to say something...

"Sergeant!" shouted Wunsch. "Stop that couple!"

Dragging her after him, Damas darted into the crowd, the Verheyden woman looking back, crying out now — shrieking, "The suitcase, Mijnheer Wunsch! The suitcase!"

Two Belgian army trucks were approaching. As they crept through the crowd, their drivers leaned repeatedly on the horns and shook their fists at the refugees.

The air-raid sirens started up again. Suddenly the milling crowd panicked to take cover. Freed of them, the Belgian soldiers were getting down from the trucks to quickly fan out across the road and the tracks. Their weapons... what was it about their weapons? Not Belgian... not Belgian... "Captain, that suitcase!"

A sheet of flame burst in front of Wunsch. Blood rushed into his eyes, his nose and ears as he was flung into the water. The half-ton was upended. The strongboxes it had contained were tossed about, some to split open and spew their diamonds into the blood, the bits of flesh, an arm, a leg, a hand as the sound of gunfire caught them up.

Out on the water and just downriver from them, Hagen heard the explosion, then the pop-popping of small-arms fire and the staccato chatter of machine guns.

"Can't this thing go any faster?" he shouted.

Leo Ooms gripped the wheel in one hand and pointed to the plume of smoke that had risen from among the docks. "Cut one of the barges loose," he shouted back. "Toss some of your men overboard."

The diamonds had been given priority one. Now a dozen Belgian marines had joined them. Two of the men manned the machine gun in the bow; another two had set up their gun on top of the deckhouse. But the barges, the drag they caused... "This old engine," said Ooms. "If it does nothing else, my friend, let us hope it gets us there at all."

His partner banged his gums in dismay. Knowing there'd be trouble, Walter Vreeken had removed his false teeth and had put them safely away in his locker. Armed with the shotgun, and holding Leo's gun in the crook of his left arm, he watched the quays along the river, hoping that they'd somehow get out of this alive.

Running, barging through the crowd, Arlette heard the scream of the dive-bombers overhead. The crash of a bomb came, then the pull-out as the plane tore itself up from the river. She'd left Lev far behind her, had to get to the *Megadan*, had to help them.

When she reached the Kempischdok, she began to thread her way among the warehouses. Sniper fire was pinning the Belgians down. Again and again she heard the shots as the firing around the diamonds became more ragged.

There were even brief moments of silence, of consternation, of hunting the skies and the rooftops. Then the Stukas would come in again and the whole mad rush of cannon shells would start up once more to trickle off in machine-gun and small-arms fire.

She searched the rooftops of the warehouses. People stared at her. People wondered why she stood out like that, so exposed and with a gun in her hand.

When she found the source of the sniper fire, she found the iron ladder and went up it.

Dieter Karl Hunter had the Stuka's pilot fly him over the area again. Things were not going well. They were meeting more resistance than expected. Caught on the wharf, the Belgians were putting up a stiff fight in spite of everything.

"Make a run of the estuary, then return to base for more bombs."

Splitting off from the squadron, they flew northwest along great, sweeping meanders whose marshes, islands and poldered shores opened out before them.

When they saw the destroyers entering the estuary, Hunter told the pilot to notify Eindhoven and ask for reinforcements.

When they flew in over the river again, they caught the tour boat and its barges and raked them with fire until the guns were empty.

Splintered wood, glass, blood and smoke filled the tiny wheelhouse of the tour boat. Hagen tore Ooms's hands from the wheel and stepped over the body. The Stuka had made one hell of a mess, had killed or wounded half the men. The forward machine-gun crew were still okay; the men on the roof hadn't had a chance.

An arm hung over the shattered windscreen in front of him. Blood dripped from the fingers. The wristwatch kept on ticking. It was after one o'clock now. An hour...? Had it really been an hour since he'd heard the first explosion?

"Snipers...on top of that warehouse."

The burly Belgian marine shouldered his way into the wheelhouse. "Take cover, *mijnheer*. They'll have seen us."

Arlette crept across the roof toward the rusty shed on which the two men had positioned themselves.

The sharp, flat report of one of their telescopic rifles came. First one would shoot and then the other with ruthless determination.

As the Stukas flew away she heard the sound of distant artillery and knew that the Allies must be falling back again. Soon streams of Belgian soldiers would enter the city to take up their final positions.

Out on the water a badly hit tour boat with two barges was trying to reach the quay where some of the strongboxes were now piled.

Choosing her moment, she ran across the roof at a crouch, to throw her back against the wall of the shed. Then she started up the short iron ladder that would lead to the roof.

The two of them, spread-eagled on the corrugated iron, lay at the far corners. Each man had a satchel beside him. On this was a pile of cartridges that glistened in the sun.

Arlette heard them talking quietly to each other. Apparently their commander, the Untersturmführer Theissen, was gathering his men for a final rush. It was now or never.

Arlette crept up the last few rungs and when she was standing on the roof, she said, "Hey, you two!" and shot them both. The first in the face, the second in the chest.

Two shots. Only two.

Then she lay down in one of their places and calmly took up his rifle.

Theissen was the first man she shot. Then his second in command. One by one she began to pick off the others until, realizing what had happened, they took cover.

The diamonds began to move from the quay to the riverside. The tour boat and its barges had docked. There was still lots of firing, lots of fighting.

She found another man, their wireless operator. He was hidden behind one of the trucks. Only a leg was showing.

The cross hairs settled on it, the man was flung over onto his stomach to stare beneath the truck and wonder what had happened. She shot him in the face, and began to hunt the warehouses again.

Racing to load the diamonds, Hagen knew only that a small miracle had happened. Someone had given them breathing space.

Word came that the destroyers had entered the estuary. A tugboat was heading upriver to them to replace the shattered tour boat.

As the sound of the Stukas returned, someone handed him a pair of binoculars. Angular against the eastern sky, the Stukas rushed towards them. And on the roof of that warehouse one lone speck had pinned the Germans down.

It was a girl with short-cut, dark brown hair and a beret.

Hagen lowered the glasses. Lost in thought, he didn't hear the cry to take cover.

Then the Stukas descended and it all began again.

"Bernard ... Bernard, can you hear me?"

The chatter of machine-gun fire, the stench of cordite. Water ... water in the shell craters, mud everywhere. Rain ... had it been raining? Flanders, 1914 ... or was it 1915? No, it was 1918. Yes ... yes, it must be.

Wunsch tried to open his eyes. Sand ... the sandbags had been split apart. There was sand under his legs. Cobblestones ... the torn-up iron of railway tracks.

Again the sound of machine-gun fire came to him but louder this time, heavier, more persistent.

Out over the river, a Messerschmitt had joined the Stukas.

He shut his eyes and lost consciousness.

Later there was sporadic firing. Single shots, the crump of mortar shells, but still the whine of the Stukas.

"Bernard, Arlette's alive! I've seen her."

"Lev..." Wunsch wet his throat. The pain in his chest wouldn't go away. Blood...had he lost his hands? "Lev, the diamonds," he gasped.

"Out on the river, Bernard. On two barges."

"Richard...?" asked Wunsch, only to pass out again.

The Stuka climbed, the sound of its engines dwindling as it flew high above the tidal flats of the Oosterscheldt before banking.

Hagen waited tensely. The barges were connected to the tour boat by a hawser. The Germans had sunk the tugboat that had been sent to take over.

The sound of the Stuka's engines ceased, and for a moment he was thrown back to the airfield at the Heinkel factory on the Baltic, to Dieter and the Krupp.

The thing seemed to hang up there, to remain motionless. Then it started down, came hurtling at them!

Hunter watched from the rear gunner's cockpit behind the pilot. As the tour boat and the diamonds came closer and closer, men fired at them and he saw Richard standing out on the deck. Defiant always, a rifle in his hands.

The plane lifted with a lurch as the bombs fell away and the scream of its siren came to him. Then they were climbing back up into the sky again, and he was straining to look back to see what had happened.

The tour boat had gone down. The barges had been cut adrift.

"Go back. Machine-gun those who are in the water."

"I have my orders, Baron. We are to return to base to attack the destroyers."

"Go back! One pass."

Perhaps it was the tone of voice, perhaps the fact that the baron had a close association with the Gestapo Krantz.

Horst Ungermann lifted the Stuka's nose before banking in a wide turn that would bring them in over the river again. The Belgian AA batteries opened up. The Stuka dived. His wing guns began to fire. Splash points raced across the water, killing the men, catching them as they struggled to get away. "Richard...Richard," shouted Hunter. "Kill him! You must kill him!"

The barges drifted aimlessly downstream, the diamonds under canvas. No one was with them. No one. Eight tons of diamonds. Eight tons...

"Baron, we must go back."

Only bodies floated where men had once swam. Richard would have been killed instantly.

Suddenly exhausted, Hunter slumped back in the seat and didn't reply.

Watched helplessly from the quays by men who had raced to rescue them, the barges continued to drift. In time they reached a point opposite the lighthouse at Bath but fetched up against an island on the far side of the shipping channel. As Belgian marines clambered aboard a pilot boat, gulls came to watch. The lead barge had wedged itself in the mud; the trailing one now tugged at it, a contest of wills.

There'd not be time; the Stukas would come back.

Downstream some forty miles, an anxious Duncan McPherson searched the skies. Even at a speed of twenty knots an hour — far too fast for a crowded channel — it would take the destroyers *Halifax* and *Torbay* a good two hours to reach the port of Antwerp. Would the diamonds still be there? Would they be able to take them off?

"I pray to God we have the cover of darkness, Captain. Och, it's a fool's notion to wish for it."

At 1532 hours the rusty hulk of an East Indian freighter stood oddly out in midchannel, stern down and sinking. Abandoned with its deckhouse and hold in flames.

Off Hansweert and the canal that linked the Scheldt estuary to that of the Oosterscheldt there was more wreckage, drifting bodies, the roof of a Ford sedan that had been driven off a pier in haste, another motor car that had been hit by cannon shells. Milling villagers, farmers still stunned by what had happened and standing out in their fields. Fishermen watching the skies.

The life preserver from a ship, a drift of oil slick and splintered boards...

McPherson knew it was hopeless. The Stukas would come back and with them would be a squadron of Messerschmitts.

At 1650 hours someone nudged his arm — a midshipman. "Message received, sir. Reads: Diamonds on two barges. Last seen drifting off Antwerp. Believe will be taken in tow by Belgian marines. Xavier."

Arlette Huysmans... Odette Latour.

McPherson felt his throat tighten. He had wronged the girl, had wronged Richard...

When the midshipman asked if there was any reply, he shook his head. "She'll have shut down the set and beat it, if I know that one."

The Stukas came back as the sun was in the west, but by then he had the barges in sight and the destroyers had hoved to in the center of the channel. Sitting ducks. "Oh Jesus," he said, "we're for it now."

They came in waves, five Stukas first, diving from the heights to release their bombs but followed swiftly by ME-109s that came in low to savagely rake the decks and meet the hail of antiaircraft fire.

As the barges came abreast of them, McPherson tried to shout above the din of the guns. Men raced to throw the boarding ladders over the side. The barges were secured. Someone cut the pilot boat free and it started out, the Belgian marines taking cover as best they could.

A Stuka screamed. Exploding as it pitched into the river, the plane threw its spinning wreckage at the pilot boat. All around them now there was fire, the smoke and clamor of battle. McPherson found himself straining on a hawser, lending a hand to load the strongboxes. One cargo net and then another — again a Stuka, now an ME-109 . . .

As the last shell casing spat from one of the deck guns. the skies cleared and the long twilight began.

The *Halifax* was being turned around. The *Torbay* had been sunk, a direct hit, the Stuka having never pulled out of its dive.

Survivors were being picked up. The diamonds were being stacked forward to be taken down into the hold.

"Sir, Captain reports ship under way."

"Tell him to pick up as many of the *Torbay's* crew as possible. Have Sparks send this to the prime minister: Diamonds secured, now in transit."

The sound of kettledrums came up from the street below the office, that and the clip-clopping of countless hooves and the tramp of soldiers' boots.

Wunsch ached as he'd never ached before. All the hair had been singed from his face. His head was swathed in bandages. His eyes had been blackened. The right arm was in a sling — broken in three places by the blast, the collarbone, too, and three ribs. A chunk of shrapnel had taken the lobe off his left ear, death missing him by a hairbreath.

The diamonds . . . there'd been a terrible battle for them, but they'd got them safely off to England. They'd be in London by now, thank God.

Somehow he'd been fished from the river but had lost consciousness so many times he could remember little.

And now, a city on its knees.

"Lev, you cannot do this thing."

"Bernard, it's the only way. Will you and Martine help us?"

What could he say? "But of course, my friend. Lev, the Germans, they cannot possibly want to — "

"What, Bernard? Round up every Jew? I'm not thinking of that, but of my value to them as a cutter and my apparent interest in their Red Cross parcels. It was one thing for us to supply them for as long as we did. It's another for me to work under them. They know me at the Red Cross depot. What else need I say? Besides, there is my Anna to think of. They might try to separate us, Bernard, and I can't have that."

"But the loft above the fabricating shop? What if they should decide to look there or wish to store things?"

None of them could predict what would happen.

Lev was stubborn. "They won't find us because I'll build a secret room. Believe me, Bernard, this will be best. At least until we see how things go. Look, if it was good enough for German parachutists, then it's good enough for me. Besides, they won't think to look there, having used it themselves."

Already the Nazis had run up their swastikas above the Central Railway Station and all other important buildings. They'd commandeered the De Keyser Hotel, the Waldorf, the Empire and the Metropole. They'd taken over the National Bank, the wireless broadcasting station, telephones — everything.

Even the town hall.

Antwerp's citizens were to present themselves at the *Kommandantur* to apply for the necessary residence papers. Lev and Anna would be singled out — Wunsch knew this. "Tell me what you need and we'll work out a system for getting it to you. There are some old boards in the shop yard. Nails... you will need old ones, Lev, so as to make the partition appear as if built long ago."

"A false ceiling, Bernard. I've already thought about it. Anna's waiting there for me."

Had it come to this so soon? They'd need water, food, spare clothing — how would they do their laundry, their cooking? The many everyday things one had taken so much for granted?

To live like fugitives, to be hounded down — was that how it would be?

He didn't know.

"I will walk a ways with you, Lev. It's better if there are two of us. Then if we are stopped, I can say we are simply going to the fabricating shop."

Lev shook his head. "Come only after dark and watch out. That schoolmaster may still be interested in us. Richard and Arlette... the Nazis will want them, Bernard. Me, I only hope they've managed to get away."

Arlette had gone into hiding — where he didn't know.

And Richard? Wunsch asked himself. Apparently she'd not met up with him, couldn't even know that he had been on that tour boat. Was he out there some place lying dead or wounded, or trying desperately to reach the Allies, who were fast falling back toward Dunkirk? Two young

people who had been torn apart. They'd been like a son and a daughter to
him...

"Herr Wunsch?"

"Yes...yes, that's me."

"You will come with us, please. The Gestapo Krantz wishes to ask you
some questions."

Lev...Lev had gone back through to the cutting shop for something.
Wunsch reached for his hat, then decided the effort wasn't worth it.

They would ask him about Richard and about Arlette, and he would
have to tell them nothing.

Fourteen

A S A PATROL made its way through the darkness toward the Central Station, Hagen stepped into what had once been his office. The floor was littered with papers. Some caught the moonlight, others hid from it. All the furniture had been taken. Only the telephone, singled out by moonlight, stood sentinel to remind him of the past.

It seemed an age since he'd first met the Dutchman here. Arlette had been so worried. Arlette and Bernard and Lev.

The whole of the diamond district had been vacated. The bourses were empty, their tall windows shattered. Some of the buildings were gutted shells. Roof timbers cried out to the sky.

Arlette had waited for him that first night. Arlette...

He went through to the foyer, empty like everything else. The door to the vault was open, but it was too dark to see anything. The memory of her came to him, the sweet, soft feel of her in his arms.

He wished they could have had children, wished she was alive.

The shop Lev had kept so meticulously was barren. Dieter must have escaped the fire. Dieter had had everything shipped to Munich.

And Lev? he wondered. Had Lev been forced to go there? Bernard... where was Bernard now? Killed in the battle for the diamonds, or sent to Munich, too?

Somehow he had to get out of Belgium. Krantz and Dieter would hunt him down, and if not them, then Heydrich.

He'd need a set of papers, a change of clothing — so many things. He'd have to pick up Heydrich's dossiers at the farm and the brown paper wrappings from the Red Cross parcels that must have contained diamonds from the Congo.

Returning to his office, Hagen reached for the telephone, was startled to find the line still connected.

Cecile had been sleeping with Dieter. Cecile would have to be forced into helping him escape.

Hesitating, he rang the club and asked for her. She answered soon enough, asked who it was. He waited, saying nothing, then hung up.

She put down the receiver. "It . . . it wasn't him. I'd know Richard's voice anywhere. It was just someone inquiring about the club."

Krantz took in the shapely figure, the sequined sky-blue sheath, the long blond hair and stunning blue eyes. Gestapo Antwerp's listeners would soon tell him who had called and what, exactly, had been said.

Still showing the effects of the fire in Munich, Dieter Karl stared at her back. She'd been so beautiful in bed, had had such a splendid body.

But it had all been a lie. "Let us get Richard first, Cecile, then I will see what I can do for you."

The Berliner smiled inwardly. Heydrich would need heads — Hagen's, the woman's, the Huysmans girl's, and another's.

"You do that, Baron. I'm sure Frau Verheyden will appreciate a little help, but just so as she understands how things are, she's not to leave the club or do anything but what you tell her."

There, he'd turned responsibility for the woman over to Hunter in front of witnesses — the SS Hauptsturmführer Lechner of the Interrogation Squad, and his all too able assistant, the SS Sturmmann Helmut Schultz.

Schultz was a sadist. Krantz knew he was lowering himself into the slime of Poland, but what else could he do?

Heydrich had given them an ultimatum. Find Hagen within two weeks or else.

BRUSSELS 0310 HOURS	JUNE 4, 1940
TO THE CARPENTER	FROM XAVIER
BLUFF CHECK INCLUDED	TRUE CHECK INCLUDED
	LOCATION TRANSMITTER
	MOVED FROM ANTWERP
	TO BRUSSELS AREA

Message reads: IN PLACE / AWAIT INSTRUCTIONS

Arlette Huysmans had safely reached Brussels. From having helped to save the diamonds, she could now go over to gathering intelligence in a Europe that had all but collapsed under the weight of the Nazi heel.

The final evacuation at Dunkirk had just been completed. A beleaguered Winston Churchill, now Britain's prime minister, ran his tired eyes over the telex again.

In Britain's darkest hour a single ray of light had appeared, the first of what he fervently hoped would be many.

"Signal this: Am recommending you for the George Cross. When prudent, attempt recover Red Cross parcel diamonds Congo Antwerp.

"Sign it, White Rabbit."

"And Richard?" asked McPherson. "Shouldn't we let her know he might still be alive and somewhere in the Antwerp area?"

Churchill hated to say it but knew he must. "They won't stop hunting for Hagen, not until they have him, but the girl . . . she must remain free for as long as possible. God willing, we shall see her again."

There were thousands of men on the run in Occupied Europe — stray soldiers of the BEF who'd become separated from their units, downed bomber and fighter pilots. The girl could help them there as well, once she'd settled the diamond thing.

The dungeons of Antwerp's Steen Castle hadn't been used in well over two hundred years.

Mold, slime that looked like leaking pus in the lantern light, stinking drains and airless walls greeted Krantz as the heavy door of the cell was shoved open.

Half-hidden in the gloom, the shabby figure stirred. Painfully, Bernard Wunsch got to his feet but was forced by his condition to lean against the far wall.

Krantz noted the haunted look, the quivering of swollen lips. Setting the lantern on the straw-littered floor, he told the guard to leave them. Then he sat down on the iron cot Wunsch had momentarily forsaken and dragged out his cigarettes.

"Richard Hagen, Herr Wunsch. We know he must still be in the area, that he could not possibly have got through our lines to join those who were fleeing at Dunkirk."

"Then you don't know Richard."

"Oh, I do, I can assure you. A cigarette? Don't be so stubborn. Certainly you can refuse to talk. I merely offer the cigarette as I would to a man I can respect."

"I don't like your tobacco. I never have."

"These are Dutch — straight from Eindhoven. Don't be stupid. Say the right things and you can go home to your wife. No one need ever know."

Wunsch took the proffered cigarette. The Gestapo lit it for him.

"Arlette Huysmans, Herr Wunsch. Your diamond cutter . . . ?"

The Belgian's eyes betrayed him. The diamond cutter and the girl must have met. Damas had been right.

"I thought so," said Krantz. "So, you will tell us, please, where this diamond cutter is."

"How should I know?"

"Because you do. He'll have news of the girl, and she'll have news of Hagen."

"That's highly unlikely."

"Oh? Why is this, please?"

Piece by piece the Nazis had put together what must have happened on the docks, but they could have no firm knowledge of Arlette. "She was drowned in the sea off Ostend," said Wunsch.

"But came back to life. Has she linked up with Hagen? Are they hiding out in some other city — Brussels, perhaps?"

Though it must have hurt his broken ribs and shoulder, the Belgian shrugged.

"We can have your wife brought in for questioning," hazarded Krantz.

"She knows nothing. It would only be a waste of your time."

"And of a life?" he asked, hating himself for making such a cheap threat. A good policeman should be able to pry everything out of his prisoner without a hint of violence.

But the times had changed.

The Belgian budgeted the cigarette, taking small puffs lest the smoke make him cough.

"Tell me the names of Richard Hagen's friends in Antwerp — all of them, his contacts, too. Look, we know he's in the city. He telephoned the Club Chez Vous."

"Then I have nothing more to say to you."

Wunsch took a final drag. The Gestapo looked across the cell at him, then dropped his eyes to the lantern.

"I shot Hagen's father. Of course, I didn't know it at the time — how could I have? But the Oberstgruppenführer Heydrich had someone dig into the records. That zealot put two and two together, Herr Wunsch, and came up with my name. So now, my friend, I'm stuck with the son."

The gray cod eyes lifted from the lantern. "I must have the names of all of Richard Hagen's contacts in Belgium. His friends here and in Brussels perhaps. Those who are elsewhere."

"Why not ask Cecile Verheyden?"

"I will, but first, I prefer to hear these from yourself."

Two hours later Wunsch was blood-spattered and in tears.

At dawn they dumped his naked body from a car and left him in the street. People came to look at him, others turned quickly away or did not cross the Meir at that intersection.

There was no means of identifying him, no papers, no way whatsoever beyond the lacerated skin and the bloodied pulp of what had once been his face.

Damas stood on the roof of the shed, fingering the spent brass cartridge casing of a 7.92 mm bullet. The bodies of the two snipers had long since been removed, so, too, those of the others.

The freighter *Megadan* still lay on its side. There was still debris about from the battle.

The girl had been well trained. She hadn't hesitated, had known exactly what she must do. First Theissen and then his second in command, then their wireless operator.

There was no customs record of her entry into Belgium, therefore she had come in on the quiet. Therefore, too, she'd been given good papers and a suitable cover.

Since losing the diamonds, the Germans had shunned him. They'd need him, of course. Far too many were on the run. Belgians, knowing Belgians, would have to be used to find them.

The girl would have gone to ground somewhere, have taken a job most likely and fitted right into things because that would be the only way she could hide.

Again he thought her cover must be good, since she'd been so well trained.

Had the British sent a wireless set with her? Gestapo Brussels and Antwerp had tracking scanners. Perhaps they'd picked up her signals? She'd have been brief. She'd have known all about the threat of detection, would have wanted to move her set about the country.

But would she be able to do such a thing? Would her cover have included this?

A secretary...a receptionist. Wouldn't it have been wise to have placed her into something with which she was familiar? A shop? he asked himself, remembering that her parents in Ostend had had a shop before the bombs had removed it.

All about him German engineers readied the port of Antwerp while others emptied the warehouses, shipping the goods by rail to the Reich. Still others looked to its antiaircraft defenses.

Climbing down from the shed, Damas went along the quays until he came to the fabricating shop. Independent of Krantz, he'd had one of his men watch the place. So far there'd been nothing to report. Hagen might come. The girl might come. Had the Wehrmacht turned off the electricity to the building? The girl would need that for her wireless set. She'd have batteries, of course, but no means of recharging them, and so would want to conserve them whenever possible.

When he found the dried crust from a slice of rye bread on the lowest step to the loft, he thought nothing more of it.

When he stood beneath where once there'd been a roof vent, Lev and Anna smelled the smoke from his cigarette. But then he went away, and when, after several hours of anxious waiting, he didn't return, they began to relax.

"I told you it was nothing," whispered Lev.

His wife of over forty years didn't answer. Without de Heer Wunsch's help, Ascher had had to leave the place each night in search of food. She knew he needed all the encouragement she could give him.

"It is nothing, as you've said. So, another game of gin rummy, or would you prefer to read?"

"Let's have that game and then perhaps a cup of tea."

Thank God the power was still on. He'd rigged an electrical cord up to them and had brought in a small hot plate. It had made all the difference in the world.

"There's lemon — real lemon, Anna. From the back steps of the Club Chez Vous. Someone must have dropped it."

He'd had to have a look at what was going on. He'd had to see for himself that the place was still open for business.

Steam rose from the heavy iron kettle. The children, seated at long benches around the table, watched with consuming interest. Arlette stirred the soup, drew in the aroma of it and shut her eyes. "Ambrosia," she said. "Chicken stock, lentils, onions...Mmm, it's good."

They were all hungry, all tired, confused, so many things. Refugees — never had she seen so many displaced people. The cellar of the church was full of them, the hostel but one of twenty the Red Cross operated in Brussels.

Some of the children had lost their parents, others had simply been separated from them. Every day there were new ones to care for; every day word would come in that someone's parents had been found.

As she filled their bowls, Arlette made certain that each received exactly the same amount. No more, no less.

The boy, Michael, the oldest, started in. Annette, who sat beside him, stiffened in alarm. His spoon stopped. He shut his eyes and waited for the reprimand, but felt Mademoiselle Latour tousle his hair. "So he's hungry, everyone. Michael's only telling us that we should eat while it's hot."

Arlette broke the bread, and here there were some differences, but any who felt cheated got a little more to make it up. Then she filled their glasses with milk and each got exactly the same amount, even though the littlest ones often spilled theirs or couldn't finish them.

Franz Boeck was impressed. Of all his helpers in this hastily thrown-up kitchen, the girl had fitted in the best. She never complained, did ten jobs at once, was always happy, always smiling — and such a smile — always willing to stay late and do a little more.

She had even stayed overnight a few times to calm the children, yes, but also — and here he was impressed — to get to know them better.

The hostel was in the basement of the Church of St. Julian, not far from the southern end of the Park van Woluwe. If he'd had to choose, he couldn't have asked for better. At least some protection from the bombs and shell fire.

But now that the fighting had stopped, now that the country was occupied, he would like to have had space on the ground floor. One never had much warning of when the Nazis would make a sweep. Sometimes their henchmen came for the stupidest reasons — fully sixty percent of the people here were children under the age of ten. At other times...

Windows would have given them a little warning.

The girl, one of a staff of twenty-five, found the dregs of the soup kettle and began budgeting out a little more for those who had been very, very good, perhaps? Ah no, not that one. For those who had suffered the most and were feeling so very lost.

"You seem to have found your niche, Mademoiselle Latour."

Arlette brushed the back of a hand quickly across her brow and gave him a generous smile. "It's nothing. They're so good today, I'm going to take them all for an especially long hike in the park this afternoon."

Boeck nodded. The children looked at one another. Escape! Escape from this place.

He could read it in their eyes. The girl had charge of forty children. She could sweet-talk them into anything.

Boeck was a Fleming, tall, thin, of middle age. Fastidiously tidy, and of a tidy mind, he was inclined to be overly serious but seldom without good reason.

Tugging thoughtfully at the iron-gray goatee, he asked her to step into the aisle with him. There were over fifty tables in the hall, nearly three hundred people, yet they could talk quite quietly when needed.

"*Mademoiselle*, a small word of advice. I don't know from where you come or how you came to us — my supervisor, de Heer Vervoordt, who has signed your papers, was killed at the front. Perhaps he had been informed by others, but I ..."

The earnest blue eyes swept over the room. "What I want you to know, Mademoiselle Latour, is that for someone as capable as yourself, there are no questions from me. I will say exactly what your papers say. You do understand, don't you?"

Arlette waited tensely. When he didn't elaborate, she said carefully, "I try to do my best, *mijnheer*: I really have been with the Red Cross for as long as my papers say. I'm much saddened by what has happened to my children and want only to help them."

"But there are others, *mademoiselle*. Our head nurse, Mevrouw Demeulemeester for one, who will say you have not worked for us as long as your papers claim."

"Then they are wrong!"

Boeck gripped her by the arm. "Please, all I'm suggesting is that you be aware of this. For now you're fitting in extremely well, and as I've said, I'm only too happy to have you with us. God knows we need you."

Walking home in the twilight from her tramcar stop, Arlette found herself remembering things she hadn't thought much about in months and months. The beach at Ostend, the shop of her father, the smell of cedar and spices, of things from so far away, all mingled with the aroma of his pipe smoke and the sound of quiet conversation.

Her mother in the kitchen baking bread or making pastry, in the shop, too, beside her father. Willi... Willi de Menten. The *Vega* ... had Willi managed to escape in her?

The *Vega* ...

Her pistol was hidden in the flat beside the wireless transceiver. Beneath the lining of her coat collar there was a capsule of cyanide.

At 2200 hours she rolled back the sitting room carpet to check the wireless set. The compartment had been well made — it fitted right into the floor — but she knew a routine search would soon find it.

At 0310 hours she lay awake, wanting desperately to contact London, to reach out for guidance, yes, but for friendship, too — that was the thing she missed the most.

The convoy passed along Antwerp's Kammenstraat, heading away from the river by a roundabout route that would take it to the Central Station. Long lines of prisoners of war had been crossing the river for days. Belgian, British, French, all so gray with fatigue, dispirited, silent and hungry as the tramp of boots brought home the message of defeat.

Many of the men were wounded. Without exception, all were dirty. They'd be packed into waiting railway cars just as so many others had been before them.

Would they ever return? One could see this question in the faces of so many.

After the convoy had passed and the thin crowd of onlookers had broken up, Hagen quickly crossed the street to enter the bakery.

Jani Lutjens saw him and turned quickly away to busy herself in wiping down the shelves. "So, what can I do for you?" she asked tensely, knowing only too well it would be something she'd not want.

"Where's Anders?" The shop was empty but for the two of them.

"Gone... gone to hell or heaven for all I know. Jesus, why have you come to me? Haven't I had enough?"

Hagen reached for the doorknob. She had two small children. She had a sister, Berke, who ran the Club Chez Vous.

"No... don't leave. Look, it's all right. Of course you must come to me, but you didn't think, did you, Mijnheer Hagen, that they might also be watching this place?"

Hagen stepped away from the door. "I did. I've been by twice in the past two days. I know they've been watching your sister, that they've let her go, hoping I'll try to contact her."

"Wait for me in the bake room. Don't go upstairs. My mother . . . the children . . ."

"Is Cecile working for the Nazis?"

"Of course not. Oh, I see . . . the baron. But of course you thought . . ."

She shook her head and went back to wiping the shelves.

Later they had their coffee in the room that held the bake ovens. The Old Dutch Bakery was nothing fancy. A steady clientele. Open at 6:00 a.m., closed for two hours at noon, and open again from then until 6:00 p.m. Fridays until 9:00.

Jani didn't know Richard Hagen well. Anders had always been the one to talk to him, but then Anders had got on well with just about everyone.

"He's dead. I know it," she said. "A person can feel such a thing. A wife . . ."

The hazel eyes had lost their quickness, the face was thinner than usual, the blond hair in disarray.

"Maybe Anders will be released. The Germans must want the bakery to remain open."

"Anders *wanted* to go to war. He was *glad* it had happened."

Dragging the telegram from her apron pocket, she thrust it at him.

Her husband had been reported missing in action and believed dead. The thing was dated May 16.

"Will you talk to Berke for me? Try to get a message through to Cecile that I'm still in the city and will do what I can."

"You're crazy. Did you know that? A man without papers is a man condemned."

"I need money to buy myself a decent set. I also need to know the name of a man I can trust to supply me with them."

"You and ten thousand others!" She tossed her head. "Are you carrying information the British will want to know?"

There must have been some talk. "That and much more."

They'd take the children from her. They'd put her up against a wall and shoot her.

"So, where are you staying?" she asked.

He gave her a sheepish grin. "In the streets, where else? The blackout and the curfew are blessings in disguise."

"Then you'd better stay here — in the pantry. I'll . . . I'll try to contact Berke for you."

Damas watched as the woman left the shop after the supper hour and made her way along the street to a tramcar stop. It had been a hunch, a bit of a gamble. Krantz had men watching the sister but had so far left this one alone.

When the two women met at a small café near the Stadhuis Gijdehuisen, he knew he was on to something. Berke van der Plaat was the older of the two by six years. Used to being the big sister, she frowned at the news the younger one had brought and kept shaking her head in dismay.

Cecile . . . yes, they were talking about Cecile Verheyden and Richard Hagen.

Money . . . had it to do with a sum of money?

Damas knew it had, and when the Lutjens woman left the café, he followed her to a house near the Platin-Moretus Museum.

A half hour before curfew, she left the house in a hurry to catch the last tramcar home.

With a nod, he had his men pick her up and take her to a warehouse on the river.

The splintered crosspieces of the window held shards of glass. Cobwebs were caught in the cool breeze to trail out from the shards in long streamers or bag like tents in a gusting wind.

Hagen felt so empty. Berke's sister hadn't returned at curfew. No telephone calls, no warning. He'd waited longer than he should have and then had left the bakery at a run just as the first of the Gestapo cars had turned onto the street.

They'd taken everyone from the house and had closed and padlocked the place. He had to find somewhere to hide. Krantz wouldn't stop. Now that the Berliner knew he was still in the city, he'd hound him down.

At a sound, slight and across the floor from him in the distance by the stairs, Hagen stiffened. Dieter had emptied the fabricating shop. Everything had been taken.

The sound came again. He held his breath and waited as someone came down the stairs to leave the building and stand just outside the door.

After a while the man moved away into the darkness, his trail being picked up by another.

In tandem, the two men made their way through the blackout. Infrequently the drifting clouds revealed the paleness of the moon. Once at the Grote Markt, they headed for the Club Chez Vous.

Then the first one stole up the back lane while the other one waited. A patrol came by. Music filtered from the club. There was laughter from the troops on leave, shouting, clapping . . .

The man who'd come down the stairs returned to watch the street and steal away. The other one followed him back to the fabricating shop.

"Anna, it's me. I've had the most fantastic luck. A whole pot roast of lamb. Leeks, potatoes, carrots . . . they even remembered to put the garlic in."

There was a sound like no other — anxious fingernails on wood, a partition being eased away. Small laughter, a gentle rush of words, a kiss, a hug — the casserole being lifted in. "Watch out. It's still hot. Be careful."

The fitting of the partition back into place took some time. And then . . . why then, just outside the building, there was the sharp flame of a match, hidden in cupped hands. The acrid stench of burning sulfur. The billowing of the cobwebs.

At midnight fog lay everywhere along the river and over the port of Antwerp. Droplets of mist, gray in the light of the headlamps, filtered down, bringing memories of Berlin, of nights like this between the wars. Of bodies he was about to find. Of nights when as a detective he'd been forced to "look into things."

Krantz hesitated to get out of the car, and since he was in command, the others who were with him also waited.

But they'd not know that he was thinking Hagen, being Hagen, could well be waiting for them.

"Baron," he said, "why not go and have a look? Damas, you stay where you are. You, too," he said to their driver. "Tell the others to remain in their car, Baron. The woman's right ahead of us, down that bank, in among the reeds."

Damas shouldn't have killed her. The Belgian would have to be dealt with. One couldn't leave him alone. It had been a mistake to think one could.

Hunter got gingerly out of the car but left the door open behind him. Krantz was playing games. Heydrich wanted heads. Richard was out here some place.

He'd not go near the Club Chez Vous, not Richard, not until he knew the coast was clear. Somehow Krantz would have to be led into leaving the club alone.

Cecile would be no problem. Berke van der Plaat had been taken to the cellars of the Steen, but just in case Cecile thought otherwise of cooperating, they could let her see her friend or bring her here.

Passing into the beam of the headlamps, Hunter walked uneasily toward the river, switching on the flashlight only at the last moment.

Krantz waited. There was no shot, no sign of Hagen yet. And in this fog could he really shoot from a distance sufficient for him to escape?

Hagen could kill all eight of them even as they poured from the cars.

Hunter found the woman at last. For a second the baron stiffened.

Uncontrolled, the beam of the light swung along the bank and out over the water.

She'd be floating among the reeds. She'd be lying facedown. A mother of two children, the wife of a baker, a widow...

Her hair was flaxen but dark, reminding him of Irmgard. Her legs were long and slackly parted. The clay that had squished between her fingers was a deep blue-gray, and where there were smears of it on her back and rump, they marred the pale whiteness of her skin.

"Check the face." said Krantz on joining him. "Go on, Baron, do it, and remember that your former friend was the cause of this."

Hunter crouched. The Berliner's shoes were to his right. Her face had been shoved into the mud. In terror of drowning, she'd been suffocated by the mud.

Krantz gave him a nudge. Hunter reached out over the water, avoiding the mud at all costs — teetering, nearly losing his balance — then snatching at the woman's hair, digging his fingers into it, gasping, straightening up — pulling her with him. The face...the face...Mud was jammed in her nostrils, mud drained from the cavity of what had once been her mouth.

The face was a mask of terror, the cheeks taut, the eyes clogged.

He dropped her like a stone and turned away to vomit.

Krantz calmly lit a cigarette but remained staring at the corpse as the retching continued. Berlin came back to him. The things he'd seen... Poland, too. Yes, Poland.

Abruptly the Berliner motioned to two of the men who were with them and had the corpse dragged up onto the bank.

Jani Lutjens, the sister of Berke van der Plaat, had had a passable figure — a bit too thin and bony for his liking, a bit too tall. Not beautiful, just average, a nobody really and yet...

As he ran his eyes over the badly mutilated body, Krantz realized that the schoolmaster was a natural. Unleashed, he'd find the Huysmans girl and she'd be only too willing to tell them where Hagen was.

If she knew of it. Of course that might not be — there was always that possibility. But in war one could not worry about such things until one had the answers one needed.

"Baron, find your own way back to the club. Herr Damas and I have something we must do."

The trawler was berthed in the Straatsburgdok at the far end of its quays and near the refit firm of Burgden and Lunde. She'd lost her engine but had since been ignored. She'd have to do. The cabin area below decks would be quite suitable.

Lev and Anna would be safe enough for a few days, safer by far than where they were now hiding.

As he made his way through the dark and the fog toward the Kattendijkdok, Hagen thought of their brief meeting in the loft of the fabricating shop. There'd been tears in their eyes. They'd hugged each other tightly.

He'd had to kill the two men who'd been watching the place. Time was short.

Lev had told him he'd met Arlette, that she must have been the girl on the roof of that shed.

Brussels, Lev had said. She'd come by train. But was she still in Brussels? Could he try to find her?

The tracks that ran parallel to the Willemdok Oude were slippery. In the darkness he didn't see them and went down hard. From the direction of the control, a guard shouted.

The Wehrmacht had sealed off the harbor with controls at all points of entry.

Cursing himself as he crept away, Hagen made a wide detour that could only cost them time they didn't have. When he heard a burst of shots from the direction of the fabricating shop, he knew that all was lost, that Lev and his wife had been taken.

Krantz surveyed the bodies. The Jew had clung to his wife, she to the diamond cutter as Damas had cut them down.

"Brussels...the woman said Brussels."

"Yes, yes, I know," snapped Krantz. "But where in Brussels?"

Taking the Schmeisser from the schoolmaster, he opened the breech and removed the spent clip. "Try always to keep a little in reserve so that if you have to reload, you can do so from a position of some strength."

They had stripped the woman in front of her husband and she had given them the answer the diamond cutter had refused.

But why had they been packing up? Why the rolled blankets, the hastily bagged scraps of food?

Why unless Hagen had come to offer help.

"Cecile, listen to me. If you're keeping something from us, then now is the time to tell me. Krantz has got that Belgian schoolmaster working on things. Berke's sister..."

Hunter couldn't say it. She waited, loathing everything about him, the times they'd slept together, the feel of him, the arrogance that now seemed broken.

"Is it that you were upset by the sight of what they'd done to her, Dieter?"

He reached for his glass, then thought better of it. His clothes were disheveled. There was mud on his shoes and the turnups of his trousers, more of it on the knees. The collar of his shirt was open. He'd had to run, had been afraid, perhaps for the first time in his life.

She knew he'd come to the club alone and on foot. Though he was armed with a pistol, it couldn't have been a pleasant journey for him. "Richard will kill you, Dieter, and then he'll kill Krantz."

"Not if you tell me who the rest of his friends are. Richard is still in Antwerp, Cecile. He'll have to hide someplace."

"But not with friends. Not Richard. He wouldn't do a thing like that, no matter how desperate he was."

"He's the reason Berke's sister was killed."

"Murdered!"

Hunter knew it was useless to try to reason with her, yet all he could see was the woman he'd pulled from the river. Her face, her body.

"I'm warning you, Cecile. Don't hold things back. They'll only take them from you."

"Name?"

"Odette Latour."

"Address?"

"Number 47 Boulevard Anspach, apartment 5."

"Occupation?"

"Red Cross nursing assistant." The Gestapo had sealed off the cellar and had descended on the hostel. Lunch had just been served.

The Sturmbannführer Walter Rath glanced at the photograph on the girl's papers, then at the one the Gestapo had provided.

The others were being questioned. He motioned to the children, who looked along the table toward them with fear in their little eyes. "Eat," he said. "Go on. Eat it!"

He closed her papers but held on to them. "Latour . . . ? That's French?"

Arlette acknowledged that it was. He asked if she spoke German. She said that she did.

"What places have you visited in the Reich?"

"Düsseldorf, but when I was ten years old. My mother's family were German."

"Were?" he demanded suspiciously.

"Are." She smiled. "Her sister, that is. My mother died when I was fifteen."

The girl the Gestapo Krantz wanted had chestnut hair and deep brown eyes like this one, but in the fall of 1937, the hair had been worn much longer. She'd be of about the same age. "This aunt, her address?" he asked.

"One hundred and ninety-seven Montague Street."

"Where is that?" he snapped.

"Brooklyn."

Again he asked where that was and she answered, "New York City," offering so little information it had to make him wonder about her.

The children were beginning to fidget.

Rath ran his eyes up over the girl. Krantz's orders had been clear. Report all suspicious persons but leave them at liberty unless, of course, they should attempt to make a break for it.

As he returned her papers, he said, "*Auf wiedersehen*, Fräulein Latour. Our apologies for the interruption. These things —" he indicated the search "— are necessary."

Across the all but deserted Grand Place, the guards in front of the Hôtel de Ville stood rigidly to attention in the rain. The swastika that hung above them had been wrapped around the flagstaff by the wind.

Arlette knew it was only a matter of time before they picked her up. She had to move the transmitter. She mustn't let them find it.

Starting out to cross the Place, she clutched the collar of her raincoat and held on to the handle of the plain brown suitcase a little more tightly.

A large Red Cross sticker covered the exposed side of the suitcase. She knew that her using it would mean trouble for de Heer Boeck if she was caught, but what else could she have done? He'd be in trouble in any case.

When she reached the Boulevard Anspach, she found the street blocked off. The Germans were doing a house-to-house search. Every intersection had been closed. People were running from their apartments and from the offices and shops below to line up against the walls. Never mind the rain. Never mind that there were old people, women and children, or that it was very near the dinner hour.

She could hear the cries of "*Raus! Raus!*" the slamming of rifle butts against apartment doors.

The stone balusters and tall windows, the high, crowned dormers in the steep green-copper roof sidings, drew her attention. Five floors ... the chimney pots up there ...

Terrified by what was happening, she tried to think. Had they found the flat? Had they searched it already?

Suddenly a man shrieked behind her, "Open that!"

Startled, she spun around as two Gestapo in plainclothes closed in on her.

"The suitcase," shouted the older of the two.

"But ... but everything will get wet."

The younger one tore the suitcase from her and flung open the catches.

"Bandages, Herr Neitz. Iodine, scissors ... it's a first-aid kit."

"Yes, of course it is. Now will you give it back to me, please? I'm from the Red Cross."

"What are you doing here?"

"I . . . I live over there, at . . . at number 47."

"Your papers. Papers, please. Hurry!" demanded the one called Neitz.

He scanned them. In spite of the teeming rain, he took his time and got them thoroughly soaked. "Do you know the Jewish tailor, Mandelheim?"

She shook her head and swallowed. "He deals in secondhand clothing."

"Then you do know him."

"No, I don't, Herr Inspector. I merely pass his shop twice each day, going to and from work. The shop has been closed for some time."

Still they kept her papers and the suitcase. The search went on, and for a good half hour she was forced to watch as building after building was emptied.

When the all-clear sounded, the younger one handed her the suitcase; the older one, her papers.

"Someone reported that two British airmen had been seen on the roof of one of the houses."

The Gestapo watched her as she crossed the street to walk along the boulevard. It was the end — she knew it was. They'd be waiting. They'd have searched the flat. There'd be no place to run, no place to hide.

To give herself time to think Arlette took the stairs, but each one grew more difficult and there were five floors.

Walking along the empty hall, she felt for the cyanide capsule in the lining of her coat collar. Could she really swallow it?

Ripping the lining open, she freed the thing, held it in the palm of her hand . . .

"They've gone."

"What?" she yelped.

It was Mevrouw Pellerin, her neighbor across the hall, peering through a crack in her door. "Gone," whispered the woman.

Hurrying now, Arlette pushed open the door to her flat and went through to the sitting room to roll back the carpet.

Removing the boards, she lifted out the wireless set in its plain brown suitcase and transferred the Red Cross sticker to it.

Then she hid the first-aid kit away, put the pistol in her coat pocket and took a last look around.

At the Gare du Nord the German officer in charge was very smart-looking in his uniform. A red-and-white-striped pole barred the main rampart that led to the platforms. Two soldiers with rifles raised this barricade to let the people through. Others watched from the sidelines.

Arlette set down the heavy suitcase so that he could see the Red Cross sticker. Handing her papers over, she waited, knowing they'd be on the lookout for her.

His sharp blue eyes lifted. "What is the purpose of your visit to Antwerp?"

The lie was ready. "Liaison for the collection and shipment of parcels to prisoners of war in Germany. I am to have a meeting with my counterpart at the main depot on the docks at Antwerp."

"The name of your superior?" he asked.

"De Heer Boeck." Dear God forgive her.

Her papers were returned. The officer clicked his heels and bowed. A hand was raised and the barrier lifted.

She picked up the suitcase and, willing herself not to rush, made her way through and up the rampart to the platform.

Already too many had been let through. There was hardly room to stand.

Attaching herself to a group of elderly nuns, she suggested that if they wished seats, they'd best try to get closer to the tracks.

When the train came in, the front two cars were, as usual, reserved for the Wehrmacht. Accompanying the nuns cost her a seat, and she was forced to stand with some others in the corridor.

So far so good. A patrol came along on the other side of the train. Dogs, rifles . . . nothing out of the ordinary. Not really. With the occupation only just begun, the Nazis weren't taking any chances. But thank God they'd seen fit to allow the trains to run.

The trip would take about an hour and a half, given the delays, perhaps as much as two hours. She'd have to contact Cecile, have to find a place to stay. She couldn't risk going back to Madame Hausemer's again.

Just outside of Mechelen, the Gestapo conducted a search while the train was still moving. They started at the far end and they went through like a cold wind. Everyone had to show their papers. Some had to take down their luggage and open it. Food, cigarettes, wine and booze — they seemed uninterested in these things, and the knowledge of this fled on ahead.

Arlette clung to the leather strap. The car rocked from side to side. They passed a switch box and she saw a railwayman signal to the engineer. They were putting the train onto a siding. They were going to do a thorough search. They'd pull her off the train. They'd hit her — tear the wireless set from her. Open the catches . . . Run . . . should she try to make a run for it?

Calm . . . she must remain calm.

As the Gestapo entered the car behind, Arlette went along to the one ahead and asked if she might sit down.

Her German was good. She was pretty, and she did look tired.

The Hauptmann Martin Berger stood up to address the man who sat opposite him in the otherwise empty compartment. "Herr Generaloberst, may we allow this young woman a seat? Her luggage..." Berger indicated the suitcase with its Red Cross sticker.

The general, busy with some papers, gruffly said, "Yes, yes, of course."

He indicated the seat opposite him and went back to work, only to pause and say, "Martin, why are we stopping?"

"It's nothing," said Arlette. "They're just taking on some more passengers."

The Gestapo never thought to look for her in those two cars. They questioned everyone else, opened every suitcase no matter how small.

Reluctantly they were forced to let the train proceed, but by then she had agreed to have lunch with the *Hauptmann*. He wouldn't have taken no for an answer, and she hadn't had the courage to refuse for fear of being discovered.

They reached Antwerp's Central Station after a journey of two and a half hours. The *Hauptmann* helped her down with her suitcase, even suggesting they give her a lift.

This she refused but thanked him warmly. They shook hands and said goodbye until the next day.

Alone like her, Karl Christian Damas fell in some distance behind her. Krantz had told him to watch the station just in case the Huysmans girl should manage to slip through the Gestapo's net.

The suitcase with its Red Cross sticker puzzled him, but there was no mistaking her.

When, seemingly on impulse, she headed for Antwerp's docks, he knew exactly where she'd try to hide.

The streets of Antwerp were gray in the twilight mizzle that had swept in from the North Sea. Bundled in his trench coat and hat, Krantz was tired, hungry and fed up.

The girl had successfully eluded them. One possibility did exist, and that was the schoolmaster. But then the girl could well have killed the Belgian.

"Hagen," he said. "Let us try to find him. The Club Chez Vous first and then perhaps a little something to eat."

Increasingly he'd come to believe that although the odds were overwhelmingly in his favor, it could well be Hagen and not Heydrich who would kill him.

THE ALICE FACTOR • 353

Trapped, and unable to escape, the diamond salesman would have to go on the offensive.

Hunter and the Verheyden woman were downstairs in the club. Krantz didn't bother to check his coat and hat but waded through the Wehrmacht crowd.

Gray in the smoke-filled air, gray in the sea of uniforms, the Verheyden woman had chosen to wear that color as well.

He ignored Hunter. "So, Frau Verheyden, a few short words. Hagen's father would have had Belgian friends. So, too, then the son could well be friends of those friends. You've left a little something off your lists of his contacts, and this I must now have."

The baron tensed but said nothing. Nervously the woman stubbed out her cigarette and turned to say something to the leader of the band. The music stopped so suddenly there was a distinct lull in the accumulated conversation.

"Don't make me do it," breathed Krantz.

"Cecile, tell us," said Dieter, standing now.

"Why?" she asked. "Richard was my friend, my lover, yes — my ex-lover."

The conversation began to fall off — here a stifled laugh, there a broken guffaw.

The Berliner dragged out his cigarettes. For a moment he was lost to the silver-plated case and the dented head of the kaiser. Again when he spoke, it was as if he breathed the words. *"Now*, Frau Verheyden, or do you wish me to have you stripped naked and beaten in front of all these nice young men?"

The implication was all too clear. Lust and violence so often went together. Unfeeling, the cod eyes took her in. Counting ... was he counting to ten?

"Laeken ... Father Gerald. He ... he was an old friend of Richard's father from the Congo days. Richard ... Richard and I used to visit him."

"The address?" asked Krantz, knowing he had slipped back into the slime of Poland and hating himself for it. But knowing, too, he had had no other choice.

"Forty-four Van Eycklei, just across from the —"

"The Stadspark. Yes, yes, I know the street. The apartment number?" She gave him that, too, then turned her back on him.

"Baron, don't let her out of your sight. Post extra men inside the doors and wait here for me. Business as usual, you understand? If Damas turns up, tell him to sit tight. Hopefully we'll have work for him."

Damas waited in the deeper darkness of the loft above Dillingham's fabricating shop. The distant and infuriating sound of a winch came to him again, intruding on the silence he so desperately wanted.

The Huysmans girl was here — he knew it, felt it, could almost reach out to touch her she was that close. She'd found the bodies of the diamond cutter and his wife, had thrown up in spite of all the training. Had taken the time to cover the corpses with a blanket.

He had men watching all the exits, men downstairs in the empty shop, two men with him now.

"The roof," he whispered at last.

Arlette lay very still. The currugated iron was cold. The suitcase with its wireless set was to her left — she'd use it as a barricade if possible. The Browning was in her hand.

Leaving the suitcase, she eased herself over to the edge of the roof. With the blood rushing into her head, she sought out the deeper pockets of darkness and tried to remember where the ladders were.

A tiny metallic clink was followed by the scraping of a coat button. Without a light, in fog, mist and darkness, they were creeping across the roof toward her.

When the silhouette of one of them became a little clearer, the urge to fire was almost more than she could bear.

Squirming back to the wireless set, she began to pull it after her.

They would reach the vent and find her gone. They would stand up perhaps. She'd have a better chance then. She mustn't panic, must shoot at each of them and only once.

Damas searched the darkness ahead of them, picking out the line of the roof and then the housing of the vent. Since all exits were covered, there was no possible escape.

Arlette drew the heavy suitcase a little closer. Her feet had come suddenly to the end of the roof. She couldn't let them take the wireless. She hoped it would be destroyed. If only there was some way she could escape with it — no sight of her, no sound. Just gone from them into the night.

Lowering herself out over the end of the building, her shoes touched and touched again the steel I-beam of the hoist boom that ran from there a short distance out into the yard behind the shop.

There was a chain-operated hoist on the boom. They had used it for lifting the heavier crates onto the trucks.

Easing the suitcase after her, she backed away from the outline of the roof until coming to the end of the I-beam. Then she lay flat and huddled against the girder with the suitcase turned lengthwise to them.

Broad tree-lined thoroughfares surrounded the triangle of the Stadspark — the Quinten Matsijslei, the Rubenslei and the Van Eycklei, the one they wanted. Across the streets there were houses — rows of them. Blocks of flats.

Krantz had cars posted at the apexes of the triangle. Even though there were Wehrmacht troops billeted in the park, he sent men into it while others took up their stations in the web of streets immediately to the south.

Given the shortness of available time and the lateness of the hour, it was the best he could do.

In three packed cars, himself in the lead, they headed down the Van Eycklei — very nice houses, very baroque — Flemish and old, high and gabled . . . heavy doors, locks and locks, centuries of them. Dark, so dark . . .

In a rush, they hit the front door but the flat was on the second floor. The stairs were steep, the thunder of their shoes was now everywhere.

As one, he and the others hit that door, too, splintering the wood — staving the thing in and flinging on the lights. Shouting now.

Blinded by the glare — bewildered — terrified by the noise, the missionary's housekeeper of fifty years and her sister were hustled into the sitting room, clutching their nightdresses. One had the temerity to make a dash for a spear — there were several of these standing in a corner. Shelves that contained bits of carving, mementos, gourds . . .

A burst from a Schmeisser filled the room with plaster dust, screams and broken glass. All too soon the two old sisters lay dead in a pool of blood.

"Hagen!" shrieked Krantz, swinging at the man who'd killed them. "I wanted Hagen, you idiot!"

"Gone . . . he's gone, Herr Krantz. There's no one else in the flat," said one of the others.

Gone . . .

The missionary had died a year ago at the age of ninety-seven. The Verheyden woman had known this and had thought to use it to buy herself a little more time.

The bitch!

Krantz shoved past the men. There were four bedrooms, a book-lined study, kitchen, dining room, bathroom . . . Suddenly exhausted by the effort of rushing the house, he switched on the bathroom light and ran a finger around the basin.

No bristles, but Hagen would have rinsed the thing out.

Coffee cups on the drainboard in the kitchen. Three teaspoons, two cups, now why?

There was a gap in the rack of the clothes closet in one of the spare bedrooms. Right in the middle too. A place for a pair of shoes below. Mud . . . was that a bit of mud on the floor?

Hagen...

A whistle sounded from the roof, three stories above him. The all-clear. No second blast.

He pulled the blankets back and felt the sheets, but old girls like those would have done their underwear every day, so, too, the sheets.

A wave of fatigue rushed in on him. Closing his eyes, the Berliner held the bridge of his nose. Hagen...Where would he go next? He'd need food, water, dry clothing, a place to shave.

"Herr Krantz...?"

"Yes. Yes, what is it?"

"Shall I tell the *Hauptmann* to call off the search?"

"Comb the streets and laneways. Look up on the roofs. Get more men from the park. Find Hagen and bring that bastard to me."

There was soup enough for five or six good strong men on the back of the stove, bread enough for an army in the larder box, cold chicken, some cheese, a bottle of pickled onions and a half liter of red wine.

He'd eat as Hagen must have eaten, and then he'd catch a few winks.

Though he hated to admit it, the salesman was getting the better of him.

Just before dawn Damas let himself into his flat. As Hagen watched, the schoolmaster went through to the tiny kitchen to light the gas ring and put the kettle on.

Two tablespoons of coffee beans went into the hand grinder. Fed up with such a menial task, Damas began to turn the thing.

Filter cone, pot and filter came out of a cupboard. As he waited for the kettle, he fidgeted, drummed his fingers on the drainboard, moved about constantly.

The gas supply must have been reduced. The pressure...there was hardly any pressure. In anger, he reached for the valve, only to find it wide open.

A cigarette was needed. Taking one out, he bent to light it at the gas ring, momentarily lifting the kettle away. Then he went back to fidgeting, to loosening his tie, to pulling off his jacket. The girl...the Huysmans girl...

Something was really bothering him. As Hagen watched, the schoolmaster dragged out a handkerchief, only to notice there was blood on it and to fling the thing from himself. He hit the counter with a fist.

The coffee didn't settle him. Standing there remembering the chase, the hunt for the girl, he gripped the edge of the counter and rocked back on his heels.

Krantz had wanted the girl to be taken alive. Could nothing go right?

When the schoolmaster came into the bedroom, he tossed his pistol on the bed and pulled off the tie before going over to the window to yank the heavy blackout curtains closed.

He'd try to get a little sleep, try to think what was best. The girl had been so very clever — cold as ice. So pretty.

A girl with a secret wireless transmitter. One of the enemy . . .

Damas reached for the light switch, only to discover he wasn't alone.

Fifteen

A T DAWN THE CLUB CHEZ VOUS was closed and empty looking.

Still very afraid, still very much on the run and knowing they'd nearly caught her last night, Arlette pushed off from the curb. The stolen bicycle blended in with the streams of others. The wireless set was strapped to the carrier behind her.

Everything about the club looked normal enough, but could she chance it? She desperately needed help, a place to stay, a change of clothing.

There were no cars in the street, not even a Wehrmacht lorry. No uniforms for that matter.

Jostled by the other cyclists and forced to keep pace, she rode past the club but turned up at the nearest side street.

Again there were no signs of the Nazi presence. The streets were far too empty of them.

Five and a half blocks from the club, the cars started to appear. Those few that were parked at the side of the road looked as if they belonged, and since few Belgians were allowed cars, they were, of course, of the Nazis.

Getting off the bike, she walked it quickly along the sidewalk. She'd have to find a telephone, have to hope that Cecile or someone else would warn her if the place was a trap.

Peeled black letters gave faint testament to former businesses: Konstanz, Electrical Contractors; Van Dern the house painter . . .

Bold ones gave the new occupants: The Offices of the Todt Organization.

It would have to do.

The German businessman who stopped her in the hall was in his early fifties. In many ways he reminded her of de Heer Wunsch. He asked what she was doing in the building and she said, "Please, I am looking for the offices of my uncle, Monsieur Adrian Beaumont, the lawyer."

His name had once been on the door.

Horst Reugen gave her a fatherly smile. "He used to have his offices here, *Fräulein*, but I'm afraid we required the premises."

1

The fullness of her big brown eyes swept over him. The girl gave such a frown. "Would it be possible for you to tell me his new address?" she asked. "I've only just arrived in the city and would like very much to see him."

She spoke excellent German, had a look about her that intrigued. The brown beret and trench coat suited, but there were dark circles under her eyes, suggestions of hunger and exhaustion.

"If you'd care to come upstairs, I'll see if I can find it. We should have a forwarding address someplace. You can leave your suitcase in the hall. No one will touch it."

"These days I'd rather not."

"Then you must allow me." A portly man, Reugen took the suitcase from her, only to grunt at the weight of it. Had she rocks in the thing?

"It's a typewriter," she said modestly. "I'm a secretary. I've come to Antwerp to look for work. I was hoping my uncle . . ."

Herr Reugen stepped aside to let her enter the lift. If she had to kill him, Arlette knew she'd have to do it between floors.

The office was spacious and equipped with several drafting tables. As Reugen led the way, he worried about the threat to security, then dismissed this. The girl was so like his daughter. The same age as Ilse, the same height. And in the city alone.

Arlette ignored the drawings that must be of coastal defenses the Todt were constructing at the mouth of the Scheldt. She asked to use the telephone, and he left her to it. No one else was in the office as yet, but she could hear the sounds of others down the hall.

Reugen was either an architect or an engineer.

There was trouble getting a line through to the club and more than once she thought to leave it. Cecile worked late. She'd be asleep . . .

"Hello . . . Hello, who is it?"

Had Cecile been crying? "A friend. Look, I need a place to stay. Would it be all right for me to come to see you?"

There was a pause, a split second's hesitation. "Of course. About six? Would that be all right?"

Six p.m. was hours away.

Arlette set the receiver carefully down, only to look up into the warm brown eyes of Herr Reugen.

"Bad news?" he asked. She shook her head.

"Just a friend who is too polite to say she's indisposed."

Reugen straightened his tie. "Would you care for a cup of coffee and a biscuit? It would please me very much. A little company. Please . . . come, come . . . my office is just next door. Then I can, perhaps, drive you to your uncle's new address as it is on my way."

"The bicycle . . ."

He smiled and waved a reproving finger. "We will tie it to the luggage compartment, as I used to for my daughter before the war."

He'd been in Poland since the late fall of 1939, and now Belgium. Three periods of leave, that had been all they'd given him. Six weeks in total.

A lonely man.

The schoolmaster was hanging from the end of the hoist beam in the shipping yard behind the fabricating shop of Dillingham and Company. He'd bitten through his tongue. Flies had collected over the gash on his forehead, they'd crawled into his nostrils, were searching for moisture and salt in the eyes.

Hagen had made a little side trip with the Belgian. They'd gone to the warehouse Damas used and had picked up more than three dozen sticks of dynamite, sufficient blasting caps and fuse.

They'd taken a Schmeisser, 1700 rounds of ammunition and a Mauser rifle.

It was this last that troubled Krantz the most, and as he sat in the car waiting to give the orders, the body turned and he was taken back to the docks and the death of the Lutjens woman — that same feeling of desperateness, of knowing Hagen was out there someplace, that he'd try to kill him if he could.

"So, Baron, we take a walk. You first, or me, I wonder?"

"Richard isn't that stupid. It's broad daylight. There'd be no escape."

"Good! Then perhaps you'd best go first."

The Berliner lunged across the seat to wrench the door open. "Be my guest, Baron. Go on. Get out! See what it feels like to stand alone knowing a man is out there trying to kill you."

The wind was from the northeast, cool and in off the sea. The sun was high, and all around the car there were warehouses.

Dieter got out of the car. The body turned. He began to walk toward it.

At a signal from the Berliner, the others remained in the cars.

Krantz leaned forward to glance in the rearview mirror, to look down the road behind them to the roofs of the most distant warehouses. Come on . . . come on. Shoot if you must!

He sat back and waited. Anxiously he turned to look behind them. When the shot came, it didn't hit Hunter. It hit the side of the rear door, ripping the metal and taking the back off Krantz's left hand!

The Berliner flung himself across the seat. A shot shattered the rear window, killing the man who sat in the right front seat.

In the tense silence that followed, Krantz managed to cradle his wounded hand. Splinters of bone stuck through the mass of bloodied tissue. "Bastard . . . bastard," he cried in anger. The hand was numb, no feeling at all. He tried to move his fingers and found they wouldn't respond. "Some brandy," he gasped. "A cigarette."

Hagen ... had he got away?

Only the road, the long line of the tracks and the warehouses faced him as he crawled out of the car.

The lace of the curtains was Flemish and very old. Horst Reugen watched as the girl called Odette Latour fingered it. Had she an uncomfortable interest in the Tolstraat or the Scheldt Monument? They'd been to the uncle's address only to have found the man gone.

"Please say you'll stay. No one will bother you, and in a day or two you can, if you so choose, find other lodgings."

Arlette let the curtain fall. It was now nearly ten o'clock in the morning. She'd asked him to drive by the docks, and he had become suspicious and had refused.

"I know you cannot have the proper residence papers, Fräulein Latour. For me this is no problem, but for the authorities ... "

Reugen left it unsaid.

Through the lace she could see his car parked on the street below. The bicycle was still tied to the back of it. "Is it so obvious?" she asked, not looking at him.

Encouraged by the sadness in her voice, he said, "I could perhaps help you to secure the necessary documents."

"Have I any choice?"

Reugen reached for his hat. Again he was struck by her tender years, by the resemblance to his daughter. She'd been in the office. He'd have to report her.

"For now I think not, but please don't worry. Everything will be all right."

Arlette let him leave the flat. Later she'd ask herself why she'd done such a stupid thing. She heard the lift come up to their floor. The architect got in.

When he reached the street, Herr Reugen thought about the bicycle and decided not to untie it. He'd want her to sleep with him. He'd question why she had so few clothes.

As he drove away, the utter loneliness of her position came to her.

It was not far to the docks and the main Red Cross depot. She could take the wireless and leave the flat before it was too late. He'd only ring up and immediately know what she'd done.

When he drove past the building a few minutes later, she stepped away from the window. He'd thought to find her in the street.

Five minutes later the telephone rang. Herr Reugen was worried. She said, "I was just about to take a bath. I hope you won't mind."

A girl from the countryside. "No, please, I insist. Use the place as you would your own. I will try to be home a little early and we can talk about things then."

Long after he'd rung off Arlette remained by the telephone. Then slowly she went through to the bedroom to stand in its doorway.

It was all so tidy. The bureau held photographs of Herr Reugen's wife and family, a daughter and a son, both of whom were in uniform. There were nice warm woolen socks in the top drawer, some extra money at the back, the smell of mothballs.

The corduroy trousers in the second drawer would be far too big in the waist for her, the sweaters too large, but should she pack a few things and some food?

Would he come back again?

Quickly she went through to the sitting room to stand at the window, listening for the lift and looking down at the street.

Herr Reugen's flat was on the top floor. True, the windows were exposed...

Leaving the door ajar, she went along the hall and up the stairs that led to the roof. The door there was padlocked but that posed no problem. She could force it easily and string the aerial where no one would think to look. She could contact London just before dawn and ask for more time.

If only he would say nothing for just a little while.

"Herr Reugen, it's me, Odette. Please, I am sorry to have troubled you at work but would you like me to prepare something for supper? There is a piece of steak. I could..."

He said that anything she had in mind would be fine.

Cecile Verheyden clung to life in filth and bathwater, naked and shivering on the floor. The terror of not being able to breathe was always there. Cold, like ice, she had cried out to God, had screamed at them, only to be plunged back in and forced down, down, down...

As the terrified woman clutched her shoulders, Krantz held his throbbing hand and said, "You boys are slipping."

The two interrogators were stripped to the waist and soaked. The Verheyden woman hadn't been easy. She'd thrashed about so much they'd had to hit her several times.

When they reached for her again, the Berliner said, "Let me show you how it's done. Baron, help her to kneel beside the tub or is the sight of her too much for your stomach?"

Hunter turned away in anger. Krantz shrieked at him to take hold of the woman.

"Now drag her to her knees."

"She hasn't any strength, damn you!"

"Nor will you have, if she doesn't tell us what we need to know."

Irmgard had had this done to her. Irmgard ... Hunter caught Cecile under the arms and lifted her to her knees.

The Berliner grabbed her by the hair and jerked her head back. *"Hagen!"* he shrieked. *"Who are his contacts?"*

They'd done a job on that pretty face. Bruised and badly battered, she could hardly focus. She tried to speak, and when he heard her whisper, Krantz tore her from Hunter and shoved her into the bath.

Like a man throttling a dog, he held her under. There was still strength, still resistance. She kicked, thrashed out her arms — tried to breathe!

He yanked her out and she choked, threw up, bent double vomiting water.

Poland ... it was so like Poland.

"Count to three with this one. Down, yes? Then up to give the hint of release, then down again right to the bottom, then up at last. It is best that way."

Krantz shoved her under. The cheeks of her seat stiffened in panic. The legs began to straighten, the feet to fight for purchase on the slippery floor, her body twisting, her arms reaching outward ... the voice coming to Hunter as he watched and could do nothing. "Dieter ... Dieter, no!" A scream. "Please don't let them do this to me! Please!"

Irmgard ... Irmgard.

As Hunter watched, Cecile evacuated her bowels. Krantz pulled her head out and flung her into the waiting arms of the interrogators.

When she died, they left her naked body half in and half out of the tub, kneeling on the floor.

The steak had been cooked to perfection. There'd been onion rings and fried potatoes. The cabbage soup had had little bits of sausage in it, just like at home. "Of course my wife doesn't like my being away so much, but she understands it is the war. What else can one do?"

Arlette took a sip of her wine. "Find a mistress perhaps."

The accusation flustered Herr Reugen. She smiled wisely and said, "There are five other Belgian girls living in this block of flats. One more won't be noticed — isn't that what you've been thinking ever since you first saw me?"

He reached for his cigarettes and offered them. Her fingers touched his.

He blurted, "Would it be too much to ask for ... for the little favor of ..."

Again there was that smile. "Of your saying nothing, Herr Reugen?"

"Horst, please, Odette. I . . . we . . ."

"Could be happy?" She tossed her head. "Yes, I suppose we could. Fair's fair. My body in exchange for my freedom. I don't exactly relish the thought of jail."

Did she have to make it hurt so much? "Will you at least consider it?"

"How long do I have?" she asked.

He picked at the last of his meal. "A week, two weeks . . . I place no time limit on it. Let this be your home. I've enough for the two of us."

Their glasses touched, they sipped their wine. She trembled once and said, "Your offer is really very kind."

"The 'uncle' was not a relative of yours, was he?"

Flustered, she set down her glass and almost cried.

Reugen reached across the table to comfort her. "Odette, I had to telephone him for your sake. He has said you must be mistaken."

The Browning was in her coat pocket and her coat was folded on the chair behind him. There was a paring knife on the drainboard in the kitchen, but he was closer to it. The vagus nerve then. Pressure there would stop the motor fibers to the heart. Death would come, in seconds.

"Please tell me why you lied to me," he said.

She shrugged. "I had no money. I needed to use the telephone. I thought . . . ah, what does it matter what I thought?"

She was angry with him now, but it would be best to get everything out in the open. "Who did you telephone?"

"A friend. She was just somebody I'd met once."

Then the girl was truly alone in the city. "Was there a man with her?"

"A German officer. Look, she said I could go there after six o'clock. I'll leave now."

Reugen caught her by the sleeve. Her chest rose in alarm.

Apologetically he said, "Please, I beg you. Don't go. Stay here and think it over. We could try things out, and if you found them to your liking, you could stay as long as you wished."

"And if not?"

He let go of her. "I will say nothing because even now I have allowed you to stay too long, and the authorities would only want to know why I hadn't reported you."

The Red Cross parcels were thirty centimeters to the side, the regulation size. Each parcel weighed no more than ten kilograms. The addresses, in pen, gave a POW camp in East Prussia near the border of what had once been Poland.

Hunter ran his eyes over the fifteen parcels he'd had singled out from the shipment of over ten thousand that had been caught in the harbor during the invasion.

Each of the parcels would contain four kilograms of crushing boart and a third of a kilogram of mixed tool diamonds, in addition to the woolen socks, underwear, toothbrushes, soap and canned or dried food.

It hadn't been easy finding just the right person in the Congo.

A security guard at one of the mines had seemed a promising prospect but the man had had to be killed. That death, however, had softened a woman in the office of the mine manager. Georgette Augiers had been lonely. At the age of 43 she had wanted love and promises of marriage.

She'd had a friend, a foreman, one Pieter van den Oorst, half Belgian, half Afrikaner.

It had been through her and van den Oorst that he'd managed the parcels — a steady if modest flow of diamonds past the British blockade with the promise of more.

But now Richard would destroy the link, and if not him, then Arlette Huysmans.

When Krantz, fresh from having the dressing changed on his shattered hand, came into the warehouse, Hunter was ready for him.

"The girl has to have been sent from London to find these," he said. "That's why she has a wireless set. Stake out this place and you'll get her."

"And you, Baron? What will you do?"

"Once we have her, we have Richard."

With difficulty Krantz found himself a cigarette and lit it. "They're not working together. She can't even know Hagen's alive."

"Then we let Richard know she'll come here."

That was interesting. "How?" asked Krantz. The pain in his hand and arm was excruciating. He'd refused the morphia.

"By leaving the Club Chez Vous alone. By leaving only myself in there to face him. Richard will never try to make contact with Cecile if you have so many of your men in the place."

That was also interesting. "Then be my guest, Baron. You to the club, myself to stake this place out. Tell the others to leave the club in ones and twos over the course of the next hour or so. I can use them here."

Hagen would kill the Baron but hopefully not before Hunter had told him about the girl.

From the couch in the sitting room, Arlette could hear the German snoring peacefully in his bedroom. There had been times when she'd thought he'd awakened suddenly, times when she'd thought him listening for her.

Even as she crossed the room to open one of the windows a little wider, Arlette knew she'd have to kill him.

Leaning out, she looked along the darkened street, then up to the eaves above her. A corner, a ledge, a drainpipe — something — she had to get a fix on the window so as to find it from the roof.

Reugen turned onto his side when she stood in the doorway listening to him. It would be so easy to kill him now, and then what? The hue and cry as soon as he didn't show up for work?

Softly she closed his door and put two cushions against the bottom of it. If she had the opportunity to lie, she would tell him that they'd been because of his snoring.

The hallway was dark, the staircase up to the roof cramped. Crouching, she felt for the lock, found its hasp, traced out the end of its plate, the first of the screwnails...

Using a dinner knife, Arlette removed each of the four screws and set them carefully in a corner on the top step. It would take time to replace them, but if successful, this was far better than forcing the lock.

London wanted her to get into the Red Cross depot but London didn't understand how things were.

The roof was flat in its center but steep at the sides — sheets of copper that shot away to the eaves below and then the windows.

Stringing the aerial between the chimney pots, she leaned over the edge of the roof, trying to find the window of the flat. Nothing doing! Damn!

She got up and pulled off her coat, lest the gun fall out of her pocket.

Each sheet of roofing copper was flanged where it joined the next one. Gripping two of these flanges, Arlette pulled herself out over the edge of the roof and down.

Glancing along the darkened street as the sound of a patrol came up to her, she waited, straining now, the blood pounding into her head.

Where... where was the window? Two over — at least two. Three? she wondered.

Working her way back up onto the roof, she gave herself a moment. She had to be sure. There wasn't all that much wire left.

At 0310 hours London time she sent the briefest signal: ENEMY CLOSING IN / WILL TRY TODAY

In the morning there was soot on the cuffs of the girl's trench coat, and this, Horst Reugen could not understand.

Krantz rested his throbbing arm on the table and reached for the cup of coffee. The café, much frequented by dockworkers, was almost directly across the road from the Red Cross depot.

The Huysmans girl still hadn't shown up. Had the baron's hunch been wrong?

He found his cigarette case and pried it open. So many cigarettes, so much coffee — still no morphia. Heydrich wanted Hagen and the girl. Heydrich . . .

He'd be lucky if he didn't lose his arm.

The whole area was sealed off. They'd let the girl through, then watch for Hagen.

With luck, he'd get them both, but had luck turned against him?

Blood and pus still leaked through the bandages. The splinters of bone made their ridges. He couldn't move his fingers, couldn't move his wrist, either. Felt only constant pain.

He touched his brow and rubbed it a little, took another sip of coffee.

Outside, the day was warm. The door to the Red Cross depot was open. The girl at the desk was looking through the venetian blinds.

Several blocks away from where the control should have been, Arlette stopped at the curbside to look questioningly down the long length of the street toward the docks. It was all so like before the war, she had to wonder about it.

A woman with a baby in a carriage went past, an old couple — there were shops here, the whole complex of the port of Antwerp opening out before her at the far end of the street.

The Café Nordique caught her eye, the Restaurant de Paris. There was a milliner's . . . Should she continue down the street? Should she?

Everything in her said to turn away.

At the Club Chez Vous the blackout curtains were still drawn, and the place had that closed-up, deserted look about it. No one seemed to be watching the club. There were German soldiers on leave. One tried the front door only to find it locked.

The man tried to look in through a gap in the curtains but soon gave up.

Arlette turned the corner and went around the back so as to pass the service entrance. Some garbage bins lay on their sides. Two cats were worrying over a bit of refuse. The garage doors were closed. There wasn't a sign of anyone.

From a café, this time, she called the place but there was no answer.

Unsettled, she crossed the street and started up the back lane. Here it was hot, the sounds of the street soon muffled.

She stopped to peer into the garage through one of the small triangular panes of glass that were set in the doors. Puzzled that Cecile's car was there, she glanced apprehensively toward the back door of the club and then up to the windows.

Cecile couldn't help her. Cecile had been in trouble herself. "Don't do this," she said, a whisper. "Just try to get out of the city."

Leaning the bicycle against the wall, she gave the lane and the street beyond it a last glance before sliding her hand into her pocket and over the butt of the Browning.

Someone had placed a red silk rose on the lower step that led to the door. A shred of boiled cabbage lay nearby; not far from this, the overturned casserole from a pot roast of some kind.

The door was slightly ajar.

"Arlette, Cecile's dead. Come away from there."

Unable to move, she waited. It couldn't be. Not Richard. Not him.

"Richard, is it really you?" she asked, not turning. He'd be in the garage. He could quite possibly have seen her looking into it.

"Dieter Karl Hunter is in the club. Take the bicycle and walk slowly back down the lane but do so against the inner wall."

Hunter would call the Gestapo if she left. At least this way Richard might escape.

Shaking her head, Arlette nudged the door open and stepped into the club. At once the silence of the place hit her. A short entrance hall soon led to the kitchens. A faucet dripped. A mouse scurried along a shelf above the central counters.

The warm, greasy odor of curried lamb came to her. "Cecile, it's me. Where is everybody?" she called out suddenly.

The swinging doors were closed. Beyond them the postage stamp of the dance floor, stage, bar and tables lay in the half-light from the ceiling.

Where once there'd been a plaster rose above the dance floor, there was now the darkness of a stain. Water dripped from the center of this stain but, like the faucet in the kitchens, it made no sound. The plaster rose was fast becoming a mush of ruins.

Furtively Arlette glanced at the staircase, then swept her eyes over the place again. The bar had been looted — the Gestapo hadn't been able to resist that. The till drawer was open.

Step by step she climbed the stairs. The Browning was in her hand, but for how long had it been there? She had no memory of having taken it from her pocket. Where . . . where would this Dieter Karl Hunter be?

The door to the office was open. Cecile's accounts ledger would be at the side of the desk. She'd been such a good businesswoman, so meticulous, so very beautiful Richard had . . .

Darting up the remaining steps, Arlette flung her back to the inner wall. Pressing the muzzle of the pistol against the door, she nudged it more fully open.

The office was empty. Half a battle of Scotch whisky and an empty glass were by the chair next the window.

Arlette turned suddenly at a sound, but when she went back out into the hall he wasn't there. The door to the sitting room was open, that to the bedroom closed.

Richard would come after her — she knew this, had known it all along. But would he stop to cut the telephone wires? Would there be time to save him?

"Cecile, what has happened?" she asked, her voice too loud.

There was no answer, but now they both would know where she was.

The door to the bathroom at the far end of the hall was also closed. The German would wait for her to open it. Timing would be everything.

Otto Krantz glanced at his watch. Winding the thing was almost an impossibility. He'd liked to have it on his left wrist. That, too, was an impossibility.

It was almost 0900 hours and still there'd been no sign of the girl.

"Send a car round to the Club Chez Vous and ask the baron to join us. Better still, give him a call."

Though the flat above the club was warm, the door to Cecile's bathroom felt like ice.

Arlette turned the doorknob slowly, so slowly.

As the door swung gently open, the sound of trickling water came to her.

Hunter saw the girl hesitate. Had she changed her mind? Did she suspect what awaited her in there?

Where was Richard? Where? To have caught them both, to have killed the one and wounded the other... that would be so good, that would satisfy Heydrich. All would be forgiven.

The door to the bathroom opened a little more. There was water on the tiles, threads of sickness, the smell...

A foot, her ankles — the thighs, the seat... Cecile...

Hagen crossed the hall and moved along it swiftly. Arlette saw the body. Water still flowed over the rim of the tub in a thin sheet that found its way to the floor.

Cecile's arms had floated out. Her head... she was facedown in the water.

"Arlette!"

She spun round and fired, cried out in anguish, *"Richard!"* and emptied the gun.

Dusk had settled over the city. Haunted by doubt, Horst Reugen left the car at the curb and went up the stone steps to the apartment block. The Gestapo were out in force. He'd seen their cars parked at several of the nearby corners. By the National Bank there'd been a truck full of SS troops, another at the Church of St. George. Guard dogs had been tethered to a tree.

He'd made a little survey of the area, then had driven down the Volkstraat to the Arts Museum only to find a truck there. More dogs, more men . . .

The Gestapo were going to cordon off the area and do a house-to-house search. What a fool he'd been! Even as he went into the building, he knew that the girl who had called herself Odette Latour could not possibly have been of that name. The "typewriter" in her suitcase would have been something else.

He waited for the lift, a stuffy, somewhat overweight man, with sad brown eyes.

The cage came down. Like an automaton he got in. Was there no one else in the building? At the last moment the front door opened and a Belgian girl cried out, "Wait, please."

He held the lift door for her. She smiled, had such excitement in her eyes.

She got off at the third floor and suddenly the loneliness and the fear swept in on him again. What was he to do?

The girl called Odette Latour wasn't in the flat. It didn't look as if she'd been there all day. The place had that empty feeling about it. Quickly he went through the apartment.

There was no sign of her, only a pair of stockings and a blouse in the bathroom.

He began to search for her suitcase. It wasn't on the chair by the couch, nor over by the wall.

In panic, he swept her laundry from the bathroom and wondered how best to hide it. The Gestapo mustn't discover he'd had the girl staying with him. He must deny all knowledge of her.

Hurrying into the kitchen, he thought to stuff her things into the garbage, then thought they'd be sure to look there. Struck by the futility of what he was trying to do, Reugen put the things into a jacket pocket.

She'd hidden the suitcase under his bed. She was planning to come back after all!

Lugging the thing over to the window, he set it on the radiator, but would the Gestapo not see him opening it here? He took it into the sitting room and set it on the chair where she'd placed it before. The catches were stiff, the leather quite good but made so as to appear a little shabby.

Some underwear, another blouse . . . it was all so neatly packed he was afraid to touch a thing.

A portable typewriter, one of the latest Underwood models, lay beneath the clothing.

The girl had been telling the truth. Hating himself for having doubted her, Reugen wondered where she was.

The light across the moors was deepening. Through the hush came the endless turning of the windmill.

There were three wooden bridges, three drainage canals that crossed the road near Cecile's farmhouse, and this was the last of them.

When Richard was done, he would fix Heydrich's briefcase of documents, then they would decide what to do with the rest of the dynamite.

Dieter Karl Hunter had died instantly. Richard and she had almost been out of the club when she'd told him about the wireless set.

Cecile had had a typewriter and Richard had said they must go back for it. They had taken her car and had driven to Herr Reugen's flat to make the switch and recover the wireless set.

Standing in the shallow water beneath the bridge, Richard fitted a bundle of three sticks up among the timbers.

Satisfied, he took it down. Without a crimper, he had had to bite on the ends of the blasting caps to hold the fuse he'd inserted into each of them.

Again, as he did so, he looked up at her, but this time there was more than sadness in his eyes. "We could kill ourselves this way," he said, indicating the blasting cap. "Arlette, I really wish you'd let me cover for you. Alone, you might stand a chance."

Behind the farmhouse, the light touched the tops of the sand hills. Cradling the Schmeisser under her right arm, she again searched the empty road.

A windmill turned. The wind brushed the tops of distant reeds. "I wish we could have had a child, Richard. I wish we could have had a house of our own, a flat, a farm like this. I don't want to die. I want to live."

The charge in place, Hagen climbed out of the canal to put an arm about her. She leaned her head against him. Suddenly neither of them could speak, and in silence, they walked back to the farmhouse.

KEMPEN AREA BELGIUM   2047 HOURS JUNE 28, 1940
TO THE CARPENTER   FROM XAVIER
BLUFF CHECK INCLUDED   TRUE CHECK INCLUDED
                                 LOCATION TRANSMITTER MOVED
                                 FROM ANTWERP AREA TO THE EAST
                                 NEAR THE DUTCH BORDER

    MESSAGE READS:

ALICE CONFIRMS CONGO DIAMONDS GETTING PAST BLOCKADE RED CROSS RELIEF PARCELS LEOPOLDVILLE ADDRESSES AUGIER MLLE GEORGETTE / OORST PIETER VAN DEN / ARNOLD HENRI / KLOOS JOHANN...

Some other names followed and then, HUNTER DIETER KARL DEAD / AWAITING NAZIS

Krantz spread out the map on the hood of the car. Direction-finding centers at Antwerp, Brussels and Eindhoven intersected in a thin triangle well to the east of the city near the farm of Cecile Verheyden.

Hagen had chosen well. The wind was down; the moors were flat; the trajectory of a Lee Enfield rifle would zero in at one thousand meters, no problem. Not with Hagen or with his father, only the rifle wasn't British. It was a Mauser 98K, the German *Landser's* standby. Five rounds in the box clip, one in the breech and the desolation of Flanders through the sights. Fog, mud, shit, death, shattered tree trunks, wrecked gun carriages, tattered bits of cloth and shell holes — everywhere there'd been the shell holes. Which one had the father been in? A cigarette? Could he risk it? A hand to his pocket, a movement so slight the force of the impact had carried him back.

"Hagen's crazy. He must know we are aware the Verheyden woman had a farm out here and that this is where he'd hole up."

They crowded around the map. A *Feldwebel* named Jorgen, who was tough and experienced; the Hauptmann Ernst Kunzler, ruthless and desirous of proving himself to Berlin. Others: Gestapo in plainclothes, the two trucks with Armed-SS contingents, the Wehrmacht with one of theirs.

"It's the drainage canals I don't like," said Krantz. "Hagen will try to kill me."

"Then stay in the car and let us go in and finish him off."

This had come from the *Hauptmann*. Krantz sized up the man in one look. He should be tolerant but had no patience, was in too much pain for that. "No matter what Herr Heydrich has told you, my friend, Hagen is far too smart for that. He'll have planned a retreat into those sand hills behind the house and barns. From there he can pin your men down all by himself."

The *Hauptmann* returned the look. Old battles were best forgotten. War was different now. The Oberstgruppenführer Heydrich had commanded that Hagen and the girl be killed at once.

"I have my orders, Major."

"Fuck your orders. Send men along the road to check the bridges for explosives. Otherwise Hagen will make you walk, Herr Hauptmann, and then he'll shoot you down."

The smell of gasoline, coal tar and kerosene filled the barn in which they'd hidden Cecile's car. Arlette watched as Richard stuffed a rag wick into the last of the wine bottles.

"How's the road?" he asked.

She slung the Schmeisser over a shoulder. "Still clear but I don't like it. What if they've surrounded us and are waiting until dark?"

Hagen cleaned off his hands and came over to her. "Then we'll leave and make our way through them on foot."

Together they went out to watch the road, which ran almost due north and south past the farmhouse and was some five hundred meters from them.

A kilometer to the north there was a drainage canal that cut across the road at one of the little bridges. South of this, the lane from the house met the road just before another of the bridges. Here one of the canals angled off to the northwest. Then, a kilometer to the south, there was another canal and bridge. The ground between the canals and the road was exceedingly flat. Only behind the house and barns was there any relief.

"Richard, let me come with you. What happens if you should get..."

"Nervous? I've slit the ends of the fuses. All I need to do is light them."

"Please, I... I would rather be with you. The two of us together. Me to give you cover, while you..."

He shook his head. "Go while there's still time. Please, for my sake."

Arlette threw her arms around him and kissed him one last time.

The Germans came so suddenly both of them felt sick. One moment there was nothing on the horizon, the next, a smudge of gray that grew rapidly and then a car and two trucks to the north of them, another car and a truck to the south.

"Love me, Richard, as I'll love you always."

He gripped her hand, then ran to the barn. The lead car to the north of them came to a stop some distance from the bridge. At once two soldiers leaped out of the truck behind and began to walk forward along the edges of the road. They looked so angular in their helmets with their weapons at the ready. Richard would never reach that bridge. He'd never be able to throw those bottles or light the fuses...

Hagen swung the car in beside her. "Arlette, don't even think of trying. Promise me you won't."

"I cannot watch you die!"

Even as he drove Cecile's car down the lane, Hagen knew Arlette was running across the flats, trying to reach the most southerly of the canals.

The soldiers stopped. In two arcs their Schmeissers came to bear on the car. Hagen jammed the throttle down. They began to fire, shattering the windscreen and showering him with glass...

As Krantz watched, the girl pitched herself into the nearest canal and Hagen drove the car straight at the *Hauptmann* only to leap out at the last moment. The two cars collided in a burst of flame that shot over the truck behind.

All hell broke loose. Some of the men were on fire. Hagen had disappeared into the canal.

The girl was gone — she'd be racing toward the bridge!

Arlette slid down the muddy embankment and ran in under the timbers. Clawing, dragging herself up, she fought to find the matches and reach the fuse.

Three minutes...that was all Richard had said he'd have. Forty seconds a foot for the fuse. Four and a half feet of it!

She tried to light a match. Black powder from the end of the fuse spilled over her shaking fingers. The matches... Steady, she must keep steady.

The sound of hobnailed boots rang on the timbers above her.

Too slow...too slow...she dragged out the Browning and fired at them. The fuse began to splutter. Run...she'd have to run!

When the thing went off, the blast pitched her along the canal and tumbled her head over heels in the water.

Dazed and bleeding, she got up and ran.

Hagen saw her crawl out of the canal. Suddenly everyone had gone to ground. She ran for about one hundred meters — they let her get that far. The tac-tac-tac of an MG-42 came to him. The earth was kicked up around her and she fell to lie there.

He turned and ran himself. "Arlette!" It was a scream, a cry. Hagen raced for the next canal and leaped into it. At a crouch, he made for the farmhouse. She'd be about three hundred meters out in that no-man's-land. Krantz would have a rifle, too.

Oily black smoke and flames billowed from the truck and the two cars. All but one of the bridges had been blown.

Arlette hadn't moved.

Quickly the Berliner and the others took up positions behind the embankment of the road. Reports filtered in. The *Hauptmann* was dead. Several others had gone with him. Six were badly burned or otherwise out of action.

The girl still lay out there. Hagen would try to reach her. Krantz asked for a rifle and rested it on the edge of the road, cursed his luck for not having the use of his left hand.

"Herr Krantz, the briefcase is on the last of the bridges."

So it was. "Send someone for it."

"Hagen will only kill him."

"Get it, damn you!" The girl — had she tried to move?

The man reached the bridge. A length of fuse ran from the briefcase down between the timbers to join up with another length that stretched away along the canal in which Hagen was hiding.

Krantz waited. The man stooped to pick up the briefcase. Hagen fired. Krantz leaped and fired. The man crumpled into a heap, and the reports of the shots chased each other over the moors.

The Berliner cursed. He'd torn the bandages from his hand, had tried to use the thing. The pain was excruciating. Damn Hagen. Damn the girl. "All right, you bastard. We're coming for you!"

A man stood up at a crouch and fell to the road. The girl had moved. She was now nowhere in sight.

Hagen lit the fuse and together they ran toward the sand hills. Arlette flung herself down behind some cover as the dynamite went off. Richard went past her and on up into the hills. Higher and higher still . . .

She heard the crack of the rifle twice and then again.

When she threw herself down beside him, he fired twice more. Reloading the Mauser, he pinned the Germans down.

"Are you okay?" he asked, not looking at her.

"Are you?" She touched his cheek.

Krantz scanned the tops of the hills. Again there was that feeling of utter loneliness the battlefield at Ypres had brought. The girl was now with Hagen but lying some distance to the north so as to cover that flank.

There was only one thing to do. He had to nail Hagen, but when he looked again, the salesman was nowhere to be seen.

An hour dragged by. Finally the Berliner could stand it no longer. The pain in his hand . . . he'd need a shot of morphia.

He took out the cigarette case. As so many times since the First War, he ran a thumb over the dented head of the kaiser.

Then he asked for a light and drew in gratefully. Ah, that was better.

Hagen shot him through the head. The report echoed like a cannon. The man who had caught the Berliner in his arms died as well.

Then Hagen faded back along the canal and up into the hills.

Arlette lay still. For an hour now the sun had been up. Dragonflies came and went, or hovered overhead. The reeds were thick, warm, the sound of water near, that of the dogs more distant.

A shout came and then another. Across the moor, at gaps of thirty yards, men were spread out, and the line of them stretched for at least a thousand meters on either side of them.

At five-minute intervals the men would change places, cutting diagonally to the left and the next time to the right. They were wading through the tall grass with their rifles held before them. Fresh troops, far too many of them.

Hagen reached for the Schmeisser, easing the satchel of ammunition toward himself.

Exhausted, Arlette slept on. The wind came to touch the reeds but made no sound. Her chest rose gently. Another breath.

He hated to awaken her and wondered if he should, if it wouldn't be better to let her die like that. Happy to be with him, secure in the knowledge he was beside her.

When he turned away to part the reeds, Arlette opened her eyes to lie there tensely listening. Opalescent in the early light, the transparent wings of a dragonfly were so very beautiful. The thing hovered directly above her — she'd have sworn it looked down — but then it zoomed away.

Richard had such a nice smile. It spread gently from his lips to fill his eyes and make her feel warm inside.

He jerked a thumb toward the south. Blinking, she turned over onto her stomach and reached for the rifle. The sound of the dogs came again, then a shout from the *Feldwebel*.

Would they die together? she wondered anxiously.

Hagen motioned her to retreat. Stubbornly she indicated the flattened reeds. The dogs would only find them.

Silently he said, Trust me. She moved away reluctantly, pulling herself through the reeds until perhaps ten meters separated them and she was faced by a barrier of water.

It was a canal, about five meters wide. If only they could cross it. If only . . .

Just downstream of her a small flat-bottomed punt lay tethered to a pole. The rifle would have to stay.

Sliding into the tepid water, Arlette swam silently toward the punt and was soon in the slim wedge of shade that lay behind it.

The canal wasn't all that deep. She could just touch the bottom. When Richard reached the bank, she signaled to him and at once he slid into the water.

Carrying the guns and the satchel just above his head, Hagen swam slowly downstream until he had joined her. There were some burlap bags in the bottom of the punt, things that had been used for eels perhaps. Quickly Hagen hid the guns and the satchel under them, then broke off two lengths of reed.

Together, each holding on to the other, they sank below the surface. The sun began to climb, the dogs to bark again. At a shout from one of the men, the barking ceased.

At dusk they gave up the search.

Spring came early to the Dorset hills. On Black Down Heath the wild-flowers were in bloom, and if one shut one's eyes it was so very far from the war.

Out on the moor Arlette heard Richard call her name. He waved. He'd a letter in his hand. Orders now to report for duty. Damn!

Each of the parcels would contain four kilograms of crushing boart and a third of a kilogram of mixed tool diamonds, in addition to the woolen socks, underwear, toothbrushes, soap and canned or dried food.

It hadn't been easy finding just the right person in the Congo. A security guard at one of the mines had seemed a promising prospect but the man had had to be killed. That death, however, had softened a woman in the office of the mine manager. Georgette Augiers had been lonely. At the age of 43 she had wanted love and promises of marriage.

She'd had a friend, a foreman, one Pieter van den Oorst, half Belgian, half Afrikaner.

It had been through her and van den Oorst that he'd managed the parcels — a steady if modest flow of diamonds past the British blockade with the promise of more.

But now Richard would destroy the link, and if not him, then Arlette Huysmans.

When Krantz, fresh from having the dressing changed on his shattered hand, came into the warehouse, Hunter was ready for him.

"The girl has to have been sent from London to find these," he said. "That's why she has a wireless set. Stake out this place and you'll get her."

"And you, Baron? What will you do?"

"Once we have her, we have Richard."

With difficulty Krantz found himself a cigarette and lit it. "They're not working together. She can't even know Hagen's alive."

"Then we let Richard know she'll come here."

That was interesting. "How?" asked Krantz. The pain in his hand and arm was excruciating. He'd refused the morphia.

"By leaving the Club Chez Vous alone. By leaving only myself in there to face him. Richard will never try to make contact with Cecile if you have so many of your men in the place."

That was also interesting. "Then be my guest, Baron. You to the club, myself to stake this place out. Tell the others to leave the club in ones and twos over the course of the next hour or so. I can use them here."

Hagen would kill the Baron but hopefully not before Hunter had told him about the girl.

From the couch in the sitting room, Arlette could hear the German snoring peacefully in his bedroom. There had been times when she'd thought he'd awakened suddenly, times when she'd thought him listening for her.

Even as she crossed the room to open one of the windows a little wider, Arlette knew she'd have to kill him.

Leaning out, she looked along the darkened street, then up to the eaves

their escape came back — Ostend in ruins, her parents still in the harbor, tied up with all the fishing boats.

out to begin again? Another nightmare?

by the hand. She said, "Well, what's it to be?"

and the Congo. Churchill's convinced the Germans are lied with diamonds."

face him. Reaching out, her trembling fingers touched his made love time and again, each with an eagerness that to get greater.

ell you something, my husband. If it's a girl, I'll call her then Bernard first, I think, and after that, why, Lev."

in his arms. The tears were there, the sadness in her earning. He lifted her up and let her slide down to the him it made them both think of things.

hey walked out over the moor. She knew of a place. ietly in the sun, just the two of them.

e," she said. "Out here. I haven't told your mother yet. ntil I'd told you first."

irchill will want you to go there, to help them train

lready thought of that. I'll have the baby there and k..."

ns, he in hers. It was as if they had started all over re could be no tomorrow for them.

above her. A corner, a ledge

The days of their escape came back — Ostend in ruins, her parents dead, the *Vega* still in the harbor, tied up with all the fishing boats.

Was it all about to begin again? Another nightmare?

He took her by the hand. She said, "Well, what's it to be?"

"Mbuji-Mayi and the Congo. Churchill's convinced the Germans are still being supplied with diamonds."

She turned to face him. Reaching out, her trembling fingers touched his cheek. They had made love time and again, each with an eagerness that had only seemed to get greater.

"Then I must tell you something, my husband. If it's a girl, I'll call her Cecile, if a boy, then Bernard first, I think, and after that, why, Lev."

Hagen took her in his arms. The tears were there, the sadness in her lovely eyes, the yearning. He lifted her up and let her slide down to the ground so close to him it made them both think of things.

Hand in hand they walked out over the moor. She knew of a place. They would sit quietly in the sun, just the two of them.

"Make love to me," she said. "Out here. I haven't told your mother yet. I...I was waiting until I'd told you first."

"Kincalda...Churchill will want you to go there, to help them train others."

"Yes...yes, I've already thought of that. I'll have the baby there and when you come back..."

She was in his arms, he in hers. It was as if they had started all over again, it was as if there could be no tomorrow for them.